LIMITED EDITION

S.C. WILES

For my Family

AMPHITRITE'S TALE

Dancing on Naxos, twirling wild and free,
unaware of catching the eyes of thee.
The god of the sea, Poseidon that is,
decided at once, that she would be his.

Unwilling to bend to his marriage bid,
she fled to Atlas, with her heart she hid.
But not long after, a Dolphin was sent,
urging her return, clear with his intent.

Pulled to Naxos with strong invitation,
earning Dolphin his own constellation.
The queen of the sea, whose voice could reform,
Poseidon's temper, calming his storm.

1

THE TUNNEL AT THE END OF THE LIGHT

"ALWAYS STRETCH after your run or you'll pay the price later."
The words of Hali Edie Shawn's high school track coach, Mr.
Souza, cycled through her mind as she lay in bed, wide
awake, her legs burning with pain. It was 11:53 p.m. on the
eve of her eighteenth birthday and Hali had no clue what
she had done to deserve the hellfire spreading through her
lower limbs like a small-town rumor. In the two weeks since
Hali graduated high school, she hadn't done a lick of stren-
uous activity.

In fact, the most active Hali could claim to be—though
not without a hit to her pride—was the daily trips she made
to the beach. And even then, beach-going required minimal
physical exertion on her part—unless baking under the
relentless sun could be counted as exercise. In Hali's book—
it didn't. Even when the sun's rays pulled her worries and
energy straight from her like an exorcism, sweat glistening
her skin, there was no comparison. The sun could never
substitute the dripping sweat produced from pushing her
body to the limit, like running had almost every day of her
life for the last four years.

For this reason, Hali deduced that her current pain—which was equivalent to soaking her legs in a bath full of gasoline and setting it ablaze—could not be from any recent physical activity. A hindrance considering she still had no idea the cause of her pain. But also, a relief to know that she didn't need to give up her beach time anytime soon.

The beach was her safe place. An escape from the uncertainties of life that plagued her when she let her mind wander. A new chapter awaited her on the horizon. Soon, she'd start college, and there wasn't enough stagnate heat in an Emerald Cove summer to help her forget that fact.

College represented a loss to Hali in a way that she hadn't quite grasped. Before graduation, most of her peers reveled at the idea of starting the next chapter of their lives. So much so, their daily planners transformed into graveyards with X's enthusiastically marking out each passing day. Hali's planner, on the other hand, remained tucked away in her book bag for the entirety of the year. Avoiding the daily reminder that her childhood was coming to an end, she opted to write her homework assignments in a composition notebook instead.

Hali wasn't as certain that adulthood held the hidden promise of better things to come that her peers believed it did. Adulthood, college ... it was all just another way of saying change. And to Hali, the word *change* was synonymous with being uncomfortable.

Hali's dislike for change dated back to her freshmen year of high school, when the puberty fairy paid her a visit. Hali's bra-size had gone from nonexistent to full-C's practically overnight, bending her wiry lean figure into womanly curves. Not only did her body change, but the taunting did, too. Boys who had derided her flat plains began ogling her hills. Whereas the girls who had usually laughed along with the boys who mocked her child-like figure, looked at Hali with disgust, questioning the authenticity of her new developments.

The experience had been a mess for Hali whose sudden blossoming cost her a state title in track freshman year, when her self-consciousness got the best of her. She had been favored to win the mile event, but instead, she had altered her running form to cover her curves, holding her arms awkwardly across her chest so her girls stayed in place. She somehow managed fifth place, but something in Hali snapped that day as she watched the lithe competitors pass her on the track, snagging up medals as they went. To add insult to injury Hali had been neck and neck for fourth place and was only overtaken in the final seconds because she refused to pump her arms. Standing on the sidelines when the race was over, disappointed, she resolved to never let her new figure cost her a race ever again—and it didn't. Frustration fueled determination, earning her three first-place state medals in the coming years, which proudly hung from her bedroom wall. Though despite Hali's turnaround, the experience left a bad taste in her mouth where change was concerned, and the idea of college felt a lot like a déjà vu.

For one, college meant she wouldn't see her only true friend, Camille, every day since they would be attending different colleges. Hali had decided to stay close and go to Emerald Cove Community College, while Camille, being the more adventurous of the two, picked a university two hours away. It wasn't that Hali couldn't be alone. In fact, it was quite the opposite. She actually enjoyed the solace. What troubled Hali was the expectation to be a full-fledged adult when the four years were over. Hali was certain that Camille would rise to the challenge without issue. She'd be in a new city, with new friends, enjoying a new exciting life full of possibilities. While Hali would be at Emerald Cove Community College, pretending to still be in high school, unsuccessfully willing adulthood away.

Those facts alone were the reasons Hali committed herself to having zero plans for the summer other than to be another body strewn on the sands of the Emerald Cove Beach with her best friend beside her. But her plan to avoid adulthood and responsibility for as long as possible didn't include waking up to legs writhing in pain mere minutes before she would turn eighteen and technically be an adult. But like most things in life, it didn't matter what Hali's plans were, life's plans always won out to her own.

After massaging her legs and rolling to several positions, Hali was no closer to relief. The insistent pain demanded Hali's attention, but her eyelids rebelled. With her eyes still closed, Hali threw her sheets from her body and drew her knees to her chest. Four years of running track in high school had never produced muscle cramps even close to her present miserable condition. Not even training for a half marathon the previous summer had left her feeling so terrible. Hali imagined the throbbing pain as a living organism swimming in her veins corralling other cells to join it—misery as their mission.

Losing hope of falling back to sleep, Hali's eyes opened to see that she had been tossing and turning for almost an hour.

12:47 a.m. June 17th. Happy Birthday.

Giving up the notion that sleep was possible, Hali stood up from her bed, throwing on an oversized sweatshirt that enveloped her petite frame, including her curves that she tried to forget she had most days. After standing a moment at her bedside, Hali cautiously put her left foot forward;

touching her toes to the carpet as if testing the temperature of a pool. Hali grimaced, expecting pain. When it didn't come, she relaxed hesitantly, proceeding forward to her desk. *Right foot, left. Burning pain. Right foot, left. Pain. Right foot, left. Warmth?*

A few steps towards the desk and Hali was relieved to find her pain had dulled and warmth had taken its place.

Maybe her legs had fallen asleep and just needed the blood to circulate, she thought.

Laying her hands flat on her desk, while she got her bearings, Hali peered up to see a small forgotten item tucked in the corner. Her desk, which was normally cluttered with binders and school papers during the school year had been cleared at the start of summer, except for the music box she had had ever since she could remember. Sitting down at her chair, she pulled the simple, cream box from the corner. She ran her thumbs along its smooth edges until they hit the solitary, violet stone that served as a knob to open the box. As she began pulling up on the stone, a flash of light in her peripheral caught her attention, distracting her from her diversion. Pushing the closed music box back into the corner, Hali stood up from her desk chair, slightly alarmed by the unknown light. Then another flash of light lit her room, and another, and another. Hali could almost count down to the second when the next flash would occur. Curiosity bubbled within her as she felt the warmth in her legs pulsating to the same rhythm as the light. Hali walked to her window on shaky legs. As she peered out, she discovered the source of the flashes to be coming from the Emerald Cove Lighthouse. The beam carved a circle of light into the night sky, as if it had been doing it for years, when the reality was, the lighthouse hadn't been functional for almost two decades.

The popular landmark closed down seventeen years before—only about a month shy of eighteen years—after it stopped working mysteriously. Hali's parents would joke that her arrival brought so much light to the world that the Emerald Cove Lighthouse retired itself when it couldn't compete. But that didn't stop the town from trying to bring it back to life. Problematic wiring was blamed for the sudden ceasing of the lighthouse after a burn mark was discovered on its outer surface. After many attempts to locate and remedy the wires responsible for causing the small fire, no specific problem with the lighthouse's wiring was found. In fact, no problem was found at all, which puzzled everyone involved with its repair. Without a known source to pin the mysterious singed spot on, and with no clear direction on how to prevent it from catching on fire in the future, the Emerald Cove Lighthouse was deemed unsafe and permanently closed with all its wiring capped.

Hali watched the light she had never seen before from a distance, mesmerized, as it passed across her body standing in the window. The bright beam bathed her in its strangeness and somehow, her legs grew even warmer.

Feeling drawn by the hypnotic circles of the beam, Hali grabbed the keys to her Honda Civic that was older than she was by a couple of years. Without too much thought, she headed for the door and walked downstairs, quietly praying she would not wake up her parents. Gently, she grabbed the handle to the front door and closed it behind her. It wasn't until she had made it to her car that she realized she hadn't left a note behind. Not wanting to wake her parents up by going back in the house, Hali told herself she wouldn't be gone long and leaving a note wouldn't matter. It was a mistake that would have little impact on the outcome of what was about to happen, except to offer a morsel of reassurance to her parents. A few scribbles on a napkin or an old receipt to tell them where she went and why she left the house at such an hour, would have made a difference—in their minds at least. If only to let them know that she had thought about them, for even a moment, before she left.

Five minutes later, Hali closed the door to her car with the same ginger touch as the front door of her childhood home. The warm winds whipped and clawed at her as she walked towards the ominous beacon harassing the night sky. The heat that had invaded her legs just before leaving her house had now filled with a new sensation that made her legs feel like two electrical currents. Fear coursed through her as realization set in that coming to the beach hadn't been voluntary. She tried turning back and going home, but her body was magnetized to the lighthouse. The closer she got to the circling light the greater its pull, like a fish being reeled in by a fisherman's line.

The experience reminded her of the time she had watched a cowboy lasso a cow at a rodeo when she was five. At the time, Hali focused on the cowboy as he wrangled the rope in one hand and firmly held his horse in the other. The cowboy's movements were controlled and precise as he homed in on his target. Not once during the show had Hali considered the cow's plight. The massive bovine spotted with black and white patches ran for his life in a square dirt box with no chance of escape, while the audience gawked at his pointless attempts. Hali's stomach twisted with bile at the memory. She was now the cow.

But who was the audience? she wondered, as goosebumps prickled up from her skin, unrelated to being cold.

As she approached the lighthouse door it opened automatically, as if waiting to welcome her to a fate she had yet to discover. Hali had always been cautious. But her body moved in spite of her brain's good sense. She looked up to the night sky once more, finding only a few stars that hadn't been covered by thick, gray clouds that concealed the beauty of the night. Stepping into the lighthouse, Hali could only hope that she would awake from a nightmare. But she wasn't that lucky.

Slam!

The door closed. The light beam surged on the ocean one final time before retreating. The Emerald Cove Lighthouse returned as a lifeless silhouette towering above the land and sea. Leaving the warm air a bit cooler than before and the night sky a bit darker.

2

THE DAY THE MUSIC STOPPED

ABIGAIL SHAWN AWOKE to her alarm clock blaring a twangy country song which pissed her off immediately.

Theo's idea of funny.

Abigail thought of getting a few ice cubes to stick in his shirt, but her husband of twenty-three years was no longer in bed. Tomorrow she'd get him back. It didn't help that he consistently woke up before the alarm went off—which made his little game of switching radio stations on her all the more convenient. What made it worse was Abigail never knew when it was coming.

For the first year of marriage she thought her alarm clock was broken. It took three alarm clock exchanges at the local Wright-Mart for Theo to finally confess his deceit. However, instead of feeling guilty, he laughed. And not the typical chuckle, but the bellyache-blue-in-the-face-lose-your-breath kind of laugh. Abigail still remembered him dropping to his knees with tears in his eyes.

Tears.

She could count on one hand how many times she had seen that man cry. Theo Shawn wasn't a man who believed in wasting tears. But on that day, almost twenty-two years ago, he gushed them out like a fire hydrant. He even had the nerve to admit that he only told Abigail the truth so that Wright-Mart wouldn't flag her as a customer to watch. Abigail was livid and didn't speak to Theo for a week. After four years of behaving, Theo decided to give his prank another go and had been hijacking Abigail's alarm clock ever since for the last eighteen years.

Eighteen years.

The thought awakened Abigail to a state of reminiscing. Her annoyance at Theo forgotten for the time being while she remembered pleasant memories of a little auburn-haired, pigtailed girl eating chocolate cake with vanilla frosting, bordered with violet and yellow-frosted flowers. Looking at the clock, Abigail pondered whether she had enough time to make breakfast before she headed to the aquarium for work. And if she made it, would Hali even be up to eat it? Abigail and Theo served as veterinarians at the Emerald Cove Aquarium, where punctuality was imperative for the sake of the animals.

In the midst of her contemplation, Theo entered the room, sitting next to Abigail on the bed. Planting a kiss on her head, he said, "I got breakfast setup. Would you mind putting some French toast on the skillet so I can get my shower in?"

Abigail stretched her arms up, gently scraping the headboard with her fingertips. "Oh, good!" she yawned. "I was just thinking about making her breakfast but didn't know if she would rather sleep in than eat."

Giving in to temptation, Theo yawned, allowing his body to collapse next to Abigail's until they were both looking at the ceiling. "She's got the rest of her summer vacation to sleep in, she can get up and share one last birthday breakfast with her old mom and dad. Plus, she can go back to sleep when we're done."

Abigail sat up from Theo, placing her hand on his chest to look into his eyes. "What do you mean, 'one last birthday breakfast?'"

Theo sighed. "I didn't literally mean one left, I just meant ... she's getting older and we don't know what will happen. After two years of Emerald Cove Community College she might be running to the furthest college from here."

"Do you really think so?" Abigail asked, worry crinkling at the edges of her eyes.

Theo shrugged. "Don't know. She's never been one to venture too far from home. But who knows what could happen within the next few years. Emerald Cove isn't known for much besides the beach. And as much as I'd hate to see her go too far, I won't stop her from seizing new opportunities or even traveling abroad. So, if and when that day comes, I just want to make sure we take advantage of this time with her before she starts her own life."

Theo's words felt like an anchor dropped in Abigail's stomach. Over the past eighteen years she had been counting firsts: first foods, first steps, first bike ride. The thought of counting Hali's lasts was like one-hundred bee stings to the heart.

For Theo and Abigail, Hali was an answer to forgotten prayers. From being a couple struggling with fertility to finally receiving a long-awaited miracle in the form of a happy, baby girl. The years of waiting for Hali felt like an eternity, but the time with her flew by too quickly. All the happy memories leaked from Abigail's eyes as she stepped out of bed and made her way to the kitchen, without any warning to Theo.

"Ahhh Abby, don't cry," he said, running his hands through his hair, while following Abigail to the kitchen. "She's going to community college for now, we don't have to worry about that yet." But the thought had already manifested in Abigail's head, taking hold like an incurable parasite.

Abigail sobbed to the kitchen island where the cold skillet sat on a burner. A bowl filled with a cinnamon-egg mixture sat on the counter beside it, ready to transform bread into French toast. Theo followed Abigail closely behind, wearing a grimace that held the knowledge he had put his foot in his mouth, and worry in his eyes that showed he hadn't quite figured out how to get it out.

"I know," Abigail said through shaky breaths. "It's just gone too fast. I think you're seeing how many emotions you can get out of me this morning."

Theo tilted his head in confusion. "Huh?"

"The alarm clock, Theo. First you irritate me with music I don't like, then you rip the rug out from under me, forcing me to think about the day Hali will leave us."

"Oh," he remorsefully chuckled while turning on the news. "I did that last night because you zonked out as soon as your head hit the pillow. I couldn't resist. I wouldn't have done it had I known I was going to upset you first thing."

As Abigail listened to Theo, her eyes glanced at the television where a newscaster—a young woman dressed like she was going to Easter brunch, rather than the beach—reported about a mysterious light that residents claimed to have seen coming from the Emerald Cove Lighthouse the night before. In the background of the frame, with the young blonde newscaster, was an old Honda Civic with a pink Hawaiian lei hanging from the rearview mirror. Dazed,

Abigail pointed to the television, and asked, "Is that Hali's car?"

Abigail turned off the burner before she could even cook the first pieces of French toast with a wave of worry passing through her like a current of acid. Theo's expression twisted in concern once his gaze caught sight of Hali's 2000 Honda Civic in clover-green pearl on the television screen. There was no mistaking the car to be Hali's, since it was practically a relic in Emerald Cove, where cars didn't generally age past the five-year mark before being replaced with a newer model. Despite the town being small, it was affluent. Retired millionaires wanting a reprieve from fast-paced living hid in every corner, wearing faded shirts and sandals with frayed straps for good measure. Outsiders were none the wiser.

Why would Hali's car be at the beach?

A heartbeat passed between them before Theo charged to Hali's room, ahead of Abigail. Something was wrong. Hali didn't just go to the beach without warning. She wasn't rebellious, and she had never snuck off. To some, it may have seemed that Theo and Abigail were overacting, that maybe Hali had just decided to go out to the beach for a bit and would return. But to the few that really knew Hali, Theo's and Abigail's reaction was just what it ought to be.

Rampaging through her room for what felt like an eternity, both Theo and Abigail left the room heavier than when they walked in. They double-checked outside for her car and then buzzed around the rest of the house, calling for Hali like they were in a one-sided game of Marco Polo. Their minds raced faster than their legs would allow. Abigail's heartbeat pulsed in her ears as her ability to reason became impossible.

"You stay here and make some calls and I'll go the beach to see if I can find anything out. Maybe she went with

Camille to the beach last night. Call her first," Theo demanded as Abigail clung to Theo's rationale with hope.

"O-kay," Abigail managed to stammer out through constricted breaths. Her whole body felt like she was wearing a corset from her head to her toes. But her mind felt loose and disorganized as she tried to think clearly.

"Abby, we'll find her. Don't think the worse. Breathe," Theo instructed. "I'll call you as soon as I know anything. I love you." Theo gave Abigail a kiss to the lips before rushing out the door. Abigail was too numb to feel it.

Hours later, the search for Hali grew rapidly. Search and rescue continued, and speculation soared. Abigail spent two hours on the phone answering one question after another, an endless loop of insanity. One-hundred and twenty minutes went by and she hadn't received any answers of her own. She was sure she had been asked the same questions ten different ways. Abigail willed herself to stay calm in case her answers proved helpful in some way. But by the end she was left antsy. She decided to join Theo, needing a more proactive approach in the search for Hali.

Abigail was known as the finder of all things lost in the Shawn household. From lost socks, phones, or keys—there wasn't much she couldn't sniff out. Sitting back, letting others take over on something as important as her own child, sat as well with her as a puppy watching a tennis match. It didn't.

The waiting had driven Abigail to madness as she worried her bottom lip with her teeth until it was chapped and bleeding. Grabbing her cell phone and car keys, she headed for the front door. She only hoped that nothing had been mucked up or missed while she had paced and waited at home.

3

SHEDDING A LAYER

"WE ARE GOING to comb every section of the beach. Each of you will be assigned to a group and you will be responsible for your section. Do not, I repeat, DO NOT, go out into the water. We have a crew designated for the ocean. However, if anything washes up onto the shore let the officer assigned to your section know immediately."

Camille listened to Officer Lancey go over search and rescue protocol while her mind drifted into the previous day. The day when her best friend wasn't missing. A day when she was on the very same beach but for a very different reason. What a difference a day could make. Camille and Hali planned on spending their last summer before college at the beach every day. Despite having opposite personalities, the two girls were both smart, goofy, and loyal in their friendship to one another. But that was where their similarities ended. Camille was loud and outgoing to Hali's shy and reserved. In fact, Camille was Hali's only real friend. When Camille was absent from school Hali preferred the company of her books at lunch rather than people. Camille secretly envied Hali's indifference to constant companionship. She had never felt secure in being alone. It didn't feel natural. It wasn't natural. Not to Camille and not to zebras or any animal that traveled in a pack or a herd. Zebras knew that separating from the herd could mean imminent death via lurking lions. Camille shuddered at the thought of Hali being the lone zebra in this scenario. Not only alone, but alone at night, not telling one soul where she went. Hali hadn't even left a note behind to clue anyone in.

When Camille was questioned by Officer Mick a couple of hours earlier, she was forced to consider everything she knew about Hali. Did Hali have a boyfriend? Was she planning on running away? Did she get along with her parents? Did she have any enemies?

Each question forced Camille to examine every detail of her friendship from a new perspective. Up until yesterday Camille could answer each question with certainty. No. No. Yes. No. But today, Camille wondered if she had missed something in all their years of friendship.

She desperately searched her brain for a logical explanation to why Hali would go to the beach by herself at night, without anyone.

Had she left something behind the prior afternoon?

Camille didn't think so. Sunscreen, sunglasses, water, car keys and a beach towel were the only items they had ever brought to the beach. And except for the sunglasses, which Camille remembered Hali wearing on the car ride home, and car keys, which you really couldn't leave the beach without, nothing was valuable enough to return to in the middle of the night. Nothing was amiss except for reports of the Emerald Cove Lighthouse coming back to life after years of being dormant and Hali's car in the parking lot. Yet something had to be, because Hali was gone.

Emerald Cove had become the scene of a game Camille would play on the back of a cereal box where you were supposed to compare two similar pictures and find what made them different. Except with the cereal box, you had the advantage of being provided with the first picture. The before and after. The yesterday against today. The problem was, Camille knew Hali's yesterday picture better than anyone. Which made her wonder, had she ever really viewed the first picture clearly to begin with?

As Camille reflected on it all she heard a shout from a man down by the shore, stopping her dead in her tracks. She peered up from the sand to find a crowd formed around him. Camille's heart sprang to action, pounding in her ears. She stood frozen a solid five seconds before her legs finally ran over to the group. The thick, loose sand slowed her stride with every imprint her feet created until she made it to the packed, wet sand on the shore and could run faster. Making her way through the crowd she received some sympathetic looks as she pressed forward. The yelling man stood next to an officer who held an evidence bag in one hand and a soaking item of clothing, with what looked to be tongs, in the other. The officer gently unfolded the balled mass of wet cotton to reveal a huge sweatshirt. A sweatshirt that Camille had seen many times in the past four years, including yesterday. Camille's throat formed a knot that she was certain would silence any words she could speak if she had any. Crying would have been a relief, but her tears were like a stubborn child holding her back to a closed door; begging to be left alone yet wanting nothing more than to escape the prison she built for herself. Camille's pain at seeing the article of clothing summoned a four-year-old memory to the surface from the summer before freshmen year.

"You're not really going to buy that thing, are you?" fourteen-year-old Camille questioned Hali in the junior's clothing department of Wright-Mart.

"Yes. I. Am," Hali stated with confidence and a little pride.

"Camille," a voice belonging to Camille's mother, Diane, warned in a sweet southern drawl. "Let Hali get what she wants." Turning to Hali, she said, "Turquoise will be a beautiful color on you, but perhaps you might try to get a size or three smaller," she motioned to the other sweatshirts on the rack for Hali to consider.

Ignoring her mother, Camille kept her attention on Hali. "Why?"

"Why, what?" Hali asked, holding the sweatshirt to her body, indifferent to Camille's badgering.

"Why would you buy a touristy sweatshirt from Wright-Mart of all places?" Camille responded with irritation.

"Camille don't be a snob, the sweatshirt is fine," Diane stated more firmly this time. "But I would look at a smaller—"

"We live at the beach for crying out loud. WHY not buy an Emerald Cove sweatshirt at an Emerald Cove Beach shop?" Camille interrupted, turning to her mother for help. "Mom! Tell her, please. Aren't you the one always telling us that we should support local businesses if we can?"

"Well, yes I did, but ..." Diane faltered between holding her ground on her current point and not going against her previous preaching.

"So, why would you buy that sweatshirt, Hali? It would fit an ogre better than you, and it's almost the same color as one, too."

"Hey, there is nothing wrong with ogres," Hali rebutted with a Scottish accent.

Camille stared at Hali, not amused.

Hali huffed out a breath of air, rolling her eyes, then said, "I want to have something that's easy to throw on at the beach. I *don't like fufu cover ups, because they don't actually cover anything."* Hali was modest then, even before she had any curves.

Neilan scoffed. *"Like you have anything to cover,"* Camille's seventeen-year-old brother mumbled before being scolded discreetly by Diane.

"Plus"—Hali glared at Neilan—*"this is cheaper."*

"Your parents would be proud you are spending money wisely, Hali, but I already told Camille I would stop at a local shop on the way so she could look at cover ups, if you would like to wait?"

"I appreciate it, Mrs. O'Riley, but I'm going to stick with this one."

"Now that that is settled, can we get our snacks and sunscreen and get out of here? We've wasted five minutes on this, and dad will leave for his fishing trip without me if we don't get to the beach soon," Neilan asked in a snarky tone.

"Neilan, don't be rude. As proud as I am at how seriously you are taking these fishing trips, we still have another forty minutes to meet your father," Mrs. O'Riley countered. *"But if you're happy with the sweatshirt, Hali, we should get a move on."*

"I am," Hali affirmed.

"Wait," Camille said. Camille could see in Hali's eyes that she expected for Camille to pester her more about her sweatshirt choice. Maybe throw a few more digs at it and tell her that it was made by some poor kid in a sweatshop halfway across the world. But Hali's face lit in surprise as Camille said her next words.

"I want to get one, too."

Neilan threw back his head while rubbing his palms across his eyebrows. *"Just shoot me now."*

Camille was taken out of the memory with a woman crying to the left of her. Abigail Shawn. Theo Shawn cradled his arm around his wife with his head down, shedding his own silent tears. The search party dissipated in a reticent agreement that Camille missed while she was lost in the memory.

She turned her gaze to the once vibrant, turquoise sweatshirt that now appeared gray and tattered. The whimsical, orange, calligraphy-styled font scrolled across the chest, and the black and white lighthouse was chipped, cracked, and unrecognizable from its formal glory. The old letters and image, now faint shadows, devoid of the life that once filled them.

4

SWISH SPLASH

"Ugh," Hali groaned while the right side of her face pressed into the sand. The mid-morning sun rays punished her shoulders, holding her in place like a toppled bookshelf, while the other half of her body sank into the cooler grains produced from her shadow. The squawking of seagulls shrieked above as a steady *swish swish* sounded over the unwavering thrum of the ocean waters push-pull dance with the shore. Fear gripped at Hali as awareness set in.

Why was she lying in the sand like a drunken tourist?

A few truths trickled into her foggy memory. Today was her eighteenth birthday. She had a terrible dream—a nightmare. One so intensely real, she had slept walked and driven to the beach. The memory of throwing on her favorite sweatshirt, grabbing her car keys, and leaving her house was so vivid it had to be true.

Swish. Swish.

Hali's eyes opened slightly at the sound to see a gruff, disheveled man sitting on a discarded log that hovered halfway in the ocean and halfway onto sand, sharpening a tree branch with what looked to be a shell. Adrenaline coursed through her veins as she pushed herself out of her sand burrow. Hali stared at the man mere feet away, word-lessly, while wiping sand off one side of her face.

Unaffected by Hali, the gruff man continued sharpening his tree branch, not sparing her a look. Beside him sat a pile of clothes on the sand. Hali spotted a few cheerful beach dresses and board shorts, which did not appear to belong to the vagabond, whose own clothes were tattered, dingy, and lifeless.

"Who are you?" Hali questioned, wrapping her sunburnt arms around her waist. She shifted side to side, feeling exposed in only her tank top and cotton shorts that she had worn to bed the night before.

Where the heck had her favorite sweatshirt gone?
Swish. Swish.

The melodic shaving continued as the man remained focused on his task, ignoring Hali as if she wasn't there. After a few more attempts at conversation, Hali gave up. Confrontation had never really been her thing and she had enough concerns of her own at the moment.

Filled with confusion, she decided to head back home. Her parents had to be wondering where she had gone, with the sun moving towards its afternoon position in the sky. How she had managed to sleepwalk and drive to the beach was a mystery. She pushed the unsettling thought away, vowing to confront it again only after she had returned home.

As Hali started turning for the parking lot, a light shined in her peripheral, eliciting a déjà vu, that had her stopping in her tracks. The foreboding feeling startled her as she lifted her arm to shade her eyes. But when the light changed directions suddenly, no longer blinding her, she was met head on with its source. Her stomach dropped to her feet as she witnessed a giant wave erupting out of the waters that had been mellow moments before. Sunlight glared from the precipice of the liquid mountain, as it threatened to crash down onto the shore.

Hali's feet twisted the opposite direction towards the Emerald Cove parking lot to escape, her upper body lagging behind like a cartoon character with wide, panicked eyes to match. But once her head caught up to her lower body, her panic turned to horror when she found there was no parking lot. Instead, a forest of pine trees stood before her, with some trees cut down, but uncleared. Out of options, Hali continued running towards the forest, until new sounds had her coming to a halt.

Voices.

A safe distance from the crushing wave, Hali whipped her head back around to discover the looming wave had vanished and in its place were seven figures. Three men, three women and a boy, who couldn't have been older than twelve, stood stark naked and dripping wet.

"Hello there," one of the men greeted. The three men, who appeared a few years older than Hali, erupted in laughter. She spun away from them as quickly as she could, her cheeks hot with embarrassment, the ominous wave forgotten. Irritation swelled within her at every chuckle they had at her expense. Last time she checked Emerald Cove wasn't a nude beach. She hoped a police officer would happen on them and slap the cackling hyenas with an indecent exposure charge. Maybe that would silence their arrogant hysteria.

"Cut it out, Kai. Let her get her bearings," she heard a woman say. Her approach was stern without being harsh. Hali guessed it had come from the oldest of the women she saw based off her mature tone. "You can turn around now, we are decent." Hali reluctantly swiveled, meeting the gray eyes of the oldest woman, who didn't look much older than thirty, with blonde hair and peach skin—Hali had been right. Her eyes were kind and concerned when she looked at her and said, "I'm Marilla. Are you hungry?"

Hali took a few steps closer, no longer fearing for her life, but still wary of the strangers. They stared at her with curiosity and a bit of uncertainty as Hali stared the same at them. Outnumbered, she looked away from their invading eyes many times, pulling at her pajamas nervously and failing to cover more of herself.

After what felt like an eternity, Hali spoke, remembering that the blonde woman named Marilla had asked her if she was hungry.

"No, I'm good," Hali lied, attempting to fill the silence as quickly as she could. "Actually, I think I've gone further down the beach than usual and got myself a little turned around. Do you think you could point me in the right direction for the parking lot?"

Being a native of Emerald Cove it almost pained Hali to ask for directions. But after seeing the unimaginable wave appear from thin air and vanish just as quickly, she grew desperate to get back home. Even disoriented, Hali couldn't recall ever being to this section of beach before. A fact she felt best to keep to herself. She didn't think it would be wise to tell the strangers the circumstances that had led her there. Mostly, because the details were still murky for her, but also because she didn't want their judgements. Not that the opinion of nudists on a public beach mattered much to her anyway, but even still, she didn't need the extra aggravation.

The strangers continued staring at her and Hali recognized that they were all uniquely beautiful. Each with mixtures of mocha, bronze, and peach skin. Hali assumed that the young boy, that stood next to Marilla, belonged to her since they both shared the same gray eyes, though his skin was a few shades darker.

Each person in the group carried wooden spears similar to what the gruff man sitting on the log was making when she first awakened. However, these spears impaled about one-hundred fish each. The young boy held his spear up like a torch, pride threatening the seams of his reserved smile. The group finally broke eye contact with Hali, changing their focus to Marilla. Their shifting gazes passing a figurative torch to the eldest woman to answer Hali's question.

As if on cue, the blonde woman answered. "This isn't Emerald Cove." She paused, before adding, "You are on the Eyes' Land."

"The Island?" Hali repeated, uncertain she heard the woman right.

"No," the dark-bronze skin man named Kai interrupted. Pointing to each of his wide-opened eyes, he said, "the Eyes'"—ensuring to emphasize each word with as much condescension as he could muster. Then to drive his point home even more, or to be as big of an ass as possible, he expanded his arms upward, circling around like a travel guide, ending his show with the word—"Land." Hali glared at him as he circled and laughed obnoxiously, summoning the other men to join him.

"That's enough, Kai," Marilla interjected.

Tired, burnt, hungry, and in need of a bathroom break, Hali was about to crack. Not a morning person on the best of days, the futile conversation with the strangers was putting her on edge. She had fulfilled her daily beach and crazy people quota for the day—maybe even for the week—without Camille. Her burnt skin would need the break and her frazzled mind would need the solace. But first, she needed to get home.

"Well, this has been ..." Hali started, uncertain how to finish her sentence, so she changed the subject instead. "Do any of you have a cell phone I could use?"

At the ripe age of eighteen, Hali hadn't owned her own cell phone, since she hadn't cared enough about having one. Her parents had encouraged her plenty of times to carry one in case of emergencies, offering to add her to their cell phone plan. But she had assured them there was no need since she was either always near someone who had a cell phone or never far away from home to require one. She cursed herself now for her stubbornness.

Again, the group looked back and forth amongst each other. Searching for the next victim to convince Hali that they weren't crazy. Kai clasped his hands behind his head while squeezing his arms around his face in frustration. Sighing in annoyance he paced towards the water. The other two men followed him, with what looked to be an attempt to calm him.

Hali tilted her head, watching the men's interaction, puzzled. They were acting as if Hali was the one not making sense. She wondered for a moment if Kai's frustration was all for show just to goad her some more. But his irritation was too real not to be genuine.

As the thought tumbled through her mind, the young mocha-skin woman's voice broke through the silence.

"What's your name?" she asked.

"Hali," Hali reluctantly answered as her heart started to pick up speed. Something didn't feel right. Being lost only made it worse. Her heartbeat drummed in her ears as her fight or flight instincts idled.

The mocha-skin woman with caramel eyes looked to the others and then back to Hali. "I'm Carmya," she supplied. "Listen, I know that this all seems very strange to you—it certainly is to us—but you are not on Emerald Cove anymore."

Hali grimaced. She felt the smallest amount of relief mixed with dread at the tiniest bit of clarity the young woman offered. Maybe Hali had gone to a beach further away. It wasn't ideal and extremely alarming considering she had traveled so far in an unconscious state. But it also answered the question of why the Emerald Cove parking lot wasn't where it was supposed to be. Hali waited for the woman to continue, while she mentally listed all the other beaches near Emerald Cove that she could have ended up on.

"Emerald Cove is not far away from here," Carmya stated, filling Hali with hope as she waited for the woman to provide directions. But that's not what happened—not even close. The nervous looks shared by the others should have been Hali's first clue to not expect it, but Denial was a lovely place to visit when the outside world stopped making sense.

Carmya's eyebrows drew together slightly before she spoke, and Hali for the life of her couldn't understand why it was so hard for the woman to spit out some directions so she could be on her way. Carmya placed an arm on Hali's shoulder—which should have been Hali's second clue that this news wasn't going to be pretty, and said, "But you won't be able to go back ... ever."

Wasting no time, Hali sprinted at the word "ever," like it was a whip and she a horse. In the midst of her terror-induced dash she could have sworn she heard Kai tell Carmya "good job," but she couldn't be sure with air whistling in her ears as she whizzed away. She hadn't run since high school ended. But with muscle memory and fear coursing through her body she was sure she could set a personal record even with the sand slowing her tread. Not wanting to go back towards the forest and risk getting even more lost, Hali ran along the packed sand of the shore knowing that was going to be the fastest way to escape. She prayed for a familiar landmark to appear and help guide her way home.

Escaping the crazy seven, she hurdled over the log that still held the gruff man shaving branches. As she ascended on her leap of freedom Hali's legs were met with a splash of water by the gruff man himself.

Really? she thought, as water drenched her whole body.

Bracing for her descent, the lower half of Hali's body pulsed with a sudden surge of electricity. The sensation surprised her, as she peered down to discover her legs were no longer legs but had transformed midair. Anxiety and awe consumed her to find that her legs had fused together and were covered with pale violet scales that shimmered under the sun and fins had replaced her feet. An iridescent bra of the same making was all that covered her upper body, leaving her stomach exposed. Milliseconds passed before her astonishment cost her and she thudded to the earth. Landing on her side Hali flailed like a dying fish—albeit a beautiful dying fish. As the thought of what she must look like passed through her mind, she could hear Kai's rolling laughter in the background—once again, finding amusement at her expense. Just when she thought things couldn't get worse, she looked up to see her prayer had been answered.

Across the ocean sat a landmark that jarred her from her

new form. Despite seeing the sight from her bedroom window all her life, she had never seen if from this viewpoint. The Emerald Cove Lighthouse sat miles and miles away in the distance. The image assaulted her memory with one word.

Captured.

5

FIRST SWIM

"IF YOU DON'T WANT us to see you naked you better get in the water," Kai yelled, before proceeding to cackle with the other two men; one was tall and gangly with ashy brown hair and peach skin, while the other was shorter and stockier with black hair and olive skin.

Startled, Hali looked down to see her newly acquired fins turning back into feet. The tank top and shorts she had started her day with sat on the sand next to her, ripped to shreds. Not taking any chances with exposing herself, Hali frantically rolled into the ocean like fire on a gasoline-drenched wick. Electricity pulsed through her feet as they transformed back into fins.

Was she dreaming? Maybe she had sun poisoning and her new fins were only a hallucination.

As Hali back floated to the surface, she examined her body a little closer. Carmya joined her in the water, sporting her own fins, but turquoise. "You'll get used to it," Carmya reassured.

"What's happening?" Hali asked, through chattering teeth. "Am I a ..." Hali's breath caught in her chest as she blinked away salty, ocean droplets from her eyes. There was too much information and not enough all at once. The sand still shimmered, and the ocean waters were the same blue she had known all her life, but she was now different.

Changed.

Hali struggled not to stare at her body. She studied her pale violet scales glistening in the sun and couldn't make sense of any of it. As a young girl, she would glide through a pool or the ocean with Camille, their hair flowing, pretending to be mermaids. But even as a child, Hali knew that mermaids existed in the fantasy world only. They weren't real. And she definitely never believed herself to be one—not then or now. She tried to remind herself of those facts as she gaped at herself, waiting for her eyes to stop playing tricks on her, and for her human form to reappear. That, or she would wake up from the nightmare that had gone on long enough. But as she stared and stared, she remained the same.

Growing up in Emerald Cove, Hali knew there were small islands that surrounded it. She even visited a few throughout the years on her family's boat. But she had never heard of the Eyes' Land. Not once. With Emerald Cove still being within sight, none of it added up. Why had she never heard of it? How could she be found if no one knew where to look? She couldn't be discovered in a place no one knew existed. The thoughts sent a shiver through her spine.

Images of her legs burning, driving to the beach, and a magnetic lighthouse with a slamming door, bubbled to the surface of Hali's recollection. Her stomach was left with a sinking feeling at the memories while her body buoyed in the ocean. But who was her captor, or captors? She didn't remember seeing anyone the night before at the lighthouse. And if Emerald Cove was so close, why couldn't she just go back? Carmya had said she couldn't go back ... *ever*. What was preventing her?

Hali was a decent swimmer. Not Olympic worthy, but able to get back and forth in a pool. But swimming in the ocean was nothing like swimming in a pool. Rip currents were known to disarm even advanced swimmers who were unfamiliar of how to handle their pull.

Looking unsure, Carmya hesitantly answered the question Hali couldn't finish through her shallow breaths.

"You're a mermaid, Hali, as you've always been. Or Anchor, as we call ourselves, since we are anchored to both land and sea, existing in both worlds. But we live more of our time out of the ocean than we do in it."

Hali shot an incredulous glance at Carmya. "But I haven't been a mermaid or Anchor. I think I would have noticed."

Carmya's calm countenance never faltered. "But you have. It's just been sitting dormant within you, like grass in the winter."

Dormant?

"If that's true, then what caused the mermaid part of me to un-dormant all of a sudden?"

Carmya chuckled at the made-up word. "I don't know exactly," she said reluctantly, before hiding behind a forced smile that didn't reach her eyes. Hali sensed that Carmya knew more than she was comfortable saying. Their conversation was cut short when the other two women entered the water.

Marilla approached, swimming to Hali and Carmya, with the other young woman who had tan skin, dark brown hair, and chocolate eyes. The tan mermaid wore a genuine white smile that illuminated against her other features. Her orange scales were as vibrant as the sun.

"Hi, I'm Delphia," she said, her tone chipper. Hali only managed a small nod and a quiet "hi" in return.

"I sent the boys back to take lunch to camp," Marilla said, flapping her pink fins. "And to bring you back some clothes." Marilla's compassionate smile managed to settle Hali's nerves, if only a little.

"Your fins are much more fun to use than they are to look at," Delphia smiled, nudging Hali softly with her elbow. "I'll race you." Delphia tunneled to the horizon, like an orange falling star shooting across the ocean, before Hali had a chance to register her words.

Marilla looked at a shaky Hali, whose eyes flitted along the path Delphia swam. "No time like the present, Hali. Let's find out what your fins can do."

Blood drained from Hali's face, tangling with the nerves fluttering in her stomach at the sight of Delphia's speed. A cold sweat dotted her nose and forehead. It was like waiting in line for a roller coaster, watching riders plummet down the first drop, knowing it would soon be your fate.

"Will I be able to c-control how fast I go?" Hali stammered; shivering even though the air and water were warm. "How will I breathe?"

Marilla smiled tenderly, placing a comforting hand on her shoulder. "Trust yourself Hali, you are built for this."

Hali took a breath in, overwhelmed. Twenty-four hours ago she was sunbathing at the beach with Camille, with not a care in the world. The recollection was a rabbit hole of sadness, provoking her to worry about what her parents were going through. At this point in the day they must have discovered she was gone. Even when she did sleep in, they always came in her room to kiss her forehead before they went to work. Most of the time she was awake when they did, too comfortable to leave the warmth of her bed just yet.

Remembering where she was, Hali refocused on the present, reigning in her tears that threatened to spill in front of the strangers. Trading wistfulness for motivation, Hali decided to let her memories fuel her with purpose.

She would find a way home, she told herself.

Gathering as much courage as she could muster, she stopped treading; holding her breath before her face lowered into the water. Once completely submerged, and her air had run out, instinct told her to take in water. But Hali stubbornly resisted, afraid of the unknown. A fire ignited in her chest from the lack of oxygen. Her temples throbbed. Hali's body screamed at her, as she continued holding on to her breath, too embarrassed to come to the surface for air and admit defeat. When the possibility of gulping water had become a less painful option than holding her breath, Hali gave way to her instincts.

At her first intake of water Hali's body adjusted, like a newborn baby taking its first breath. She could feel the shift of her breath go from her mouth to her scales. The pulsing in her head went away instantly as Hali's body absorbed what it needed. No longer deprived and pained, but fulfilled and relieved.

As soon as she adapted to the new environment her nerves calmed, but her heart galloped in excitement. Every color on the spectrum, even ones she hadn't seen before, came alive, highlighting life below the skies. The saltwater washed against her eyes without burning and she could see everything under the horizon line with such clarity. It was as if she had been watching a grainy black-and-white television that had suddenly turned 4K, but even more striking.

Breathing and sight in check, her body streamed forward with seamless speed, that felt exhilarating without being too intense. Cheers erupted above water that sounded as if whoever was cheering was standing right next to her. The sounds weren't even muffled. In the distance, she could hear the high pitch squeals of an animal that she had never heard before, but once she heard the sound there was no mistaking the source.

Dolphins?

"I can understand dolphins?" Hali said aloud to herself. The sound of her voice had her take pause. "And I can talk underwater?" she added, as she touched her throat. The novelty of the new experience had her so immersed that she hadn't even noticed when she was no longer alone.

"Amongst other things," a voice answered, startling Hali.

Hali whipped around to the male voice, finding that it belonged to the taller friend of Kai. He swam around her, his merman transformation not concealing his lanky frame. He sported green scales and his smile held mischief that put Hali on edge.

"I didn't get a chance to introduce myself earlier. The name's Jett," he said, staring at Hali intently. "And I didn't *catch* your name."

"Hali," she answered, keeping her voice steady as she tried to decode his intentions. "What other things?"

As if on cue, Kai appeared from behind Jett with his other shorter friend. "Things that would frighten the fins out of you," Kai said.

They circled Hali, slowly at first before picking up speed, never taking their eyes from her. Swirls of navy blue, forest green, and black enclosed her like an ice cube in a tall glass.

"Worse than sharks," Jett added.

"Or any nightmare you've had," reinforced their black-haired friend.

Fins began poking at her arms as she tried to time an exit that didn't get her knocked down in the process. A cyclone of colors blurred around her. A display as equally impressive as it was frightening. The brief elation she had enjoyed earlier from being underwater quickly dissipated, trepidation taking its place.

When realization set in that waiting for a gap to slide through the ominous vortex wasn't going to happen, an idea occurred to her. The high jump hadn't been Hali's event in track, but equipped with the speed of her new fins, she knew she could make it work.

Lowering herself to the bottom of the ocean floor, her tormentors followed, never ceasing their spinning. Unnerved and annoyed, she hoped they would get dizzy, pass out, and eaten by the unnamed danger they threatened her about.

With great speed, Hali undulated her body, with her arms pointing straight up to the sun. She launched from the ocean floor to the surface in a perfect arc, evading her cyclone of harassers. As soon as her entire body was airborne, she pushed outward toward the shore. Reentering the water on her descent, she swam as fast as she could until her fingertips met the sand. On the shore she flopped near the gruff man. He tossed clothes in her direction. Hali peered down at the garments in her hands, confused. Until she noticed her fins fading to feet, quickly changing her back to her unclothed human form.

In a race against time and modesty, Hali threw the clothes on as fast as she could, thanking the gruff man as she did. No reply was given as he continued shaving branches with a shell. But Hali hadn't expected one. She had learned that much from her short time on the Eyes' Land.

After putting on a cotton sundress that could best be described as a long tank top, the three women—Marilla,

Carmya, and Delphia—came out of the water and quickly put on their clothes. Hali was sure they did it for her sake more than their own and she appreciated the gesture more than they knew. But she thought better than to tell them so.

Carmya approached Hali on a mission. "What did you do, Hali?" she asked, her tone laced with accusation.

"What do you mean?" Hali questioned, wondering if she had accidentally voiced her thanks to the women for getting dressed without realizing it.

"You know exactly what I mean," Carmya stated, staring Hali down. Her demeanor had switched from gentle to indignant. "Explain to me, what I just witnessed."

"Carmya ..." Marilla warned, wearing a grimace that held a hint of guilt.

Now Hali was irked.

What did she have to explain? And what was Marilla not saying?

Irritated, Hali begged the question, "Explain what? I'm not sure how I got here, I'm apparently a mermaid or Anchor as you call yourselves, three of your friends thought it would be funny to surround me like sharks and torment me in the water. And to top it all off, I just had to pee in the ocean, which I haven't done since I was really little. Well, except that one-time last year when they locked the bathrooms at the beach, but other than that—"

"Why do you *glow*, Hali?" Delphia asked, adding another marble of information to Hali's already full marble jar. Delphia said the word "glow" as if it scared her to say it aloud. Both girls gazed at her with suspicion, as if she was an alien they were trying to decide what to do with. Hali was just as surprised by the information as they were.

Was glowing not something mermaids did? she wondered.

Up until a few hours ago mermaid-ing wasn't something

she did either, but the strangers seemed to be okay with that part of her. She wished that her nightmare would end, and she'd find herself home, in bed, with the smell of French toast wafting through her nose, waking her up.

"Like I said, *your friends* ambushed me in the water. I jumped out to escape. That's all I know," Hali answered. "What does it mean to glow?"

Marilla's worried eyes relaxed as she set her very comforting hand on Hali's shoulder. Hali didn't miss the leery glances Carmya and Delphia shared. She wondered what they weren't saying.

"Hali let's get back to camp, so you can meet some of the others," Marilla offered, diffusing the situation. "I think this has been a long puzzling day for us all and it's not even noon yet. Let's get some lunch in our bellies so we can figure all this out."

Marilla's idea was the first one that had made sense to Hali all day. She was fully ready to eat something, but as luck would have it, Hali's abrupt departure from the water brought consequences.

A waterspout formed in the ocean out of nowhere, compelling the women to spin in its direction. The powerful column of water was completely out of place against the otherwise calm waters, as the massive wave had been earlier. Unlike the surge from before, the women appeared surprised by this anomaly, to which they had no involvement.

Suddenly, three figures catapulted from the spray. Kai and his friends flew out of the ocean towards the group on the shore. The shock and horror Carmya and Delphia wore on their faces at the display, revealed to Hali that mermen flying out of waterspouts wasn't a common occurrence. Hali suspected the women held her culpable, since her own leap from the water most likely created the water pressure responsible for their ejection.

The flying trio thudded loudly and painfully on the shore, groaning as they rolled around in the sand. Hali tried her best to suppress a grin. The women shifted their gazes to her as if waiting for an explanation. She had none.

The women went to the men. Hali held back with the gruff man, feeling no remorse. Rolling her eyes, she looked away from the spectacle, scoffing as the men accepted the women's nurturing.

They deserved what they got and more, she thought.

When the waterspout had erupted in the ocean, Hali noticed that the gruff man had stopped shaving, and she could have sworn she even saw him glance her way during the ordeal. But as soon as Hali noticed his pause from work, he resumed as if he had never stopped. The three women had been too distracted by the waterspout to notice.

Swish. Swish.

Once dressed, the men walked to camp with their heads down alongside each of the women. Hali hung a few steps behind, observing Delphia comforting Jett, while Carmya comforted Kai. Marilla, on the other hand, lectured the black-haired Anchor she walked with, on not only his behavior towards Hali in the ocean, but Kai's and Jett's. Hali learned his name was Toru through Marilla's scolding, and had to contain a chuckle on his unfortunate luck on walking companions. Not that Hali felt sorry for the fact that he was receiving a tongue lashing, but he wasn't any guiltier than Kai or Jett, who were receiving compassion for the same offense. Hali smiled to herself to see the men so defeated and in need of mothering—amazed that they were the same men that had evoked the tiniest bit of fear in her earlier. Boys in men's bodies were all they were. As they made their way to camp, Hali noticed the younger boy who had stood with Marilla at their first meeting hadn't returned to the water after taking the fish back to camp.

As she thought this, she heard the snap of a branch behind her. Turning around to look, she found the gruff man following. Hali gave him a closed mouth smile, nodding her head at him in recognition as she continued walking. Her smile wasn't returned, and he kept as equal of a distance to Hali as Hali had with the pairings in front of her.

No one said a word to her, and she didn't say a word to anyone else. She took in the pine trees: their scent, their shade and their beauty. Pine trees and the beach always made her feel at home which she thought somewhat ironic in her current predicament. Now the pine trees and the beach felt like a trick. She was thankful for her calloused feet, the result of spending plenty of time outdoors without footwear. Otherwise, her feet would have most likely bled on the rough path to camp which was littered with little rocks and pine straw.

While Hali was taking in her surroundings the group arrived at camp. A glimmer of relief fluttered through her stomach as she looked on to hundreds of Anchors bustling around fire pits. Old and young worked together to prepare the afternoon meal. The aroma of fish and something sweet made its way to Hali's nostrils making her salivate. She didn't eat fish too often, but her impatient stomach wasn't picky. Sustenance of any kind would help her foggy mind and waning energy level.

Maybe she could get more answers from the others at camp.

It hadn't escaped Hali's notice that Marilla evaded her question about what it meant to glow. But Hali would worry about that after she'd eaten.

The simple promise of a warm meal let the spark of hope grow within her as the prospect of going home sooner than later started to become a real possibility. She thought with a meal inside of her and fins, getting to Emerald Cove would be no problem. Hali grew almost impatient planning out her journey home. But the spark that had kindled quickly, extinguished just as fast, when an unfortunate encounter stood in her way, before she even stepped foot into camp.

6

HURDLE

"Who is this?" an angry man stopped them at the entrance of camp, glowering at Hali with the same bitterness as his tone. He was around the same age as Kai and his sidekicks.

"Cas, this is Hali," Marilla said evenly as she moved to stand next to her. "I think she may be the one Mamie told us about." Hali turned her head away from Cas's cold blue eyes to gape at Marilla, as more questions erupted in her brain.

What one? Had the strangers expected her? Who was Mamie?

Cas's imposing figure guarded the entrance of camp. Despite not being really tall, he was extremely intimidating. Height wise he was average for a man, but taller than Hali. Then again Hali was short, so most people were taller than her. But Cas's fit build stood with authority.

"How do you know that, Marilla?" Cas shook his head in disbelief, crossing his arms, unconvinced of Marilla's statement. "It's more likely she is one of *them* than the *one*. How do you know she's not going to flay us down to nothing?"

"Ugh," Hali sounded aloud her disgust at the image of flaying *anything*. The group glanced at her as she wrapped her arms around her waist, comforting herself from their judging eyes and Cas's brutal accusation. A killer she was not.

Figuratively, Hali had wished for the three mer-boys to be eaten by the unknown danger in the water that they had terrorized her about; in reality, she would have been mortified if her wish had come true.

"Who do you think I am?" Hali asked, but her question went unanswered as the others debated about that very topic without ever consulting *her* thoughts on it.

"She also glows!" Kai added in the middle of their debate. Hali turned her head to a smug Kai smiling back at her. He had the nerve to wink, which made Hali briefly reconsider how upset she'd actually be if Kai ended up a sea monster's dinner. Though the fact that he mentioned her glowing to Cas gave Hali clarity on one thing; glowing definitely wasn't an Anchor thing.

Hali's empty stomach growled as if sensing the chance for a warm meal slipping away with every spoken doubt of her trustworthiness.

While listening, Hali began nervously pulling sand from her fingernails and was surprised when Cas abruptly stepped towards her. Lifting her chin to look at him, he inspected her. Hali's wide-opened hazel eyes met his piercing blue ones, out of shock more than desire. His nostrils flared and his beryl eyes appeared darker up close. Had he not been scowling at her Hali might have thought he was attractive with his warm peach skin and dark brown hair. But his looks were the last thing on Hali's mind as he treated her with contempt; her hunger and thirst growing by the second.

A sheltered girl as well as a bit of an introvert, Hali had never found herself in such a precarious position. As an only child, she valued independence and her books, steering clear of people and situations that complicated those values. Emerald Cove was a small community, and though she was generally liked by her peers she didn't feel it was necessary to have a large group of friends.

However, Hali's parents believed it was important for their only child to socialize with children her own age. And if they hadn't encouraged her friendship with Camille when she was young, Hali may not have had any real friends.

Oddly enough, Camille was the complete opposite of Hali. Camille could approach a group of people and start a conversation in a way that Hali never could, and she secretly envied Camille for it.

She was reminded of Camille's courage, as she gazed into the bitter man's eyes, wishing nothing more than to be Camille in that moment. She would know what to do. The awkwardness of being face-to-face with another person while others watched the interaction play out, was almost too much to handle. But Hali was determined to not break eye contact. She would not give Cas the satisfaction of knowing he made her uncomfortable.

In all Hali's life, she had never experienced being hated so fiercely, especially by a person she didn't know. The snickers and dirty looks she received when she had gone through puberty were mild in comparison. Cas's resentment practically radiated from his pupils like a laser. There was nothing at all funny about her predicament, but there was a part of her that felt like laughing at the absurdity of her conundrum. Hali's depleted state kept her hysteria in check.

"What are you?" Cas demanded, still holding Hali's chin. Hali noticed a scar above his right eyebrow that reached to his temple and she had the oddest urge to touch it. As she fixated on his scar the gruff man "hmphed" in what sounded like disapproval.

Did he hear her thoughts? Hali wondered.

Embarrassed by her treatment and wandering mind, Hali snapped her chin to the right to get out of Cas's hold, retreating a few steps away from his grasp. Wrapping her arms back around her hollowing waist she glared at Cas with the same vehemence he showed her.

"Your guess is as good as mine," Hali answered. Her reply didn't hold half the indignation as Cas's question, but she knew her stubborn withdrawal from his inquisition rattled Cas and threatened her goal of a warm meal. The rest of the group looked at her with uncertainty and Cas's eyes lit briefly with befuddlement. His frustration brewed and he became eerily quiet.

Not saying a word, he loomed over the group, but his eyes remained only on Hali. She refused to look at him after tearing her chin away; no longer sure if appearing strong was the right move. Uncertain and scared, she grimaced at the trees.

Silence hung in the warm air, stagnant and unforgiving. As she focused on the trees for comfort more than enjoyment, she regretted her moment of rebellion. Hali wished she could find the right words to settle his concerns, but she had no answers. Her foggy mind couldn't think straight.

Hali had always chosen her words carefully, contemplating then speaking. As a result, she didn't say much most of the time. It helped her stay out of trouble up until now. But how could she explain why she glowed when she wasn't sure herself? She hadn't even noticed herself glowing. Anything she said would be a lie.

Angry at Cas as much as herself, Hali stewed—ruminating over all that had been said while trying to find the words that would unlock Cas's compassion, and allow her into camp. But no words came. Her crossed arms hid her hands squeezing the fabric on the sides of her dress. The rest of the group, including the three mer-boys, remained silent. Carmya gazed at Cas with adoration, while everyone else looked to him with respect. Even Marilla didn't question Cas's outrage, despite being the oldest. Hali was curious how someone of his age could hold so much power and why he was using it to hate her. There was so much she didn't understand about these people that she wasn't sure how to eliminate their fears of her when she didn't know what their fears were to begin with.

After an uncomfortable amount of silence had passed, Marilla spoke. "I think we should listen to what she has to say and make an informed decision. She genuinely doesn't seem to know anything. I don't believe she is dangerous."

Cas scoffed. "I'm sure she wouldn't want you to *believe* she's dangerous. Taking Anchors out is much easier if we don't see it coming."

"Cas, please," Marilla pleaded, "we need to hear her out. If she is who I think she is—"

"And if she isn't who you think she is?" Cas questioned.

"Then—" Marilla hesitated as the edges of her eyes crinkled in contemplation.

"We outnumber her," Kai interjected.

Confused by the helpful threat Hali glanced at Kai briefly. The glare he beamed in her direction expressed that his words had no intention of helping her. But Hali was no longer afraid of him or the other two mer-boys after watching them walk back to camp with their tails between their legs. Launching the three mer-boys had been an unintentional result of her own launch from the ocean, but their wounded egos didn't know that. Hali certainly wasn't about to mention the incident in front of Cas, knowing it probably wouldn't tip the scales in her favor. But as Hali soon figured out, that didn't mean the rest of the Anchors were as willing to keep the incident to themselves.

Carmya glanced at Kai, but quickly looked away. Her guilty look wasn't missed by Cas.

"What is it?" Cas asked, his suspicion growing.

Marilla, Hali's only advocate and the only person who seemed to understand that she wasn't there by choice, looked at her with an apology in her eyes. Hali knew then, she was not going to enter camp. Angry disappointment replaced her clawing hunger.

Hali half-listened to Carmya as she divulged the earlier catapulting incident to Cas, her focus remaining on the trees. It should have made Hali feel better that Carmya spoke with no enjoyment. But as she listened, something in her shifted. Pride grew from the last dying ember of her hope. Despite her stomach's angry protest, she turned around and left; heading back towards the beach where only the ocean could be heard. No food was worth being ripped apart over. She refused to be a beggar.

"Where are you going?" Cas called to her, but Hali didn't turn around. What was the point? The anger in his eyes when he lifted her chin was evident. She wasn't going to stand trial for an unknown crime she couldn't defend or deny. Hali knew that she might regret the decision later but doubted that if she stayed Cas would have allowed her into camp anyway. Leaving made the decision hers at least.

After sitting under a tree that sat closest to the beach for about an hour, Hali heard someone walking through the brush. The gruff man plodded into view coming from the worn-down path that led to and from the camp. He hobbled like a man twice his age down to the water wearing a holy shirt and pants that looked to be made out of burlap. His hair was coarse, curly, shoulder length, and mostly salt with a dash of pepper. The gruff man sat on his log that straddled the ocean and sand, taking something out of his pocket—a shell, she presumed. Removing a branch from his stack he resumed shaving.

Swish. Swish.

As Hali watched from a distance, she heard another movement in the brush. This time it was the young boy that had been by Marilla's side when she was fishing earlier in the day. He had grilled fish piled on top of a large shell plate along with grilled figs. He looked around before handing the plate over to Hali.

"You are a godsend!" Hali exclaimed in relief at the bounty.

The boy looked embarrassed by Hali's excitement as he handed her a smaller shell. Hali's confusion must have been evident, because the boy added, "It's to eat with ... so you don't have to use your hands. I would have brought you a fork, but Cas takes inventory and I wasn't close enough to home to grab from our own utensils. Mom said he'd probably notice it missing when it was time to wash the dishes. I wasn't sure if I could sneak it back into the dirty pile without being noticed, since I'd already finished eating."

"This is perfect," Hali said, scooping a rather large portion of fish into her mouth. The muscles in her body responded to the protein with relief. In the next bite she included some grilled fig. She let out a sigh as the sweetness made its way to her stomach. The hollow space filled with warmth, quieting the howls of her hunger.

"Here, drink this," the boy said as he handed her a canteen filled with water.

Hali took several gulps of water, then asked, "Where did the canteen come from?"

"Enchanters," he said. "This one is our personal one, so Cas won't notice it missing."

Hali expected him to laugh and tell her he was kidding. But he never did. "Enchanters? Like ones that cast spells?" she questioned with a full mouth.

"Yep, those are the ones. They also send clothes and other supplies."

"Why?" Hali had to ask.

"Guilt."

"Guilt?"

"Uh-huh," he said, offering no other information. "Mom wanted me to let you know that we will teach you to fish tomorrow afternoon when it is our turn to feed camp. It will be about the same time as we did it today. We can eat the fish raw in our mermaid and mermen form, but it makes us sick to eat it raw in our human form. Plus, it tastes better cooked, I think."

The thought of eating raw fish repulsed Hali, especially after eating it grilled with the figs as she just had. "Thank you," Hali said. "I'd have to agree with you on that."

The boy tipped his head.

After several bites in silence, Hali asked, "Is your mom, Marilla?"

"Yep," he nodded. "We'll try to bring you some more food tonight if we can. Dinnertime is at six, so if I'm able to come it will be after that time. If not, then breakfast is at seven in the morning and lunch is at noon. Hopefully you'll be able to fish with us tomorrow. We fish two hours before we plan on eating so we have time to catch and cook, and we fish in groups for protection, so you shouldn't go out in the water by yourself." He looked to the sky as he recalled the information as if he was trying not to forget any of it.

"Did your mom tell you to tell me that?" Hali asked.

The boy nodded again and then pulled some uncooked figs from his pockets.

"Here," he said, "in case we can't bring food tonight. Mom said we will show you where to find the fruit trees tomorrow, too. The orchards are near the windmill and well."

Hali was overcome with gratitude by the boy's bravery and kindness. "Thank you, so much ..." Hali stopped mid-sentence, realizing she didn't even know the boy's name.

"Ronan," he shared.

"Thank you, Ronan," Hali said, trying his name out. Pointing her head in the direction of the gruff man, Hali asked, "What's his name?"

Ronan shrugged. "He doesn't have one." Hali cocked her head at Ronan's answer, prompting Ronan to add, "At least not one that we know. We just call him Mr. Gruff, although no one actually talks to him and he hasn't talked to anyone else."

"That's a fitting name, but it's a shame no one knows his real one. He doesn't use sign language either?"

"Nope," Ronan answered, unaffected. "Well, I should get going before someone notices that I'm gone."

Hali nodded. "Thanks again, Ronan."

Ronan smiled slightly before slipping back onto the path. Leaving Hali alone once again with the ocean, sand, trees, and Mr. Gruff down by the water. With a full stomach and a headache that made her eyes sting to stay open, Hali was overcome with exhaustion. The food, as delicious as it was, was not enough to take away her fatigue and sore body. Wanting to find a way home, but unable to think straight,

Hali rested her head down on the sand. Reasoning with herself that if she slept for a little bit, she'd be refreshed enough to attempt the swim home. Tears began rolling down her cheeks as she closed her eyes and curled up in the shadow of a tree.

To be officially an adult and cry like a child. Ronan was probably more mature, she thought, before dozing off into a dead sleep with sand-streaked tears. The cool sand lulled her to sleep instantly.

She awakened to a dark navy sky, speckled in the brightest stars. A sliver of moon was hidden behind a small patch of dark clouds, undetectable. With bleary eyes sticky from tears and sand, the stars blurred into tunnels of light similar to the beam of the Emerald Cove Lighthouse. As reality set in that her day hadn't been a bad dream, so did disappointment. Sitting up, Hali found herself covered with a red blanket.

Ronan? Had he tried to bring her dinner after all?

Hali made a mental note to thank the boy for his kindness the next time she saw him, as she looked for traces of food like a raccoon. After finding none, she remembered the figs he had given her in case he couldn't bring dinner. Hali wiped one off with her dress, removing as much sand as she could feel in the dark. As she took a slightly grainy bite, she did her best not to think of eating unseen bugs that may have gotten to the figs while she slept. After finishing two figs, Hali looked out to the ocean to see the silhouette of the Emerald Cove Lighthouse. Anger boiled inside of her. She'd missed her opportunity to swim during the daylight hours and the idea of swimming in the dark filled her with anxiety. The mer-boys had alluded to a danger in the water that she really didn't want to encounter in the dark. Hali sighed a silent acquiescence. Logic beating out desire, she decided to wait until morning to swim home.

Leaning back on her elbows she peered up to the sky. A star shot across, then another, and another. The sky tormented her with shooting stars, but out of defiance she couldn't bring herself to make a wish like she had done in the past whenever she spotted one. Hali couldn't remember a night she had seen so many or had as good of a reason to make a wish as she did on this night. But she let each one streak across the sky without ever making a wish.

In her anger, she lost the awe she used to have for their dashes through the sky. Now, she could only see them for what they were and not for what they weren't. They weren't the minuscule fires at the end of birthday candles or the better part of a wishbone or even a full dandelion.

They were just meteors hurtling through space, minding their own business, until summoned by Earth's gravity. Uninvited rejections with no intentions of barreling into Earth, were all that skimmed the atmosphere, like rocks skipping across water. But intentions mattered not, the consequences were determined and unavoidable once their path had been set.

7

THE FISHING POLE

AFTER STARING up at the sky deciphering constellations and planets to pass the time after her long nap, Hali was astonished to wake up the next morning to the sun rising in the sky. Surprisingly, it wasn't the sun's rays that stirred Hali awake, but the distant murmurs of voices. Amongst the different voices was Cas's baritone. Filled with curiosity and a more positive frame of mind than the night before, she stood up, wrapping the blanket around her shoulders, and spied on the group from behind the tree she slept under. As she snooped on the group, she only recognized Cas. The other five adults were not part of the lunch group she had met the day before. Independent of the fishing group, Mr. Gruff remained perched on his log, shaving his branches.

As Hali wondered what Mr. Gruff did with all his branches, she moved from the shadows slightly to get a better look at the scene, only to step on something.

Snap!

A branch cracked under Hali's foot. Afraid of being discovered eavesdropping she ducked back behind the tree. Cas turned from the group and scowled in her direction.

Picking up the empty canteen, Hali tiptoed along the tree line with the intention to avoid a confrontation with Cas that would jeopardize learning to fish and eating in the afternoon.

With her headache gone, and her hunger not as desperate as the previous day, Hali went for a walk further than she expected. On her stroll she happened on a solitary windmill, a well, and an orchard of fruit trees. She sighed in relief to know she would not have to go without breakfast. She even kept a few figs to snack on later, cupped in the red blanket wrapped around her shoulders with the canteen.

On her walk she thought of more questions that she could ask Ronan and Marilla. Despite her confusion on basically everything, she felt better. Refreshed. Ready to figure a way off the Eyes' Land. She wondered how far a distance Emerald Cove was and if she could make the swim. It couldn't be hard in mermaid form.

Could it?

The task didn't seem impossible as she looked out to the lighthouse on the clear sunny day. But despite her improved condition she still felt weak and sore. She exhaled deeply, stuck between logic and desire. Erring on the side of caution, Hali decided not to attempt her swim home just yet; with the thought that she'd be much stronger to make her journey home with another meal in her stomach.

On her jaunt, Hali discovered that the Eyes' Land wasn't very big. If she had had more time she could have walked around the entire circumference within a day, but she didn't want to lose the opportunity to fish with Ronan and Marilla and miss another meal.

After returning to the same tree she had slept under, Hali was pretty hungry and thirsty. With nothing to do besides wait for her turn to fish, she examined her skin. Her normally bronze shoulders were pink and flaky as a result of no sun protection the day before. Without any sunscreen she decided to put mud on her shoulders to give them a break. Her nose felt a little tender as well, so she slathered some mud on the bridge of her nose, cheeks, and ears. The coolness felt nice on her skin. Before she knew it, every part of her not covered by her dress was covered in mud.

It would do, she thought.

When Hali finished mudding her body, she attempted building a sandcastle. Though she didn't have a sufficient amount of water to build a good one. Hali made do with what she had, deciding it was best to avoid going down to the shore and risking another run-in with Cas. She had already chanced going down to the shore once that afternoon to get water for her makeshift sunscreen. And even being a good distance away from where the fishing group entered the water, Cas still managed to pop out of the ocean like a Jack-in-the-Box to scowl his disapproval of her being there.

Hali had just rolled her eyes back at him, tucking the canteen she hoped he hadn't seen under the red blanket she knew he had. A big, red blanket wrapped around one's shoulders was impossible not to see, but she hoped it wouldn't get Ronan and Marilla into any hot water with Cas for having it.

After the morning group moved on, Hali waited for her turn to fish with the afternoon group. With nothing else to do besides watch Mr. Gruff shave branches and take in the view of the ocean, Hali got antsy. To pass the time she lay on her side with one hand holding her head and the other cupping sand. Hali watched the sand waterfall out of her palm to rejoin the rest in a state of distraction. She wondered what kind of rocks the little specks originated from before they were broken down and scattered along the earth. Were the tiny grains aware they were no longer part of something whole and solid but something broken and unstable? Was stability only an illusion? Could a rock be considered whole when parts of it eroded away?

In the midst of her existential crisis she heard voices coming down the path. Ronan and Marilla were the first to come into view, and Hali felt her face light into something that felt like excitement. Following behind were the three mer-boys, Carmya, Delphia, and ... Cas.

Hali's smile faded into discouragement.

Why was he here? He wasn't part of the fishing group yesterday afternoon.

Hali stayed behind the tree. Ready to walk back to the fig trees she had found earlier to grab a few to eat for lunch once the group went out into the water. She could feel her positive outlook slipping. Hali hoped that Cas had switched a shift with someone and wouldn't be part of the dinner fishing crew too. Her mind flooded with possibilities, rationalizing a reason to hope for the best. But she had a strong inkling that Cas fished with the afternoon group out of his own desire to keep her away rather than a need for an extra person. It hadn't escaped her notice that there was no one missing from the lunch fishing crew that had been present the day before, proving that Cas was an addition not a substitution.

Still, she prayed that maybe she could eat more than figs for lunch. But more than that, she craved being able to talk with someone. She wasn't a needy person. Socializing wasn't a priority for her. However, she had never had the option taken away from her before either. To be left with only your thoughts was maddening. There was no distraction: no books, no television, no computer, or music. Hali was half-

tempted to help Mr. Gruff shave his branches just for something to do.

To make matters worse, Ronan and Marilla had discour-
aged her from going into the water without the group. The
same group that Cas was now blocking her from being a
part of. Hali was frustrated and on any other day she would
run off her worries. But with no promise of a next meal, Hali
didn't think it would be smart to burn through calories so
foolishly. Especially when she needed those calories to
swim her way home.

As she worked through her thoughts, she had an
epiphany. If she could explain to Cas that she was only on
the Eyes' Land until she could find a way home, then maybe
he would be on board with allowing her to join the fishing
group. Considering he despised her being on the Eyes'
Land, it would be a win-win for both of them.

By the time Hali was done sorting through her plan, she
had convinced herself that Cas would be just as motivated
about it as she was. Gathering her courage, Hali ran down to
the shore to the group before they could disrobe.

"Wait," Hali yelled as she approached. The group turned
towards her. Cas aimed a speared branch at her heart, separating her from the rest of the group. If she moved an inch
closer, it would impale her. Hali held her hands up in
surrender, not feeling quite as confident about her plan as
she had moments before.

"Please, just hear me out, and I think I have a way to
make us both happy."

Cas's seriousness gave way to a genuine chuckle, that he
desperately tried to restrain but failed. No sooner had his
chuckle escaped was it replaced with disbelief and hatred.
The rest of the group, except Marilla, didn't recover as
quickly, and continued laughing. For what reason, Hali

couldn't guess. Marilla soon quieted the group with her perfected glare.

Gaining composure, Cas challenged, "Who says I'm not happy? What do I care to make you happy?"

"You're not happy I'm here, right?" Hali reasoned.

Cas huffed, which Hali took as agreement and continued, "Well, then that makes two of us. But I think I can leave and then I won't be a problem for anyone."

Cas's eyebrows furrowed like she was speaking a different language. "Hali, is it?"

"Yes," she confirmed.

"How old are you?" Cas asked. Hali noticed the nervous looks of the others standing behind Cas. She wasn't sure what she had said wrong, but by the way their eyeballs were flying around to each other she imagined she was going to find out soon enough.

"Eighteen—as of yesterday," Hali answered, cringing as soon as she divulged the last unnecessary detail.

Why would these strangers care about her birthday being yesterday?

Cas let out an exasperated breath. "Do you think that we are stupid?"

This wasn't looking good.

"No, I don't think that," Hali stated, scanning the others for clues of where the conversation was headed.

Cas cut in, "You've been here all of a day. There have been people here as long as you have been alive. You think if there was a way to get off the Eyes' Land we wouldn't have found it already? You think we need some eighteen-year-old kid to figure it out for us? There is a barrier in the ocean that was made to seal us off from the rest of the world, and the rest of the world from us. Not one Anchor has been able to cross it because it was designed to be unbreakable." Annoyed, Cas shook his head.

Cas's distrust of her made her nervous. The sharpened tree branch he held to her heart didn't help. The steam her courage was fueled on to confront Cas, slowly began leaking the hot air it was built on.

"I think we've gotten off on the wrong foot," Hali back-tracked, while her heart beat out of her chest so hard, she thought it might successfully stab itself with the tree branch. Cas was the stubborn door Hali needed to unlock if she wanted to fish with a group and not wait around for Marilla and Ronan to throw her scraps when he wasn't look-ing. Time was ticking by and Hali had no time to waste waiting on the charity of others. But she still needed their help.

Asking for help wasn't a strength of Hali's, but she was desperate, and not against begging if it meant she could sleep in her own bed sooner than later. It didn't escape her, that just yesterday she had rejected the very idea of being made a beggar. She had never felt so pathetic in all her exis-tence, but she didn't care. There was no place for vanity when it came to survival. A night alone on the beach listening to nothing but the waves and leaves rattle—from what she told herself was only the wind—had taught her that much. Because the reality of her situation was that she needed the Anchors, and they didn't need her.

"Why? Because I won't subject *our* kind to getting killed off by *your* kind? Is that the kind of foot you would have liked us to get off to?" Cas bit out.

"You're the one holding a spear to my heart," Hali pointed out as calmly as her racing heart and shaky voice allowed. "What do you think I am? I just found out that I'm an Anchor yesterday. I am from Emerald Cove and was captured and brought here somehow. All I want to do is go back home." Hali pointed across to the lighthouse, recounting every detail she remembered. Hoping that if she was honest on what she could recall, Cas would trust Hali on the details she couldn't. She started from how she was awakened with severe pain in her legs all the way up to the moment she landed on the Eyes' Land; including her memory of being pulled to the lighthouse beam by some force and trapped inside. She spoke as if she had a gun to her head. The sharpened spear didn't feel much different.

"I don't know what you think I am, but I am telling you the truth of how I got here," Hali concluded.

"Cas, may I have a word with you?" Marilla stepped away from the group, expecting Cas's compliance to her request. Cas reluctantly dropped the spear from Hali's heart and walked with Marilla a little further down the beach out of earshot, but never out of eyeshot of Hali. With the spear no longer threatening her life, Hali's body crumbled, but miraculously remained upright even when her knees buckled. The rest of the group intentionally avoided eye contact with her. Instead, they made small talk amongst each other to fill the awkwardness that was placed on them by Hali being present. But not Ronan.

He stepped towards Hali, squinting up to her with big, innocent, round eyes, appearing confused.

"Why are you covered in mud?" he asked. The group continued avoiding her, but Hali noticed their failed attempts at concealing their grins. Hali groaned, as it became clear what their laughter had been about when she had approached them on the beach.

Hali straightened, determined not to care what the strangers thought. She tried not to dwell on the fact that slathering mud all over her face was not a great impression to make on people who already didn't trust her. "I'm trying to avoid being burnt today."

Satisfied by the explanation, Ronan shrugged in acceptance, then added, "He'll come around when he realizes you aren't one of them?"

"One of what?" she asked.

Ronan tilted his head at Hali's question, surprised that she didn't know the answer herself, before responding, "An Eye."

Hali's eyebrows knitted together. "What's an Eye?"

Without missing a beat, Ronan answered, "A leprechaun."

Of course! How could she have not guessed that?

"Is there a hidden camera on this island? Is someone going to pop out at me and tell me that this is all one big birthday prank. Please tell me that's what this is, Ronan."

"Mom told me about cameras, once. They sound like Eyes. Why would you want that for your birthday?"

At this point the others were lost in their own conversations, disinterested in Hali's and Ronan's. "Because at least I would know that things would go back the way they were when the prank was over." Hali answered more to herself than to Ronan, but his eyebrows furrowed as he pondered Hali's meaning, while she puzzled over what he had said about Eyes being like cameras.

After a few moments of not speaking, Hali whispered, "Thank you for bringing me the blanket last night."

With a scrunched nose, Ronan asked, "What blanket?" Before Hali could investigate any further Cas called out to the group.

"Everyone, *besides* Hali, come here."

The group, including Ronan, traipsed over to Cas and Marilla obediently. Hali watched on in curiosity, dying a slow death from her unsatisfied thirst and hunger, while they discussed what to do with her. She couldn't help but stare like a lost puppy on a porch. Cas stood with his arms crossed and his face was unreadable as Marilla made her case. Occasionally, one of the others would talk, but their faces did not give away whose side they were on. When someone would talk, Hali would try to gauge whose team they were on by whether Cas's reaction appeared to be in agreement or not. After ten minutes of waiting, Hali got bored and sat at the shore. She watched as the tide rolled over her feet and retreated in a game of hokey pokey. Observing her feet as they transformed to fins then back again when they dried.

As she dawdled, she looked up to see a gray cloud appear in the sky. Goosebumps covered her skin, tingling with anticipation. Like the night before, her body reacted, like a fish on a line being pulled from the ocean. Except this time, she wasn't the one being drawn. She felt her skin breathe in the cloud. She wasn't sure what was happening, but it felt natural as energy swirled beneath the surface of her skin. She should have been scared, but all she felt was peace. Hali's hunger pangs intertwined with the energy as she took in a deep inhale. The energy was as constant as a ray of light. It moved through her like a current and she felt the strain of her body as it pulled. Hali opened her eyes, not aware of when she shut them. Hundreds of fish fell at her feet as she inhaled.

Surprised by the sight, she shuffled herself backwards, pushing the sand into a ledge with her feet. The energy dissipated in her veins.

Was this an Anchor ability? she wondered.

Hali got her answer when she looked to Mr. Gruff who had stopped shaving a branch to look at her with a blank expression. It didn't last long until he was back at shaving again.

Maybe he was taking a break.

Hali then looked over to the group who stared at her with a mixture of awe, disbelief, and fear. Marilla ran over to Hali and crouched down to her level looking from her to the fish and then back again.

"How did you do that?" Marilla asked. The rest of the group walked over, but still kept their distance.

"I don't know," Hali responded, shaken at what she had just done. "I think I absorbed the cloud." Afraid to ask, but needing to know, Hali grimaced, "Is that something Anchors can do?"

Marilla placed her hand on Hali's wrist. "No," she answered as she shook her head. Such a simple word, delivering a kick to her gut, even though deep down she knew absorbing a cloud wasn't an Anchor ability.

"Does that mean I'm a—"

"A leprechaun?" Cas said as he walked up. "Yes, it does." His mouth was a solid line. Hali immediately looked away from him. His hatred was too much when she had her own turmoil to sort out.

"And an Anchor," Marilla added with encouragement while attempting to reason with Cas with her eyes. Cas avoided eye contact with Marilla like she was Medusa.

Hali stared at the fish, ignoring anything else. Her own parents rarely argued. And when they did, it was usually over her dad switching the radio station on her mom's alarm clock. Hali was uncomfortable being the reason for discord amongst the Anchors, but she couldn't seem to avoid it.

"Marilla, this is on you," Cas said before disrobing. Hali went out of her way not to look at him, staying focused on the fish.

"I'll take full responsibility for Hali." Marilla sounded like a child persuading a parent to get a pet. When Hali heard Cas's splash in the water, she glanced up to Marilla, with a small smile forming on her lips.

Ronan smiled wider. "I told you he'd come around."

"But how?" Hali asked. "I'm a leprechaun. Aren't leprechauns what he was afraid I was?" Hali could hardly believe what had just transpired.

Marilla laughed. "Yes, but you *are* an Anchor."

Hali tilted her head, unsure how being an Anchor made any difference if she was also still a leprechaun.

"Cas was convinced that you were *only* a leprechaun, specifically an Eye. Eyes are the leprechauns around Emerald Cove that can come on and off the Eye's Land as they please. Cas thought you were an Eye using an enchanter spell to disguise yourself as an Anchor to trick us into trusting you," Marilla explained.

Perplexed, Hali asked, "What changed his mind?"

Marilla's smile grew bigger, "Guising spells don't last more than a day when used by leprechauns or anyone that isn't an enchanter. It's been a day and the water still turned your feet to fins."

8

THE SPARED AND THE SPEARED

"How about you and Ronan help me spear the fish to take back to camp," Marilla instructed, a subtle grin touched her cheeks and eyes, humbly declaring her victory.

"Yes, ma'am," Hali smiled back. Ronan collected spears from Mr. Gruff and put the pile in the middle of them.

"Is this what all the spears are for?" Hali asked.

Marilla and Ronan glanced at each other before Marilla answered, "Not all of them. Most of them are saved."

"Saved for what?" Hali asked while she skewered the fish onto spears with Marilla and Ronan.

"Do you see the fallen trees, Hali?"

"Yes," Hali answered, certain that her own question was being brushed off.

But Marilla continued. "The Eyes spied on us through the trees about ten years ago. That's how the leprechauns in our vicinity got the nickname, Eyes, and why this island came to be known as the Eyes' Land. They attacked us at night. Not everyone lived." A flicker of sadness crossed Marilla's face.

"Is that why Cas has a scar?"

Marilla nodded. "He was just about Ronan's age when it happened. Lost both of his parents, but he still managed to warn most of us before we were all killed in our sleep."

"I thought Cas was eleven when it happened. I'm twelve," Ronan's eyebrows furrowed at the discrepancy.

"Yes, Ronan, he was eleven. But I did say he was close to your age when it happened not exactly your age," Marilla clarified.

"That explains why he hates me."

"He doesn't hate you, Hali. You're just the first person to end up here that wasn't born here or sent to shear us of our scales. Cas was a toddler when he got here and doesn't know anything outside of the Eyes' Land."

"Why do you trust me then?" Hali asked, wondering if she could be as trusting as Marilla if she was in the same position.

Marilla thought about Hali's question. "Because I wasn't born here. I still remember what it was like outside of the Eyes' Land. When it comes to character, every assortment of beings comes in the good, bad, and in-between variety; whether or not they are mortal, Anchor, leprechaun, enchanter, etcetera."

Hali admired Marilla's kindness despite her own history. Even though it was a history Hali hadn't quite grasped. "Why is the Eyes' Land here? And what did you mean when you told Cas that you thought I might be the *one* expected?"

Marilla chuckled. "You caught that, huh?" Hali nodded in response. Marilla placed the last fish on her very full skewer. "I will answer all of your questions in due time. But right now, we need to get these fish to camp before everyone starves." For the sake of knowledge, Hali hoped that *due time* was sooner rather than later, because Hali had no plans to stick around.

The three stood up, fish-strewn skewers in hand. Hali had forgotten how hungry she was before the group had shown up that afternoon. Her stomach rumbled as her fear-laced adrenaline settled. A wave of exhaustion swept through her underfed body. As they walked towards camp, Hali stopped, peering back to the ocean. The clouds had cleared in the sky as the sun warmed her mud-caked skin and the tip of the Emerald Cove Lighthouse brushed the blue sky above the horizon.

She would eat, rest, and then swim home, she told herself.

But a small seed of doubt planted in her mind that maybe she had underestimated the Eyes' Land and overestimated herself.

Hadn't Cas said the very same thing to her? What if he was right?

But despite all the others believing there was no way off the Eyes' Land, Hali had to believe otherwise. Hope was the backbone to her sanity. She couldn't lose it. Reality would be too bleak otherwise. She would do whatever it took to figure out how to get off the Eyes' Land and back to her family. But she had to do it in a way that didn't upset the others at her attempt and risk losing the little trust she had gained.

The walk back to camp felt like déjà vu from the day before. Anxious and fatigued, Hali begrudgingly prepared herself to be refused admittance.

Would some other Anchor step forward and take issue with her presence? Or would Cas change his mind about allowing Marilla to oversee her, leaving Hali to her own devices on the beach?

What started as the small flutters of butterflies in her stomach, quickly turned to the quaking expansion of a hawk's wings. So much was at stake. But Hali had little control of the outcome. A headache bloomed from the stress, coupled by her basic needs being unmet. Hali craved the use of a shower and a real bathroom as much as a warm meal.

Marilla must have sensed Hali's apprehension, as she gingerly took Hali's fish skewers from her shaky hands to pass to Ronan, along with her own.

"Ronan, you go on and take these to camp to be prepared and meet us back at the cabin."

"Yes, ma'am," he agreed, running off with his body weight in fish skewers. Hali would have felt bad if he hadn't been so happy to do it.

As they walked around camp, Hali hadn't realized she was holding her breath until she had gotten to Marilla's and Ronan's cabin. Relieved to make it there without a confrontation, she exhaled, her heart pounding to catch up from the deprivation.

Stepping through the doors of the small abode she noticed its simplicity. There was a square living space with a couch and an overhead fan with a light. Two simple rectangular windows lit the space inside, bordering the couch. Makeshift curtains that looked to be made of the same material as Mr. Gruff's clothing were rolled to the tops of the windows and tied with string on each end to stay in place. A rectangular kitchen island made of wood sat off to the far side of the square room—nearest the windows— with a round kitchen table with three seats in the middle. Cupboards lined the entirety of the kitchen wall up until it reached a doorway to a hall that led to three doors. Hali learned that behind two of the doors were bedrooms and the middle door was a bathroom with all the essentials: sink, toilet, and a shower bathtub combo. The kitchen was well appointed too, with a refrigerator, stovetop, oven, microwave, toaster and coffee maker—all the essentials that

Hali had at home. The space was quaint but surprisingly adequate, cozy and bright.

A recess of shelves was tucked between Marilla's bedroom and the bathroom carrying the cabin's linens and towels. Marilla left the living area and gathered a towel and a sponge that looked authentic. Walking back into the living area she handed the items over to Hali. As Hali took in the space, Ronan whipped open the front door, his tan cheeks blushed from his run and his hairline matted with glistening sweat.

"Did all the fish make it to camp okay?" Marilla asked.

"Yep," Ronan answered. "They started cooking it before I left."

Marilla nodded, bringing her attention back to Hali. "You go ahead and get washed up. There are jars of body wash, shampoo, and conditioner already in the shower. When you're done you will take Ronan's bedroom and I'll put some fresh sheets on his bed while you shower. The boy carries his body weight in sand every time he comes back from the beach and there is no amount of walking or showers that gets rid of it like getting into fresh sheets."

Hali laughed. But Ronan wasn't pleased at his mother for outing him as anything but a budding adult.

"Mom!"

Quick to assuage his wounded pride, Hali said, "It happens to me too and I'm technically an adult now."

He smiled at their commonality. His exasperation for being discovered altering quickly to acceptance.

Turning to Marilla, Hali said, "Thank you so much for taking me in but I really don't want to take Ronan's room from him. I can sleep on the couch."

"Not happening. You'll take the bedroom and that's final," Marilla stated.

Flooded with awkwardness, Hali smiled a tight, closed-mouth smile to avoid challenging the issue any further. Though as welcoming as Marilla was being, she couldn't help feeling like more of an imposition. She had to remind herself that Ronan's room would be returned to him as soon as she was gone.

"Thank you ... again. Is there anything I can do to help while I'm here?" Hali offered, stifling a yawn.

Marilla shook her head. "Having another person to talk to that has been outside of the Eyes' Land recently will prove use enough. Our day-to-day can be pretty monotonous. It will be nice to know what has been going on in the outside world."

Hali's gaze fell to her feet, struggling with a response. Though Marilla's words were meant to placate Hali's discomfort for imposing, it had the opposite effect. Marilla spoke as if Hali's stay was permanent, like she was caught in the same impossible web as the rest. She hadn't considered the Anchors being in the exact same position as herself; captured from their previous lives and thrown into a tropical prison. Cas had alluded that the Anchors had attempted their own escapes.

But had they?

If they had, they were unsuccessful. So, what were Hali's chances of success? Since arriving she hadn't imagined they weren't on the Eyes' Land by choice. Foreign but familiar, the Eyes' Land was like another dimension. The landscape was similar to what she knew, but the inhabitants were not at all the same.

Bringing her gaze back up to meet Marilla's eyes, Hali said, "I will probably have more questions about the Eyes' Land than you will have about what is going on outside of it. There has to be something else that I can do."

Hali looked around the small living space, scanning for a way to be useful. The immaculate home didn't need cleaning, so offering to clean as payment to Marilla's and Ronan's kindness didn't seem to be enough. As she gleaned the small cabin, she wondered how it ever existed at all.

"How are the cabins here?" she asked.

Marilla brushed her hand across the countertop, wiping imaginary crumbs into the sink. "Everything that we have that isn't part of the land or sea comes from enchanters. Any supplies we need are kept in the lodge. When the weather is bad, we eat in the lodge too. But it's also where schooling takes place, so we do our best to keep out when the children are learning."

Hali remembered Ronan telling her that the canteen came from enchanters' guilt. Every answer she received only seemed to create more questions. Marilla hesitantly offered each morsel of information, as if testing whether Hali could handle the next course. Unnerved, Hali accepted the small morsels, starving for more, but reluctant to ask.

She was still coming to terms with what she had learned about herself, barely having a chance to try out her new abilities. Her first swim as an Anchor overwhelmed her senses. The short time she was in the water felt like being at a rock concert; her heightened senses resulting in a terrible headache. The most puzzling part of her situation rested in possessing more physical power but little freedom.

Accepting Marilla's answer without pushing for more information Hali glanced around the room before her gaze settled on the kitchen. It was such a happy space. That's when she got an idea of how she could be helpful. "Maybe I can bake some cookies if you'd like."

"You don't have to do anything to stay here, Hali," Marilla quickly assured.

"But you can if you want to," Ronan perked up.

Marilla's eyes cut towards Ronan. "Ronan! Where are your manners?"

His hands flew up in exasperation. "What? Who is going to turn down cookies?"

Hali laughed, but Marilla huffed.

"Really, it's fine. I want to make them."

And that was the truth. Baking cookies was an activity that reminded Hali of home with her family. At Christmas she would bake so many different types of cookies with her mom and sometimes Camille would join in their efforts. Most of the cookies would be placed in brown paper bags, tied up in festive ribbons, and then given to neighbors, friends, and the coworkers of her parents. The memory warmed Hali briefly, until she remembered where she was, leaving her in a state of nostalgia-induced melancholy.

"Well, all right then," Marilla said, "but only if you want to. Don't feel you need to do anything extra. Like I said, we are just happy to have you here. You can use whatever ingredients that we have. We usually get a bounty at every full moon. I will say, that anything you make, you need to make enough for everyone on the Eyes' Land."

"That won't be a problem," Hali's nose crinkled, grinning at Ronan, whose eyes shined with excitement. With the matter of dessert settled, Hali excused herself to take her long-awaited shower.

The warm water washed away layers of sand and dirt down the drain before Hali ever used the sponge. Sand and mud stuck to her hair, taking several finger combs to loosen. But once she applied soap, shampoo, and conditioner, she began to feel like herself again. After a day and night of living outside, Hali welcomed the creature comforts she had taken advantage of all her life. Although the shower presented another unanswered question.

If water transformed her into a mermaid, why did she stay in her human form in the shower?

After her long glorious shower, she went to the bedroom and found clean clothes that looked better suited to her size than the soiled t-shirt dress. There were undergarments, shorts, and a t-shirt along with sandals that were as comfortable as shoes. After dressing, she lay on the clean sheets, promising herself she would close her eyes for only a few minutes.

Hours later, Hali awakened, her eyelids heavy from the effects of deep sleep. She jumped up from the bed, worried about the time she'd lost, knowing that she had slept much longer than she had intended. Stepping out into the living space, she was greeted with the sweet aroma of coffee and noticed Marilla sitting on the couch with a mug in her hands. Ronan sat on the floor, his legs stretched under the coffee table, engrossed in a book.

"Feel better?" Marilla asked once Hali came into view.

Ronan looked up from his book, glancing at Hali before looking up at his mother with hope in his eyes. Marilla squinted at him, while slyly shaking her head. Ronan let out an irritated sigh, pouting. Watching their interaction, Hali thought that she knew what the silent request and denial were about. She smiled to herself, remembering what it was like to be twelve. Too old to ask for exactly what you wanted, like you could when you were younger, without considering the needs of others.

"I do, thank you," Hali answered.

"There is a plate from lunch on the counter," Marilla stood up, gesturing to Hali where to find it. "I didn't want to wake you. I know you must be exhausted."

Hali's eyes zeroed in on the plate filled with fish and sautéed cinnamon apples. Her hunger rekindled.

"Wow, what time is it? I'm so sorr—"

"Don't even complete that sentence, young lady. No harm done. You need your rest after all you've been through. It's only 2:30 in the afternoon."

Marilla handed the plate to Hali with a fork this time and Hali gratefully accepted, wrapping her hands around the white disc topped with very needed calories.

"When I'm done eating, would you like to make some cookies to take to dinner, Ronan?" Hali nonchalantly asked, mischievously grinning to herself as she lifted up onto a barstool to sit.

An instant smile spread across his face and then Marilla's.

"Yes!" Ronan exclaimed, turning to his mother. "And I didn't even have to ask, mom."

Marilla and Hali chuckled, as Hali took the first bite of fish. Her heart and stomach fed.

After finishing a late lunch, Hali began preparing dessert with Ronan. She hoped dessert would soften any Anchors who were reluctant about her presence at camp. Scanning the cabinets for ingredients, Hali decided on baking a butter cookie, for two reasons: one, the ingredient list was simple, and two, the cookies were delicious. Initially, she wanted to make sugar cookies, but it required rolling the cookie dough balls into sugar before baking. Normally that wouldn't be a problem, but after spending the better part of a half hour scraping her skin of sand and dirt in the shower, she decided that the grainy sugar felt too much like sand.

Several hours later Marilla, Hali, and Ronan left the cabin, each holding a tray full of cookies. The baking project was a welcomed distraction to all the stressors Hali had encountered over the last day. Ronan seemed to enjoy a change in his daily ritual too. Hali only hoped that the other Anchors would accept the cookies, but ultimately, she wanted them to accept her. Being an outsider amongst a group of people who weren't accustomed to getting outsiders was daunting in and of itself. But being part leprechaun, the very outsider who was responsible for killing their families and friends years ago, was terrifying.

Maybe the others would take the perspective of Marilla and not Cas, she hoped.

Marilla and Ronan ventured to camp, relaxed and happy, with a skip in their steps. Hali walked with her shoulders practically hitting her ears, clutching a tray of cookies like her life depended on it.

Maybe it did. Cas did hold a spear to her heart just hours before.

She knew better than to believe she didn't need to worry. If Cas disliked her and the others valued his opinion, then that couldn't be good for Hali. Cookies wouldn't fool anyone into letting their guard down for a potential threat.

Who was she kidding?

With her doubts increasing with each step closer to camp, Hali considered handing her platter to Ronan and Marilla, and taking off to the beach. But before she got the chance a warm hand landed on her shoulder. She turned in the direction of the trespasser, coming face-to-face with an elderly woman who inspected her with kind brown eyes that crinkled around the edges. The woman's mouth lifted in a closed-mouth smile, her hair was pulled back in a bun and was a shade of gray that would look pale blonde on a younger person. Platter in hands, Hali stayed rooted in place as the woman continued to examine her before moving her hand from Hali's shoulder to her face. The woman gently rubbed her thumb along Hali's jawline and looked at Hali pleased.

At first, Hali feared the confrontation would be what she had expected; a trial of her identity followed by another rejection. But the older woman's gentle touch and loving eyes, told another story. Hali surprised herself, holding the gaze of the woman with a sense of familiarity, mirroring her grin with her own. The moment strangely comfortable in spite of its intimacy and Hali's own hesitation at affection.

Marilla broke the spell with an introduction.

"Mamie, this is Hali."

"Hello, Hali. It's nice to finally meet you," the woman greeted with a feminine gravelly tone.

Confused, Hali looked to Marilla then back to Mamie, unsure of how to respond. But eventually settling on a simple, "It's nice to meet you, too."

"Hali and Ronan made butter cookies," Marilla said before Mamie turned to look at Ronan.

"Ronan can't make cookies, he's still a baby," Mamie teased.

"Mam Mam! Really? I'm too old for this game!" Ronan declared.

"Nope! Can't be true. You'll be too old when I'm dead. And I'm still here. So, you're not too old, baby Ron Ron," Mamie cackled.

Hali laughed at Mamie's feistiness, but was also afraid of being slayed by Mamie's wit next if she laughed too hard at Ronan. Ronan pouted, but the twinkle of love in his eyes he had for Mamie betrayed the annoyed expression he wore.

Being the mature one out of the group, Marilla stated, "We are going to walk these cookies down to the camp now. You coming, Mamie?"

Ignoring Marilla's question, Mamie studied Hali further.

"You're nervous," Mamie stated rather than asked.

"I am a little," Hali answered honestly.

Mamie laughed a youthful laugh and said, "Good."

The enigmatic old woman's discomforting words managed to comfort Hali as they reached the epicenter of camp. If spears were waiting for her, she was ready.

She hoped.

9

CAMP

HALI FOLLOWED Marilla's and Ronan's lead and set the cookies down on an empty table. Mamie had decided to come to camp with them after all and strolled beside Hali, humming the short distance like she was taking a stroll through a park. The tune she hummed was slightly familiar to Hali, but her mind was too preoccupied with how she would handle a confrontation with another Anchor to give it too much thought.

After placing the cookies down, Delphia and Carmya walked over to the them.

"What do you have there, Ronan?" Delphia asked with a spring in her step.

"Butter cookies," Ronan smiled with pride. Marilla cleared her throat, nudging his arm.

Embarrassed, Ronan added in a low voice, "Hali did most of the work."

"Mmm, butter cookies, mind if we give one a try before dinner?" Delphia waited for approval before she dipped her hand beneath the towels of one of the platters and grabbed out two cookies—one for her and one for Carmya. Once both girls took their first blissful bites, their faces curled in delight like they had never tasted a sweet in their lives.

Carmya daintily wiped the corners of her mouth with her fingers. "These are delicious."

"Very," Delphia added.

Carmya's golden eyes, flawless ebony skin, rouge cheeks, and curly, sun-kissed tresses made her look even more youthful than her twenty-two years as she munched on the cookie like a little girl at a tea party trying to display her best etiquette. Delphia was not as delicate with her cookie, tearing into it as ravenously as she swam. Hali smiled at how different the two friends were, which made her think of Camille.

"Thank you," Hali responded. "Ronan did a lot more work than he is taking credit for."

Ronan grinned at the compliment; his pride restored.

"Let us know the next time you bake, and we'll help," Delphia offered.

Carmya nodded in agreement and said, "The amount the two of you made had to take a lot of time. But I bet it was fun. Can't remember the last time I had a cookie."

Delphia nudged Hali playfully in the elbow, "You've sure gotten Cas to bend a lot today."

The comment immediately filled Hali with dread. Carmya's demeanor appeared to dampen as well, but Hali had no idea why.

What else had Hali done to make Cas bend?

Before Hali's mouth could open to ask, she was interrupted by the three mer-boys walking up, grabbing handfuls of cookies and stuffing them into their mouths. They were the frat boys she thought she would avoid by going to community college as opposed to a four-year university.

Guess not.

As they grabbed their second handful, they came to a halt, setting their cookies down on the table. Baffled by their sudden awareness of manners, Hali followed their gazes and spotted the source of their epiphany. Mamie cleared her throat, crossed her arms, and delivered the three mer-boys a death stare that Hali couldn't believe the sweet, old woman was capable of.

Kai looked to no one in particular and asked, "Could we have some cookies ... please?" The forced question was as painful to hear as it was for Kai to say.

"Isn't it a little late to ask since they were just in your mouths?" Ronan scoffed.

"Probably," Toru mumbled, while chewing on his left-over crumbs.

"Gentlemen, let's remember our manners next time," Marilla reminded. "The children look up to you." Marilla poured the guilt on as the foolish trio softened into puddles faster than a popsicle under a Southern summer sun.

"Also," she continued, "Hali and Ronan made the cookies, so they're the ones you need to apologize to."

In unison the three mer-boys raised their heads to the sky and released a collective groan; like three huge defiant toddlers being asked to put a jacket on in a snowstorm. Bringing their heads back to eye level, they avoided eye-contact with Hali, settling instead on Ronan—the easier of the two to mutter a reluctant apology.

"Sorry, may we have some cookies?" the three mumbled so quietly it could barely pass as one person speaking.

"Yes," Hali blurted out, wanting their embarrassment to end for their sake as much as her own. The growing crowd around them brought more attention than Hali ever desired. The trio said a quick thanks before scooping up their cookie piles and speeding away. Hali was relieved.

The rest of the night went on without a hitch with all the Anchors besides one. Cas avoided Hali and her baked goods like they were both poisoned, keeping an eye on her like she was a violent prisoner on the loose. But other than having Cas's cold blue eyes following her every move, there were no other awkward encounters. Kai, Jett, and Toru behaved, steering clear of Hali and the cookies the remainder of the night. The grilled fish, rice, and warm cinnamon apples were delicious. Even the other Anchors easily accepted Hali, complimenting the butter cookies even though they were a little surprised by their presence.

Hali couldn't help but wonder if she had done something wrong by baking them, despite Marilla's approval. Even though the cookies were eaten by everyone except Cas, Hali couldn't help but notice that the Anchors looked at them curiously and ate them with guilty pleasure.

At first, Hali chalked up Cas's disinterest in the cookies to his overall distrust of her. But when an older merman approached her and said, "Atta' girl, set 'em straight early. Let 'em know what he's workin' wit," Hali knew that something was up.

Her olive branch was turning out to be the Trojan Horse, and she was the only one who didn't seem to know why. But she knew the answer rested with Cas. Hali asked around, but everyone evaded her inquiry. They would just tell her how wonderful the cookies were, filling their mouths with the sweets so they were too full to answer. Either that or they would start conversations with other Anchors and avoid Hali altogether. When she questioned Mamie about it, Mamie would pretend she couldn't hear Hali, asking her own questions instead.

Eventually, Hali gave up, spending most of her night with Mamie discussing what it was like outside of the Eyes'

Land. Sometimes others would join and listen, before tending to babies or children, but Mamie remained the entire time. When Hali would ask a question, Mamie managed to deflect it back to her. Hali wasn't even sure how she ended up talking most of the time, but Mamie had a gift. The old woman was the sweetest master manipulator Hali had met in her eighteen years and she couldn't help but wonder what Mamie was hiding.

"Mamie, I've basically told you my life story, but you haven't told me a thing," Hali finally said.

"Not true. I told you that Anchors can only turn into mermaids and mermen in the ocean," she said.

"Mamie ..." Hali challenged.

"Oh, to be old, my circuits don't seem to run quite like they used to."

"I'm finding that hard to believe, Mamie," Hali chuckled. "Your circuits seem to be firing on all cylinders."

"You see, I haven't heard of cylinders in many, many years. Have cars changed a lot?"

And before Hali knew it, she was talking about cars with Mamie. The types, the different color options, and if they were still running on gasoline. Mamie even asked if cars were flying yet. Hali just smiled and replied, "not yet." The lively woman had the curiosity of a child, with a mind as sharp as a spear. At camp there were over two-hundred Anchors, but Hali was content in the corner shooting the breeze with Mamie. Hali had initially hoped that she would finally have her questions answered and be a step closer to getting off the Eyes' Land, but before she knew it the Anchors were putting out fires and cleaning up.

"I should help clean up," Hali shot up from the picnic table she shared with Mamie, looking for a way to be helpful.

Mamie got up too, and started folding the linens off the tables, then carefully placed each tablecloth in a basket that she had lifted out from under the table. Hali followed suit. When they finished the task, Mamie gave Hali a hug.

"I'm going to retire young lady. You've made an old woman very happy tonight. Next time I won't monopolize all of your time so you can chat with the others closer to your age."

"Thank you, Mamie, but I was perfectly happy chatting with you. But next time maybe you won't ignore all of my questions."

"Maybe," Mamie said with a weak smile, that held a hint of sadness.

When Mamie departed, Hali looked around for Marilla and Ronan but saw Mr. Gruff instead. He held a large piece of wood over his shoulder and headed towards the path that led to the beach. Hali began to follow him but was intercepted by Cas, whose expression was unyielding.

"Why did you make cookies?"

Was he just finding reasons to hate her? Hali thought. *Who has an issue with cookies?*

"I wasn't aware that there was a rule against cookies," she stated sarcastically.

Hali did her best not to laugh. She really did. But the intensity of his stare and the fact that he had literally come after her for trying to do something nice put Hali over the edge and she got a case of the giggles.

"You think this is funny?" Cas asked incredulously.

"I do. Let me ask you a question. Are you actually against cookies or just *who* made them?"

Hali claimed full responsibility on dessert, deciding it would be best to not throw Marilla and Ronan under the bus.

He already hated her, what's the difference? She'd be gone soon anyway, she thought.

"This has nothing to do with cookies."

"I figured as much."

"This has to do with being independent."

"I'm not following. Please explain to me how cookies deprive you from being independent on an island that you are all captives."

"You're not following."

"I said as much."

Cas took a deep breath in and out, like Hali was an idiot for not understanding such a simple concept. Hali waited for his explanation in silence, taking the opportunity to examine his scar, while he looked down. The mark was deeper than the surrounding skin, as though it hadn't healed properly. Her sympathy for him grew, as she pictured Cas as a boy facing off against the Eyes who killed his parents. The experience shaped him and that made Hali sad for some reason. The scar must have been a constant reminder of the event and all that was lost.

How had the Eyes so easily hurt a boy?

She realized then that she didn't want to fight with him or upset the balance. "I'm sorry," Hali found herself saying. "If baking cookies is a problem, I won't bake them anymore." And she meant it. Hali just hoped she would find a way off the Eyes' Land soon so she wouldn't have to go without cookies forever.

Cas looked up at Hali with confusion as if he was expecting a bigger fight from her. Hali was just as surprised with herself. She had no desire of upsetting the harmony of somewhere she didn't plan on staying for long. Cas had his own issues to deal with and Hali had hers. There was no point in making an enemy out of someone who had been captive for much longer than she had.

"Are you ready to head back?" Marilla approached with Ronan, looking back and forth between Hali and Cas, quizzically. "Is everything all right here?"

"Yes, and yes," Hali stated as she turned and walked away from Cas.

They hadn't walked more than a few steps before Cas called out to Marilla and Ronan. Marilla and Ronan gave him their attention. Hali did too, even though her attention hadn't been requested. Cas hesitated, then said, "Be careful. You know what she is." He walked away before anyone could reply.

When Cas was out of sight, Marilla attempted to comfort Hali, wrapping an arm around her shoulder. "He'll come around, Hali."

"Cas is being a jerk, mom," Ronan countered.

"It's okay," Hali replied. "He is just looking out for you guys. I did wonder why everyone seemed surprised by the cookies."

Marilla looked guilty. "I should have prepared you before we came into camp that Cas wouldn't be onboard with the cookies, but I didn't want to stop you from making them."

"But why? I don't want to cause any problems."

"How many people enjoyed the cookies, Hali?" Marilla asked.

"Everyone who had one, which was everyone, besides Cas."

"Exactly. Only one person had a problem with you making cookies. Why does one person get to dictate what is best for the rest of us?"

Hali didn't disagree, but she didn't answer. The Eyes'

Land was a strange place, with strange rules and customs. Hali was still hung up on how baking could hurt their independence.

"I'm confused, why did Cas's opinion matter yesterday, but it doesn't matter today?" Hali was beginning to wonder if the camp had a true leader. Maybe the Anchors picked a new leader for the day by pulling a name from a hat and today was Marilla's turn.

"Cas's opinion always matters, Hali, everyone's does."

Hali was waiting for the "but" in Marilla's statement, but it never came.

"Cas doesn't want us to be too dependent on the aid of enchanters in case they ever stop providing. It's the reason we fish three meals a day. Enchanters have given us anything we've ever asked for, but when it comes to food, Cas wants us to be as self-sufficient as possible. Ever since the Eyes attacked the camp and he lost his parents he became very concerned about relying on anyone other than ourselves."

"And you don't agree?" Hali asked.

"I don't know anything for certain. To think it could never happen would be foolish. I lost my husband, Ronan's father, during the attack. Life here is unpredictable, but always monotonous. We work, eat simply, swim, and sleep. I see no harm in enjoying a butter cookie or two if given the opportunity. I'm certainly not giving up coffee unless it is an absolute necessity."

"Me either," Ronan stated. "Well, except for the coffee, because it's disgusting, but I agree with everything else my mom said. What kind of cookie will we make next?" Ronan looked at Hali with hope in his eyes.

Hali felt torn, she didn't want to displease Marilla and Ronan because they had been so kind to her, but she also didn't want to go back on her word to Cas. Whether or not he trusted Hali, or ever would, was beside the point.

"I'm not sure if I can, Ronan. I just told Cas I wouldn't make anymore, and I don't want to go back on my word." The disappointment in Ronan's eyes pulled at Hali's heart strings. So much so that she thought about going back on her word with Cas but knew she couldn't do that without creating a bigger riff.

"Then we will have a vote," Marilla declared, looking determined. "Hali, I respect that you are a woman of your word, so we will vote, so you don't have to betray it."

Ronan shouted a triumphant, "YES!" balling his fist and bringing his elbow into his stomach. Hali felt a twinge of guilt over his elation, since she had no plans to stay on the Eyes' Land. She certainly had no intention of causing a cookie revolution.

"I don't feel right about this," Hali stated. "Won't Cas be the only one that votes against cookies, since everyone else ate one?" Hali refrained from giggling at her own question. Never in her life did she think there would need to be a vote on whether making cookies was acceptable. But she'd also never been on the Eyes' Land before.

"You never know," Marilla said. "What people say and what they do are entirely different things sometimes."

"They shouldn't be," Hali countered.

She wasn't sure if she should feel better that Cas wouldn't be alone in his vote or not. Being defiant and a newcomer was not what she was going for or how she wanted to spend her energy. She cursed herself for baking cookies in the first place. Of all the tasks she could have offered to do, she chose one that would bring about contro-versy. One she had no desire in taking part in.

"Marilla, are you sure this is a good idea? I don't want the rest of the Anchors to despise me."

"It will be fine. There is nothing for you to worry about. As much as the Anchors can disagree, we can still come away from a vote not hating each other. You are one of us now, Hali."

One of us.

Marilla's statement unsettled Hali as much as it comforted. Hali couldn't believe the faith that Marilla placed in her. She held no false ideas that the other Anchors looked at her the same way that Marilla and Ronan did, but in the end it didn't matter.

She wouldn't be there long, she kept telling herself.

She just hoped Marilla's plan didn't backfire.

As she lay in bed that night, Hali had no plans to sleep. Instead she waited for the first light of dawn, solidifying her escape plan as she waited. The night had been a welcomed distraction to her disturbed thoughts. But she was no closer to understanding how she ended up on the Eyes' Land, or how the others did for that matter. The Anchors were as elusive as Marilla on its origins. Mamie especially, who perplexed Hali more than enlightened. She could make no sense of becoming an Anchor and then a leprechaun. With her thoughts and worries running in circles, she accidentally fell asleep.

10

THE LIGHTS OF DAY

FLASHES OF LIGHT speckled above Hali: invading, confusing, and blinding her vision. Initially, she thought the lights were a result of her eyes adjusting to the morning sun rays, but the small flares kept occurring. Inconspicuous, but then impossible to ignore, like fireflies. Hali lay still in the twin bed watching and wondering if it was an Anchor or leprechaun manifestation or something else entirely. The little lights came down and rested above her heart, bobbing up and down only an inch, looking like a field of illuminated wild sunflowers. The small eruptions set Hali at ease, although she had no idea why. Ever since arriving on the Eyes' Land she hadn't gone one day without a surprise. Day one, she learned she was an Anchor and on day two she discovered she was a leprechaun.

What would day three bring?

As she watched the little lights dance above her, she remembered what she planned to do. Outside her window —Ronan's window—it was still dark, but there was a tinge of brightness to the darkness, indicating it was closer to morning than evening. When Hali stood up, the little flickers vanished, like smoke in the wind. She looked around the simple room but found no signs that they were ever there. The little bursts of warmth they provided left with them.

Hali left the cabin, much like she left her childhood home, except without the persistent pain in her legs. This time she had nothing to lose by leaving, though if she stayed any longer, she could see that not being the case. The sooner she left, the easier it would be for everyone. She had no intention of imposing on Marilla or Ronan longer than needed, nor did she want to stay so long that her departure felt like a betrayal.

Nerves rattled within Hali as she moved closer to the beach, fearing what lay ahead and beneath the ocean that she hadn't seen on her first swim as a mermaid. The three mer-boys successfully planted the seed of doubt that something terrifying lurked under the horizon; Ronan watered the seed when he warned Hali to not go into the water alone. Convinced and determined there was no way to return home without literally plunging face first into the depths of the unknown, Hali trudged on in the direction of the beach. She'd just have to suffer with her anxiety while she swam and pray nothing would come for her during her —hopefully successful—attempt.

Walking along the tree-lined path to the shore, where the brightening sky broke through the treeless spaces, the humming static of the ocean met her ears. She was close. Thank goodness, since the morning fishing group, would be down to the shore soon. The shore was empty when she emerged from the path out of the trees, with the exception of Mr. Gruff shaving wood in his usual spot. Hali wondered if he ever went out into the water or if he was even an Anchor. The man was an enigma, shaving wood until mealtime and then resuming his work when he finished eating.

Did he even sleep?

The night she had slept near the beach he had been down by the water, but she hadn't noticed if he had been there through the whole night. All she knew was that he was in his same spot when she woke up the next morning.

When Hali arrived at the edge of the shore, the apex of the sky was still navy blue, fading to teal as it touched the ocean. A sliver of sun peaked above the line that separated the sky and sea. It was enough for basic visibility of shapes and muted colors, but still dark enough to not identify details. It would be minutes until the sun shined in all its glory and uncovered what the night sky hid. Hali could be grateful for that much.

Walking a few hundred yards down the shore away from Mr. Gruff's back, Hali scanned the surrounding area. With not a soul in sight, she slipped her clothes off into a pile far enough away from the water to not get wet, but close enough to retrieve in the event she was unsuccessful in getting home. Hali had no clue what she would cover herself with once she made it to Emerald Cove, but she'd worry about that once she got there.

Her empty stomach did flip flops and goosebumps prickled on her skin as she sheepishly met the approaching tide. With the sun only moments from unveiling her, she stepped into the water as it washed away her human form. The transformation took her breath away like it had the first time it had happened.

How would she ever tell her parents? Would they understand? Had they known what she would eventually become?

Guilt gnawed at Hali for departing without leaving a note and for going out into the water by herself. But she had told herself it was better to make a clean break, even though another part of her didn't believe it. Marilla and Ronan had generously taken her in, and she repaid them by not even giving them a heads up of her plans. Maybe it was because she didn't want to be stopped, but her excuse no longer felt valid. Whatever her reasoning for not telling anyone didn't matter, it was too late to go back.

Below the water, Hali came alive and her nerves disappeared with her human form. Her body revved like an engine. Where the land above was soft and dim the sea below was sharp and vibrant. Zooming from the shore, the schools of fish Hali passed had nothing on her speed. She dipped down further than she had ever gone and faster than she had ever swam, all while not losing clarity of the details all around her. It wasn't only her legs that transformed, her whole being did. Before Hali knew it, she had traveled several miles offshore, coming to the barrier that separated her from Emerald Cove.

Treading like a sea horse Hali stared down the impediment. Home waited for her on the other side. The excitement of swimming dampened by her reality. Despite being told there was no way to get across the barrier, Hali had to try. A sea turtle glided by as Hali moved closer to the obstacle. Hope and dread see-sawed within her heart. Hali didn't want to find out what everyone already knew and be left with only defeat. Within inches from the barrier, Hali stilled, raising her right hand up to the invisible wall. She pushed her hand forward until it was less than an inch away from the obstacle. The barrier looked like a web of bubbles swirling around, across, and around each other, over and over again. It didn't seem impenetrable like the others had insisted, but harmless. Hali thought she heard the soft swoosh of another creature coming from behind her but saw nothing when she twisted her head to check. Turning her attention back to the barrier, Hali connected her hand to the bubbling wall. An electric charge lit up her hand and shot through her body.

"HALI!" She heard a voice yell, before the vibrant world below the sky faded to black and little yellow lights swarmed her lifeless form.

11

BOUNDED

SWEAT FELL into Hali's eyes as she ran towards the finish line. She would clear first place by a solid three seconds as long as she kept her pace. But she made a mistake that runners should never make. She turned around and looked behind her. The runners she had run alongside more or less for the past four years looked different. Their ears were pointy and instead of looking exhausted they looked possessed as they charged for her. Adrenaline burst through Hali as she readied her body to sprint hard to the finish, but she was held in place. The ground below her moved fast in the opposite direction, like a treadmill. She couldn't keep up. Hali was losing a bigger race than the one written across the banner of the finish line. Her heart pounded so hard she could feel it pulsating in her temples. Suddenly, the ground below her liquified and swallowed her whole.

Now in her mermaid form she began to swim but was stuck once again. But this time she was trapped in a rope net. Above the water, the pointy-eared runners circled and peered down at her, each holding a sharpened knife and wearing maniacal grins. Looking around, Hali realized that she wasn't in a large body of *water but in a sphere container similar to a fishbowl. There was no room to swim away or escape upwards.*

She was trapped.

In the distance Hali could hear a sound. At first it was faint, but it was definitely familiar. Her pounding heart made it difficult to hear the sound clearly as her pulse drummed in her ears. Hali focused on the sound, attempting to silence her fear so she could hear it better. She closed her eyes to avoid the losing battle above her and stilled her body. Mamie's voice came through, humming the tune she had heard her croon at dinner the night before. A tune she had heard during a simpler time before Mamie had purred it. The notes connecting her old world—the one she knew—to the one she was still discovering.

But where had she heard it?

She was running out of time to figure out the riddle as the knives above her lowered towards her. Squinting, she awaited the piercings she could sense before they ever touched her skin. Mamie's crooning grew louder like a warning or an answer. Hali wasn't sure as she tried to solve a mystery that was tethered in her old life as much as her new one. Her pulse sped out of control in sync with the increasing volume. Mamie was nowhere in sight.

The knives dipped into the water and headed for her scales, ready to clip the newly acquired appendages straight from Hali. Pushing down further into the net, Hali attempted to escape the inevitable. As she awaited her fate with eyes closed an image flashed in her mind like a bolt of lightning. The music box that had sat on her desk the entirety of her life appeared as her ears were assaulted with its sweet music. Unopened for the better part of a decade, Hali recalled the beautiful auburn-haired mermaid inside of it, swimming back and forth to the melody it produced.

Why was Mamie humming its music and what did it all mean?

Pain shot through her body as one of her scales was snipped

off by a greedy bystander she didn't recognize. At some point the
familiar faces that had charged for her had changed into blurred
voids that barely passed for human.

Maybe they weren't.

"Why are you doing this?" Hali yelled with bubbles encasing
her face. But she was ignored as a second scale was carefully cut
from her body. She swatted their knives with her hands, but her
hands were abruptly captured and tied behind her body. The evil-
doers continued like surgeons, clipping Hali's scales one by one
with precision. Anger rose within her and the little lights
appeared around her chest. They stretched into lines across her
upper body as she titled her head down to watch something other
than her own mutilation. The small orbs looked like a string of
Christmas lights at first, but once Hali really looked, she saw
words.

"Boundless as ..." Hali read the words as the little orbs began
to rearrange into another formation. She cringed in pain, feeling
weaker with the loss of every scale. As the little lights began
forming a new set of words, she was pulled upwards.

She survived—somehow—despite being breathless for a
stretch, while her body adjusted to taking in oxygen as a
human and not a mermaid. She squeezed her eyes shut,
bracing herself to come face-to-face with her captors.

"Hali!" a voice called. "Hali!" Her shoulders were shaken
up and down every time the voice cried out her name.
When her eyes opened, she awakened on the shore; her
nightmare now a fuzzy memory. Cas's face loomed above
her outlined by the sun that sat above the horizon, fully
exposed. Hali looked down at herself, a blanket draped over
her nude, human form. She clutched the blanket up to her
neck, wondering how much Cas saw before putting it
over her.

"What happened?" Hali asked, casting her eyes down

from the blinding halo of light that bordered Cas's body. But as her eyes peered down, she realized that he wasn't dressed either. "Why aren't you dressed?" Hali immediately snapped her head away.

Cas sighed. "Hold on." In her peripheral, Hali could see him getting up, seamlessly sliding a shirt over his head and then his board shorts. He sat next to Hali when he finished dressing, angled in a way that she could still take in all of his features.

He said nothing for a while, as if deciding whether to talk to her at all. With his knees propped up, he encircled his arms around them, with his left hand holding onto his right wrist. He stared at the ocean, exhaling deeply. Dark, wet tendrils of hair hung near his eyes, amplifying his cold blue eyes that Hali discovered actually had flecks of gold in the irises.

Maybe he was disappointed that she awoke.

His show of concern belied her thoughts. Not expecting any intel from Cas, Hali tried to recall what landed her on the beach, naked and confused. She had hardly come to terms with the existence of the Eyes' Land. Distinguishing between dream versus reality felt impossible when existing in an uncertain state of consciousness most of the time. But in her current state of being, that rolled much slower than her nightmare, she was pretty sure she wasn't dreaming.

As her breaths stabilized, snapshots of her recollection surfaced. Images of running against her peers who turned into pointy-eared captors emerged. The memory was disoriented and fragmented like shards of glass on a shag carpet, solidifying the idea that because the memory wasn't lucid it had to have been a nightmare after all.

But the memory of leaving Marilla's and Ronan's cabin and attempting the swim home was vivid and rooted in her thoughts. Yet she couldn't remember how she ended up on the shore.

Why was Cas even at the beach?

"The wall shocked you," Cas answered, surprising Hali out of her own musings. So much so, she barely caught what he said. She stopped herself from asking him to repeat himself. Instead, she mulled over his hazy mutterings; retrieving his words from her mind before they fell into a black hole of forget. Cas looked down, indifferent, but he sat there anyway. He didn't lecture Hali as she would have expected or appear angry that she pursued the wall that he had already warned was impossible. Though his face still contained an expression Hali couldn't figure out. The wrinkle between his eyes made him appear either perturbed or reluctant to ask a question. There was definitely something rolling around in his mind, but Hali didn't know him well enough to guess what.

Piggybacking off of Cas's answer, she asked, "What has happened to the others that have tried to get passed the wall?" She waited for an answer that she wasn't sure she would get. She waited for anger, annoyance, or anything that showed Cas's wariness of her, but it didn't come. His quiet contemplation confused her.

"Nothing," Cas replied.

Hali wasn't sure if Cas was answering her question or blowing it off completely, but then he continued.

"Everyone who has gone to the wall has failed to break the spell that holds it in place, but no one has made the wall react the way you have. The wall has been just like any other wall, solid but harmless. After years of attempting it, we've all just stopped trying."

"What does this mean?" her body shivered. The jolt from earlier left her body cold and jittery, despite the sun rising further up in the sky and the red blanket covering her up to her neck.

"I don't know," he answered, his eyebrows knitting together.

Steering to a topic that Hali thought he could answer, she asked, "Why did you follow me in the water in the first place?" A beat of silence passed between them. Hali's eyebrows shot up in horror when her thoughts began making sense. "Did you see me ...?" her voice raised then lowered as she hugged the blanket tighter to her. She couldn't even finish the rest of her sentence—at least not out loud. His silence made her cringe. Cas hadn't even bothered denying he had seen her strip down, even after she had made sure to check her surroundings before entering the water. Hali wasn't sure why it took her so long to figure out, considering she was hiding under a blanket without any clothes.

Sensing where Hali was going with her questioning, Cas stopped her, "It was still pretty dark out when you first went out, so I didn't see too much."

Cas unsuccessfully hid a smirk that touched his eyes. Hali huffed in annoyance, sobering Cas's momentary lapse in seriousness.

"I get that where you come from it's a big deal to be in your natural form, but here it isn't. It's part of life. Plus, your body's fine, so I don't know why you're embarrassed."

Warm blood rushed Hali's neck and cheeks, overflowing to her ears. Not only had he watched her like a stalker, he didn't even seem sorry about it.

"I'm not embarrassed of my body," Hali lied. "But you're right, it *is* a big deal where I come from to see others naked, especially when they aren't *aware* they're being watched. At least for most people it's that way."

Frustrated, Hali attempted to get into a standing position with the blanket secured around her as tightly as a boa constrictor. Cas quickly stood up, his expression turning to confusion once again. As soon as Hali was upright, she realized her clothes remained piled on the sand. Forgetting her blanket-compromised mobility, she bent down to retrieve them, only to lose her balance. In that moment, Hali was left with two choices, neither one ideal. She could either let go of the blanket in order to free her limbs so she could catch herself or risk free falling with her limbs and modesty secured, but with the possibility of face-planting in the process. There was no chance she would willingly expose herself to Cas for a second time in one day, so she chose the latter.

But instead of falling on her face like she had hoped for, Cas decided to be chivalrous. Hali barreled into his chest, awkwardly bouncing back up until their noses were touching. Cas steadied her by the shoulders, holding Hali in place so she could regain her footing. For a brief moment they both just stared at each other, dumbfounded, like two deer caught in headlights. Cas's blue eyes cornered her hazel ones. Seconds that felt like minutes passed, and Cas made no move to let go. His expression was stern, but not furious like it had been during their first encounter at camp. A taco of her own making, Hali couldn't remember how she had ended up in such a mess—her brain short circuited.

Her flush had grown so many brilliant shades of red. A different hue for every emotion she was feeling; crimson for her embarrassment, maroon for her annoyance, and rose for an emotion she couldn't quite pinpoint. The latter emotion stemmed from the awkwardly intimate proximity to Cas, and it was the most disturbing emotion of all.

By the time Hali entered middle school she had learned

the art of avoiding "close" encounters at all costs. Hali's training started with middle school dances that Camille tirelessly begged her to attend. Hali only caved once, accompanying Camille to a fall dance in eighth grade in which she ended up spending half the evening hiding out in the bathroom whenever a slow song threatened. After that dance Camille tried to get Hali to go to others but failed.

In high school Hali wasn't any more comfortable. When prom season approached, she always planned something to do those weekends months in advance so she would have her excuse ready in case she got asked. Hali avoided any activity that required physical touch from the opposite sex.

Which is why for the life of her she couldn't figure out how at eighteen years old, out of high school, in the least likely place of all, while attempting her escape home, she found herself falling into Cas's arms. Not only had she fallen in his arms like a damsel in distress nonetheless, a blanket was all that separated Hali from being completely exposed to this guy who despised her. Hali couldn't help but grimace at the predicament she found herself in without even trying.

"You all right?" he asked, his tone steady. Quickly, he released her shoulders as if it had never happened.

"I'm fine," Hali said, without looking up.

Cas lifted Hali's clothes off the ground and wordlessly held them up for her to grab.

Willing herself to look up at Cas, who had a small smile playing on his lips, Hali straightened herself. Carefully adjusting the blanket to hold up in one hand, Hali accepted her clothes from Cas in the other. "Thank you," she managed to say, her tone miffed. Irritation was all she had to work with to help fuel her shaky confidence.

"I didn't mean to spy on you. I was up early and figured I'd watch the sunrise before fishing. We don't typically go out into the ocean on our own, so when you did ... I followed."

"Well, thanks, I guess," she gritted out. "I'll return the blanket at lunch." Hali nodded her farewell with as much composure as her mortification would allow. She turned away from Cas, flustered, wanting to bury her head in the sand. But most of all she wanted to get dressed again to not feel so vulnerable. Hali didn't wait for a response as she traipsed back to Marilla's and Ronan's, kicking the blanket up as she walked. Moving away from the shore, Hali noticed the rest of the morning fishing crew emerging from the path, while Cas headed over to join them. She swiftly ducked into the trees, narrowly avoiding another uncomfortable encounter. Her skin buzzed and she wasn't even sure if the shock of the wall was to blame. Dipping further into the tree line Hali looked around more carefully this time for watching eyes. Dropping the blanket on the sand and letting her clothes fall on top, she quickly dressed and walked the rest of the way to Marilla's and Ronan's cabin. When she picked up the blanket, Hali noticed the tag on it had the same professionally stitched capitalized letters on it as the one she mysteriously received her night alone on the beach.

"RANA," she read aloud.

The enchanters must brand their linens.

But Hali wondered what the letters meant. Was it an acronym? If it was, Hali couldn't guess what they stood for. Just another unanswered question she would have to ask Marilla or Ronan about and hope to get an answer.

Hali barely made it inside the cabin before Marilla wrapped her lean muscular arms around her back.

"Thank goodness, you're back!" she exhaled in relief. "Where did you go?"

"I'm sorry I worried you, Marilla. I just went for a walk and ended up swimming. I know I shouldn't have, but I haven't had a chance to really try out my fins." With the worry already etched on Marilla's face, Hali decided to leave out the part of her swim where she got shocked by the barrier and Cas had to pull her out of the water.

The coils of stress that held Marilla upright, loosened as the wrinkles that etched into her face relaxed. "I'm sorry Hali, you're right. I guess we didn't take you out like I had promised."

Feeling guilty for Marilla's guilt, Hali backtracked. "It's not your fault, Marilla. I understand. It's not like anyone knew I was going to become a leprechaun yesterday and ruin our swimming plans."

"That's true," Marilla smiled as she sipped on coffee. "But next time you get an idea to go swimming before we are awake. Don't."

Hali laughed. "Okay."

"I'd tell you to wake us up, but I'm useless without a couple cups of coffee in my veins and Ronan is typically not a morning person. Plus, sharks aren't the only predators in the water." As if on cue Ronan sat up from the couch like a zombie from a grave.

"What mom?" Ronan asked. His eyes peered around, disoriented. Tufts of his brown hair stuck out in every direction but down and was the most alert thing about him.

"Go shower up or we're going to miss a hot breakfast," Marilla ordered.

"Any cookies left?" Ronan asked with eyes half closed.

"Ronan ..." Marilla warned.

"All right, all right, I'm getting up."

Hali hid a smile as Ronan blindly ambled to the bathroom, guided only by memory Hali could imagine, since he rubbed his eyes the entire fifteen-step journey.

"Marilla?" Hali held up the blanket into view. "What does R-A-N-A stand for?"

A flash of recognition spread across Marilla's face when she looked at the blanket. "Where did you get this?"

Would Hali ever be able to have a question answered with an answer and not another question?

Hali felt a blush creeping up her neck again, while she tried to figure out a way to explain her encounter with Cas in a way that didn't make her sound like a foolish girl or a girl trying too hard not to sound like a foolish girl. Hali realized that she took too long to answer when Marilla tilted her head and squinted her eyes at Hali, like she was already busted. For what, Hali couldn't guess. But Marilla's stare made her squirm all the same. Coming up with no logical excuse for why she would have the blanket she told a little white lie.

"I just found this one on the beach walking back, but I actually got one just like it my first night here when I slept near the beach. I thought that you or Ronan had put it on me when I was sleeping." A surprised snort escaped Marilla and Hali wondered what she had said that was so funny.

"Those are Cas's blankets. RANA isn't an acronym. It is Cas's family name—Cas Rana. His father was excellent at needlework and stitched every single one of their linens with their surname. I have to say, I haven't seen him carrying these around for a long time. I'm surprised that he would leave any of these blankets at the beach. After his parents passed away, he always carried a blanket around. But he never left them behind, even when he was a little one."

"Oh," Hali responded. The blush that crept up her neck

earlier threatened to choke her into oblivion. "Well, I guess that makes it easier to know who I need to return them to."

"I guess it does," Marilla smirked before taking a final sip of her coffee, placing her cup in the sink. Changing the subject, Marilla looked at Hali with concern in her eyes. "Are you okay, Hali?"

"I'm fine," Hali lied, what felt like the tenth time that morning. It was her automatic answer whenever someone asked her that question. Whether it was true or not didn't matter. As much as Hali liked Marilla, she was still a stranger. And Hali had never been one to unleash her problems to someone she barely knew. If she was being honest with herself, she wasn't any better at it with people she did know.

"Something seems to be eating at you," Marilla pried, "Did you see something when you went swimming?"

Hali felt her stomach sink at the question "I ..." Hali didn't want to lie, but she didn't want to add any worry to Marilla. She also remembered that she did have a question. "Actually, I saw little lights surrounding me this morning. I was wondering if you could tell me what they mean?"

Marilla's inquisitive expression relaxed into a smile. "Hali, I think it means you're part enchanter." Marilla made the announcement as if she hadn't just told Hali something life altering.

"What?" Hali's eyes widened in shock at the discovery.

"I suspected as much when you glowed the first day, but I didn't want to overwhelm you."

Hali paced, sorting through her jumbled thoughts. Moving a step forward, then three steps back, she wore the wooden floors down with her disorganized dance. "I can't even think straight right now. This is like a terrible dream or a joke, but this can't be real. What's on the menu for tomorrow? The Loch Ness Monster? No, maybe a yeti, or better yet, a unicorn. What is possibly left for me to be on this crazy island?"

"You'd be surprised," Marilla added.

"What does all this mean?"

Evading Hali's inquiry, Marilla stated, "Let's go eat breakfast with the others."

"Marilla, please tell me. Not knowing is worse than whatever you could tell me."

"I'm not sure that's true," Marilla said. "But I agree you should know."

Hope and fear sprouted in Hali.

Would she finally get answers?

"But you should hear it from someone who knows the whole truth," Marilla concluded.

Confused, Hali begged the question, "Who?"

Marilla exhaled a breath. "Hali, I promise I'm not trying to withhold information from you. It's just that some information is not mine to share. As much as I might want to."

"Can you at least tell me whose information it *is* to share?"

Rain began pattering on the quaint cabin. Ronan stepped out of the bathroom fully dressed in shorts and a t-shirt, looking way more alert than when he walked in minutes before.

"Guess we are eating in the lodge today," Ronan stated, disappointment clouding his typically happy features. The rain sounded like footsteps on the roof of the little abode, halting Hali's conversation with Marilla.

Ronan's and Marilla's eyes flooded with panic at the sudden heaviness of the raindrops. Trepidation filled Hali as she tried to understand what was happening. She stood quiet and still, waiting for a cue from Ronan and Marilla on how to proceed. The little orbs rose from her skin and hovered, pausing an inch above her as if awaiting an order. Ronan's eyes rounded at their appearance. The little lights zinged with an energy that Hali felt connected to her being. The pounding rain was not rain at all, but footsteps that threatened to cave in the roof of the small cabin.

"What's happening?" Ronan whispered while still staring at the orbs. They stood frozen in place. Marilla's chest rose and fell with panicked breaths that she tried to conceal with a calm face. That's how Hali knew something was terribly wrong. The pitter patters of feet that definitely belonged to full grown adults of some species came to an eerie halt. The little orbs—that Hali hadn't figured out what to do with—pulsated, matching the energy within her.

Bang!

The front door of the cabin snapped off its hinges and flew away.

"Eyes!" Ronan yelled.

12

A FAMILIAR FACE

WIND with the force of a tornado pulled at Hali, Marilla, and Ronan. Before Hali could think, she was pulled to the opening in the wall that used to hold the front door. With arms spread wide, she held her body across the space while Ronan's and Marilla's bodies pushed against her back. The wind felt like a vacuum, kicking up sand and ocean spray that whipped at her face. Hali's arms held strong as she closed her eyes, turning her face down against her hair slapping at her eyes. If she let go she had no idea where she would end up with Marilla and Ronan following behind. But the angry foreboding winds knew it wouldn't be anywhere good. The force was stronger than the night she was captured from Emerald Cove and that terrified Hali. Especially since she felt responsible for Ronan and Marilla now. As Hali's grip began loosening on the doorframe the little orbs flew to each of her hands, spreading their light with the strength of a thousand vice grips around the frame.

"Your hands are glowing!" Ronan shouted over the wind.

"I noticed!" Hali yelled in return.

"Why are your hands glowing?" he asked, his tone a mixture of awe and terror.

"I have no idea, but right now it's very helpful." The wind walloped Hali as if she was in a wind tunnel, ripping at her vocal cords every time she spoke.

A storm brewed overhead, transforming the sky into angry layers of gray clouds. Another energy twisted within Hali with the clouds hovering above. She inhaled the swirling clouds like a sponge, the same way she pulled the fish to shore only the day before. The rattling cabin quieted and the pressure of two beings pressed into Hali's back subsided. She dropped to her knees within the doorframe. The blue sky had returned, and the sun shined above as if nothing had happened.

"Are you okay?" Marilla asked, dropping to her knees with Ronan to inspect Hali.

"I think so. But I'm a little dizzy. What was that?"

"I think it was the Eyes," Marilla answered. "The last time they actually came to the Eyes' Land they ran across the roof just like they did now, before attacking."

"Are they coming for scales again?"

"I don't think so," Marilla said, looking unsure. She bit her bottom lip appearing full of fret, her racing mind almost popping out of her eyes. "We need to get to camp."

"What if they are still out there, mom?" Ronan questioned, his worry revealing the little boy he tried so hard not to be.

Marilla said nothing at first as she contemplated Ronan's question. "Grab a knife from the butcher block," Marilla ordered, frantically. "Stay behind me. If we stay here, we are sitting ducks. The game plan for an Eye attack is to get out in the open with the others so we can work together."

"That makes sense," Hali agreed.

Marilla quickly moved to the kitchen, grabbing three knives of varying sizes and three large serving forks resembling pitch forks. Marilla handed out the kitchenware to Hali and Ronan with trembling hands. Hali prayed that they didn't need it. Even though she had only known Marilla for three days, she knew Marilla wasn't a person that was easily shaken. Whatever waited outside of the cabin couldn't be good if Marilla was arming everyone with cooking utensils.

Knives and forks in hand, the three cautiously stepped outside with Marilla leading, Ronan in the middle, and Hali covering the back.

"If there's any trouble don't be afraid to use your leprechaun powers like you did earlier, Hali," Marilla whispered without turning around.

"Copy that," Hali complied. Beads of sweat popped up on Hali's nose as they ventured further down the path that led to camp. As they got closer, the sound of arguing voices arose.

"Where is she hiding?" an unfamiliar gravelly voice bit out. He was a squat man, with salt and paprika waves that hung to his shoulders. His ears broke through his uncouth hair and came to sharp points halfway up each side of his head.

At the sound of the gravelly-voiced man's words, Marilla gestured for Ronan and Hali to hide behind the trees just outside of the eating area. Their position behind the trees gave them a slightly obstructed view of Anchors standing off against what she assumed to be Eyes. The Eyes looked like humans, except their ears were pointy. Grabbing at her own ears, Hali noted that hers were the same as they had always been.

"There's more than one *she* that lives amongst our kind. You're going to need to be a little more specific than that," Mamie countered.

No one could ever say Mamie wasn't a savage.

"Don't toy with me old woman," the gravelly-voiced Eye shot back. "You know exactly who I'm talking about. None of you fish could have pulled our clouds out of the sky."

"What clouds? I don't remember seeing any clouds," Mamie stated. A collective chuckle escaped from the Anchors and even a few Eyes, which annoyed the gravelly-voiced Eye enough to turn around and scowl at his betrayers. Hali wasn't sure how Mamie was even able to hold a straight face, considering Marilla's cabin door literally sat a few feet away from Mamie. It was impossible not to see.

"So, you want to play aloof, do you? We didn't come for scales, but we can make that happen if you want to keep playing your games."

The threat launched the Anchors into fighting stances, ready for battle. Hali could see the glint of knives being pulled from their hiding places. The elevated tension could be felt in the air. Ronan sucked in a breath and Marilla embraced him in a hug to shield his eyes from the horror.

Moving out of the protection of the trees, Hali walked towards the two groups. Marilla's fingers trailed Hali's arms as she did, but not in time to stop her. Hali wasn't brave. But she also didn't want to endanger Mamie any more than Mamie was already doing to herself. As she was steps away from being in view of both groups she was pulled down behind another tree.

"Stay out of sight," Cas growled.

"What about Mamie? I can't just let her get hurt protecting me," Hali rushed the words out in a panicked stream. Her heart raced at the uncertainty of the situation and the possibility of fatalities if she remained hidden behind a tree. She tried not to think about the likelihood of her own demise if she handed herself over to the Eyes.

"There are only ten of them and hundreds of us. He's bluffing," Cas assured Hali. "Mamie's smart, she knows what she's doing."

Hali didn't doubt that Mamie was smart and sly, but she was also a little bit crazy from what Hali could tell. The kind of crazy that didn't know when to stop poking the bear.

"What if you're wrong?" Hali rushed out, earning a glare from Cas. Realizing her words didn't come out right, she corrected herself. "Not about Mamie being smart, but about the Eyes not attacking." Hali struggled to watch on and do nothing as the scene played out.

"I'm not wrong. Trust me."

"You don't trust me, but you expect me to trust you?" Hali bit out, shocking herself with how snarky she sounded. Fear, indecision, and Cas's arrogance had gotten the best of her.

"You're a stranger with no one to vouch for you. I may be a stranger to you, but you have no reason not to trust me," Cas huffed, stating his words as fact.

"That is a terrible argument. You have not earned my trust just as much as I have not earned yours."

Cas appeared flustered by Hali's point. As if he couldn't comprehend not being considered trustworthy by all who made his acquaintance.

"Now let's just all settle down now and there doesn't need to be any fighting today." The gravelly-voiced Eye raised his hands in surrender, a nervous chuckle escaped his weather-worn lips, but the Anchors remained in position. As Hali glanced at Cas, she noticed his fists were clenched so tightly that his knuckles were white from the tension and the muscles in his jaw twitched. Hali wasn't sure how his glare alone hadn't set the Eyes on fire already. His hatred of them was evident and even though Hali knew why, she couldn't understand why he would tell her to hide.

"If you hate leprechauns so much and I'm part leprechaun, why not just hand me over to them so they go away?"

Cas turned his gaze to Hali, which shifted from hateful to just plain aggravated that she posed such a stupid question. "Because, all leprechauns are schemers with no good intentions, especially the Eyes. Eyes have made it their goal to hunt us down when we have nowhere else to go. There's a reason this place is called the Eyes' Land, Hali. If they are trying to take you, it's to benefit themselves."

Feeling dumb that she hadn't come up with that practical line of reasoning herself, Hali responded with a simple, "Oh." But then she had an epiphany. "How would they *take* me anywhere if I can't leave?"

Cas sighed. "They wouldn't *take* you away. They would use you here for some personal gain and our detriment. And that's all I know. Considering you're part Anchor and leprechaun I'm sure they have plans for you that would hurt us."

Hali shuddered at the thought of being used in such a way and accepted Cas's explanation by silently remaining behind the tree. She dared not tell Cas that she was most likely also part enchanter. Though she doubted possessing another magical strain could really put him off any more than he already was by her. Besides, Ronan had said the enchanters brought supplies to the Anchors. But he also said they provided supplies out of guilt—whatever that meant. Another mystery Hali had yet to solve.

"Just hand over the mutt and we'll leave!" The gravelly-voiced Eye shouted at Mamie, provoking the Anchors to draw their knives and move closer around her. That's when a familiar younger Eye stepped forward. For a moment, Hali thought her eyes would fall out of their sockets from opening so wide.

Neilan?

Excitement bubbled within her to recognize someone who was practically family, until the reality of her situation snuffed it out, and skepticism began to take its place.

Why was he here? And why was he standing with the Eyes?

Hali squinted trying to get a better look, knowing that it couldn't really be Neilan O'Riley. But it was. Besides his ears being pointy, sporting shorter hair, and his once scrawny body filled with muscles, he was the same. Camille's older brother, who had been like a brother to her, was on the Eyes' Land—in the flesh.

She would need to hear him speak to fully believe what she was seeing. Hali hadn't heard anything positive about Eyes since arriving on the Eyes' Land. The chopped down trees scattered everywhere proved that Eyes would stop at nothing to get what they wanted. But what did that mean for Hali who was part leprechaun? There was nothing Hali wanted enough to kill someone over. Were all leprechauns the same kind of terrible like the Eyes were? Hali liked to think not. She wanted to believe that Marilla had been right when she said that there was good and bad of every kind of being. If her eyes weren't playing tricks on her, what did that mean about Neilan? For a moment, Hali almost forgot where she was at and ran up to the closest thing to home she had seen in three days. But with Cas demanding that she stay put and the tension high between the Anchors and Eyes, Hali didn't think it would be a good idea. All the Anchors besides Mamie were jumpy. The spry old woman held her ground and seemed to be intentionally egging on the gravelly-voiced Eye. The last thing Hali wanted was to start a battle by running out of her hiding spot and inadvertently scaring an armed Anchor into a fight.

Neilan rested an arm on the gravelly-voiced Eye's shoulder holding him in place, while looking to the Anchors while he spoke. "Let's take a step back. We aren't here for a fight, or your scales. We just want to know where *she* is."

Yep, definitely Neilan.

Mamie let out a sigh. "Like I said before, I'm not sure to which *she* you are referring."

Neilan stayed calm as he looked at Mamie, but the other Eyes were growing impatient by the second.

"We're looking for Hali," Neilan stated. "Do you know her?"

"Hal and Lee?" Mamie questioned. "I thought you were looking for one girl. That sounds like two people to me. Hal is an interesting name for a girl. Is it a nickname?"

At this point, Hali didn't know whether she was more scared for Mamie or impressed by her boldness. Even Neilan's resolve cracked just the slightest at Mamie, revealing a brief smile. Cas, on the other hand, didn't lose his laser-focused glare even for a second.

"Do any of you know Hali?" Neilan addressed the crowd of Anchors, bypassing Mamie's antics.

"Stay here," Cas ordered, before walking out of the protection of the trees.

"What are you doing?" Hali asked, but he was already gone.

All eyes fell on Cas as he stalked towards the two groups

like a lion in the Serengeti. Neilan watched, his expression unreadable.

"Hello," Neilan said imperviously.

Cas ignored his greeting. "We don't know a Hali. You can leave now."

Neilan stared at Cas. In all the years of knowing Neilan, it wasn't a look that Hali had ever witnessed him wearing. He appeared to be sizing up Cas, standing a little straighter as he did.

They are going to kill each other, she thought.

Losing all semblance of cool that he had had with Mamie, Neilan's tone became indignant.

"We know she's here. Just tell us where she is and we'll—"

"Leave," Cas growled. "We owe you nothing." Despite not having a view of Cas's face, Hali saw the tension corded in the muscles of his neck, shoulders, and back.

"We will. Once you show us where she is," Neilan countered.

There was a stare down for what felt like an eternity. Hali couldn't understand what the Eyes would want with her. Cas had implied that the Eyes would use her to their advantage.

But what?

If they were after scales, then why would the Eyes not try to flay all the Anchors for their scales right then and there. Her leprechaun abilities wouldn't be special to a group of leprechauns. Unless they knew about her being part enchanter. She wished she could speak to Neilan in private—the old Neilan, not the Eye Neilan. Old Neilan was predictable, Eye Neilan, not so much. She wanted to find out how her parents were doing and to see if he knew how she and all the other Anchors could get off the Eyes' Land. But now she wasn't so sure what his intentions were.

Did Neilan want her dead?

Hali shuddered at the thought.

Neilan finally spoke. "If you aren't going to help us, we will just have to conduct our own search."

Tingles broke out on Hali's skin as the little light orbs made an appearance. Breaking away from her skin, the little lights crawled up the tree, like the illuminated paths of a movie theater. Taking the hint, Hali followed, while they helped her grip her way up the tree as they had with the doorframe earlier. When she felt like she was high enough to be out of easy viewing distance of the Eyes, she tested a thick branch for sturdiness, before stretching her legs across it and keeping her back against its trunk. She was so high in the tree she had a full view of the ocean. No one would be able to see her if they looked straight up. Hali only hoped that climbing up trees wouldn't be part of the Eyes' search. Once in place, Hali anxiously waited.

Many agonizing hours later, after numerous close calls and a thorough investigation of the Eyes' Land and the Anchors—including a collective effort of the Eyes to pull the ocean around like a blanket off a child's head during a game of hide and seek—the Eyes finally left. To see the Eyes manipulate something as big and powerful as the ocean almost had Hali falling right out of the tree. The stunt was the last in the Eyes search attempts and Hali could see why. All the Eyes looked completely wiped out despite it being a group effort.

When Marilla finally gave Hali the green light to come out of the tree, Hali realized that it was well into the afternoon. Marilla walked with Hali to camp as Ronan ran ahead for lunch.

"Are you okay, Hali?" Marilla asked.

"I know Neilan," Hali blurted out.

Confusion crossed Marilla's face as she waited for Hali to continue.

"The younger Eye is my best friend's brother." Hali paused, gathering her thoughts. "I had no idea he was an Eye. I really don't know if I did the right thing by waiting in the trees. What if he was here to help me get back home, Marilla?" Desperation coated Hali's words. Neilan was like seeing a glass of water in a desert and being told she couldn't drink it because there was a fifty-fifty chance it could contain poison. Maybe her situation wasn't as dire as that, but at that point it didn't feel too differently. It didn't take long for regret to seep in after the Eyes left.

Had Hali missed her one shot of going home?

"You did the right thing by hiding, Hali," Marilla assured her.

"But even you said that there is good and bad of every—"

"Hali, this situation is different," Marilla rushed out, biting her bottom lip when she finished.

"How do you know? We don't know what they wanted from me. Maybe it wasn't bad."

Marilla looked exhausted. "Trust me."

Trust had become Hali's least favorite word on the Eyes' Land. For Anchors, trust was no more than a demand to not act against their wishes—given without being earned first. For Hali, trust meant believing what a person said, because that person had built a solid reputation of not letting her down—earned before giving. There were very few people that Hali trusted, so it didn't come easy for her to give trust away without the recipient of her trust passing a significant trial period.

"If the Eyes had good intentions for you, then they would have had no issue saying what they were. But they didn't. They spent hours looking for you. Not many people are driven to spend hours looking for something without expecting something in return."

Hali thought about what Marilla was saying. She wanted Marilla to be wrong. Neilan was a jerk at times but she never knew him to be evil. But she didn't argue, because for the first time since knowing Neilan, she wasn't sure who he was.

Did he know what Hali was to become their entire childhood? How long had he himself been an Eye?

"Hali ..." Marilla started, indecision clouding her features. The pregnant pause caused Hali's pulse to jump with anticipation as she waited for Marilla to speak.

But what was Marilla undecided about? Would she finally tell Hali the origins of the Eyes' Land and how she got there?

With a sigh, Marilla finally spoke. "Come with me," she said.

Hali followed Marilla to camp, where the tangy and sweet smells of grilled fish and warm apples permeated the air, causing Hali to salivate. Anchors bustled around, chatting somberly and preparing the afternoon meal, as smoke billowed off the fire pits and rose above camp in gray clouds. They wove between tables of famished Anchors that waited patiently for sustenance, as children played tag on the outskirts of the tables, unfazed by the unwelcome visitors from earlier. They found Mamie sitting alone at a table with her head resting in the palm of her propped-up elbow, appearing taciturn. Everyone at camp seemed to be shaken as they cooked the fish that was intended for breakfast. As they approached, Mamie brought her gaze up to Marilla, then Hali, then back to Marilla where it settled. For a moment, Marilla and Mamie spoke with their eyes. One not giving in to the other in some battle Hali couldn't comprehend, leaving her more anxious than before.

Mamie exhaled. "Fine. But we need to go somewhere private. Let's at least bring lunch with us. Missing one meal was quite enough on this old body." Mamie patted her growling stomach.

After filling their plates, the three walked down to the beach, laying a blanket down provided by Mamie. Stretching the blanket out reminded Hali that she still needed to return Cas's blankets back to him. The task was hardly a priority considering the other pressing concerns that had presented themselves that afternoon. But Hali felt a sudden urgency to rid herself of the linens. Having the blankets brought two experiences to the forefront of her mind that she wished to forget—her arrival on the Eyes' Land and her failed departure back to Emerald Cove.

The three ate in silence and Hali wondered if Mamie was just going to give her the run around again—not that she was certain where the conversation was going anyway, but Hali had her suspicions. Both Marilla and Mamie wouldn't have bothered having a private conversation with her, if it wasn't something important. Not wanting to give the old woman a reason to stir up her antics, Hali patiently waited, not asking a single question. Hali knew that her curiosity would only give Mamie strings to tease and tug at and Hali would get nowhere in the end. The woman's crazy game was strong, and Hali would not fall prey like the gravelly-voiced Eye had. When Mamie finally spoke, Hali tried not to look too surprised.

"The Eyes' Land has been here just under eighteen years, Hali. Before its existence we were free. We worked, we loved, we lived, just like the rest of humankind. The only difference was that we could transform into mermaids and mermen, becoming Anchors of the land and sea."

Hali listened intently, while attempting to appear indifferent; fearing that if she interrupted, Mamie would veer off track. The truth, Hali believed, would guide her escape off the Eyes' Land and provide her clarity in her muddled situation. But what Hali hadn't expected was the truth to be so devastating.

13

ARCELIA'S STORY

"I'M GOING to tell you Arcelia's story now, Hali," Mamie announced, feeling drained before she even began. Hali's eyebrows twisted up in confusion to the name she had never heard before. Though Mamie was certain when she finished, Hali would be irrefutably cured of that blessing. Not that Arcelia was not worth hearing about—it was quite the opposite. But Hali would soon find out what she thought she so desperately needed to know. Information was like that when you were young—tantalizing and necessary. If Mamie learned one thing from getting older, it was that some knowledge wasn't power, but just plain debilitating. Period. But with the return of the Eyes, there was little choice in the matter. Mamie had put it off for as long as she could and now it was her sole responsibility to break the full history of the Eyes' Land to Hali. She had hoped for a little more time with her before this day became necessary. But really, she had hoped this day would never come at all—or that she'd at least be dead when it did.

Realizing that she wasn't so lucky, Mamie swallowed,

treasuring Hali's innocent eyes one last time, and then began.

The Eyes' Land was an island created by a leprechaun named Cillian who had an unrequited infatuation of an Anchor with unique abilities. The Anchor's name was Arcelia and not only was she beautiful, she was also half enchanter. Unfortunately, Arcelia's mother, who was a full-blooded enchanter, passed away when Arcelia was only a baby. Leaving Arcelia to learn how to use her magic completely on her own since she was raised by her father who was an Anchor. Cillian was drawn to the power Arcelia possessed, caring little for her heart. Though that didn't matter because Arcelia had already given her heart away to Cillian's younger brother, Murchadh.

When Cillian learned that Arcelia and Murchadh were together his anger boiled over. His infatuation for Arcelia quickly turned to hatred for not only her, but Murchadh, who was the complete opposite to himself. Although leprechauns were seen as thieves and liars, Murchadh never stole or lied to anyone. He lived honorably, earning gold fairly and without deception, no matter how easily he could.

However, the same could not be said for Cillian. Cillian was not above lying, cheating, stealing, or stooping to whatever violent means necessary to get gold. Growing more and more dissatisfied by the material items afforded to him through leprechaun and mortal means he began trading his gold for magic. Cillian enjoyed the power of it within his hands, though he was never fully satiated with the amount he was given.

Enchanters only gave out simple magic in exchange for gold to other magical beings. For instance, an enchanter might transform a piece of paper into a lollipop for a child or capture a three-dimensional memory inside a snow globe for an adult. Under no circumstances were enchanters to produce magic that altered a life or lives without permission from the Enchanters' Assembly, an assembly of witches and warlocks that made laws and decisions on the proper use of magic. An enchanter who violated rules set forth by the Enchanters' Assembly could be sentenced to banishment, execution, or whatever punishment the Enchanters' Assembly found fit. But that didn't stop Cillian from coveting enchanters' power and becoming obsessed with acquiring as much magic as he could, even if he needed to find a banished enchanter to help him succeed with his goal. Wayward in his singular thinking, he resolved to let no one stand in his way of gaining power through magic, not even his younger brother.

Things got uglier when he found out Murchadh was planning on marrying Arcelia. In Cillian's mind, Murchadh was purposely sabotaging his plans to capture and use Arcelia as his personal spell maiden. Cillian threatened to kill Murchadh and Arcelia if Murchadh didn't stay away from her. What Cillian didn't know was that Murchadh and Arcelia had already been married in secret for four months. Knowing there was no reasoning with Cillian, Murchadh and Arcelia ran off together without telling anyone, in the hopes that Cillian would come to his senses. While away they received word from a leprechaun close to Murchadh that that hadn't been the case.

Cillian's anger brewed with every passing day they were gone, as did his plans. So much so, he resorted to trading gold for two potions with a banished enchanter named Rowina.

When he spotted Arcelia and Murchadh strolling the shores of Emerald Cove, several months after they had originally disappeared, he snuck up on them with both potions in hand. Cillian bashed a rock in the back of Murchadh's head, killing him instantly, without a shred of remorse.

Distraught and overcome with grief, Arcelia's mouth hung agape at the shock of watching the life exit her husband of only ten months, so alive one moment and gone the next.

Seizing the opportunity of Arcelia's shock, Cillian poured the binding spell potion he had procured from Rowina, down Arcelia's throat. Which instantly, though temporarily, shut Arcelia off from accessing her own magic for one to two hours. Leaving Arcelia numb in all senses of the word.

Unfazed by his atrocities, Cillian cackled. With each obstacle conquered easier than he could have imagined, he felt empowered and indestructible. He began rejoicing over his victories before he had even begun the real work. Growing more arrogant, devious, and greedy, he thought of ways of amassing more magic and power before he had even handled Arcelia's magic. He had only succeeded in restricting Arcelia from using her magic for no more than two hours, nothing more. But that didn't stop Cillian from thinking ahead and growing concerned of losing her magic in the event that she died. Unsettled by the thought, he developed a backup plan.

Unhinged, Cillian plotted to pull and trap all the Anchors in the region to one secluded place. Allowing him access to their scales whenever he wanted, so he'd never be without power. Since scales could be traded for magic, they were equal to magic in his mind. However, Cillian's plan rested in the belief there would be plenty of exiled enchanters willing to trade with him. He concluded that with the strict rules enforced by the Enchanters' Assembly, there would be no shortage of ousted enchanters who couldn't adhere to those rules at his disposal. He reasoned that he had found one enchanter to trade with easily enough, how hard would it be to find others? The wheels in Cillian's brain spun at so many possibilities. What had started as a simple spark of attraction for Arcelia's magic, evolved into an uncontained wildfire of obsession to rule over every creature of the land and sea. Only death would stop him.

Mamie watched Hali's expression swell with anger as she uncovered each layer of the truth that intertwined with her own fate of being uprooted to the Eyes' Land.

"Why would an enchanter give Cillian *any* power? Did the enchanter not see how evil he was?"

Mamie rested her hand on Hali's arm. "Sometimes people become so desperate, or swayed by another, their brains deceive them into thinking that the wrong thing isn't so bad. They believe they are doing good."

Hali wordlessly shook her head in disgust and Mamie wished she could take all of her pain away. She would be the pin cushion to all of the grief, if it meant she could spare Hali from the agony of Arcelia's story. Instead, Mamie was left to be the knife, only finished when the final kill had been delivered. After gathering her composure, Hali sighed and said, "I'm sorry for interrupting Mamie, please continue."

"It's all right, child. I'd be more worried if the story didn't bother you." Mamie took a sip of water, cleared her throat and began again.

Rowina had not known Cillian would capture an entire region of Anchors with her potions, nor did she agree with it. She hadn't been a malicious enchanter in her previous life, just extremely generous, or as some thought, careless with bestowing her magic to humans. Rowina found it difficult to stand by and watch humans die of diseases she had the ability to cure, so she did exactly that. Even after being warned several times by her coven that it was not her place to meddle with the outcomes of mortals, she continued on, unworried of the consequences. But as promised by her coven, she was eventually punished by the Enchanters' Assembly by means of banishment and left to her own devices.

Rowina passed decades in solitude after being removed by her coven, before being approached by Cillian. After more than thirty years of only talking to herself and the forest animals, it was nice to have someone converse back.

Cillian, charming and convincing, shared his woes with Rowina. Claiming that his brother was placed under a love spell and taken from his family by an Anchor that was also half enchanter. Alleging that Arcelia planned to use Murchadh for her own selfish gains, strengthening her own powers by employing Murchadh's abilities with the elements.

Flabbergasted, Rowina could hardly believe such a being as Arcelia existed and that she would exercise her powers so selfishly. Animosity took hold of Rowina, as she felt wronged by her own punishment all over again, when there were enchanters freely practicing for their own greedy agendas and the Enchanters' Assembly did nothing about them. Blinded by her own injustices, Rowina agreed to help Cillian put a stop to Arcelia. The gold he promised was an added bonus she couldn't bring herself to refuse when he offered, even though she would have helped him just on his story alone.

Rowina produced two potions for Cillian, one to restrict Arcelia from using her own magic and one to open Arcelia as a magical vessel for Cillian. When Rowina questioned Cillian on why he would need to access Arcelia's powers, he simply explained he only wanted to bottle some of Arcelia's magic to take to the Enchanters' Assembly to demonstrate that her magic had been used for deceptive purposes. Magic could be tested for what good and bad it was used for, like the blood of a mortal could reveal disease.

Satisfied with Cillian's answer, Rowina received five gold bars for her troubles, which made her salivate at all the delicacies she hadn't enjoyed for so long that she'd now be able to buy from mortal marketplaces.

Prior to Cillian approaching her, Rowina was living a simple existence. Being an outcast, she didn't have the luxury of living or associating with enchanters from any coven, including her own. Meaning that she had to provide for herself without the typical conjuring work her kind was extended. Side work for an outcast was unusual to receive and typically outside the moral codes of enchanters.

When she was banished from her coven she was not only banished from her livelihood and place to live, but her freedom to shop in the Enchanter's Marketplace. This meant gourmet magical foods, exotic potions, charms, trinkets, and other magical items were off the table. She was stripped of any extras, or enhancements to her natural magic.

Rowina was even excluded from gaining employment through mortal means as part of her punishment. But she wasn't excluded from shopping at mortal marketplaces. Though how she could afford to, without any means of honest work, she had no idea. The reason given by the Enchanters' Assembly for not allowing her to work for mortals was that Rowina needed to survive solely by her own devices. But Rowina knew that wasn't the only reason. The fact was, the Enchanters' Assembly no longer trusted her to be around mortals for an extended period of time.

Especially since mortals were mostly ignorant to the existence of enchanters and enchanter law had frowned upon letting mortals know any different. This made bartering spells for common items like food and toiletries with mortals impossible.

Luckily, Rowina had gotten by in her abandoned shack in the woods. The forest provided, even when her magic was limited without the use of the goods available at the Enchanter's Marketplace. Rowina existed on a series of daily routines, easily losing herself to the consistency and banal nature of her new normal. Life tasted bland on her tongue and there no longer was the excitement of the occasional peaks and valleys; only flat planes, like a prairie, except without the occasional tornadoes to sweep her off her feet. For Rowina, the worst part of living in the woods, other than feeling unneeded *by anyone, was needing to take up the monotonous task of hunting for her own food.*

So, when Cillian crossed her path in the forest with a problem she could help with and the resources to do it, along with gold for her time, Rowina felt alive again after many years of merely existing. She hadn't forgotten about the rigidity of enchanter law and that the decision to help Cillian could result in her own demise. But that didn't matter, because her own life had turned into something she wasn't sure she wanted anymore. If she was going to die, at least she could remember what it was like to live again and have a purpose.

Spells that resulted in the removal of rights from its subject, like the potions Rowina concocted, always required a vote from the Enchanters' Assembly and a randomly selected jury of twelve, similar to a mortal jury. The seizing of one's natural and magical rights were taken seriously and overlooking such laws were considered an abomination, with the consequence being death or worse.

Mamie paused, bracing herself for the next part. When Hali asked, "What happened next?"

Mamie peered into Hali's hazel eyes, without any intent to withhold the information, but wishing she could. For Mamie, telling the story was like uncovering a wound that never healed. The wound ugly and gruesome, its impact carried shrapnel, spreading to every part of her. The shrapnel was the invisible pain that she carried daily. Her burden. Sharing the burden of the story with Hali only intensified her own pain. But there was no way around it. Mamie sighed, reluctant to push forward with the story that had felt like a train blazing a path with a missing track. Once started, it couldn't stop until it crashed, derailing so many lives in the process.

"As you've come to discover, leprechauns are tricky creatures in that they have the unique talent to pull energy from the elements, but not the ability to cast spells.

"They are able to harness power from rain, clouds, lightning, and especially rainbows to pull their subjects close to them. However, sun power is too much for a leprechaun to channel, which makes rainbows the perfect solution. The energy from the sun would level out even the most proficient leprechaun, but they are able to catch the power of the sun from the raindrops of a rainbow, which hold a significant source of power.

"Typically, leprechauns aren't able to pull from other magical beings. Those who possess magic are able to cage it like ribs cage a heart. But Rowina uncaged Arcelia's magic, using a forbidden spell, leaving it open for Cillian to use as he pleased. Does this make sense, Hali?"

Hali nodded.

"Good, because it is important that you understand this before I go on."

Mamie could see Hali's mind piecing together the different information, trying to understand how the new facts related to the story and to herself. Mamie closed her eyes to avoid seeing Hali's reaction to the rest of the story and then she continued.

With Arcelia in hand, Cillian arrived at the Emerald Cove Lighthouse. The summer day was humid with rain clouds peppering the sky. The sun played peek-a-boo in their cover. Arcelia looked to the sky, letting a lonely tear fall to her cheek. Squeezing the back of Arcelia's neck, Cillian forced the contents of another burning liquid down her throat. The open window potion coursed down Arcelia's esophagus, opening her magic up to anyone with the ability to pull it from her. Everyone, that is, except for herself. Arcelia's magic had become barely a flutter under the binding potion Cillian had already used on her.

Anxious and impatient, Cillian paced as he waited the full thirty minutes for Arcelia's open window potion to take full effect. The potion worked like eye drops used by an ophthalmologist to dilate eyes. With every passing minute unearthing more and more what lay hidden beneath the surface.

After thirty minutes had passed, Cillian dragged Arcelia closer to the Emerald Cove Lighthouse. With one hand on the lighthouse and the other hand clenching the back of Arcelia's neck, Cillian took in a deep breath. A breath that took Arcelia's own breath away as her magic ripped from somewhere within and out of her mouth. The magic rebelled at its misuse, pushing back against the pull, which pained Arcelia even more than the burning potions.

The magic circled like a spiral of smoke around the lighthouse. Smoke turning into rings of light like a newly lit Christmas tree. The cloud above unmasked the sun and a rainbow illuminated the sky in a mist of brilliant colors. Arcelia, in her human form, had never felt more mortal. With her powers being torn from her body and lacking the water required to transform into a mermaid, she felt helpless.

She couldn't depend on a passerby to stop Cillian, because the first thing he did when touched by her magic was freeze time. Everyone outside of the magical world remained frozen. To make matters worse, Cillian began pulling even more energy from the rainbow, intertwining it with her magic. The excess power lit the lighthouse up as bright as the sun, radiating out onto the ocean.

The target illuminated.

A tree-filled island in the distance sprouted out of nowhere. Cillian let out a maniacal laugh at his achievement at the same time Arcelia's knees gave out. She was dying. Cillian must have known all along that would be her fate when this ordeal was done.

The ocean waters formed a massive wave that pulled from all

sides. Suddenly, the wave transformed into a cyclone containing Anchors from miles and miles in every direction. Except for Arcelia. She remained in place next to Cillian, like the moon to the earth. She endured being pushed and pulled physically, emotionally, and magically by Cillian, until she couldn't any longer.

Arcelia collapsed under the impossible demands of Cillian, half of her face planted in the sand, as his clenched hand was forced to release from her neck. She watched on as disaster struck the sea and all its inhabitants. The only silver lining to the horrid situation was not having to watch her father suffer from the same fate, since he had passed away two years prior.

The Anchors remained trapped inside the cyclone, making the sea appear like a giant blob of glitter glue. Cillian took in another deep breath that Arcelia thought would end her and the misery of being used to hurt the others. Killed over and breathless, Arcelia believed she couldn't have much magic left inside of her for Cillian to extract. She prayed that she didn't. But somehow Arcelia survived to watch the cyclone of Anchor-water blown across the sea to the newly formed island. An incomplete glittering barrier of water sealed the Anchors off from Emerald Cove.

She knew this because her magic was like having a thought. Even though she didn't control it, her magic still spoke to her. So, she knew every spell her magic was being summoned to do. And at this point her magic was responsible for banishing an entire region of her species onto an island controlled by Cillian and his minions. An island that would allow Cillian to steal the Anchors' scales to trade for gold or magic.

The lighthouse was now wrapped in a magnet spell that would pull all Anchors to the island if they were touched by the light from the lighthouse from that day forward. The knowledge sickened Arcelia.

Something had to be done.

There wasn't much she could do about the island, but she

could stop Cillian from using the Anchors for his own selfish purposes. That's when Arcelia got an idea. Barely alive, Cillian stopped paying attention to her as her body lay flattened to the ground with her head turned to the water and her mouth gasping for relief.

Focused solely on polishing off the last bit of magic he could commandeer from her wasted body and the depleting rainbow that had been mostly covered by a cloud, he worked quickly to seal off the barrier to the island.

Arcelia stayed silent easily enough. Making any sound would have required oxygen that was being ripped from her as well as her magic. She scanned the scene and timed out her plan. While waiting, she casually turned her head up to the sky. Her heart beat faster out of a last-ditch effort to stay alive or anticipation, she wasn't sure.

A cloud crossed the sun, dimming Arcelia's once lit face as she continued counting with the twitch of her eyes.

One, two, three ... twelve-seconds total from end to end.

As the magic beamed across the ocean, Arcelia watched on. By the third row, Arcelia knew exactly where the beam would be. Light slid across her face as the shadow retreated and the cloud uncovered the sun.

The time had come.

Arcelia rolled her almost lifeless body to the ocean with energy she didn't have. Mutating like she had done all of her life from human to mermaid. She swam with a fierceness that only anger could deliver. Wrapping up his barrier spell, with horizontal strokes across the horizon, Arcelia caught Cillian's attention, but not in time for him to stop her trek. Shooting from the water like a dolphin, Arcelia caught onto the shelf-like space between the incomplete barrier that enclosed the island off from Emerald Cove and the rest of the mortal world. As Cillian was about to work across the last small area of space that Arcelia had launched to, she angled her scales in a perfect V-formation. Part of her scales pointed towards the sun, the other part towards Cillian.

"Please work," she pleaded to no one in particular as her pale scales gathered light in one direction and shot it out in the other. Cillian didn't have a chance to respond to the ambush. His body burned as he worked the last stroke of the barrier. Once completed he stopped pulling from Arcelia's power, disengaging her from burning him with the sun. Arcelia crashed into the ocean, with the shelf-like space in the sky now filled in with the magical barrier. Cillian pulled Arcelia back to shore with one inhale.

"Ha," Cillian exclaimed, feeling successful that he accomplished what he set out to do, his face and hands scorched and blistered. Peering out to the now still waters, Cillian assessed the sky, finding gray clouds forming overhead. He smiled to himself, before sucking the entirety of the clouds into his chest with one deep inhale, greedily. Arcelia lay motionless on the shore, still in her mermaid form, as the waves lapped over her body. With Cillian's chest puffed full of cloud, he absorbed it into his lungs for later use and approached Arcelia.

He stared down at her, kicking at her tail to check for life. "You thought you got me, didn't you, you washed up mutt," he said bitterly. "And you're supposed to be part enchanter and Anchor," he huffed. "You and my brother were made for each other. Both weak. Can't even last through a few spells without passing out. Pathetic." Pulling a knife from his back pocket he said, "Doesn't matter now, I got what I needed … your scales will grant me whatever I desire, that's for sure."

Squatting down, Cillian pulled on a scale that was clamped shut. "You're a pain in the ass even when you're dead," he snarled, pulling at the scale even harder. Even though Cillian knew that he would acquire more gold and magic for each scale if they were in one piece, he lost patience and began grabbing for different scales with no luck. He scratched at the scales like they were a stubborn label glued to a jelly jar, forgetting all efforts of keeping them in once piece. He became more and more abusive. As he raged on, Arcelia's eyes opened, but Cillian hadn't noticed.

"Come on," he pawed in frustration.

Arcelia watched, not saying a word, her scales bled but she held on tight. Warmth swirled within her body, thawing her like an iceberg in the desert.

"Be careful what you wish for," she whispered, her hazel eyes meeting Cillian's one last time before she unclamped her scales. Cillian had no chance to respond before blinding light, that looked like the sun had made landfall, unleashed from Arcelia's scales. She had held the sunlight within her scales when she could sense the smallest drop of her magic awakening within her again, quietly holding its heat, until that very moment.

The blasting sun incinerated Arcelia and Cillian, leaving ashes and gold coins—that a down-on-his-luck passerby bene-fited from just a day after the incident—in their wake. However, Cillian's cloud-filled body took longer to extinguish, as it sprayed rainwater for miles and miles, along with his tortured screams, before disintegrating to dust. Coincidentally, the spray was responsible for keeping the explosion contained, protecting Emerald Cove from the inevitable fires from the blast. Though it didn't stop the lighthouse from being scorched, resulting in its permanent closure.

As if on cue a raincloud above burst open, washing away the evidence of the past hour. The human world was still on pause, unknowingly waiting another hour for the time spell to wear off to become conscience again. While in the distance a new realm was just beginning.

14

TRUTHS

"Arcelia was my granddaughter," Mamie shared, her eyes filled with sorrow. "The other Anchors and I were forced to watch her demise from the ocean, trapped in the cyclone Cillian had created to pull us all to one place," Mamie huffed. "We found out the rest of the story ten years ago when the Eyes paid us a visit. They had bragged how artful Cillian had been in his plan, but not careful enough to prevent himself from being killed. Apparently, Rowina had witnessed Cillian murdering Murchadh and binding Arcelia. She felt so guilty for what she had done, she ran to the Enchanters' Assembly to put a stop to him, but by that point the damage had already been done. The Eyes rejoiced over Cillian's triumph and they wanted to let the Anchors know that even though Arcelia ended Cillian, he had still succeeded. I think part of the reason they had attacked the Eyes' Land—other than our scales—was to prove that they could."

Hali couldn't find the words to comfort Mamie, so she opted for what was on her mind instead. "She sounded very brave."

Mamie nodded in agreement. "She was very much. I wish you could have met her."

The three sat in silence for some time. No one really knew what to say next. The story of the Eyes' Land swam in Hali's head. She had more questions but wasn't sure how to ask when Mamie looked so sad. Mamie peered at Hali expectantly, as if waiting for Hali to grasp some hidden meaning from what she had shared. The day had been taxing, to say the least, and Hali was not in any frame of mind to draw any epiphanies from what she had learned, if there were any to be had. But yet they sat, silently waiting for Hali to figure it out.

Finally, Marilla spoke. "We should get back and help the others with clean up. Before you know it, it will be dinnertime." Coming to a standing position Marilla extended her hands to assist Mamie.

Reluctantly Hali followed, knowing that once they went back to camp, honesty wouldn't flow so easily from Mamie. Hali still didn't understand how she possessed her abilities and why her abilities were latent until she was eighteen.

As Mamie and Marilla began to plod away from the beach with their plates in hand, Hali called, "Wait!" from behind them. Fearing her opportunity to ask would slip away with each step closer to camp. "If all the Anchors were pulled that day, why wasn't I pulled too?"

Mamie and Marilla looked at each other. Both wearing an expression that Hali couldn't read.

Mamie took a deep inhale in and forced an exhale out. "My son, Taras, Arcelia's father, decided to go a different path than what is typical of our kind." Mamie dropped her head down, collecting herself. "He fell in love with an enchanter named Bessie and she died while delivering Arcelia. Taras was devastated. We all were. I initially didn't take to the idea of Taras marrying an enchanter very well. While Anchors don't carry the same hatred towards enchanters as they do leprechauns, we also don't trust their trickery. But that didn't matter to Taras, and he left with Bessie so they could be together. I realized too late that Bessie had a good soul and she made Taras very happy.

"When I found out they were having a child, I thought I was going to miss out on being a grandmother. Taras had completely cut me out of their lives for the ugly things I had said before he ran off with Bessie. I was afraid I'd never see them again. I know I certainly would have deserved it, if that had been the case."

Tears escaped Mamie's eyes in a hurry, and she failed to rub them dry. After a moment she stopped trying.

"A few months before Arcelia was born, Bessie came to me on her own. She wanted to make amends so we could be a family for Arcelia. Her conditions were simple; I needed to accept her for being an enchanter, since my grandchild would most likely carry magical abilities too. Little did she know, I had accepted her long before, but knew I didn't deserve her forgiveness. I wept when she offered her mercy so freely. Taras took a little longer to absolve me of my wrongdoings. He was distant and didn't go out of his way to make conversation with me like he had before. He really only tolerated me for Bessie's sake. But I understood. When I hadn't accepted Bessie right off the get-go, like I should have, my words hurt him. He took it as me not approving of him and his choices." Mamie sighed. "A few months later, Arcelia was born, and Bessie was gone."

Mamie's eyes rained fresh tears that made it even harder for Hali to control her own.

Marilla wrapped her arm around Mamie's shoulder.

"Come on Mamie, let's get you back home so you can rest. This has been a lot for one day."

"I don't need coddling, Marilla. I need to get this all out now, while I'm already worked up. Save myself the trouble of getting worked up another time. I've shared this much I might as well share the rest."

Marilla nodded and pulled her arm away from Mamie's shoulder.

A wave of worry washed over Hali, leaving an unsettling feeling swirling within her chest to see Mamie's spirits so low when all Hali had ever seen her as was lively.

What other upsetting news could Mamie have to share? Would Hali learn how she ended up on the Eyes' Land?

Hali grasped at strings trying to understand how they all tied together. But Hali still didn't have a clear picture of how she fit into all of it. The story was too terrible not to believe. She couldn't imagine even a jokester like Mamie concocting such a tale just to fool her. Mamie's emotions were too raw and genuine, and Marilla didn't seem to have a cruel bone in her body to go along with such a scheme anyhow. Only a great actress or a sociopath could pull it off. For the sake of clarity, she really hoped that Mamie was neither. Yet Hali waited for the next pieces of truth to fall from Mamie's lips like a dog waiting for scraps to fall from a kitchen table. Hali wasn't sure what Mamie would say next, but she couldn't have predicted it if she tried.

Mamie walked closer to Hali, focusing her brown eyes on Hali's hazel ones. "The reason you are an Anchor, enchanter, and leprechaun is because Arcelia and Murchadh are your birth parents."

Hali stepped back from Mamie, the information striking her like a bolt of lightning. A sharp static buzzed in her ears as if someone had turned the volume of the ocean up. She blinked several times, her eyes growing hotter each time. Hali's throat pinched together, and she was suddenly aware that she was about to cry. She needed to get away, but her legs remained planted in place.

Hali's name was called several times, sounding distant, until she realized the call wasn't far off at all—her mind was.

"Did you hear me, Hali?" Mamie asked. Without waiting for a response, she said, "I knew when I first saw you who you were. You look so much like Arcelia."

Hali couldn't breathe. If she swallowed, her tears would have escaped. Abigail and Theo were her parents. They had been for as long as she could remember. How had they never told Hali she wasn't biologically linked to them and that she looked like someone she had never met? Why did they leave her to learn this information from strangers she barely knew? After Arcelia's story had been told, Hali wasn't sure how she hadn't put it all together. It was all there right in front of her.

But why did she only arrive on the Eyes' Land now?

Wouldn't she have been pulled the same day as everyone else, since she was presumably living in Emerald Cove at the time? How did the lighthouse turn back on in the first place?

Hali searched the depths of her brain for a detail that would refute Mamie's claims. Had Hali not witnessed her own powers on display over the last three days she would have never believed what she was hearing. But she couldn't think of any reason they would lie to her.

"Hali, your father was a kind leprechaun," Mamie added. "He was an exception. Most leprechauns will hurt you when push comes to shove. Which is why you needed to know how the Eyes' Land began and why you must be careful from here on out."

Hali had heard enough for one day. She wanted the

mother who raised her for the conversation she was having with Mamie and Marilla. Her eyes burned with tears she refused to let spill. The liquid a mixture of grief and anger. Ever since she had arrived on the Eyes' Land, she wanted nothing more than to understand the story behind it. But now that she knew the truth, she wasn't sure why she wanted to know it in the first place. Hali was left devastated by her losses. Not only had her parents lied to her all her life, but her biological parents were dead before she could ever meet them. But what also disheartened her was that she was given up in the first place.

Mamie looked at Hali with mournful eyes as if reading her thoughts. "Hali, I want you to know that Arcelia and Murchadh wouldn't have given you up if it wasn't something they thought they had to do to keep you safe."

Hali nodded.

"Arcelia and Murchadh tried to keep their marriage hidden from Cillian in hopes that he would come around to their union. When they saw how angry and dangerous Cillian became with each passing day, they knew that it wasn't likely his feelings were going to change. And then when Arcelia found out she was pregnant ..." Mamie stopped, while Hali died a little inside waiting for the rest of the puzzle to unfold. Knowing the ending of the story didn't help her feel any less anxious.

Taking a deep breath Mamie continued. "Arcelia just had a bad feeling that Cillian would try to hurt you. That's why she left with Murchadh to Emerald Cove with every intention of raising you themselves. But then Murchadh received word that Cillian's feelings towards them had only turned more alarming and they knew that the only way to truly keep you safe was to give you up. Arcelia used her magic to cast a spell that would bind your abilities until you were eighteen. Enchanter law doesn't generally allow for such a thing. But parents can exercise that right if it is in the best interest and safety of their child or if the child's abilities pose a risk to society. But once one who is in possession of abilities enters adulthood, the binding spell is undone."

Marilla moved closer to Hali and brought her in for a hug. Hali's tears pooled to the bottom of her eyelids, but she refused to let them fall.

Marilla released Hali from her embrace but held onto her shoulders to look at her. Hali looked away from Marilla's slate eyes. She wasn't sure if she could handle her pity. "Is it okay if I go back to the cabin?" Hali asked. She focused on a spot in the sand, fearing that her tears would rebel against the wall of her lids if she looked up.

"Did you want to talk about it? I know since you've been here it has been a lot all at once. Since your arrival, I have felt guilty for not telling you the truth." Marilla's own voice sounded shaky, remorseful even. Arcelia's story was that of fairytales and nightmares, but the pain expressed by Mamie in its retelling was palpable. Even Marilla wore the badge of pain that only those close to a tragedy could understand. Hali felt interconnected yet disconnected. Only time would allow her to fully grasp what she had just heard. Yet the more time that passed the less likely it seemed she would find a way back to Emerald Cove. Each passing day presented new obstacles that steered her away from her goal of going back home. Instead of the story giving her insight on how she could figure a way off the Eyes' Land, it left her feeling more trapped.

"I need some time to sort all this out in my head," Hali admitted.

Marilla nodded and they walked back to camp. Once they approached, Hali decided to leave Marilla and Mamie and head around camp instead of going through it. They didn't question her motives, though they did caution Hali several times to be careful walking alone. They shared an unspoken understanding that Hali wasn't in a place to socialize. Honestly, Hali wasn't sure if they were either. They had all trudged slowly away from the beach without speaking, their faces vacant and drained. Mamie's especially.

Lost in her thoughts, Hali walked amongst the trees that let her pretend she was home for a little while, letting her wall of tears fall with each step. Mosquitos feasted on her, but she didn't care. Hali wanted to be completely wrung out of her tears before making her way back to the cabin. The sound of a cracking tree branch brought her out of her sulking. The little orbs rose from her skin, alerting her of danger nearby. She picked up a stick as protection. Fight winning over flight. With eyes wide, Hali spun, whipping the stick as she went.

Out of nowhere a figure jumped from a tree, directly in front of her. Hali didn't waste time by getting a look at her assailant before her legs were in sprint mode—flight taking over. But as she ran, she was pulled back down with a force that had her immediately remembering being pulled to the lighthouse. Before she could turn and kick her assailant, a familiar voice had her coming to a halt.

"Hali, it's me."

Relief flooded Hali as she looked up to confirm the speaker.

"Neilan?"

15

NEILAN

"Hey Hali, how are you doing?"

"I'm doing fantastic, Neilan. What kind of question is that to ask me right now?" Hali dusted sand and dirt from her legs as she came to a standing position, trading relief for annoyance.

"Sorry. Manners. Remember what those are? It's how someone usually begins any conversation," Neilan quirked an irritated eyebrow, crossing his arms.

"I think my current situation is an exception, all things considered. How are you even here? And how long have you been an Eye? Does Camille and your family know?"

Neilan lifted his arms, palms facing Hali, as if it could stop the slew of questions she sent his way. "Whoa, whoa, whoa. One question at a time. A tree. Forever. No and some."

"Who in your family knows what you are?" Hali interrogated.

"Have the fish people ignored you or something? I don't think I've heard you talk this much in all the years I've known you."

"Neilan, please. Are my parents doing okay?"

Neilan breathed in slowly, exhaling loudly, stalling to answer the stream of questions he hadn't prepared for. "Your parents are doing as well as any parents would be doing in their situation," Neilan answered.

"And my other question?" Hali grilled.

Neilan shook his head, eyes widening, before bringing his palms up to smooth out the lines forming on his forehead.

Hali placed her hands on her hips, her gaze unwavering as she waited for answers. Several moments passed and neither one spoke.

Finally, Neilan sighed, his hands falling to his sides. "My mom and Camille don't know that I'm an Eye. My dad does. And that's all that you need to know."

"Is your dad an Eye?" Hali pressed. "Wouldn't he have to be if you are?"

"Hali!" he exclaimed, waving his hands. "I know this is all new to you, but one of the first rules of being part of a magical realm is that you don't go outing people's abilities. I told you what I'm allowed to tell you. Anyways, that is not why I'm here."

Hali scrunched her nose. "Then why *are* you here?"

Neilan ran a hand over his shaved blond hair that appeared darker than usual. His newly pointy ears—or new to Hali—were more pronounced without hair to mask them. "I came to warn you."

"Warn me of what? And how did you even know I was here?"

Neilan looked away from Hali. "Magical beings gossip just as much as mortals do. I don't have all the details, but there are Eyes that will stop at nothing for power. It's in our genes. Some of us can control our greed and some of us can't. All I know is that some of the Eyes are looking at you as a priceless commodity that they want to get their hands on."

Hali said nothing at first. She wondered how anyone could find out about her when she was literally on a deserted island—unless the Eyes could still see them through the trees. Enchanters delivered supplies, so maybe they had seen her. But since being there, she hadn't run across any.

At least none that she knew.

The thought surprised her.

"What are they going to do to me?" She wasn't sure why she asked. After listening to Arcelia's story, she already knew what the Eyes were capable of.

"Nothing good, Hali," Neilan replied somberly.

The words sent a cold shiver down Hali's spine. It's not that she didn't already know that whatever the Eyes had planned for her was less than ideal, but it was like dying—as long as you could pretend that the end was far away you could ignore it. But when you were being told the end was soon, it changed things.

"How can I get off the Eyes' Land, Neilan? There's gotta be a way."

"I'm trying to figure that out, but the barrier is a mixture of so much magic, it's nearly impossible to break the spell that holds it."

Hope sprung up in Hali. "*Nearly* is not impossible. What would I need to break the spell?"

"Hali, it can't be done. I've looked at every angle and even if you *could* pull every component together, you risk dying in the process."

"Neilan. Just tell me what components are needed and I'll decide for myself if it's too dangerous."

Neilan ran a hand over his head again, cornered and exasperated by Hali's badgering. Hali could see right through his attempt to avoid her question, as he circled his foot in the dirt to buy time. When he looked up Hali nailed him with a glare, earning her an eye roll, but successfully squashing Neilan's plan to lie. He'd never been very good at it anyway.

"For starters, you need the originators of the spell that created the barrier or a descendant of their bloodline. Do you know the story of the barrier?" But what Neilan was really asking was if Hali knew where she came from. And in that moment, Hali wondered if Neilan had known who she was all along. She peered down to compose herself, scowling at the dirt to avoid scowling at Neilan. For some reason, Neilan knowing and not telling her was like she had been walking around with her fly down her entire life and no one cared enough to tell her. Despite not always getting along with Neilan, she thought they were closer than that. She looked at him like a brother and the omission stung of betrayal.

"Yes," Hali responded curtly.

Neilan's shoulders dropped with regret. "Hali, I'm sorry, but it wasn't my secret to tell."

"Whose secret was it?" Hali asked, with no intention of making his deceit easier. "Both my biological parents are dead."

"I know, Hali. I'm sorry you had to find out here, like this. But if it's any consolation, Theo and Abigail have no idea of your actual origins. They were just two people who couldn't have a kid and were offered one on a silver platter."

"Is that supposed to make me feel better?"

"Hali …" Neilan pleaded. Hali's wounds were too fresh to listen to reason. Neilan must have sensed it since he steered the conversation back to the original topic. "Do you know all the sources of power that created the barrier?"

Hali nodded, remembering the story she wouldn't soon forget. "Arcelia and Cillian."

"Yes, but the source of power also stemmed from the enchanter that originally gave Cillian his power."

"Rowina?" Hali asked, the crease in between her eyes deepening.

"Yes, and she is thought to be dead and didn't bare any children."

"Thought to be dead? You mean there's no proof? Wouldn't there have to be some other way or a loophole," Hali reasoned.

"Rowina ran off after Cillian took control of Arcelia. No one really knows what happened to her, but there was a rumor that when she went to the Enchanters' Assembly to confess her wrongdoings she was punished. That kind of crime, for enchanter law, is automatic death or some type of torture. So, if she is still alive, she is not the same Rowina and most likely not of any use to your cause. Do enchanters still send monthly supplies to the Eyes' Land?"

"Yeah, why?" Hali answered, distracted by the new information.

"Well, I'd ask if you could borrow a spell book. Usually enchanters don't lend those out freely, in fact I've never heard of it happening, so I wouldn't expect much, but if you could get a hold of one, maybe that would help you find a loophole."

The wheels in Hali's head began spinning with possibilities.

A spell book.

So far, she had only accidentally used her magic. To be able to purposely create spells would allow her better control of her powers. She just knew that if given the chance she could find a way off the Eyes' Land with the right resources.

"Hali ... Hali!" Neilan broke into her thoughts, forcing her attention back to the present. "Listen, I really need to get back now. You need to be careful. Don't do anything stupid and I will see what I can find out on my side." Neilan put his hand on a nearby tree, fingers splayed out. "Oh yeah, it would probably be best for you if you didn't tell anybody about this. Anchors don't trust Eyes and Eyes don't trust anybody who helps Anchors."

"Got it. But—"

Neilan took his hand off the tree, but still hovered it close. "What is it, Hali?"

"Could you find a way to let my parents know I'm okay?"

Neilan grimaced and Hali saw the excuse in the air before it ever came out of his mouth, her hope dangling in the silence.

"I'll try, but you have to remember that we can't go telling people who we are."

"What if you just tell them that I'm safe and leave it at that?" Hali asked.

Neilan lifted an eyebrow at Hali. "Would you?"

"Would I what?"

"Would you so easily leave it at that?"

Hali thought on it for a moment and realized that if she was in the same position as her parents, she probably wouldn't be content to not look for them.

"Plus," Neilan continued, "if I say something like that, they might think I'm involved in your ... disappearance."

"Huh?" Hali tilted her head.

"Why are you huh-ing me, Hali? You are putting me in a real shit position by asking me."

"I wouldn't want to put *you* in a shit position, Neilan O'Riley. What were you going to say?"

"What?" Neilan's cheeks reddened at his blunder.

"You hesitated before you said disappearance. What were you going to say?" Hali's teeth clenched, growing impatient.

"What are you talking about, Hali?" Neilan gazed at the tree longingly, looking to escape the conversation.

"Neilan, you are a terrible liar so just tell me the truth, so I don't put you in another *shit* position as you put it."

"You are impossible, you know that. You are probably more annoying than my sister."

Hali glowered at Neilan, unmoving and determined for an answer, as she crossed her arms.

"Fine. I was going to say, death. Happy. Everyone assumes you drowned or got eaten by a shark. I'm not sure why you needed me to say it out loud. What do you expect them to think? Someone found your sweatshirt washed up on the shore."

Silence filled the air until Hali broke it with a snort and then a roaring stream of giggles that bordered insanity. Tears rolled down her cheeks as she held her clenched stomach.

"Hali, are you okay?" Neilan asked, but he backed away from her, looking ready to flee.

Her laughter continued and Neilan's face remained unsettled. "Okay, stop laughing. There isn't anything funny about this. I just told you something horrible."

"I know." Hali's breaths teetered and tottered as she tried to steady them, which made controlling her laughter harder. "But it is when you think about it."

"I have thought about it and it's still not." Neilan's brows furrowed, appearing unamused and a bit concerned about Hali's mental state.

Neilan's wariness did nothing to quell Hali's laughter. "I was just thinking about you telling my parents what really happened to me and I am not sure what sounds more ridiculous—the truth or the lie. Why would anyone think I'd go swimming at night by myself? Ever since I've been going to the beach, I've always gone with someone, never alone. It's me, for crying out loud."

Hali's laughter subsided when Neilan's expression became eerily unreadable. "What? What's that face you're making?"

Neilan shook his head in exasperation. "Well, I'm just not sure why you're surprised anyone would come to that conclusion since your car *was* at the beach. Maybe going swimming alone at night is out of character for you, but so is going to the beach at night. Is it really that far of a stretch for someone to believe that you swam? What made you go to the beach, anyway?"

Neilan was right. His words sobering any subsiding humor she found at the idea. She ignored his first question and was surprised by his second.

How did he not know how she ended up on the beach?

"The lighthouse beam drew me in. My legs were cramping up really badly before that, but once I looked out my bedroom window, there was no escape from the pull."

"Like a moth to a flame?" Neilan asked.

"Like a moth to a flame," Hali reiterated.

"Wow, did your transformation cause the lighthouse to come back to life or did the lighthouse coming back to life cause your transformation?"

"Probably the first one, since my birth mother apparently put a binding spell on me to hide my powers until I became an adult." Hali pulled sand from her fingernails. "But you probably already knew that."

Guilt crossed Neilan's features. "I'm sorry this happened, Hali. I'll try to figure something out. I really need to go. You going to be all right?" Neilan's words were compassionate but his tone was covered in anxiousness.

"I don't really have a choice. But yes. Go. I'll make it work. The Anchors are nice. Well, most of them anyway."

Neilan looked like he was going to ask her a question, but then he didn't.

"Take care of yourself, Hali. I don't know when or if I'll be back, but I'll keep my ears open if I hear anything useful." Neilan wiggled his ears, attempting to lighten the mood. Hali smiled reluctantly, for his sake more than her own.

"Thanks," she said.

Wasting no time, Neilan placed his palm with fingers splayed back on the tree.

Before he could slip away, Hali said, "Wait. I have just two more questions."

Dropping his head down to his chest with a sigh, he kept his hand on the tree. Pausing for only a short beat, he raised his gaze back up to Hali and asked, "What's that?"

"Why aren't my ears pointy?"

Neilan shook his head. "Consider yourself lucky that you didn't inherit pointy ears. Mine are only like this when I am in a magical realm or using my abilities. What's your second question?"

Hali bit her cheek, almost afraid to know the answer to her second question. Neilan tilted his head, raising his eyebrows impatiently. "Can the Eyes still see through the trees?"

A smirk broke out on Neilan's face. "Why, you worried?"

"I am actually, especially when I am being hunted. Nothing good comes from spying on people."

"Sometimes it does," he said, almost to himself.

"What is that supposed to mean?"

"Nothing you need to worry about, Hali."

Not budging, Hali's eyes bore into Neilan's until he provided a better answer.

"If you are worried about an attack on the Anchors, don't. Like I said, I'm keeping my ears open for any whispers in that direction. We aren't all bad. You're part leprechaun, too. Don't forget that."

"How can you be so sure?" Hali asked.

"I've given the other Eyes no reason not to trust me."

Hali laughed. "I guess they haven't known you as long as I have then."

"All kidding aside, what have I ever done that made you not trust me?"

Needing no time to reflect on the question Hali immediately answered, "How about the fact that you have been an Eye your entire life and never told me. That I was actually adopted, and you never told me. And that if you had given me a clue about any of those two facts, I may have avoided having this conversation with you on a deserted island where I am now being hunted by Eyes."

"Okay, other than that, what have I ever done that was untrustworthy?" Neilan smiled at Hali, attempting to get her to smile back. But forgiving Neilan for betraying her wasn't going to be easy. But for the time being it was necessary. Survival took precedence in her current circumstances. Hali's anger would just need to stay burrowed in the back of her mind, hibernating until conditions were better.

Would they ever be?

Pushing the thought away into the corner of her brain

that held her anger, Hali looked up at Neilan and gave him a faint smile, hoping it would suffice his need for immediate amends she wasn't ready to give.

"Hey, I really need to go. No one can know I was here. Take care of yourself, be on the lookout, and see if you can get a spell book. I'll do what I can on my side." With a twist of his palm on the tree trunk, Neilan's form blurred into pixelated wind. Sprinkles of color flowed into the tree in one breath that would have been missed completely if Hali had blinked at the same time. But Hali's eyes had remained opened and her heart pounded a jealous tune as she witnessed Neilan effortlessly vanish to somewhere else. She wondered if she would ever know freedom again or if it had only been a temporary gift from her birth mother.

Placing her hand on the tree as Neilan had, she twisted her palm several times. But unlike Neilan, Hali stayed in one piece, remaining on the Eyes' Land. Irritated, she kicked the tree several times—once for every failed attempt. Heaving out a sigh, she moved swiftly through the trees back to Marilla's and Ronan's cabin.

16

TSK-TSK FISK

HALI SUNK INTO BED, her eyes and heart heavy, praying for sleep, but doubted it would come. With sand coating her legs, she opted to lie on top of the sheets, covering herself with only a blanket—one of Cas's, no less.

She would return the blankets back to Cas tomorrow, she told herself.

Today the crimson layer provided comfort and protection from the outside world. A world that had grown bigger and smaller in a matter of days. Hali had wanted to know the *why* to her situation, but now she wanted to forget everything she had learned and go back to a time when things were simpler. As worries sprung up in her mind, the little orbs popped up on her skin—surfing the surface of her arms in warm comforting waves. She watched their movements, her thoughts calmed, her breathing deepened, her eyes closed.

When she woke up, the little orbs were gone. Light shined through her window, indicating the time of day to be between late morning to early afternoon. Dried drool coated the side of her mouth, her eyes were caked with sleep that glued her eyelashes together, making opening them painful. Disorientated and groggy, she headed for the bathroom to freshen up, splashing and cleaning her face with warm water until the remnants of sleep were washed away. Once her eyes could open and close without sticking together, she proceeded to the main living area.

As she entered, she found Marilla and Ronan chatting quietly around the kitchen island, looking well rested and ready for the day. As Hali stepped into the small space, she was welcomed with their smiles. Marilla released a breath when she smiled whereas Ronan's smile was carefree.

"Morning Hali, you slept so long, you missed breakfast," Ronan greeted, then added "and dinner, technically."

Marilla frowned at him then focused her attention back to Hali. "I saved you a breakfast plate from this morning. How are you feeling?"

"Thank you." Hali stretched her arms with a yawn before reaching for the plate. "I'm better, just a little out of it still." Smirking, she squinted her nose and eyes at Ronan as she took a seat at the kitchen table. He mirrored her taunt, like a little brother. "I do have a couple of questions about yesterday, though."

Marilla nodded, looking at Hali with an openness that wasn't there the day before. Probably since she no longer had to evade the truth.

"Do the others know ... what I am?" Hali asked, forking the fish back and forth on her plate, not eating, even though her stomach growled.

"Yes," Marilla answered. "Although, to what extent I couldn't tell you. Arcelia's story is a known fact around the Eyes' Land. But it's one thing to believe on faith alone, it's quite the other to see it in the flesh."

Hali peered up from her plate, meeting Marilla's gaze. "How do you mean?"

Marilla walked to the table taking a seat across from Hali with Ronan following, sitting between them. "What I mean is, for the older generations, like myself, who witnessed the making of the Eyes' Land and saw the workings of enchanters and leprechauns, it's easier for us to believe because our belief is based on proof. We knew Arcelia, and even though she wasn't one to put her magic on display, no one doubted that she possessed the blood of an enchanter after that day. But for the younger generations it's not as clear-cut. They may have heard Arcelia's story and that she had a daughter who may one day appear on the Eyes' Land, but it's a whole other thing when a story comes to life. Up until you showed up, they believed purely on faith, if they believed at all."

Hali's eyes gleaned with revelation. "That explains why Carmya and Delphia freaked out when I glowed."

Marilla nodded, blinking solemnly, her eyes filled with compassion. "I'm sorry about that, Hali. I can't even begin to imagine how hard these last few days have been on you and you've done such a good job taking it in stride. I hope you can come to forgive us for not being the most welcoming on your first day. Just try to remember that it has nothing to do with you, but everything to do with our past visitors."

Hali smiled faintly. She understood but couldn't excuse some of the grudges she held just yet. A forgiving person she was not. Despite Marilla not separating herself from the apology, Hali could find no fault in her or Ronan. They had been nothing but welcoming. Hali was never really upset with Carmya and Delphia either, because their lashing out —or rather Carmya's lashing out—hadn't been malicious but based out of fear. She could even argue the same for

Cas, whose coldness could be blamed on looking out for the safety of the Anchors. But as for Kai, Jett, and Toru—who had gone out of their way to give Hali a hard time just for the fun of it—the verdict was out on whether she would come to forgive any of them. She doubted they would care.

Changing the subject, Hali asked, "What time is it, anyway?" finding the answer staring at her on the wall clock reading 9:47 a.m. She had slept close to eighteen hours. Her stomach growled angrily, reiterating just how much time had passed—two missed meals worth. She finally gave in to eating the lukewarm fish coupled with cinnamon apples. A combination she was surprised she wasn't sick of already. A biscuit also rested on her plate, which she saved for last so she could savor the infrequent delicacy. Only one meal a day included a baked good. One baked good kept the Anchors from rebelling too much at the lack of carbs, but it also wasn't enough carbs for the Anchors to grow dependent on the enchanters' aid. As Hali bit into the buttery biscuit, relief that felt a lot like happiness coursed through her body. "I'm not sure how I can eat fish for three meals a day and not get sick of it," Hali joked.

"It's all about the spices." Marilla smiled proudly. "We'll be taking off in a bit to fish for lunch. Cas volunteered to help out since Delphia and Carmya are out of the water this week."

"Why?" Hali found herself asking before she thought about it. Ronan squirmed in his seat, the subject matter revealing itself in his pinked cheeks.

"Oh," Hali responded, her eyebrows pinched in confusion. "I don't understand. Don't the enchanters provide *those* types of products?"

"Ugh," Ronan covered his face with his hands, smoothing his eyebrows out with his palms.

Marilla shook her head, smiling in part to amusement and the other to relief that there was still some boy left in Ronan.

"There is Hali, but it's not *that* part of the month we're concerned about."

"La la la la la," Ronan chanted as he covered his ears.

"Well, what other part of the month should I be worried about?"

Ronan's chant grew louder. "LA LA LA LA LA LA LA LA LA."

"Ronan! Cut that out. It's a natural part of life and if you can't sit here and listen maturely then you should go on ahead and I'll catch up with you," Marilla scolded.

Ronan finally stopped his chanting, jumping up from his seat. "You don't need to tell me twice! I'll see you guys later." Ronan sped towards the dilapidated front door, that was rehung not quite level of its previous state. Light slid through the outside cracks, where bits of wood had chipped off the perimeter during the Eyes' intrusion. Ronan was gone before Marilla could change her mind.

A silent count to ten filled the room once he left. Marilla's eyes lingered on the door. Shifting her gaze back to Hali, she rolled her eyes as a grin played on her lips, breathing out a sigh. "As mermaids we show our fertility differently than we do in our human form. We still carry pheromones like any other human woman does, but when we ovulate, we emit a much more powerful signal that indicates when we are at our most fertile. In our mermaid form, the signal can attract a lifelong mate, but it also can attract unwanted attention too."

"Like sharks?" Hali asked, still reeling from an overabundance of information rolling around in her head that she hadn't sorted out. Asking for more didn't seem like such a great idea.

"Not sharks. But let's not focus on that right now. You've already gone through so much and learned more than anyone should in a short amount of time. Besides, it's not a concern as long as you stay out of the water when it's your fertile time of the month."

"Marilla, I know you are just worried and trying to protect me, but I don't want to be kept in the dark anymore. I already feel like I've been lied to my whole life. I want the truth from now on."

Marilla considered Hali's point. "Okay," she voiced a quick agreement, needing little convincing. "There are Anchors that live full time in the ocean. Because of that, they are more animal than those of us who live on land most of the time. When we first arrived on the Eyes' Land there was a group of us that decided to take to the water permanently. My husband had tried to convince me that that would be the safer choice. He knew from the beginning that being on land in our human form would leave us vulnerable to an Eye attack. But I didn't want us to lose our humanity." Marilla huffed out a laugh that held no humor to it. "In the end, I lost him anyway." Marilla straightened, as if a change in posture could ease the unpleasant memory.

"Anchors avoid the water during their fertile period because of the mermen of the sea, who are Anchors that gradually change over time after remaining in the ocean— becoming what we call sea creatures. Their skin morphs into that of a chameleon but is usually bluish green in color and their teeth are similar to that of sharks. They are completely adaptable and are the reason we always swim in groups. Their courting instincts are different than ours. Once a male has targeted a female, he's extremely persistent in his attempt at convincing an Anchor woman to be his companion and becoming a sea creature. The sea creatures aren't bad, but just operate on a different set of rules than we do."

Now Hali felt just as distressed as Ronan had and wished she could be on the beach with him, thinking about anything else but what Marilla was serving. At the same time, she was very curious. "How do you know all of this, Marilla?"

"The hard way," Marilla laughed. "I was sixteen and completely unaware that I was in my fertile days. My future husband, who was just sixteen at the time as well, had picked up my fertile signal even before I knew I was emitting it. But he had been way too embarrassed to tell me." Marilla chuckled again as she plunged herself into the memory. "Later, he told me that my signal was like putting his body in an electrical socket."

"Is that what it's like for everyone in the water?"

"No, it isn't, the more compatible the match the stronger the signal. But for everyone else in the water the signal is just a little ripple of a current, completely unnoticeable. The sea creatures pick up on just about any signal, so it's hard to say if compatibility is a concern for their kind. Poor Carmya had a mishap once a few years back." A laugh escaped Marilla, and she quickly covered her mouth with her hand to regain control. After taking a breath, she said, "Carmya was practically back at camp before the sea creature would leave her be and go back to where he came from. Kai wasn't too happy about that."

"Kai?"

"Oh, yeah. Kai has been sweet on Carmya ever since they were little, but he has a lot of maturing to do before he is ready to form a worthwhile relationship with anyone. The same could be said for Jett and Toru."

"I can understand that," Hali said softly, picking at her biscuit.

A knowing grin crinkled at the edges of Marilla's cheeks. "There's nothing wrong with enjoying childhood as long as you can. As I'm sure you're aware, adulthood isn't always what it's cracked up to be. I think Carmya is probably ready to have a family, but most of her friends aren't there yet. Well, except for Cas. He's always been mature, even as a child." Marilla glanced at the clock on the wall and stood up from her seat. "So, the moral of the story is, know your cycle well enough to know when to stay out of the water. You'll save yourself from an awkward encounter if you do." Marilla peered at Hali expectantly when she finished speaking.

Hali nodded her head in confirmation, her closed-mouth smile was laced with a grimace.

Marilla returned Hali's half-hearted acknowledgment with an understanding grin and said, "All right young lady, I better catch up to Ronan. If you need the afternoon off from fishing, we'll make do without you so you can relax."

"I'll be out there," Hali assured. "I'm not sure how I slept as long as I did last night. Once I finish breakfast, I'll get ready and come down to the shore."

Satisfied with Hali's answer, Marilla said, "Okay. And if you think of any other questions of what we've talked about, we can talk about them later."

Like always, Hali had a million other questions. But the most important question she didn't get a chance to ask was when the enchanters would show up so she could request the use of a spell book.

But instead of asking, Hali simply said, "Sounds good," releasing Marilla from the conversation so she could be on her way. Her unanswered questions would just have to wait. She had already invaded their space, she didn't want to consume all of their time, too.

Twenty minutes after Marilla left the cabin, Hali found herself walking to the shore holding two red blankets. The waves pushed and pulled, Mr. Gruff sat on his log, and fins flapped out of the water here and there. Hali took a seat on the sand, laying the stacked blankets folded in squares beside her outstretched legs. A few clouds dotted the azure sky, leaving Hali to wonder if she could draw the fish from the ocean using the clouds as her power source as she did a couple days before. Temporarily blinded from the sun's brightness, Hali cast down her eyes, wishing she had sunglasses. As if on cue, the little orbs sprouted on both of her arms, bounding towards her face in two single-file lines. Hali spotted them in her peripheral moving along her cheeks like ants raiding a home for crumbs. They circled her eyes, tickling her eyebrows, their light subtle compared to the sun. Darkness suddenly shaded her vision. The small bursts dimmed not only their own light, but the light of the sun. They had fashioned into sunglasses.

Strange occurrences were becoming commonplace for Hali. Accepting the oddities were becoming easier, even if she couldn't wrap her head around how they happened. Tilting her head upward with her eyes now protected, she absorbed a wispy cirrus cloud. It didn't hold as much energy as a puffy cumulus cloud, but it served its purpose. Wind lashed at Hali's face, seagulls circled above, and small vibrations buzzed in the space between her bones and skin. Moments later fish laid before her feet, a reserved smile curled her lips upward as she trekked to Mr. Gruff for spears.

When she approached, he didn't look up from his shaving, but pointed with his head to the stack of spears ready to be used.

She said her thanks and grabbed a small bundle that she thought would be enough. Eyeing his piles, she noticed he had set aside flatter pieces of wood that were shaped into what she would guess to be two-by-fours. Hali wanted to know what the flatter pieces were for but knew asking Mr. Gruff the purpose would be fruitless. Marilla had said he created weapons, but Hali had a hard time envisioning what type of weapon he could create with two-by-fours. Either way, it wasn't a concern Hali needed to add to her own growing list. Though it still unsettled her to think about the weapons being needed.

Neilan's urging to acquire a spell book surfaced in Hali's thoughts. She believed the spell book would be the key to breaking the barrier, so that she and everyone else could get off the Eyes' Land. Hopefully, before Mr. Gruff's weapons were ever needed.

Settling into her spot on the sand, next to Cas's blankets, she began methodically spearing the fish. As she was on her last skewer, the afternoon group began making their way out of the water and Hali kept her head down, focusing on her task until she was sure that everyone was fully dressed. Ronan and Marilla approached her moments later with their hands full of impaled fish.

"Wow, Hali! I think you have us beat," Ronan complimented as he peered down at the fish-filled spears poking out of the sand, surrounding Hali like a cage.

Hali laughed in appreciation. "I may never need to go back into the ocean again, especially after what I learned from your mom today." Both Marilla and Ronan laughed.

"I wouldn't blame you," Ronan agreed. "The sea creatures are so weird."

Marilla winced. "They are just different from us, Ronan. I'm sure our ways of doing things are weird to them too."

Hali looked at Marilla curiously, surprised that she would defend the sea creatures, even after she had been approached by one as a girl. But their conversation was dropped when she looked up to see Cas making his way back to camp with his own contribution to the afternoon meal.

"Hey guys, I need to return Cas's blankets back to him."

"Do you need help carrying the spears?" Marilla asked.

"Would you mind? I hadn't really thought it through when I brought the blankets out here," Hali admitted.

"Not a problem. Between Ronan and I, we can carry all of it. You better go now. Once Cas drops off his fish, he usually doesn't stick around too long."

Nerves overtook Hali when she thought of giving the blankets back to Cas. What would she say? Handing him two blankets would be admitting she knew something about him that he'd yet to admit. Maybe he didn't care for her to know. Maybe Hali was making it a bigger deal than it was. But if the blankets were as important to Cas as Marilla believed them to be, then why hadn't he asked for them back yet? More importantly, why had he loaned them to Hali at all?

Of all the mysteries that the Eyes' Land held, Cas had to be the biggest one of all. He was cold and caring, ruthless but fair. Hali couldn't figure him out. Ever since she had arrived on the Eyes' Land, one of the biggest questions ruminating through her mind was why Cas had refused her to enter camp on her first night, only to turn around and place a blanket on her while she slumbered on the beach? If he had been so concerned that she was dangerous to the

Anchors, why show her any kindness? Hali could make no sense of it.

At least Hali could rationalize the second time she received one of Cas's blankets. It was right after the magical ocean barrier zapped her into oblivion, leaving Hali to float lifeless in the water until Cas pulled her body back to shore. Once on shore, he had no other choice but to cover her. If he hadn't, she would have awakened dry, in human form, very much naked, and extremely embarrassed. To Hali's chagrin, she learned that it hadn't mattered if she was naked or not by that point, since Cas had already witnessed her nude form slip into the ocean right before the incident had occurred. It's how he knew to follow her, how he knew she was in trouble, and how he was able to recover her from the water. As to why he had bothered to help or how he happened to be at the beach with a blanket readily available in the first place—she just couldn't guess. Especially when Marilla had given Hali the impression that Cas hadn't taken a blanket out of his cabin for quite some time, since they held sentimental value to him. The occurrence was nothing less than bizarre.

Returning one blanket was expected, but two—that was not only an admission, but a reminder of a not so distant past. The blankets were threaded with memories Hali wasn't looking to unravel. She certainly wasn't looking to put Cas on the spot about it, despite her curiosity. The fact that he had given them so freely to Hali, a girl he didn't trust or like for that matter, befuddled her and she wasn't sure how to feel about it. Now, all she wanted to do was return what didn't belong to her without any acknowledgement on the matter.

Before she could think through what she was going to say Hali was tapping on Cas's shoulder. Nerves, rather than the jog itself, left her a little out of breath. A halo of auburn frizz extended down Hali's braid. Cas turned around, skewers in hand, observing Hali before looking down at the blankets folded neatly in her hands. Recognition set in as he looked back up to her face.

"Thank you for loaning me your blankets," Hali said. Cas looked down again at his full hands, then back up to Hali. "Sorry, I didn't time returning these at the best time," she admitted nervously.

At that, Cas laughed. The sound surprised Hali as much as it pleased her to be the reason for it. "It's all right. You mind holding them until we get to camp?"

"Sure," Hali agreed, but her stomach fluttered. The two walked side by side not saying anything at first. She was relieved to see that his mood was improved from the last time she had spoken with him—when the Eyes had sought her out and they hid behind the trees. It was only a day ago, but it felt like a lifetime of information had passed through her ears since then. But she couldn't forget the contempt that radiated off Cas when he watched the Eyes from afar or how he had practically hissed at Hali whenever she had asked him a question or tried to intervene for Mamie's benefit.

"Hali, I'm sure you can tell I'm not a very trusting person," Cas broke the silence, pausing briefly, as he struggled with his next words. Hali glanced his direction, waiting patiently. "I've felt guilty with how harsh I've been to you."

"You have?" Hali asked, surprised by his confession.

"I have."

"Something I can't understand is that you were the one who didn't want me to come to camp."

"I didn't know who sent you."

"Then why bring me a blanket?" The question slipped

through her teeth, negating her previous wish to know nothing at all. She couldn't make sense of her own change of heart, but in that moment, standing next to Cas, she wanted to know everything. Her level of comfort was both frightening and exhilarating.

"In case you *weren't* here to murder us, I figured it would be cruel to make you sleep on the beach without a blanket."

"Yes, it would," Hali agreed, taking in the toppled trees in the near distance.

"I'm not saying we need to be best buddies or anything like that, but the fact that you have multiple abilities could be helpful."

Hali's head went up in a slow nod. "Ahhh, so the truth comes out," she stated, wondering if Cas knew that she was also an enchanter.

Cas cringed at his flub. "No, it's not like that," he countered, a deep—but brief—chuckle breaking through his resolve. "Anchors are all about cooperation. It's not in our nature to outcast anyone, but we also need to be aware of any threats. I would hate for what happened to me to happen to anyone here, especially the kids."

"I can understand that," Hali acknowledged, though Cas had never told her directly what had happened to him. But he didn't need to, since Marilla had already informed Hali of the role eleven-year-old Cas had played in the Eye attack ten years prior—warning and saving many of the Anchors from peril. The ambush left him an orphan with a scar to remember it by—as if he could ever forget. Fortunately, Cas didn't question Hali's knowing and Hali knew better than to ask any further into the matter. Instead she asked, "How do you know I'm not a threat?"

Cas quirked his head, his face scrunching in confusion. Realizing her mistake, Hali shook her head, quickly clarifying her question. "I'm not, by the way. But what made you believe it?"

Cas's eyebrows came together in thought, highlighting his eyes as they gazed at the trees, his scar like a jagged river. "I guess when the Eyes showed up here looking for you," he answered, glancing Hali's direction. A wave of heat rushed to her cheeks when he caught her staring at him, forcing her eyes down to the blankets in her arms, as if they were the most interesting thing in the world to look at in that moment.

Cas and Hali shared the silence as they walked back to camp. Once they arrived Cas unloaded his fish to an older Anchor. The older man looked at Cas, then to Hali, and back again with his clear blue eyes. His darkened, weather-worn skin was etched with deep-set wrinkles that accentuated the bright blue shade of his eyes.

"Got quite a bounty here, Cas."

"The fish were biting this afternoon," Cas offered.

Then the older man turned his attention to Hali. "I haven't had the pleasure of meetin' you yet, but I've already heard a lot about you. The name's Fisk."

"I'm Hali. Nice to meet you, Mr. Fisk."

"Just Fisk. Makes things easier that way." Hali nodded awkwardly at his request, not knowing where to go with the conversation. She was relieved when Fisk turned back to Cas.

"I guess we should thank the Eyes for their whirly-swirly trick yesterday. I'm sure that helped bring the fish closer to the surface," Fisk joked. But Hali didn't miss the twitch in Cas's jaw at the mention of the Eyes. Before Cas could respond, Ronan and Marilla walked up, setting their skewers down.

"Well, golly, how in the world did you catch so many

dog-gone fish? I thought Cas here caught a lot." Fisk's electric blue eyes glistened with a boyish wonder that belied his age. He stood from his seat awestruck, taking in all the fish as if gold coins had been placed before him. His excitement was contagious, everyone catching a smile, even Cas, though his smile was placid.

"Ronan and I didn't catch all these," Marilla admitted.

"You foolin' with me, girl? Tryin' to make an ol' Anchor think he's lost his mind or somethin'?"

"I'd never do such a thing," Marilla smiled. "Hali caught most of these. Remember, she's part leprechaun, so she has some unique abilities."

"Like the whirly-swirly trick?" Fisk asked Hali.

"The what?" Ronan cocked his head in mock surprise—a chuckle rising in his throat. Hali had no doubt that Ronan heard him clearly or that Ronan was at all surprised by Fisk's question. Even Hali, who had only just met Fisk, could tell that the older man didn't come with a filter.

"You know, boy. The whirly-swirly trick in the ocean. When them Eyes came and pulled the water off the ocean like it was nothin'. Is that what you did to git all them fish, girl?" Fisk asked.

Hali gathered as much composure as she could muster, trying her best not to laugh at his serious question packaged in comical wrapping. "Not exactly," she began hesitantly, suddenly aware of being different from the rest of the Anchors. "I'm not sure I possess enough power on my own to do what they did. Also, from what I know about my leprechaun abilities, you have to pull from the elements available. Today was a pretty clear day, so the elements were limited."

"That's too bad. It'd be nice to have a pathway in the

ocean to git to them fish," Fisk frowned, appearing truly disappointed.

"Yes, it would," Marilla agreed. "But the extra fish are just as nice."

"Sure is, Marilly, sure is," Fisk concurred, turning his blue gaze back to Cas. "Now Cas, you be nice to Hali here," Fisk gestured to her, while his eyes remained on Cas. "I know how you feel about leprechauns. But this pretty, little girl here seems to be a nice one, so don't go treatin' her like she was the same ones who come rippin' through here all those years ago." Hali cringed, wishing she could find a big enough clam shell to hide in. It reminded her of the times Mrs. O'Riley would force Camille and Neilan to hug it out after an argument when they were little. She wasn't sure it helped, since they always seemed to want to escape each other even more once the hug was over. The irony was that she and Cas had basically called a truce a few minutes before arriving at camp and now Fisk was putting pressure on the whole situation. Hali slumped into herself at Fisk's misplaced good intentions. Hali didn't want or need kindness stemmed from pity.

"Noted," Cas stated curtly, his lips pressed into a straight line. "If you have no other advice for me, I'm going to head back to my cabin."

"No, sir, just thought I'd put my two cents in while I had your ear and before you go burnin' any bridges with this little girl here."

The words "little girl" irked Hali, which surprised her considering she had no interest in being an adult. She chalked Fisk's usage of the endearment on his age.

He'd probably call any woman younger than him a little girl, she thought.

Cas collected his blankets from Hali, quickly adding, "I'll see you all at lunch."

"Thanks again," Hali offered timidly.

Cas nodded, a forced smile that never fully bloomed pained his lips, and said, "No problem."

Once he was out of earshot, Marilla scowled at Fisk.

"What?" Fisk questioned, completely unaware of the awkwardness he had created.

Marilla sighed, placing a hand on her hip. "You can't go putting people on the spot like that."

Fisk brushed her off, waving his hand through the air. "Oh, Marilly, I didn't mean anythin' by it. I've been 'round a lot of years and I see what a grudge can do to a person. And that boy"—Fisk pointed in the direction that Cas took off in —"he's been holdin' a grudge since he was a youngin'. It ain't healthy to be walkin' 'round with that much hurt and hate. Does nobody any good."

"I agree with you, but all I'm saying is next time it would be better if you talk to him in private and not in front of everybody."

"Now Marilly, I've raised a pretty good youngin' if I do say so myself. It doesn't hurt for Cas to git some tough love every once in a while. Everyone needs to be set straight every now and again. The older you git the more stubborn you git. And that boy is already as stubborn as they come."

Marilla and Fisk were at a standstill, while Hali stood uncomfortably in the middle, wrapped in the silence, wondering if she could slip away without being noticed.

The silence didn't last long. Though Hali suspected it never did when Fisk was involved.

"Think I scared him off, Marilly?"

Marilla placed a hand on Fisk's shoulder. "He'll come around. The Eyes' Land is only so big," Marilla chuckled.

"You're a smart lady, Marilly. Where'd your mother get all her smarts from, Ronan?"

Ronan's mischievous smile left Hali wondering what hidden meaning she was missing in the conversation.

"From grandma," Ronan answered.

"Darn tootin' she did. But unfortunately for you, you got your smarts from your grandpapa," Fisk belted out a laugh.

"Daddy! You're crazy," Marilla shook her head at his antics. Ronan scowled. "Well, we better get back and get cleaned up before lunch. Kai and the rest of the boys will be here before long with their fish."

"You all run along. It was nice to meet you young lady." Fisk gave Marilla a hug and mussed the top of Ronan's hair.

"It was nice to meet you, too Mi ... Fisk."

"Atta' girl," Fisk chuckled.

The heat of the day had grown oppressive the further the sun made its way across the sky. Heavy and invasive, the air had the consistency of a solid and Hali could feel it stick against her body as she walked back to the cabin with Marilla and Ronan.

Hali craved the cold sweetness of Italian Ice from an Ottavio's truck that was more than likely circling Emerald Cove at that very moment. The image of beachgoers lining up for the sweet, cold relief had Hali salivating and a little more envious than she cared to admit. She had never thought of food so much or had to work so hard to eat. If nothing else, the last four days had taught her to appreciate the convenience of her past life.

Marilla, Ronan, and Hali hadn't initially talked while they walked back to the cabin—probably for Hali's sake more than theirs. Talking would have expended energy and Hali still hadn't recovered to her full energy level since arriving on the Eyes' Land. As a consistent runner, Hali had considered herself in good shape. But her time on the Eyes' Land had humbled her, as she observed the ease to which the Anchors lived and worked such a challenging way of life.

As her shirt dress stuck to her back, Hali remembered Neilan's urging to get a hold of a spell book the next time the enchanters delivered supplies. The problem was, she had no idea what the process entailed for acquiring one or if it *was* even possible. A heightened sense of urgency, worry, and sweat dripped from her as the picture of spending the majority of summer mainly outdoors—under the unforgiving heat of a southern sun, no less—began unfolding in her mind. She needed a spell book. Hali's very sanity depended on it. That is, if heatstroke didn't take her out first.

"Marilla, when do the enchanters make deliveries?" Hali asked.

Marilla tilted her head towards Hali, her cheeks sun-kissed, but her serene disposition untouched by the heat. "Once a month, during a full moon. Which reminds me, we are voting on the use of supplies at lunch today. Why do you ask?"

Hali wished Marilla would forget about the cookies. She wasn't sure if she would need the backing of the Anchors in the future, but if she did, she didn't want to waste their time with a vote for something as silly as being able to make baked goods. She wanted to save it for a more important matter, like getting a spell book, if such a thing required a vote.

"I was hoping that I could ask the enchanters to borrow

a spell book," Hali replied, wiping the sweat from her fore-head with the back of her hand.

Marilla nodded. "I think that would be a good idea. You should get to know all your abilities, so they don't surprise you."

"I agree. Though I think I've already missed the boat on them surprising me. The little orbs come out of nowhere. As helpful as they are, I'd like to have a little more control of when they decide to come out. Do you know when the next full moon will be?" Hali pulled on the parts of her cotton dress that had glued to her skin, enjoying the small bursts of air that circulated her freed skin, even though it was warm.

"Can't say I've ever experienced that," Marilla grinned. "The moon will be full in about two weeks. The enchanters bring the supplies here at night when we are all tucked away in our cabins, asleep."

Hali grimaced. "So, no one is there for the delivery?"

"Just Cas."

Of course, Hali thought.

"Well, maybe I can take his place at the next full moon, so I can talk with the enchanters face-to-face about getting a spell book."

"You can try ..." Marilla said, not looking convinced.

"What aren't you telling me, Marilla?" Hali asked skep-tically.

Marilla sighed. "Cas has been handling the deliveries on his own for the last ten years. And even before that, he would go along with his parents when he was only a boy to receive the supplies. Anytime anyone has volunteered to take his place in the past, he has declined, which is always a relief to the volunteer. No one will ever say it, but everyone here is a little skittish to come face-to-face with an enchanter and they certainly don't mind getting to go to bed at a decent hour. But the truth is, I think Cas continues to do it out of nostalgia and I'm not sure he'd be willing to sit it out. But maybe he'd be okay with you tagging along. I don't think you should do it alone either way, since the Eyes are looking for you specifically."

Hali swiped the sweat down from the bridge of her nose with disappointment, tired of constantly needing to go through Cas for approval. Especially when he was very clear on his belief that the barrier was unbreakable. Hali could only hope that their recent truce—if Fisk hadn't completely voided it with his "be nice to Hali" speech—would warm him up to the idea of her receiving a spell book. It's not like she needed to give him the exact reason of why she wanted one anyway. She had told Marilla she wanted to have better control of her magic, which was partially true. But Hali had a feeling that Cas wouldn't solely be convinced with that reasoning alone. She wasn't even sure if Cas knew that she was an enchanter, or how he would react when he found out.

As Hali chewed on the inside of her cheek in contemplation, Ronan said, "I can stay up with you, Hali."

Hali glanced to Ronan, then to a reluctant Marilla, whose expression matched Hali's inner turmoil. "Ronan, I'm ..." Hali looked at Marilla for help. It's not that she wouldn't enjoy the company from Ronan, but she wasn't about to put a twelve-year-old in danger when she had Eyes seeking her out. But at the moment she was more in danger of hurting his ego, and she didn't want to risk that either.

"Ronan," Marilla chimed in, "you're strong and brave, but you are still not old enough to be staying up all hours of the night. If you want to grow up as strong as you can be, you need to get plenty of rest."

"I'm a year older than Cas was when he started doing it by himself," he argued.

"I won't hear another word of it," Marilla stated, not addressing Ronan's point. Ronan conceded with a groan, silently pouting his dismay.

"Ronan, the odds are, Cas will turn down my help like he has for everyone else and it wouldn't have mattered anyway," Hali assuaged. He nodded reluctantly at Hali's logic, while still carrying a hint of disappointment for not being considered old enough for such a task.

Marilla kindly wrapped an arm around Ronan's shoulder, pulling him into conversation. Ronan's head hung low and Marilla gave him a peck on the cheek. Hali stayed back a few paces so Marilla and Ronan could have their mother-son moment in private. This left Hali to mull over the one unanswered question that nagged at her the most from their previous discussion. Why would Cas be on the receiving end of the enchanters' aid when he was the one against becoming too dependent on the enchanters in the first place? A spell book was no longer the only driving force for Hali to be at the supply drop. Curiosity was now a close second.

17

THE VOTE

"ANCHORS, if I could have your attention for a moment." Everyone turned to Marilla, finishing their lunch. A hush came over the camp as Marilla stood in the center. "I would like to discuss the way we handle supplies from enchanters. Currently, we are using very little of the supplies they provide in an effort to stay independent, in case their generosity ceases. However, the Eyes' Land has been here for almost two decades now, and the enchanters have consistently contributed. We have an abundance of baking supplies that end up going to waste because we refuse to use them."

"What are you proposin', Marilly?" Fisk asked aloud.

"Well," Marilla looked around, gauging the crowd's reaction, "I'm proposing that we have a vote on whether we can use more of the baking supplies. The butter cookies we had were a big hit and it would be nice for us all to share in a treat more often."

Marilla paused as if waiting for someone to contradict her. When no one did, she spoke again. "I know it seems like such a silly thing to vote on, but I think"— Marilla glanced around again—"we've been on the Eyes' Land so long, some of us our entire lives. Life here is challenging and we work for everything. I don't think it would be the worst thing if we enjoyed a treat every now and then."

"Hear, hear," Fisk exclaimed, a low murmur spread amongst the crowd.

"Let's have a vote then," Mamie chimed in.

Hali peered around at all the Anchors, wondering what their thoughts were on the topic as the murmur grew in volume and excitement. Before she knew it, Marilla began explaining how to vote.

"All right, it's been a while since we've had a vote here, so let me remind you all how it will go. Each of you will indicate your choice by placing a shell into the appropriate 'yes' or 'no' basket that will be hidden behind this tree for privacy." Marilla pointed to a large pine tree, specifying where the baskets would be placed. "I will call one table at a time. If you are twelve or older you are eligible to vote. If you are unsure or do not want to vote, you do not have to, but please do not attempt to sway anyone's vote. Remember a 'yes' vote means you want to start using more of the baking items provided by the enchanters. A 'no' vote means that you want to keep things the way they are, and not use any more of the baking items than we currently do."

Before she knew it, Hali's table was lining up to place their votes. She didn't recognize any of the Anchors at her table besides Ronan, who had been playing table football with his shell with another boy his age at the dismay of the other adults at the table. An adorable little girl with big, brown eyes a few years younger than Ronan kept secretly watching the boys play, while a woman Hali assumed was her mother persisted that she look away. Ronan and the other boy were oblivious to the amusement they were providing the little girl or the annoyance to her mother.

Shell in hand, Hali approached the baskets, casting the first vote of her adult life. If she had been asked a week prior if her first vote would be on the important initiative of baked goods, she would have answered the question with a definitive "no," then laughed at the absurdness of the question. But as she watched her shell cascade out of her palm before clanking into the open basket of shells, she realized how much things could change within a matter of a few days. It didn't escape Hali's notice that the open baskets could easily be tampered with, allowing any Anchor to dump one basket into the other. But she didn't want to dwell on that fact.

Another matter for another time, she thought.

Once all the votes were cast, the Anchors left their tables and socialized amongst each other while waiting for the result. Not knowing where to go, Hali walked to the outside of the socializing groups, not having the energy to put on a happy facade she wasn't feeling. The heat, the constant life-changing information coupled with abilities, and the physically challenging daily tasks on the Eyes' Land had taken a toll. Despite it only being the afternoon and sleeping in that morning, Hali's body could probably sleep for a week to recover from the past four days. Most people stayed and waited for the results of the vote, but some of the older Anchors, like Mamie, had gone back to their cabins to get out of the heat. Sweat droplets coated Hali's nose, mixed with hints of chalky white. Hali was extremely grateful that sunscreen was one of the items included in the supplies from the enchanters. As Hali unsuccessfully tried to stay hidden, Delphia and Carmya approached.

"Hey Hali, want to make cookies tomorrow morning

before we go out to fish?" Delphia's smile, bright and infectious, radiated energy brighter than her orange scales.

"But they haven't announced the results yet," Hali stated.

"Did you see the baskets?" Carmya questioned. "It's practically a done deal. And my vote is chocolate chip cookies."

"Oooh, I second that," Delphia agreed.

"You in?" Carmya asked.

"Sure, as long as it's okay."

"Oh, it will be," Delphia practically jumped. Carmya smiled at her friend, whose excitement was more exuberant than her own.

A man with a slight build, brown hair, and relaxed demeanor, that Hali guessed to be in his early forties, came to the center of camp with an arm wrapped around each basket.

"Good afternoon, everyone," the man began.

Carmya leaned into Hali's ear, "That's Troy, he is the teller. He makes sure that all the votes are counted fairly."

"The result is"—

Delphia stood between Carmya and Hali, holding their hands with a death grip. Hali winced, silently enduring the pain of her fingers being crushed together. Carmya unsuccessfully repressed a grin as she peered at Hali's pulverized hand and then her own. A look that told Hali she was not alone in her pain. Delphia was none the wiser as she stared unblinkingly at Troy, a hopeful smile on her face.

—"yes, which means we will now utilize the baking items provided by the enchanters to the fullest."

The girls smiled at one other, but Delphia beamed like she had just won the lottery. Hali was conflicted if winning a battle she hadn't meant to start was a good thing, but it was too late now.

Troy walked to the woman and little girl that Hali had shared a table with earlier. The little girl who had watched Ronan and his friend play table football with their shells hugged Troy around the waist. He smiled down at her while tucking her long, brown hair behind one of her ears. But the woman, who Hali had assumed to be the little girl's mother, stared with vacant eyes at Marilla who was engaged in a conversation with Fisk.

"What time are we meeting in the morning?" Delphia asked, interrupting Hali's snooping.

Feeling embarrassed that her curiosity had gotten the best of her, Hali refocused her attention back to Carmya and Delphia with no idea what Delphia asked. Hali scanned her face, hoping that Delphia's question would ricochet back to her, so she didn't have to admit that not only was she not listening, she was also being nosy. Before she could utter her dreaded "what?" Kai, Jett, and Toru walked up out of nowhere.

"Got a thing for older guys, Hali?" Jett joked, while Kai and Toru cackled.

"Troy's wife may not like that too much," Toru added.

"Cut it out guys. What are you even talking about?" Carmya asked. Hali grimaced, wishing Carmya hadn't given them an opportunity to be more specific.

Was Hali staring? Yes.

Was she into Troy? Definitely not.

Was the truth of why she was staring any better than what the obnoxious trio were crafting? Probably not.

Hali had not grown used to the embarrassing situations she found herself in daily. Wittiness was not a strength she possessed when put under pressure, but she was sure later while she lay awake in bed pondering this moment, she'd have plenty of comebacks. But for now, they were hidden under a blanket of mortification, that did little in helping her out of her current predicament.

"Did you not see Hali eyeing Troy up and down as his daughter gave him a hug?" Jett said.

"You know what they say, some people are only into someone if that person is taken," Kai added.

Mouth agape, Hali struggled on how to refute their claims. Delphia spoke up before Hali could think of a comeback.

"Haven't you ever spaced out before? None of us have ever been through what Hali has, how about cutting her some slack."

"She was clearly staring at Troy, and not staring out into space, Del-phi-a," Toru said, emphasizing each syllable of Delphia's name.

"How would you even know that? You guys just walked up." Carmya said, as her eyebrows twisted up in a scowl.

Annoyance crept into Hali's blood at being talked about like she wasn't even there. The trio's wariness of Hali's abilities had apparently worn off as their bravado made a resurgence. Whatever the reason, she was tired, and her patience had met its limit.

"What business is it of yours who I look at?" Hali questioned, the words tumbling from her lips like spilled milk from a ledge. Shock overwhelmed the trio's expressions.

"See, she doesn't deny it," Kai stated, "that's messed up."

"No, what's messed up is your accusation. Not that I owe any of you an explanation, but since when is it wrong to observe your surroundings?"

"More like observe who *isn't* available," Toru countered. "Enjoy a challenge, Hali?"

They're hopeless, she thought.

The trio burst into rolling laughter, earning glares from

both Carmya and Delphia. The trio's forced guffaws rattled Hali, but she knew there was no reasoning with their brand of lunacy. They would enjoy her attempts all too much and Hali would most likely end up even more irritated in the end.

Taking a deep breath in and exhaling out slowly, Hali decided to remove herself from their torment. She said a quick farewell to Carmya and Delphia, ignoring the trio as she turned away to leave.

Hali had walked several steps when Carmya's hand landed gently on her shoulder. "Can you meet at Delphia's and my place tomorrow?" she asked. When Hali didn't respond right away, she quickly added, "For the cookies?"

Hali's shoulders relaxed. "Sure, what time?"

"How about after breakfast, that way we can gather supplies and walk to the cabin together."

"Sounds good," Hali agreed. Carmya grinned and nodded before turning back towards the group.

Glancing around to find Marilla and Ronan, she found Cas staring at her instead. A small grin graced his face, softening his eyes. Unaware if his grin was the result of overhearing the conversation she just left, Hali sheepishly turned away, hiding the blush that inflamed her cheeks. The idea of Cas laughing at her along with the trio, filled Hali with disappointment. Despite not knowing what to think about Cas most of the time, she wanted to believe that he was better than that. Though she wasn't sure why she cared.

"Hali"—Ronan greeted her, forcing her to bring her eyes upward—"we were looking for you."

"Here I am," Hali wore a smile that didn't reach her eyes, crossing her arms around her waist.

"I just knew everyone would vote 'yes' for the cookies after tasting the ones we made," Ronan declared, oblivious to Hali's rouged cheeks. For the first time since arriving on the Eyes' Land, Hali found a reason to be grateful for the ruthless heat. It made her embarrassment harder to spot.

Hali laughed. "Cookies aren't the only things we can make."

"What else is there?" Ronan asked.

"Pie, quiche, eggs for breakfast instead of fish every day, muffins. I'm telling you Ronan, there are endless possibilities." Ronan's face scrunched in confusion at the word "quiche" but he never asked for clarification.

"When can we start?" he asked.

Hali giggled at his impatience, but she also understood the urgency. Having only spent four days with limited baked goods, she couldn't understand how they had gone so long without cookies. If baked goods were the lasting impact Hali contributed to the Eyes' Land before she got a hold of a spell book and went back home, it wouldn't be the worst offering. After her confrontation with the trio and Cas's ambiguous smile, Hali was beginning to care less and less about gaining approval. As far as she was concerned, she had all the allies she needed; it's not like she was gunning for homecoming queen. A surge of confidence ignited in her and she began to feel like herself again after four days of being out of sorts.

"How about tonight, before dinner?" Hali suggested.

"Cool, what are we going to make?"

"Not sure, but before we do anything, I need a shower and a nap, before I fall over."

Ronan chuckled. "Tired?"

"Oh yeah," Hali agreed. "Even with all the sleep I've had. So, if you are ready, we should head back now so we have time to get everything done. If you have any paper, I can write down the recipes of everything we make so you can make it whenever you want, whether I'm tired or not." Guilt coated her words, because she left out half the truth. The plan all along was to get off the Eyes' Land, but she knew that whatever happened, she would miss Ronan and Marilla, wherever they ended up. Hali knew that her destination would be back with her mom and dad.

"That's a good idea," Ronan agreed. "Mom keeps a recipe box, too, but it's mostly on the many ways to add flavoring to fish."

"I bet she does," Hali smiled as they made their way over to Marilla and Fisk. "By the way, who was the woman and the little girl at our table."

A frown appeared on Ronan's face. "Binda is the woman; the girl's name is Petra. Binda's husband, Troy, is Petra's dad. Troy is the teller. Binda doesn't like me and my mom for some reason."

"Well, her opinion doesn't seem to be shared by Petra," Hali reasoned.

Ronan rolled his eyes at the statement. "I wish it was, then maybe she would stop following me around. It only makes her mom hate me more."

"Does Troy share his wife's feelings?" Hali asked.

"If he does, he doesn't show it. Troy has always been nice to me and my mom, but he keeps his distance."

"Do you know what reason Binda has for disliking you and your mom?" Hali was too curious not to ask.

Ronan shook his head from side to side. "Not that I know of. It's just been that way as long as I could remember. I've tried to ask my mom about it, but she just says it's something she would rather keep buried in the past. I haven't brought it up again."

It was interesting to Hali that anyone could dislike Marilla, and Ronan by extension. Marilla had been nothing but kind and selfless to Hali in her four days of being there, so she couldn't understand how anyone could dislike her.

"How's about that? Looks like this old man's gonna git some more treats in his gullet 'fore he dies," Fisk announced as he and Marilla approached.

"Daddy, I think you've been in the sun way too long," Marilla teased as she shook her head. "Maybe you should have gone back to your cabin when Mamie and the others did to get out of this heat."

"Now you listen here, Marilly," Fisk pointed his finger at her. Marilla grinned a closed-mouth grin at the mock scolding she was about to receive. "Gettin' old is all a frame of mind. When you think you're too ol' to handle the things you spent a lifetime gettin' use to, like the darn heat, then you're right. But I'm going to keep tellin' my mind that I'm young, even if my bones disagree. 'Cuz now I got me some treats to try out and I ain't missin' out on any of that. Now I know you're just lookin' out for me, Marilly, but you're goin' to end up coddlin' me to death, lit-er-al-ly."

"Okay, daddy," Marilla surrendered, patting his shoulder a few times. Then she glanced over at Hali and Ronan with an exasperated smile lining her cheeks. "You guys ready to head back?"

"Yes," Hali and Ronan both agreed.

Hali rested her head on her pillow, clean and worn out.

Was it really only day four? she wondered to herself.

The days were long, but short, challenging, yet simple. It felt so good to be out of the heat, in the cool cabin, with a light sheet covering her body. It didn't bring the same comfort as Cas's blankets did, but linens weren't going to prevent her from falling asleep. Only two weeks before she could get a hold of a spell book, or at least request one. She just hoped the enchanters would grant her request. If they didn't, she wasn't sure what she would do. Her worries jumbled into streams of pictures and plans that faded into a dark abyss.

18

GIRL TALK

AFTER HALI'S NAP, she and Ronan got started on baking as planned. They decided on butter cookies again since she knew she would be baking chocolate chip cookies with Delphia and Carmya the following morning. This time when they made the cookies, she handed over a bulk of the responsibility to Ronan, calling out measurements and directions while she wrote the recipe down on card stock. Thankfully, Ronan was a good listener, otherwise it would have been a frustrating task for the both of them.

During dinner, the butter cookies were a big hit like they were the first time. Hali happily stepped back and let Ronan bask in the compliments as she ate dinner with Mamie. The two shared an unspoken agreement to leave the past alone, at least for the time being. The open wounds needed to scab up first before Hali was ready to pick at those topics anymore. With the information put before her, she knew what she needed to know in order to figure a way off the Eyes' Land. At least she hoped she did.

Eating a plate of fish, figs, and butter cookies, Hali enjoyed the company of her long-lost great-grandmother until it was time to head back to the cabin. Marilla and Ronan had started at the same table as well until their conversations took them in different areas of the camp. Mealtimes at camp reminded Hali of a backyard barbecue on the 4th of July, full of friends and family. The only difference was the people at this barbecue transformed into mermaids and mermen in the ocean.

A few times, Hali heard those around her discussing the Eyes and a game plan. When they spoke about the Eyes coming it was a matter of when not if. So many unusual events had occurred that Hali had a hard time sorting it all out in her head. Her mind was in a constant state of overdrive that made her anxious or crashing asleep with no in between. She did find it rather unusual that the Anchors wasted any effort on voting on the use of baking supplies after the Eyes caused so much upheaval at camp. But when she brought it up to Marilla before dinner, her response was *that the Anchors needed a boost in morale and distraction during times like these*, which Hali thought was rather ominous. It only served to amplify her own fears that the Eyes were coming after her.

On top of that, she still had no idea if the Eyes still spied on the Anchors through the trees. Neilan had been very evasive when Hali had asked him in the woods, which did little in pacifying her concerns. She had told no one of their encounter, fearing it would leave the Anchors suspicious that she was in cahoots with Eyes. Hali had no desire to sleep on the beach again or to eat only raw figs. So, she suffered in silence, glaring at the trees unnecessarily long as she passed.

As dinnertime came to a close, Cas walked to the center of camp with Troy standing next to him.

"If I could have all of your attention for a moment," Troy

spoke as the conversations dwindled down to whispers. "As you all know we had a visit from some Eyes." The whispers quieted completely. "We would like to go over safety precautions, as we expect the Eyes to return."

A collective gasp sounded, and the whispers grew into hysteria, despite the Anchors having the same conversations amongst themselves just moments earlier. Hali presumed it was because the fear voiced aloud by someone of authority gave it weight and wings.

"Are they coming for our scales?" a middle-aged woman panicked, as she enclosed her young daughter's ears with her bosom on one side and her palm with the other.

"Now everyone, calm down," Cas commanded over the crowd. When the hysteria quieted, Cas spoke again. "We don't believe they are after our scales. The Eyes were *clear* on their intentions."

Hali's face flushed as heads turned in her direction. Cas never glanced her way but stayed focused on the crowd as his jaw and fists clenched, and knuckles whitened.

"We need to be prepared for anything, but there is no need for panic," he reassured. The scar on his face glistened and Hali had the urge to reach out to it—for some unknown reason—bringing with it the tingle she experienced before the little orbs appeared. She looked down quickly to block them from escaping. It wasn't the first time she was drawn to the scar, but it was the first time Hali was aware of the orbs while the urge struck. Luckily, the sensation subsided before she made a spectacle of herself.

What was that? she thought.

As she looked down at her hands, she could feel Mamie's gaze heating her peripheral. Hali glanced her way and found the perceptive old woman grinning at her with a twinkle of mischief in her eyes. Mamie appeared to know exactly what Hali was experiencing when Hali didn't even know herself. Hali tore her eyes away before Mamie blew her cover. After speaking with Marilla earlier, Hali wasn't sure how many Anchors truly believed she had enchanter abilities, but now hardly seemed the time to remind them when they were already on the brink of a full out frenzy over the Eyes. She barely absorbed what Cas was yammering on about, but before she knew it everyone was standing up and heading for their cabins for the night. Grateful, Hali said a quick goodnight to Mamie and started walking towards Ronan and Marilla, when Cas approached.

Fantastic, she thought, *of all times to single her out.*

"Hali, can I talk to you for a moment?"

"Sure," Hali found herself muttering as she contemplated how to look at him without looking at him. He began walking to the perimeter of the camp and Hali followed.

When he came to a stop, he said, "So, Marilla tells me that you want to wait for the enchanters to get a spell book?"

Confusion overtook Hali's features as she peered at Cas, gauging his reaction to her new strain of magic.

"I am," she reluctantly answered, waiting for him to banish her to the beach.

"I can do it," Cas stated, answering a question that Hali hadn't asked.

"You can do what?"

"I can request the spell book on your behalf, so you don't have to come," he clarified. Hali tilted her head even more baffled.

"But you're not an enchanter," Hali had forgotten all about the orbs and stared at Cas like he had lost his mind.

"I realize that."

"So, how are you going to get the enchanters to hand over a spell book?"

"I'm going to ask, same as you would," Cas's tone had gone from annoyed to condescending.

Hali heaved out a breath, because she was getting nowhere in this broken circle of reasoning they had going on.

"And they are just going to lend a non-enchanter one because you asked?" Hali returned the condescension.

"That's the idea."

"Okay, so let's just think about this for a moment. What happens if your plan fails and they won't lend a spell book out without the enchanter accepting it present?"

Cas's annoyance at her barrage of questions permeated the air. Hali wasn't sure if he was hesitating to answer or if he truly hadn't thought about his plan backfiring before presenting it to her.

"If you are worried about it, then you are welcome to sit and wait out the enchanters, too."

Despite not feeling *welcome* Hali surprised herself and said, "I plan on it."

"Fine, then it's settled. I'll pick you up at Marilla's on the night of the full moon. I'll come some time before midnight."

"Cas?"

He lifted his head to the sky, letting out a puff of air. "What is it, Hali?" he asked with a clipped tone.

Hesitation bloomed in the air, as words raced in Hali's mind, too fast to catch. "Nothing," was the only word she could settle on that didn't give away her thoughts on the matter. Despite being eighteen, Hali wasn't sure how comfortable she was with the idea of purposely spending alone time with Cas, even if it was for safety. But she couldn't say that to Cas. Admitting that much would mean she was making a bigger deal of the situation than it really was.

"Okay then." He regarded Hali suspiciously, but he didn't ask her any questions. Hali felt childish for feeling the way she did. Most girls her age would probably leap at the chance to spend alone time with Cas, but she was well aware that she was not like most girls.

After hitting puberty, her mind was a little slower on catching up to the changes her body boldly made. Camille stated multiple times that she envied Hali's curves and that she should embrace them. But all Hali wanted to do was hide. The teasing she had endured in middle school for her lack of curves and then the eventual gawking she received later when that was no longer true, left her both self-conscience of her body and suspicious of the male species.

"When did you know I was part ..." Hali struggled to say enchanter.

"Marilla told me after the vote," Cas supplemented. Reluctantly adding, "Listen, if you want Delphia and Carmya to join us to wait for the supplies you can ask them too. But there needs to be one guy, and I am the best option."

Hali laughed at his boldness. "And what makes *you* the best at waiting for enchanters?"

Now Cas was the one laughing. Hali shot a skeptical glance his way, wondering what she had said to make *him* laugh.

Cas's eyebrows rose, shaking his head as he turned and walked off, completely ignoring her question.

Hali tossed and turned that night. Her mind in a constant state of overdrive, while her body was in a never-ending loop of fatigue.

Hali's conversation with Cas that evening had sent her mind into a tailspin. The anger he had for her when she first arrived on the Eyes' Land wasn't there, but he still wasn't friendly either. Hali knew that he didn't want her to be at the supply drop. If she was being honest with herself, she didn't want to be there either. But there was too much at stake for her to miss it. If the enchanters didn't leave a spell book with Cas, Hali would have to wait another month and a half to ask. She couldn't risk it. Though that didn't mean she relished the idea of waiting possibly hours for the enchanters with Cas, when it was clear he didn't want her there.

Hali groaned as she rolled off the twin-sized bed and onto the hard floor, taking the sheets with her. To say her sleep schedule was out of sorts was an understatement. Staring at the ceiling she was overwhelmed with home-sickness.

After getting ready for the day and finishing breakfast she met up with Delphia and Carmya to make chocolate chip cookies. Delphia wore a grin that spread from ear to ear whereas Carmya's smile was pleasant and reserved.

Standing in Delphia's and Carmya's kitchen, Hali could see that they had prepared for this morning. Kitchen utensils, bowls, and ingredients were neatly lined up on the kitchen island as Delphia quietly beamed, awaiting instructions. Despite Delphia being two years older than Hali, she carried the endearing openness of a child ready to learn a new task.

Carmya was four years older than Hali, but even her calm nature couldn't hide her anticipation to learn something new. Hali realized then that even though Delphia and Carmya were technically women, they were sheltered on the Eyes' Land. Hali marveled at how she had taken for granted a simple task like baking cookies all her life, when two girls close to her age, only miles away, had never been given the chance. She didn't voice her thoughts or the empathy that went with them. Instead she smiled, writing down the recipe to chocolate chip cookies while simultaneously calling out directions.

Hali was surprised at how much fun she had listening to their stories of life on the Eyes' Land and telling them about life on Emerald Cove. To Carmya's dismay, Delphia told the story about the sea creature that wouldn't leave her alone during her "fertile" time.

"Ugh, did you really need to bring that up?" Carmya groaned. Delphia belted out a laugh.

"How do you know if you're in your fertile time or not?" Hali asked.

Delphia shrugged. "You don't always."

Hali's eyebrows drew together at her answer. Delphia must have sensed Hali's uneasiness. "We count our cycle days, but sometimes that can be a day or two off in any direction, so we take those days off from the water, just to be safe.

"What you need to understand Hali is that it's embarrassing for a merman to admit to a mermaid that she's emitting a signal. Sea creatures pick up the faintest of signals because their senses are heightened from being in the water full time. But since we live on land mostly, a merman's ability to pick up a signal is diluted, which means when he does pick up a signal, he has found his mate."

"Well, can't a merman be attracted to many different mermaids? That's how it works with mortals."

"It's different here Hali, the attraction isn't just based on appearance. That is part of it, but the signals we emit run deeper than that. These signals tie Anchors to their soulmates, whether they want them to or not." Delphia shot a furtive glance in Carmya's direction.

Carmya choked out a breath. "Which isn't very romantic, if you ask me."

"Oh, Kai isn't so bad, if you took the time to get to know him better," Delphia consoled.

Carmya rolled her eyes. "Easy for you to say. Tell me how you feel once your signal attracts a mate," Carmya hissed. The statement could have been considered harsh to some other girl, but Delphia only giggled, not at all slighted by Carmya's brashness.

"You're right, I'm definitely not complaining."

"So, what happens if your signal doesn't attract anyone?" Hali wondered.

"Being linked through a signal only happens for the most compatible of Anchor matches or not at all. It's possible for a mermaid's signal to never connect with a mate. Technically, if you avoid the ocean during your fertile time you could live a lifetime never knowing you're matched with anyone, although it is extremely uncommon for a mermaid to not have at least one slip up. But if you are in the water during your fertile time, then it's one-hundred percent possible you'll attract a sea creature."

Carmya shuddered. "That's definitely true."

"Do you feel any differently now that you are matched with Kai?" Hali asked, genuinely curious and fascinated by the ritual.

"Unfortunately, yes," Carmya replied. Hali raised her eyebrows, prompting her to go on.

"How do I explain this?" Carmya contemplated. After a moment, she asked, "What's your least favorite food, Hali?"

"Oh boy, I'm not sure I like where this is going," Hali chuckled. "I'd say my least favorite food would have to be ... green beans."

"Green beans, okay. Imagine one day you were told that despite not wanting green beans, that you really should consider trying them again. And then you do and realize, maybe green beans aren't that bad, but the green bean field that you're supposed to pull from needs to mature a little longer before it will be ready for you. But the problem is, you're hungry and just realized that you actually don't mind green beans at all, but your green beans aren't ready. Then you see the fig tree—you've always loved figs by the way—is just sitting there and needs no time to grow or mature and it's beautiful. But, it's not for you because what's best for you are the green beans—the damn immature green beans that might leave you starved before they are ready to grow up." Carmya blew out a breath when she finished.

Hali and Delphia peeked at each other out of the corner of their eyes, dumbfounded.

"Wow," Delphia said, "tell us how you really feel, Carmya."

"Is it really that bad?" Hali asked.

"I wouldn't know," Delphia smiled, "but someone is just being a little dramatic and impatient is all. Carmya's original pick would not have been Kai."

Hali didn't dare ask who Carmya's original pick would have been. People coupling up wasn't foreign to Hali, but in high school, it was rarely taken very seriously. Outside of the

Eyes' Land people her age focused on going to college, vocational school, working, or traveling for a year after high school. Committing to another person so early on in life didn't make sense in her world when there was so much to do. But on the Eyes' Land there was the sand, ocean, and land. With no distractions or everyday concerns, people became the focus, for better or for worse. It was a challenge for an introvert like Hali. She'd never been very good at making people her focus.

After the first batch of cookies went into the oven, Hali asked the question that had been on her mind since the night before.

"Would either of you be interested in waiting for supplies with me at the next supply drop?"

Carmya looked down dejectedly. "We can't Hali."

"We would if we could though, but ..." Delphia looked down. Hali glanced back and forth between Carmya and Delphia, confused by their instant rejection after a pleasant morning of baking and talking.

"But Cas told us you might ask and begged us to say no," Carmya rushed out.

"Carmya!" Delphia scolded.

"What? It's the truth. I'm not going to lie about it, just because he asked us to."

"Why would he do that?" Hali asked, exacerbated by Cas's deceitfulness.

Both Carmya and Delphia looked away from her. Carmya's eyes bubbled with sadness, anger, and frustration like vegetables bobbing up out of a boiling stew. Delphia stood motionless, uncomfortably silent as she took turns glancing between Carmya and Hali, looking unsure of what to say.

Hali raged inside.

What in the world was Cas thinking and why was Carmya more upset about it than her?

"Come anyway," Hali concluded.

"No thanks," Carmya answered. "I'm not going to go where I am not wanted."

"But you *are* wanted. *I* want you both there. It's Cas who doesn't need to be there," Hali declared.

"Hali, we aren't blaming you at all, but Cas said he didn't think it was a good idea to risk anyone else's safety," Delphia reasoned.

"Do you really believe that?" Carmya challenged.

What else could his intentions be? Hali wondered.

Delphia's mouth opened then shut, as she searched for the right words.

Carmya's head shook back and forth in victory lacking triumph. "Exactly."

"Now wait a minute, you didn't give me a chance to answer, Carmya."

"I didn't have to; your reaction was answer enough."

"Carmya ..."

"It's okay, Delphia, it's over and done with."

Suddenly feeling awkward for starting something she didn't know how to fix, Hali began doing dishes. Minutes passed, dishes filled the drying rack, but not a word was spoken. Delphia dried and put the dishes in their place. Carmya brooded while scooping cookie dough balls onto empty pans. Hali wondered if the girls would notice if she left. Under normal circumstances silence didn't bother her, but it pained her to be the reason for it.

"I'm not mad at either one of you," Carmya finally said, breaking the awkward silence. Hali had been in the midst of cleaning the counter for a second time. "I'm just struggling to make peace with the fact that Kai is the one chosen for me and not Cas. When he asked us not to come, it just made it more real, I guess."

Disheartened, puzzled, and frustrated, Hali said, "What doesn't make sense, is that he was the one who told me to invite you guys. Why would he do that if he was just going to go behind my back and un-invite you?" Noticing the time, Hali said, "I'm going to ask when we fish this afternoon."

"You can't do that, Hali." Carmya put the remaining trays in the oven. "He can't know that we told you."

"I won't tell him you told me."

"How do you plan on doing that?" Delphia cast a quizzical glance in Hali's direction.

"I'll make him confess on his own."

19

SOMETHING FISHY

AFTER FINISHING THE COOKIES, it was practically time to go fishing for lunch. Wanting to confront Cas privately, Hali headed straight for the beach. Luckily, she didn't need to wait for Ronan and Marilla since they had agreed that morning to meet at the beach once Hali was done baking. Marilla had thought Hali, Carmya, and Delphia would take a while and she had been right.

Hali was the first of the afternoon group to show up. As she waited, she sat closer to the trees than the shore watching Mr. Gruff shave his branches. The process was relaxing and maddening all at once.

Who had that kind of patience?

While burying her toes in the sand, she realized she didn't exactly know if Cas would be the first to arrive or if he would even arrive alone. She didn't even know if he was taking the place of Delphia and Carmya again like he had before or if another Anchor would assume the responsibility. But as she thought of all the possible outcomes, Cas stepped out from the trees, immediately zeroing in on her.

"You shouldn't be out here alone," were the first words out of his mouth.

"I'm not," Hali responded while swinging her arm in the direction of Mr. Gruff, sitting more than a hundred yards away. "And neither should you."

As Cas closed the distance between the two of them, Hali went over what she planned on saying. Keeping in mind that whatever she said, she needed be careful not to give away that Carmya had betrayed his confidence.

Cas sat a few feet from her on the sand, extending his legs out from his body while resting back on his elbows. He gazed out to the ocean, ignoring her last statement.

Hali's annoyance with him slowly drained from her as she watched him in her peripheral. He looked peaceful and handsome. She brooded unsuccessfully, attempting to conjure up enough anger to remember why she was mad at him in the first place.

Gathering some courage, Hali exhaled a breath, which got Cas's attention.

"What is it, Hali?"

"I, uh, think I am going to skip getting the spell book and I'll let you just get it. If you don't mind?" The two sentences had her out of breath like she had just completed a five-mile run. Lying was such a taxing exercise.

Shooting an eyebrow up, Cas tilted his head. "If that's what you want to do." He resumed looking at the ocean, completely unaffected by the change in plans. "Guess Carmya and Delphia couldn't come then," Cas blurted out nonchalantly, while his eyes remained fixed on the horizon.

Before Hali could respond, the rest of the afternoon group, except Delphia and Carmya, trickled in through the trees.

"Hey there, Cas," Toru looked between Hali and Cas, not

acknowledging Hali in his greeting. "Are we interrupting something?" he joked.

Cas stood to a standing position, stepping in front of Toru. Hali couldn't see or hear their exchange, but whatever happened had Toru taking a step back and casting his eyes down like he was avoiding the sun.

Ronan and Marilla came to her side, oblivious to the heated interaction between Cas and Toru that Hali discreetly tried to watch.

"Did you bring some cookies?" Ronan asked with wide, hopeful eyes.

Hali grimaced while shaking her head. "Sorry, Ronan, I didn't think about it." And that was the truth. Hali had been so preoccupied with talking to Cas before everyone showed up that cookies were the last thing on her mind. "Not to worry, though, we made plenty for lunchtime."

Ronan grinned. "Good, because I've been looking forward to those cookies all day."

"Oh goodness, Ronan," Marilla chimed in, "you've lived your entire life up until now without cookies and now you act like you can't live without them."

"But I don't think I can, mom."

Marilla snorted, which set all three of them laughing as they caught up to the rest of the group near the shore.

Hali stood back scanning the sky, finding enough clouds to allow her to fish leprechaun style, which she preferred over spearing fish mid-swim. Hali enjoyed being a mermaid, but she still wasn't comfortable with undressing to do it. Not knowing when her fertile days were also made Hali hesitant to enter the water. Being pursued by a sea creature sounded absolutely terrifying but being told she was fertile by someone on the Eyes' Land didn't sound ideal either.

Hali grabbed some spears from Mr. Gruff—who shaved

his branches while ignoring her as usual—and found a spot to plant herself on the shore. A few minutes later, she quietly thanked the clouds, and began sliding fish down her spears.

The activity provided her time to think, plan, and wonder. Her conversation with Cas had not gone exactly how she wanted.

Had he figured out that Carmya or Delphia had spilled the beans on him?

When Hali told Cas she had changed her mind about going to the supply drop for a spell book, she wasn't sure what she had expected. Her initial plan was to say she wasn't going to gauge whether he seemed relieved. But instead he appeared indifferent. Until he mentioned Carmya and Delphia not going, and indirectly highlighted her insecurities of waiting alone with him. At least that's what Hali thought happened, but she could have imagined the last part. She really didn't know Cas well enough to judge the meaning of his ambiguous statement without asking for more information. Unfortunately for her, she wasn't given the opportunity.

But maybe that was why he had asked Carmya and Delphia not to come, she thought.

What if Cas was using Hali's insecurities against her? Knowing that if Carmya and Delphia didn't come, Hali likely wouldn't either. She already knew that he didn't want her there, so the idea wasn't too far-fetched.

What she couldn't understand was why it was so important for him to go to the supply drop alone? Hali planned on going either way, even though she told Cas otherwise. He had underestimated her desire to leave the Eyes' Land if he thought for one second she wouldn't go the supply drop without backup. The opportunity to acquire a spell book was just too important to miss over possible awkwardness.

Her head was spinning with every scenario she came up with. Spearing fish granted her way too much time to think. The activity gave her a new appreciation for Mr. Gruff's ability to shave wood into sharp points all day, every day. A job Hali was certain would drive her insane within the first week if she had been tasked with it.

But something other than her spears was fishy about the situation. Maybe it was because she was an outsider and could see what the others couldn't. Maybe her natural distrust of people put her on edge and she was reading too much into things. But she didn't think so. Her intuition had been on high alert ever since learning that Cas took primary responsibility of supplies—the one Anchor who didn't believe in depending too heavily on the aid of enchanters. There was more going on at the supply drops than anyone realized. Whatever it was, Hali planned on figuring out what. But first, she had to figure out how.

20

SUPPLY DROP

THE NEXT TWO weeks had gone by uneventfully, except for the constant rain. Apparently, summer storms didn't escape the Eyes' Land. It was the perfect weather to crawl into an air-conditioned cabin, settle into a cozy seat by a window, and read a good book. Hali settled for snuggling up on Marilla's couch and counting rain drops on the window-pane, doubting she could focus on anything else with her mind ruminating on how the night would go. The anticipation, the secrets, and the task itself had Hali wondering how she would manage to go through with it. But when she thought about her parents waiting for her at home, not knowing where she was, she knew she was making the right decision.

Once night finally descended on the Eyes' Land, Hali retired to Ronan's bedroom. After hours of lying in bed with her mind and heart racing, the time to leave the cabin finally came. Marilla and Ronan had been fast asleep for hours, completely unaware that Hali was waiting for her chance to sneak out.

Guilt burrowed in her stomach like a groundhog as she

snuck out of Marilla's cabin for the second time in less than two weeks; premeditation making the act that much worse. She could have just told Marilla that she and Cas would be waiting for the supplies, but she didn't want that information to get back to Cas. He couldn't know that she was coming after all. Cas had a secret and Hali needed the element of surprise on her side to uncover it. So, she told no one of her plan.

As she tiptoed through the trees, she questioned the soundness of said plan while forced to execute it in the shadows of night. Every chirping cricket, croaking frog, and singing cicada frazzled her nerves. She wondered if she would even make it to camp before dropping dead of a heart attack. The pounding muscle in her chest drummed so strongly it hurt. The trees loomed, half lit by the moon and half in the shadows. The leaves of the trees rattled, from the wind or an Eye, Hali couldn't guess. The uncertainty transformed her measured steps to a full out run.

When she finally made it to camp, she panted in the shadows of a pine tree. She spotted Cas next to a table, glancing around then lifting his head up to the moon. Suddenly, Cas walked away from the table.

Where was he going? Hali thought.

She followed him through the trees, making sure to keep her distance as she hopscotched into the shadows from one tree to the other. She played a similar game with Camille when she was younger in the grocery store, with its checkered-tiled floors. Jumping to the scarce blue tiles meant safety, landing on a plentiful white tile meant death by alligators. Similar game, different stakes, but the same familiar anxiousness buzzed under her skin.

Hali trailed Cas down to the shore, coming out of the

trees far enough so she could witness whatever he was about to do. Nothing made any sense.

Why was he down by the water when he was supposed to be waiting for supplies at camp? Was he going to get into the water?

Fully clothed, Cas sat where the water met the sand, letting a wave envelop his legs. His knees down to his toes became fins with dark blue scales that matched the water, glimmering in the bright moonlight. Hali was thankful for the moonlight, otherwise she wouldn't have been able to see so clearly. He pulled something from his cargo shorts, that Hali couldn't identify at first.

A knife? Why would he have a knife?

Hali watched on, feeling hypocritical that she had given Cas a hard time for spying on her not too long ago. But she couldn't look away, she was too invested in whatever it was that was happening.

All of a sudden Cas brought the knife to one of his scales.
Was he ...?

Hali couldn't believe what she was witnessing. Cas clipped one of his scales, his jaw clenched in the process. Hali gasped at the bloody sight, then quickly covered her mouth at the realization that she had yelped out loud. The scene was like watching someone fall from a building; the reaction happened before she could stop herself.

Cas twisted at the sound, scanning the area, but Hali had hidden behind a tree before his eyes could find her. At least that's what she had hoped. He turned back to the ocean, pocketed the knife with the scale, and removed his fins from the water. Once his legs replaced his fins, he stood up and began walking in the direction of camp. Hali exhaled a breath she didn't know she was holding. Her head fell in relief for not getting caught.

"I thought you weren't coming?" Cas's voice broke into her short-lived relief.

Hali spun to face him. The moonlight lit one side of his face and darkness shrouded the other. The visible side of his face displayed an annoyed smirk, the shadows hid his scar. Considering the circumstances, Hali should have been afraid of Cas, but for some reason she wasn't. Curious but not afraid.

"Why did you cut off your scale?" she asked, ignoring his obvious question.

He quirked an eyebrow up. "You sure you want to know?"

"At this point, I might as well."

"It might disappoint you. You think you can handle that?"

Honestly, Hali wasn't sure how she could be disappointed any more than she had already been since her arrival. She foolishly felt immune to bad news by this point, believing the worst had passed—oh, how wrong she was. Testing fate, she said, "Try me."

Cas nodded. "It's probably better if I show you."

"Okay," Hali agreed.

Hali and Cas walked the short distance back to camp in silence. Cas didn't seem as angry with her crashing the supply drop as she would have expected, which left Hali pondering if Cas had known she would come all along.

Was she prepared for the burden of his secret? Would his secret aid in helping her find a way home? What would Hali be disappointed about?

Thoughts raced between both ears before arriving at camp. Cas made it to a table that had a clear view of the moon and stars and stopped, looking at Hali once more with the question, "are you sure you want to know?" in his eyes. Without saying a word, Hali nodded.

Cas shrugged. "Suit yourself, then." His voice, deep and stern, dripped with part relief, part uncertainty as he gave his final warning. Plucking his scale from his pocket, it shimmered in his palm under the moonlight. Cas's scale was beautiful while still being masculine, clean but with an edge coated in his drying blood. Hali gazed at it in awe. Even though Hali was new to the world of Anchors, she knew that having their scales flayed by Eyes topped their fears.

So why would Cas do it intentionally?

Holding his scale up to the sky, Cas closed his eyes as he muttered something indecipherable. Trees began shaking their leaves as the wind picked up speed. Hair came loose from Hali's braid and her efforts to brush it out of her face were fruitless.

Cas's grasp never wavered on the scale. Hali didn't want to miss what was happening, but the wind made it difficult to keep her eyes opened.

Squinting, Hali struggled to hold her head up. The wind dried her eyes so much they began tearing up as she blinked. Cas stood like a statue, completely unaffected by the pull, the twitching muscles of his lifted arm were the only indication of his battle with the wind. The familiar tingle of the orbs danced under the surface of Hali's skin as a new energy filled the space that wasn't her own. A light, unrelated to the moon illuminated above them, and Hali opened her eyes long enough to see Cas's hand and scale glowing as her own hands did on the doorframe.

Seconds later, the scale vanished, like a feather in the wind, and the table filled with supplies. With the scale gone, the wind returned to a gentle breeze, and the glow of Cas's hand ceased. If the table hadn't been full of supplies, Hali wouldn't have believed what had just occurred. Flour, sugar, eggs, butter, baking soda, and an assortment of personal hygiene, household, and clothing items lined the table. All supplied by Cas.

Hali found herself sitting at the table without remembering how she got there. Stunned, Hali whispered, "Are you an enchanter?"

"Yes," he nodded. "I'm an Anchor and enchanter." Cas found a seat across from her, looking vulnerable and unsure. It was the first time since being on the Eyes' Land that Hali noticed Cas appear anything but confident.

"How long have you been an enchanter?"

"Forever. Both my parents were Anchors and enchanters. Though they kept the enchanter part of themselves hidden from the other Anchors."

"But why?"

Cas glared at Hali. "Why? Have you learned nothing from your parents' story?"

"A leprechaun *and* an enchanter were responsible for Arcelia's and Murchadh's death." Being part leprechaun, Hali was getting tired of leprechauns getting all the blame for every evil. Hali loved her leprechaun ability of pulling fish from the ocean, but that same ability got her captured on the Eyes' Land in the first place by another leprechaun's greed. She felt at odds, loving and hating herself for the same gift.

Cas's glare faded and he appeared almost compassionate. "I'm sorry." He exhaled a breath while closing his eyes. "I don't remember anything before being on the Eyes' Land. I was three when I ended up here, so this is all I've known. But ever since I could remember, Arcelia's story has been ingrained in my memory. My parents were constantly instilling in me that I needed to be careful and not to trust anyone, including other Anchors, with my enchanter powers." Several seconds passed where Cas said nothing, and Hali thought that he was already regretting sharing his secret with her, but then he spoke again. "It was okay at first, because I had them to share my powers with. I was content. After they died, I took over providing goods for the camp. My parents did it before me. I know they would have wanted me to keep the tradition going."

"Has it only been you and your family that have been providing for the Eyes' Land this entire time?"

Cas nodded.

"And why did you cut off a scale?" Hali asked as she pieced the information together.

"Supplies aren't free. Everything comes for a price."

Guilt plagued Hali as her heart sank to the bottom of her stomach. She had no idea that Cas was making such a sacrifice over cookies. Ever since the vote had happened, there hadn't been a day that cookies weren't made. Hali didn't think she would be able to look at a cookie the same way again. Her face must have expressed her remorse because Cas began consoling her.

"It's okay, Hali. You didn't know."

"It's not okay, Cas." Hali didn't know what it felt like to cut off a scale, but she knew that when she had scraped against a rock on her last swim it was like a thousand paper cuts, throbbing and sensitive. Cutting off your own scale had to be the equivalent of losing a finger or toe. The thought alone made the blood drain from her face.

"Hali, it's fine. Our scales regenerate like skin. The loss is temporary."

"I'm just trying to wrap my head around this. I guess now I *completely* understand why you were against relying on the supplies. What I don't understand is why you continue to conjure them?"

Cas shrugged. "Cutting a scale off isn't fun, but it's not *why* I'm against using more supplies."

Hali tipped her head to the side slightly, perplexed of what other reason it could be.

Cas met her questioning eyes with his stoic ones. "A full moon rose in the sky three weeks after my parents were killed. I was eleven. Everyone on the Eyes' Land was still recovering from the Eye attack, including me. I hadn't used my lawpnies in weeks and they began reminding that it was a full moon." Cas chuckled at the memory. "Lawpnies can be pretty persistent when they want to be."

"Lawpnies?" Hali asked.

"It's the magical light every enchanter has within them. Except it's less of a light and more like illuminated soldiers that help guide and protect an enchanter."

Hali's eyes widened. She finally had a name to attach to the little lights that had already come to her defense several times since being there.

"Then what happened?"

"I went down to the water, not sure if I was going to go through with any of it. I had watched both my parents over the years make the sacrifice and to be honest, I was still a kid, and I really didn't want to cut off a scale. But then I thought about my parents and what they would want me to do. I guess when I thought about it, the ritual became a way for me to stay connected to them, and my powers, even though they were gone. I just had this gut feeling that they would want me to continue on in their memory.

"At the time I wasn't even thinking about how the Anchors would react to suddenly not getting a supply drop after eight years of getting supplies without fail. Why I do it? It boosts morale, just like Marilla said. But as for why I don't want the Anchors to rely on it all comes down to the fact that I won't be around forever. When I'm gone, I want everyone on the Eyes' Land to know how to make it without the additional supplies."

The picture became clearer for Hali. "It all makes sense now," she whispered reverently. After a few beats of silence, Hali said, "So I guess that means I won't get a spell book." As the disappointment of it settled in, she noticed that a small smile crept onto Cas's face. Hali's eyebrows drew together in question. "What aren't you telling me?"

"Help me get all this stuff put away and then I'll show you."

ONCE ALL THE refrigerated items were put away in the lodge along with the baking supplies, toiletries, and cleaning supplies, Cas led Hali to his cabin. As they approached his front door he stopped, closing his eyes for a second as he winced at the thought of someone coming into his space. Correction, not just anyone in his space, but Hali.

"Now it should go without saying that anything I've told you so far and anything that you see inside stays between us. Not even Marilla can know."

Hali took a step back to get a better look at Cas. "What's in there?" she asked, looking somewhat amused by his request. "You don't have Eyes' ears in jars or something, do you? Because I'm not sure I'd be able to keep that to myself."

Blank faced and not offering any reassurances, Cas said, "It's not too late to back out." Though deep down he hoped she wouldn't.

Standing a little straighter, Hali scowled at him. "I'm not backing out Cas, are you?" A smirk replaced his blank expression, as he opened his door in response, all the while watching Hali for a reaction. Her eyes widened briefly in what looked to be panic, but she quickly returned his gaze in challenge. The two knowingly egged each other on, waiting for someone to cave into their senses. But neither did.

Cas wasn't one to waver. Once he made a decision, he stuck with it. But he was more than a little surprised at himself that he was about to share a prized possession with a girl he barely knew, and not for the first time since she had arrived on the Eyes' Land.

He observed her hazel eyes dancing around to every corner of his cabin, as she stayed close to the front door. He didn't like how exposed her scrutinizing eyes made him feel or how uncomfortable she seemed to be there.

Maybe she really did think he was harboring Eyes' ears, he thought.

Her gaze stumbled across his blankets that rested on the back of his couch, remaining fixed there a little longer than any other part of his place. When she finally broke her gaze and looked away, her cheeks appeared flushed, embarrassed almost.

The blankets, made by Cas's dad, were the only shred of comfort that could be found in the quaint space. The red cotton rectangles had almost become a memorial to his parents, turning into place holders where they would sit together on the couch. Before Hali had blown into his life, the blankets hadn't left their spot in his cabin for years. But the day Hali arrived on the Eyes' Land, that all changed.

It was the same day she had stalked off to the beach when Cas had questioned her intentions for being on the Eyes' Land. When Ronan unsuccessfully snuck off to bring her lunch, Cas had followed him, making sure to stay hidden behind a tree while he did. He wasn't sure why anyone thought they could keep information from him, but he'd let them have their secrets. Keeping one step ahead of their schemes gave him something to do. That day, Cas planned on keeping tabs on Hali's whereabouts for the safety of the Anchors. But after she finished her lunch, he hadn't expected to hear her crying. Especially when she was supposed to be plotting the Anchors' demise. At least that's what Cas had told himself she would be doing. Immediately, he felt like a jerk. But he wasn't about to waver over a possible threat just because she cried. Though to be fair, to waver, he would have had to struggle with a decision he *actually* made. He hadn't made any decisions. He never got the chance, since Hali banished herself before anyone else could.

After her sobs ceased and her breathing slowed to soft snores, Cas sat, just watching her sleep. It wasn't the most exciting job, but living on a deserted island for most of his life had made him an expert at dealing with boredom.

After hours of watching and waiting for Hali to go into attack mode, unleashing the real reason she was there, the dinner hour arrived. Reluctant, Cas left Hali to sleep under the tree and headed to camp. He ate quickly, made sure to show his face to all who would question its absence, and spent an obligatory amount of time at camp to prevent hackles from being raised on his whereabouts. When he finished, he returned to his hiding spot at the beach, but not before grabbing a blanket from his cabin. He stayed there watching Hali from a distance, long enough for the darkness of night to crush the light of day under the horizon and cool the warm air. Leaving his tree, he approached her curled up form with her arms wrapped around her waist. He laid the crimson layer over her exhausted body that was peppered with goosebumps up and down her shoulders and arms. Her hair was a mess of loose dark coils sprawled across the sand. When she had approached camp that afternoon, Cas had noticed her strands shined with gleams of red tones when lit by the sun. In the darkness, her wild mane appeared black, spread around her head like Medusa —the antithesis of her peaceful face. But unlike the real Medusa, this one wasn't at risk of turning him to stone. The Eyes had already surpassed her on that front ten years before.

He had watched over her that entire night to ensure the safety of the other Anchors. But ultimately, Cas knew if his mother was still alive, she wouldn't want him to leave Hali there alone. He hated Hali for being on the Eyes' Land. Life was hard enough without adding another wild card. The jury was still out on if she was worth protecting, or if the others needed to be protected from her. Either way, it infuriated him that her presence meant extra work.

"This is setup like Marilla's and Ronan's place. Did you conjure all the cabins here too?" Hali asked, breaking Cas from the memory.

Cas pulled his eyes from the blankets to look at Hali. "No, my parents did. Each cabin required ten scales."

"Ouch," she grimaced. "Do the enchanters know that the Eyes' Land is here?"

Cas shrugged. "I don't really know to be honest. But if they did, there is really nothing they can do to help."

Tilting her head, she asked, "Why is that? They're enchanters."

If only it were that simple, he thought.

"Part of the spell that created the Eyes' Land gave passage to the Eyes through the trees. Now, technically, another magical being could get here, but leaving ... that's another story."

Hali's eyebrows rose, in a way that formed a triangle of

confusion between her eyes, "So if an enchanter came here, they wouldn't be able to leave?"

Cas sighed, as she looked at him with curiosity. "Not from what I've read about spells. I've been trying to break this spell for as long as I can remember, but there are too many components holding the barrier in place. Without access to other enchanters, I'm not sure what can be done."

What Cas hadn't said, was that he wasn't completely sure he wanted to break the spell anymore. It had been over a year since he tried and, in that time, he had come to accept that the spell holding the barrier in place was unbreakable.

He used to believe he wanted to escape the Eyes' Land, despite not knowing what awaited him outside of it. Every day he walked down to the shore, staring across at the Emerald Cove Lighthouse, fascinated. His parents had shared stories with him of what it was like to be free. They talked of restaurants they missed, shows and movies they enjoyed watching on something called a television, and traveling to far-off places where there were mountains and unique landmarks. Cas was only three when he ended up on the Eyes' Land, and if he ever had any recollection of the things they had spoken about it vanished once his new life in captivity began.

At twenty-years-old, Cas stopped wishing for a life that would never be his. He accepted his lot and he thought with acceptance there would come peace. It had worked, for a little while at least.

A year later, a few days after Hali arrived, he found himself tossing and turning in his bed, unable to stay asleep. A nagging feeling had overcome him, his mind a jumble of confusion he couldn't silence. He started to question himself.

Had he given up too easily? What would his parents think of him? Why was Hali there?

His thoughts rattled him and when he could no longer take it anymore, he decided to go down to the shore to clear his head. As he was readying to leave the cabin, he spotted the lone, red blanket splayed across the couch without its match. Hali still had his other blanket, since he hadn't asked for it back. For some reason, he had a hard time admitting to her he was the one who loaned it to her in the first place. But as he contemplated the solitary blanket, it saddened him to see it without its counterpart. Without a second thought he snatched it off the back of the couch and headed down to the beach.

Once he made it to the line of trees, with the blanket wrapped around his shoulders, he had been surprised to find Hali standing at the edge of the shore. He hadn't meant to spy on her, but curiosity got the better of him. And not in the perverted-creeper kind of way, but in the what-in-the-hell-is-she-doing kind of way. Though he could admit to himself, and only to himself, that he didn't hate what he saw. And for some reason, that made him feel guilty in a way he couldn't understand.

Nudity had never been an awkward experience for Anchors, but a way of life. Cas had chalked his newfound guilt for seeing Hali nude to stem from the fact that she had gone out of her way not to be seen. Her discomfort with nudity confounded him, considering he could find nothing wrong with her form—it was beautiful.

As he tailed her in the water, it didn't take long before he knew exactly what she was doing—or rather, where she was going. When she made it to the barrier and raised her hand to it, Cas had expected the outcome to be the same as it always had been. Nothing. If he had known the barrier would shock her, he would have stopped her before she ever got close to the wall.

That day he streamed through the water faster than he had ever done in his eighteen years on the Eyes' Land, all while carrying Hali as he did. Adrenaline and despair coursed through his veins. As soon as he got her back to shore, he covered her with the last of his blankets, assessing her listless body. That day marked the second time he had willingly given Hali a prized possession, but this time, it had nothing to do with what he thought his mother would want him to do. It was on this day, Cas realized, that he didn't hate Hali quite as much as he thought he did. He didn't hate her at all.

Hali stepped further into the cabin, bringing him back to the present, her eyes large with unanswered questions. "If enchanters can't come here without being trapped, and you can't break the spell on your own, isn't there some kind of loophole?" she asked, with a hint of desperation.

"If there is one, I haven't found it. If the Eyes knew what I was, they would use me against the other Anchors."

Hali looked down to the floor, contemplating the predicament Cas had tried to bury for the past year. "As enchanters, can't we conjure weapons to fight the Eyes? It's only a matter of time before the Eyes come back, they made that perfectly clear, and we have nowhere to go when they do. There has to be something we can do."

Cas shook his head. "It's not as easy as you would think, Hali. If we were to start conjuring weapons to help, it will raise a red flag in the leprechaun realm. As you know, they pull from the elements and can sniff out when there is an elemental shift in the air when an enchanter is using an abundance of their powers."

Cas watched Hali chew the side of her mouth, as the wheels of her brain churned behind her eyes.

"I'd have to clip at least twenty scales per weapon, and I wouldn't mind doing it if I thought I could get away with it without drawing attention to the fact that I am an enchanter. I'm not trying to summon the Eyes here either."

"How many scales could you use and get away with it?" Hali asked.

Considering Hali's question, Cas's brows furrowed. "I'm not sure, but my parents always told me that if I have to use over fifteen scales, then it shifts the elements in the air; enough for the Eyes to notice."

Hali shivered. Cas could see her struggling to clench her teeth together so it wasn't obvious to him.

"Are you cold?" he asked, knowing full well she couldn't be. It was late June in the South.

"Yes," Hali answered, through chattering teeth—an obvious lie.

Cas walked over to the couch and grabbed a blanket, outstretching his arm to hand it to her. Hali acquiesced, wrapping the blanket around her shoulders. Cas knew she only accepted the blanket to hide her shivers and not because she was actually cold, but he'd let her believe that he believed her.

"Thank you," she said.

Cas nodded.

"I know that you were hoping to get a spell book tonight, but that is not something I can conjure. They are passed down from generation to generation. Even if they are stolen, they can't be opened without the rightful owner. Which is a good thing since my parents once told me they are limited, and the Enchanters' Assembly will not produce more." Cas paused, uncertain whether sharing another prized possession with Hali scared or relieved him. Both, he supposed, but mostly the latter. After years of carrying the burden of being an enchanter alone, it was a relief to have another person like himself on the Eyes' Land.

The day the vote passed to use more supplies, Marilla had revealed to Cas that Hali had enchanter blood and wanted to attend the next supply drop to request a spell book. Once alone, he found himself smiling at the news. The foreign expression confused not only him, but Hali, who caught him in his weakened state, smiling like an idiot. She scowled in response. When Ronan approached her, she cut her eyes away from him to give Ronan all of her attention. With the moment gone, Cas's unflappable demeanor returned. But he still rejoiced from within.

And now, only two weeks after he had found out he was no longer alone, he was about to share a part of himself, that had only been shared with his parents. The prospect filled him with anticipation, relief, and nausea. Hali must have noticed because her faced was suffused with trepidation, mirroring how he felt inside.

"What is it Cas? I can handle whatever you have to tell me." She laughed at a thought that came to her mind. "In less than a month, I got captured, found out I'm a magical mutt, and that I'm not biologically linked to my own parents. Just say what you need to say."

Cas sighed, realizing that Hali was right, but also hoping he wouldn't come to regret his decision. "I have a family spell book. I can share it with you so you can learn how to harness your magic. But there's a catch."

"Anything," Hali eagerly agreed.

Cas raised an eyebrow at her. "Remind me if the time comes to never let you negotiate anything."

"Cas, what's the catch?" she bounced as her shivers went

into overdrive.

Cas ran a hand through his hair.

No turning back now, he thought.

"The catch is, the spell book can't leave my cabin. I can't risk it. Which means any studying you do, must be done here." Cas wasn't sure how much Hali would like the stipulation, considering how apprehensive she was to even walk into his cabin, but it was the only way.

"That's fine with me," Hali stated, her resolve strengthened, but not her shaking.

He couldn't understand why she was shivering so much.

Maybe she was cold, he thought.

"You realize that means that pretty much any studying you do must be done at night. There will be too many questions if you are hanging out at my cabin during the day. We haven't been the friendliest to each other."

"And whose fault is that?" Hali dipped her head in judgement.

Cas rolled his eyes, shaking off her comment, then crossed his arms. "Either way, we need to be careful. We don't want any of the other Anchors suspecting anything. The Eyes are already on high alert, we don't need them sniffing their noses around here anymore than they already have."

Hali shifted to her other leg, rewrapping Cas's blanket tighter around her arms. "Cas, why are you trusting me with all of this? Do you think the Eyes will be coming back soon?"

Cas paused. "I'm not sure, but when they do, it won't be good and they'll be coming for you, Hali. You need to be prepared." Which was partially true.

Hali's eyes and nose scrunched in suspicion. "How did

you know I would come tonight? I already told you I would just let you ask for the spell book."

Cas huffed out a laugh. "I have my ways ..."

Hali scoffed.

"You want off the Eyes' Land too badly to pass up an opportunity that might help in your efforts to leave. It was a safe bet."

And it really was. Cas knew once he told Carmya and Delphia not to go to the supply drop that word would get back to Hali and she wouldn't be able to keep herself from coming. Rumors always found a way around the Eyes' Land, which was a big reason Cas always protected his secret. It was a gamble to let Hali in on it. But he knew she wouldn't screw up the opportunity to use his spell book, just to take part in idle gossip. She was too determined to go home, and she didn't seem like a busybody anyhow.

"So, you think there is a chance we could escape?" Hali's eyes shined with hope.

"If there is, I haven't found it."

"But you don't think it's impossible?"

Cas contemplated Hali's question. "Remember the day you went out to the barrier by yourself?"

"Yeah," Hali answered.

"Do you remember what happened?"

Hali nodded.

How could she not? he thought.

The jolt lit her entire tiny body up and somehow, she survived. It had been the first time Cas had actually started to believe that Hali really was who Marilla had thought she was—Arcelia's and Murchadh's long-lost child.

"If there is a way to break the spell of the barrier—and that is a big *if*—then I think you are part of the equation."

Hali stared at Cas in disbelief. "But the spell was a mixture of three powers and sealed by Cillian."

"Yeah, Cillian was Murchadh's brother, so you have his bloodline running through your veins. You are two parts of the key to break the spell, Arcelia and Cillian, but it won't work without—"

"Rowina," Hali finished, sighing in frustration. "Do you know what happened to her?"

Cas shook his head. "No one does. Everyone assumes that she was killed by the enchanters."

"What do *you* think happened to her?" Hali focused on Cas, her expression expectant. He cracked his neck from side to side, hyperaware of Hali noting every twitch and twist of his face. Her attention made him self-conscious, even though her attention wasn't directed at him per se, but on the information he could provide. Her eyes grew bigger and her eyebrows rose higher with every passing second he didn't speak.

Cas finally shrugged. "I'm not sure exactly, but I think she is still alive out there somewhere. My parents said that enchanters had stopped executing guilty enchanters on a regular basis sometime after the Salem Witch Trials. Something about too much killing of their own kind had already been done, they didn't need to add to it."

"What kind of punishment would they enforce for enchanters who didn't follow the rules?"

Cas grimaced. "My parents never told me that part. I was still pretty young. But I did overhear them talking at night one time when they thought I was sleeping. They mentioned that death was better than enchanter punishment. That the accused were stripped of themselves."

"Stripped of themselves? What does that mean?" Hali asked.

"I think it meant that they lost their powers. An enchanter without powers is not themselves anymore. Especially one who is forced to be mortal after years of being magical. If Rowina did manage to live, she is probably a slave to the enchanters."

"Would there be a way to track her if she was still alive?"

Cas squirmed, squeezing his arms tighter to his chest. "Yes, but tracker spells are dangerous. When you track someone, it opens up the location of the enchanter doing the tracking to the enchanters. Enchanters are known to be the gossipiest creatures in the magical realms and if word gets to the Eyes before we have a plan, it compromises everyone on the Eyes' Land. Couple that with the fact that we can't exactly leave the Eyes' Land to retrieve Rowina even if we knew her location. It would all be for nothing, especially if she is in fact dead."

Hali's shoulders fell, appearing truly stumped. "What *can* we do then?"

Stressed, Cas clasped his hands together on the top of his head. His head brewed with a storm of her questions he'd thought about plenty of times but could find no answer. As he brought his hands down from his head and let them fall to his sides, he exhaled, releasing the building tension within him before he spoke to her again. She gazed at him with uncertainty. Hali probably thought she was aggravating him, and in a way, she was. But he had expected this to happen once he shared his secret with her.

Taking a deep breath, he said, "Before we start tracking down a possibly dead enchanter or making any other rash decisions, we both need to prepare ourselves for the consequences that come with it. The safety of the Anchors needs to be considered before we do anything."

Hali reluctantly agreed, but Cas knew that she wasn't

done on this subject for good—not by a long shot. But she played along for the time being.

When Hali yawned, Cas said, "We'll start tomorrow night. We both need to get some sleep."

"Okay," she yawned again, turning for the front door. But then quickly swiveled back towards him, pulling the blanket from around her neck. As she did, she smacked right into his chest.

She laughed sheepishly and looked down and muttered, "sorry." But the impact produced an explosion of warmth in Cas's chest, sending tingles up his spine, similar to when he caught her fall at the beach. The sensation stunned him to stillness. She held the blanket out for him while still keeping her eyes downcast. But when he hesitated for too long, her hazel eyes met his gaze.

Ignoring the heat in his chest, he felt certain was a heart attack, he asked, "Where are you going?" while taking a step back and pretending not to notice his blanket in her outstretched hands.

Hali quirked her head, befuddled. "I'm going back to Marilla's. Where else would I be going?"

"I know that, but why are you going out the front door?"

Hali huffed, shifting her weight and bringing her arms to her chest, holding the blanket to her. "Is this a trick question? How else am I supposed to get back to Marilla's?"

Cas sighed in disappointment. "You find out I'm an enchanter, and you want to go out the front door?"

Hali rolled her eyes. "Cas if there is some other way I should get back to Marilla's I'm all ears, but please don't make me guess what that is right now. My brain is way too full and tired for mind games."

Cas held his hands up in a surrender. "No mind games. I'm just surprised is all."

Hali shot him a dagger.

Cas's eyes widened playfully; a smile bloomed on his lips over Hali's irritation. For the sake of self-preservation, he stifled it from growing any further and cleared his throat.

"I'll teleport you there. Close your eyes," Cas instructed.

"Why, what will happen if I keep them open?" Hali asked, part worried, part curious.

"Always so many questions," Cas joked.

"Seriously, Cas, what will happen?" Hali pleaded.

"Nothing. Just haven't teleported anyone besides myself since my parents. It's a little easier to concentrate if you aren't staring at me when I do."

"Oh," Hali chuckled nervously. As Cas began his spell, Hali pinched her eyes and nose together.

"No peaking," Cas demanded.

"Is this going to hurt?"

Cas grinned. "No, now close your eyes so I can concentrate."

Hali let out a shaky breath but followed his instructions. A pulling sensation circled within her core and Cas's mutterings came to a halt. She opened her eyes and found herself standing in her temporary room at Marilla's. The little cabin was quiet while her erratic heartbeat thrummed over the silence. Her hands lit up, forcing her to look down. Cas's blanket sat folded in her hands with a note.

Stop shivering.

-Cas

Hali grinned and collapsed asleep on top of the bed wrapped in Cas's blanket—her nervous quivering finally ceasing.

22

A YEAR LATER

SUN RAYS BROKE through the blinds like a burglar, waking Abigail from a restless sleep. The brightness of the rays belied Abigail's devastation. A year ago, to the day, marked the anniversary of the best day of her life and the worst— the day her child came into the world and the day her child disappeared from it. The irony didn't escape Abigail. She wished she could remove the day from the calendar just like she wanted to squeeze the assaulting sun between her fingers until it turned to ash. But she couldn't. Removing the worst day from the calendar also removed the best day. Just like removing the burn of the sun also removed its warmth and the life it touched.

As Abigail curled up in bed, staring at the strips of light on her comforter, she could hear Theo clanking around in the kitchen making breakfast, like he had done every morning for the past year. Whether the breakfast was eaten wasn't important, but he made it all the same. Unlike her husband, Abigail made a routine of visiting her grief every day, while Theo searched for the silver lining in the cloud that had permanently settled over their heads, turning all their days gray. Abigail's grief was like a novice seamstress's sewing project, one snag away from coming completely undone, and unveiling the mess of strings hidden beneath its perfect facade. Theo, on the other hand, hid his grief like a time capsule, burying it deep inside, uncovered only after some time and digging.

However, Theo and Abigail shared one commonality in their grief; they both survived it through daily distractions and unwavering schedules. Working at the aquarium as veterinarians had become just as vital to Theo and Abigail as it was for the animals they cared for. The aquarium kept them both busy, physically and mentally, making each unbearable day a little more bearable. They both thrived at the aquarium and became dependent on the rigorous schedule of their work. But once Abigail and Theo returned home every night, that was where a line was drawn in the sand.

Abigail hung on to the dangerous hope that Hali was still alive. Hope got her up in the morning, but it also pulled her down by night. Though the same could not be said for Theo, who shut down the idea of Hali being alive whenever Abigail brought it up. She knew it wasn't because he wished Hali dead, but more because he feared Hali enduring a life where she wished she was.

It had been a year since Hali vanished. Search and rescue had completed an exhaustive search combing the waters, sandbars, and small islands surrounding Emerald Cove with no luck. When Hali's sweatshirt turned up on the shore—the morning she went missing—faded and tattered, the situation became undeniably bleak. With all the evidence pointing to an ocean disappearance, a happy ending didn't look promising. But despite Hali's vehicle and sweatshirt being at the scene, she was nowhere to be found. The absolute worst-case scenario.

Life had moved on in Emerald Cove. Camille had gone away to school but visited Abigail and Theo at every break. The entire O'Riley family, besides Neilan, would visit from time to time and check in on the couple. Neilan had become a commercial fisherman right out of high school just like his father, Bram O'Riley. Though unlike his father, Neilan was never home; taking on as many fishing trips as he could to save up money. Though what he was diligently saving for, not even Neilan's mother really knew. Bram O'Riley's schedule was a little more flexible and he would visit the Shawns with his wife whenever he was home from a fishing trip. Abigail always received visitors with a smile on her face, but the effort left her drained. Camille's visits in particular were especially taxing for Abigail—serving as a reminder that Hali wasn't sharing in the same milestones as her friend.

Abigail sat up and turned off the alarm before it ever sounded. Over the past year, there hadn't been a morning since Hali's disappearance that Abigail was awakened by startling beeps or twangy country music. The fun had stopped between her and Theo. She missed the days when getting mad at Theo's pranks were her major concern. Abigail stepped out of her bed and walked to the same place she did every morning—Hali's room. For the past twelve months, Abigail had made a ritual of sitting on the unmade bed in the messy room, breathing in the faded scent of Hali's pillowcase. She would scan the corkboard containing pictures of Hali and Camille at different stages of their lives full of silliness and laughter along with newspaper clippings that highlighted Hali's running successes. Every year had been accounted for besides one.

Hali would have been nineteen.

At first Abigail would pay daily visits to Hali's room like a detective, searching for clues that would lead to answers. But she discovered nothing over several months—not a note hidden in a pillowcase or a plan written in a journal. There hadn't even been a not-quite-right visitor that tried to comfort the family since her disappearance. The room showed no premeditation of leaving on Hali's part. Abigail knew this because the room was messy, and Hali never left her room messy if she planned on being gone for long.

After months of not finding any clues, Abigail continued to visit the room, but only as a grieving mother. It had become the only space in the world Abigail could unbuckle her sadness without pity or judgement. Theo never questioned the time Abigail spent in their daughter's room, and he certainly didn't join her in the habit. Abigail found that the time she spent in the space didn't eradicate all of her grief but eased it just enough, so she didn't fall apart at the wrong place and time. It provided a kind of catharsis.

But today was different—it was the first birthday without her. Technically, it was the second, but the first one that Theo and Abigail knew it. Today, Abigail's grief was amplified, like an ant under a magnifying glass, then burnt by the sun. She had known today would be difficult, which is why she and Theo had had the foresight to take the day off from work. She couldn't handle sympathy from well-intentioned colleagues and acquaintances that had remembered what today was for Abigail and Theo or from those who were reminded by the column in today's local newspaper.

The Emerald Cove Times had called the family a few weeks prior to ask permission to run an article on the year anniversary of Hali's disappearance. Theo and Abigail easily agreed on the slim chance it could generate information from someone who might have known what happened to Hali. But Abigail refused to be out in the open when others read about her family's tragedy.

So instead, she planned to hide away until the day was over. At least that had been her plan until she heard the doorbell ring. Abigail wanted to intercept Theo and stop him, but she knew she wouldn't make it. Abigail left Hali's room and shut the door, as if closing the door would preserve the life that once inhabited the space. She rushed back to her room, while wiping her rogue tears on the sleeves of her oversized shirt. The reflection in the bathroom mirror showed a woman with sunken eyes that were at the same time red and puffy. Turning the sink water on to the coldest setting, Abigail practically stuck her eyes under the stream of cold water. After dressing quickly then brushing her teeth and hair, Abigail assessed herself in the mirror. A year ago, she wouldn't have cared, but she had become better at pretending that she had a hold on things. Pretending kept the pitying stares to a minimum.

Descending the stairs, Abigail found Camille sitting at the kitchen table chatting about her college experiences to Theo. Camille smiled at Abigail when she spotted her and held up a pink box.

"I brought doughnuts," Camille offered.

Plastering on an expression she hoped resembled a smile, Abigail replied, "Bring any Otis's old-fashioned?"

"Of course," Camille brightened.

"Well then, let the sugar coma commence."

Abigail looked at Theo whose eyes smiled at her more than his mouth conveyed. After years of marriage, she knew the look. Theo wanted her happiness more than his own. Gathering the rest of the plates containing French toast and sausage the three sat at the table eating more than was dictated by hunger. They discussed Camille's college experiences: living in the dorms, a boy she liked named Evan, and her struggle on choosing a major that she liked as much as Evan. They ate, laughed, and shed some tears sharing memories of Hali. Abigail had not wanted to see anyone outside of Theo today, but the circle they created helped her not feel so alone.

The past year Abigail witnessed the rest of Emerald Cove move on, but now, at her kitchen table, she took comfort knowing that there were two other people who hadn't. It's not that she ever believed that Theo really forgot about Hali, but he had been much better at containing his grief than Abigail. Until now, he had barely discussed Hali, keeping her memory locked away somewhere Abigail couldn't see, leaving her to feel lonelier than ever. But today, as he altered among bites of French toast, sausage, and doughnuts she could see past the wall he had created that hid the hurt in his eyes.

When Camille left two hours later, Abigail asked Theo a question that she had been wondering for some time. "Why do you avoid Hali's room?" Abigail let the hot water run down the plate she was rinsing, watching as the syrup lost its grip on the porcelain and washed down the drain. Theo resumed collecting the dishes from the kitchen table and stacked them next to the sink where Abigail stood.

"My grief is not like your grief."

Cocking her head, Abigail looked at Theo to provide a bigger explanation. He took the hint and continued.

"Your grief is like a pressure cooker. You need to release some steam to feel better."

Abigail nodded. "What is your grief like?"

"Hali's room is Pandora's box. I barely get a chance to

take in all the good before I'm getting strangled by the bad. I learned a long time ago your method was not my way of coping with all of this."

"So, your method is avoidance?"

"Yep," Theo responded.

"That's probably not healthy."

"Neither is losing a child. It's what works for me."

The couple was at a standstill as Abigail continued washing the dishes and putting them in the dishwasher. The sound of the running faucet prevented complete silence. Theo was the first to speak.

"Maybe we need some closure."

Abigail looked up from the dishwasher. "How?"

"I think we need to have a service for Hali, we've put it off long enough."

"But we don't know—"

"We do know, Abigail ... we do," Theo stated. His jaw twitched with every effort to restrain his frustration.

"She was never found," Abigail challenged.

"Not everyone that gets lost at sea does, Abigail ... for various reasons."

Theo didn't have to say one of the various reasons could have been that Hali became shark bait, but he didn't need to, they both knew.

"What if someone made it look like she was lost at sea and she is alive out there somewhere?" Abigail argued, while Theo winced at the idea that was even more haunting than the former. "We can't just give up. You know as well as I, that our situation is different."

"Give up?" Theo pointed at Abigail then instantly recoiled, sucking his words back before they exploded out of him. He turned his head into his tensed body and exhaled out, releasing the tension within himself. After a few more breaths, he calmly said, "Abby, I'm not giving up hope, I just want to choose not to live like we've completely given up on life."

Abigail stared at him, wordlessly.

Did she even want the same thing?

She wasn't sure what she thought or how to go back to living like she used to before Hali was gone. Abigail and Theo were comfortable financially but after Hali vanished the animals needed them both back at the aquarium sooner than later. A few veterinarians had temporarily stepped into Abigail's and Theo's positions at work while they grieved for two weeks, but after that, the helpers were needed back at their own sites. Life kept moving forward, despite Theo and Abigail not being ready.

Would they ever be?

Before Abigail could find her next words, Theo found his.

"I'm going to go for a run." He didn't wait for Abigail to respond when he left the kitchen. If Theo's stomach was as full as Abigail's after eating breakfast, she wasn't sure how he planned to run, but she didn't stop him. She knew that it was his way of coping, like going into Hali's room was hers.

Abigail left the kitchen a little after Theo did. Ascending the stairs, she wanted to head to her room and shower before Theo got back but detoured to the closed door at the end of the hall instead. Abigail went to Hali's untouched desk, finding the box that sat tucked away in the corner. The smooth, cream-colored, wooden box looked the same as it did when Abigail first received it on behalf of Hali when she was only a baby. It appeared seamless, like an ordinary block of wood, but an emerald-cut gemstone that was pale violet in color sat in the middle of one of its outer walls. Abigail pinched the amethyst between her fingers and lifted upwards, exposing the contents inside and the unfamiliar melody that had become familiar after years of it being opened multiple times. Abigail listened and watched the beautiful mermaid inside travel on her turquoise-waved track that shimmered. Making her way back and forth with smooth, elongated figure eights, flipping as she reached each end like a swimmer at the end of a lap. The waves moved up and down, making the mermaid appear to go against them. An inscription at the top of the box read:

Boundless as the sky at night,
Kindred as the stars.
Cherished as the sun is bright,
Burdened as the moon.

Abigail always thought the quote didn't match the delicate box and the contents inside, chalking her aloofness up to having a mind geared toward scientific rather than artistic thinking. Besides, she had always assumed the gift to be something out of a local gift shop, the inscription meaningful only to its maker and meaningless to whomever bought it. Her thought, like a linen cloth, ripped by the smallest shred of doubt.

What if it meant more?

Giving Hali the box had been the only demand Hali's birth parents ever made. Arcelia and Murchadh were adamant that Hali receive it. They had made no stipulations in regards to receiving updates, visitations, or communication with Hali—just that she must be given the music box. After years of Abigail's body rebelling to get pregnant and numerous adoptions rescinded before they ever happened, the request almost seemed too simple. Abigail and Theo were afraid to ask what the catch was in case Hali's birth parents changed their minds; leading them to agree to the request without hesitation.

They spent the next eighteen years raising Hali as their own, and as far as Hali knew, she was Theo's and Abigail's biological child. It had been the only point of contention in their marriage—other than the alarm clock—since Theo believed Hali should know her roots and Abigail feared that they would lose Hali if she did.

But now, Abigail looked at the music box a little closer, but still found nothing. Other than the strange inscription, she couldn't find anything peculiar about the box. It was just a mermaid swimming, around and around, endlessly, to music Abigail had never heard until the day the box and baby girl were placed in her arms. Abigail sighed, her head pounding from a combination of too much sugar and over-thinking. Her heart ached along with it.

She let the thought go, in a way she could never let Hali. *Would she die grieving?* Probably.

Convincing herself she had truly gone mad searching for meaning in a music box, she held it with its memories of better days to her chest.

The abrupt slamming of the front door shook Abigail from her solemn reverie. She quickly shut the box, pushing it back to its corner of the desk and slid out of Hali's room, pulling the door closed behind her.

"Theo?" she called. Panic gripped at her chest as her call went unanswered. She tiptoed down the stairs, praying she didn't just announce herself to a murderer. The sounds of heaving echoed in the downstairs bathroom. Abigail's fears dissipated and were quickly replaced with concern for Theo—even though his sudden illness was no surprise. Abigail stood outside the bathroom door cringing. But she stayed put, because Theo would have done the same for her. "You need anything?"

The toilet flushed and the door opened with Theo

emerging drenched in sweat that Abigail couldn't be sure was produced from his run or his effort to expel breakfast. She suspected the latter, considering he hadn't been gone longer than five minutes.

"A kiss," Theo said, waggling his eyebrows with mischief in his eyes. Abigail leaned in and planted a kiss on Theo's cheek, which coated her lips with his salty sweat. "And a hug," he added, holding out his arms. Before Abigail could refuse, she was swept up into Theo's embrace that left her feet dangling a few inches from the floor. Abigail squealed in surprise that was part due to her body being covered in sweat and the other part to Theo's playfulness, which had disappeared the same day that Hali did. The laughter that erupted from Abigail's belly felt alien and her stomach muscles tensed at being used. After months and months of grief being her only emotion, laughter that wasn't rooted in sadness felt good. When both of their laughs settled, Theo's eyes continued to sparkle in delight. "I guess we both need a shower now." Swooping Abigail over his shoulder, Theo jogged up the steps as if he hadn't just lost his breakfast to the porcelain throne moments before.

"Don't drop me, Theo!" Abigail yelled as she held on tightly to his chest upside down.

"Never."

"You're crazy."

"Yep," Theo agreed, "and you married me anyway."

The next day, a twangy country song blared from Abigail's alarm clock—waking her for the first time in a year. She did the unthinkable and smiled to herself. Up until yesterday Abigail hadn't realized that the past year had not only taken

Hali from them, but each other. She wasn't sure if she would ever not feel guilty for feeling anything other than grief, but for the first time in a year she wanted to.

Needed to.

But she also promised herself to not stop looking for Hali until she was found. She would do her best to live for the ones in her life who were present and hope for the one who wasn't—yet.

23

TWELVE FULL MOONS

A YEAR HAD PASSED on the Eyes' Land since the night Cas unveiled his secret. Hali was now nineteen and no closer to finding a way of breaking down the barrier than when she arrived. Life moved on the Eyes' Land like the waves: constant, but predictably changing. The Eyes hadn't returned since the morning Neilan had warned her in the woods. But Hali knew it was only a matter of time before they did.

True to his word, Cas trained Hali nightly at his cabin in fighting, spell work, and enchanter history. Initially, Hali felt unsure how the arrangement of using Cas's spell book would go, but she quickly learned that there was too much to learn to fret over possible awkwardness. Cas had become her teacher and he took the job seriously. He beamed whenever Hali got a spell right and critiqued her whenever she could have done something better. She knew training allowed him to share a side of himself that he had kept hidden for so long. It was an outlet that enabled him to pass on the gifts he possessed from his parents.

The lessons gave them both purpose and companionship. But for Hali, the lessons also instilled hope of one day breaking the barrier.

At the start of her trainings with Cas, Hali discovered very quickly that magic was like any other muscle in her body—weak unless worked and pushed. The little light orbs that Hali had learned from Cas were actually called lawpnies, were Hali's first introduction to how difficult magic was to control. Especially when they had the advantage of tuning into Hali's emotions and reacting either constructively or mischievously. More often than not, the latter was true, but whenever Hali was in any real danger her lawpnies came through and helped.

Restraining lawpnies under her skin required tightening every muscle, similar to running, but nothing like it at the same time. The exercise exhausted Hali at first but overtime she had built up her stamina and strength so that she felt in control of her stubborn lawpnies and not the other way around.

Trapping lawpnies served two purposes. The first, was to hide her powers from mortals, which really wasn't a problem on the Eyes' Land on account of there weren't any. The second, was to allow the lawpnies to charge and build in power. Cas said that charging lawpnies would be useful during a fight, allowing an enchanter to strike with more force when needed. Although he never explicitly mentioned the Eyes, Hali knew that Cas had the Eyes in mind during every training session. He wanted to prepare Hali as much as himself for when the Eyes returned, and his intense training sessions reflected that goal.

At the same time, they were limited to how much power they could use, so they wouldn't create an elemental shift that alerted the Eyes of what they were doing.

During one of their sessions, Hali asked Cas where

lawpnies got their unusual name. He didn't know, except to say that most words in the spell book weren't common. Then almost under his breath he added, *that most good things in life weren't.* Hali spent the rest of that day contemplating what Cas had meant. She never had a chance to ask him because in typical Cas fashion, he had already moved on to another training topic. Eventually, Hali told herself that she was reading too much into it, crediting her overzealous curiosity to a lack of entertainment.

Overall, life on the Eyes' Land had become routine for Hali, which made her sad when she let her mind wander into the past. She missed her parents desperately but tried not to think about them. It hurt too much to know that she couldn't see them or tell them she was okay. If it hadn't been for her training sessions with Cas, she probably would have cried herself to sleep most nights. Luckily, training drained any remaining energy she had after her full days, leaving her barely able to make it the three steps to bed after being teleported back to Marilla's each night.

Despite Hali's sneaking around, her relationship with Marilla and Ronan remained strong, even though both were unaware that Hali had been spending the last year strengthening her enchanter muscles with Cas.

Marilla had easily accepted that Hali's request for a spell book a year prior had been denied, never mentioning the topic again after Hali had told her the outcome. This relieved Hali, since she didn't want to fabricate stories she'd have to remember later. She hated lying, especially to Marilla and Ronan. It was bad enough they had no idea that Hali had attended the first "supply drop" and had consistently thereafter. Cas had said it needed to be this way to ensure the safety of the Anchors, but Hali felt terrible betraying Marilla's and Ronan's trust, even if for good reason. She just hoped that her deceit wouldn't all be for nothing and that one day her strengthened abilities would help break the spell that held everyone on the Eyes' Land.

When Hali wasn't with Marilla and Ronan, training, or completing daily chores, she met with Delphia and Carmya to bake a few times a week. Initially, baking served as a time filler to distract Hali from her worries the way the beach used to in her old life. But soon, Hali found herself enjoying Carmya's and Delphia's company just as much as the baked goods they made; chatting like they had been friends all of their lives.

At first Hali hadn't wanted to bake once she knew what it meant for Cas. But Cas convincingly argued that Carmya and Delphia would bake with or without Hali's help and that he wasn't giving up any more than he had already in the past. He reasoned that Hali might as well help them and make sure their efforts at least tasted good. Hali couldn't disagree, but still felt a pang of guilt anytime she ate a cookie.

Delphia and Carmya had grasped the art of baking quickly and began tweaking some of the basic recipes Hali had shown them. Sometimes Hali would barely lift a finger while Delphia and Carmya did all the work. Instead, she acted as a taste tester to their new creations, eating as little as she could, so it wasn't necessary for them to make more than needed to share with the entire Eyes' Land.

Hali attended every full moon ritual with Cas, since the first one she had crashed a year before, offering to cut one of her own scales every time. Cas always rejected her offers by either saying, *maybe next time* or *the Eyes may sniff out your blood* or when Cas would really want to bug her, he'd say, *I'll hunt, you cook.*

Hali hated the relief and guilt that flooded through her

every time Cas turned down her help. Cutting a scale from herself terrified Hali to no end, but it also pained her to watch Cas do it to himself every month. At least if she used one of her own scales, she might be able to enjoy the baked goods.

Maybe.

That, or she would resent everyone who enjoyed the spoils of her sacrifices—which would be everyone, besides Cas. She wasn't sure how he did it for so many years without complaint.

As Hali sat on the shore, placing the last few fish on a skewer, a seagull squawked above her, breaking her from her reverie of the past year. The afternoon fishing group was still catching their portions of lunch as Hali wrapped up her own task. After filling in for Delphia and Carmya long ago, Cas continued coming to the afternoon group even after they returned. Ronan had become a very competent fisherman over the past year and switched to the morning group, since their fish count wasn't nearly as high. Honestly, the afternoon group could have rested on Hali's catches alone, but didn't, since her ability to use her leprechaun abilities rested solely on the weather, which at best was an unreliable means to lunch. Fortunately, it was reliable enough, since Hali couldn't remember the last time she actually needed to get into the water to fish. Either way, she was grateful for her leprechaun abilities, since Marilla's story about the sea creatures that lurked in the ocean made Hali too paranoid to enter the water at least half of every month.

Completing her last skewer, Hali peered up, noticing a boat out in the distance. The Eyes' Land was invisible to mortals and the barrier had no effect on their ability to pass through it and back out of it. The entire time Hali had been on the Eyes' Land she watched several boats glide across the horizon almost daily, but this one was different. As opposed to being solid white, like most boats, this boat had a red stripe that ran around the circumference of the body. She had taken many trips on that boat throughout her life.

It was her family's boat.

Hali stripped her clothes off without modesty and began swimming before her body made the complete transformation from human to mermaid. A rocket in the water, she couldn't be stopped once the spark of hope had been ignited. She passed schools of fish, sharks, and dolphins, swerving through kelp while always keeping her eyes on the cluster of bubbles in the distance that marked the location of the boat.

As she approached, she realized that the boat had crossed the barrier of the Eyes' Land. Lifting her head from the water, she was struck by the sight of her mom and dad, Abigail and Theo, only a few feet away. Her voice, stuck in her throat, clawed to get out.

"Mom! Dad!" Hali finally yelled.

Her mother's face looked drawn and tired; her father's not much better. She continued to yell, but her words floated away like bubbles on a windy day, never reaching their ears. Abigail and Theo continued to survey the waters right in front of her, unaware of her presence, until Abigail's eyes settled on Hali's. Unmoving, she stared at Hali for several moments. Hali yelled louder, agony turning her screams hoarse as she willed for her mother's sorrowful eyes to be replaced with the flicker of recognition. Instead, Hali's longing was replaced by anguish. She had become a ghost to her old life, existing only in the memories of those who still cared.

After what felt to be a blink of an eye, and an eternity,

Abigail broke eye contact with Hali. Theo gently grabbed Abigail's arm and said something to her, to which she nodded in agreement. His words were muffled to Hali, either from the engine purring back to life or her own howling and tears, she wasn't sure. But it sounded a lot like they were saying a few parting words—a goodbye. It wasn't until her family's boat proceeded in a different direction that their purpose for being out in the ocean made sense. Their trip hadn't been for leisure or relaxation—it had been to say a final farewell ... to Hali. More than a year had passed, and they had given up in believing she was alive. Why would they think any differently? Hali watched as the little boat with the red stripe crossed back over the barrier towards Emerald Cove, growing smaller and smaller as it went.

Hali's tears mixed with saltwater, blurring her vision. The ache in her chest that she had hidden away like lawpnies for the past year broke free and throbbed painful beats as she treaded near the border of her new life and her old. The other Anchors never ventured that far when they fished. It was the only comfort Hali had, knowing she could shed her tears privately. Only the ocean would know that she had added her own mournful drops to its vastness.

In the midst of her torture she didn't sense another presence lurking near; her privacy invaded, just when she thought it wouldn't be. A slimy touch to her shoulder had her swinging herself around. Sharp teeth greeted her with a terrifying smile. A green face covered in blue dots similar to freckles attempted to close the short distance. Shock gripped at Hali's lungs restricting her air so she couldn't breathe. Arms began wrapping around her waist at the same time panic trickled down her spine.

Pulling her hands up, she pushed against the creature's chest, but his arms were like tentacles, squeezing at her every attempt of escape. She clasped her hands around the creature's wrists, attempting to pry at the source with no luck. His spindly features were strong in a scrappy sort of way.

The lawpnies rose from her skin, ready for battle. She knew that her magic should only be used as a last resort. Cas had warned her of the dangers of using too much magic and she had no desire of drawing attention from nearby Eyes. But on top of that, she hadn't practiced her magic with anyone besides Cas. Conflicted, Hali struggled with the persistent creature, while considering what consequences would result if she unleashed her power on him. With no other options available to ward off the pest, she prepared her lawpnies to zap him. She only hoped that she would get her point across without killing him. But before she had the chance to let the power surge from her fingertips, dark blue fins rose from the water behind the sea creature.

Before the sea creature could realize what was happening, he got whacked with a powerful blow to the head. The navy flippers glided back into the ocean as the sea creature's eyes rolled back into his head, crashing into the water, unconscious. Hali was pulled down with him, as his hands remained fixed on her wrists. A cloud of bubbles enveloped the sea creature as he submerged further down from the impact. His hands relaxed on Hali's wrists the further down they went, allowing her to finally unclasp his stubborn grip from her skin. After freeing herself she propelled back up to the surface, all while searching for the dark blue fins responsible. Not long after, her gaze met Cas's piercing glower.

"Get out of the water, Hali!" Cas seethed furiously, while every cord of muscle from his abs to his shoulders looked just as angry.

Cas spoke to her as he had when she first arrived on the Eyes' Land. When he thought she was sent by the Eyes to hurt the Anchors. But over the past year they had become friends. A friend that had never lost his temper towards her as he did now. Hali had never seen him quite as enraged.

She swam away from Cas as fast as she could, not because he had demanded it, but because she needed to get away. It was all too much to handle. Never looking back, Hali haphazardly threw her clothes on as soon as she made it back to the shore. Grabbing the fish-laden skewers, she ran to camp as fast as her legs could carry her.

As she approached camp, Hali did her best to temper her emotions.

"Hey there, Hali girl, how the fish bitin' today?" Fisk asked. Hali could always count on a conversation with Fisk whenever she brought fish to camp to be prepared for lunch. Fisk always had a story or a new quip to entertain Hali with that usually was a poke at the fact the she didn't "fish" in the traditional way that Anchors did. But as amusing as Fisk was, Hali couldn't stick around for it today.

Hali plastered on a smile, that she hoped would pass as genuine. "The fish were okay today. I'll see you later, Fisk." Hali set down the skewers, taking steps away from the table, hoping Fisk would let her go at that.

"Hey, wait up there. You doin' okay, Hali girl?"

"Yes, sir, just got a bit of a headache. I wanted to try and get a nap in before lunch."

Fisk squinted his eyes at her, scanning her face for signs that she was lying. Hali awaited his inspection, resisting the urge to run. The pressure building in her head, started to produce the early signs of a tension headache—her lie coming true.

"Well, okay then, Hali girl. You rest up and drink plenty

of water. The sun can be mighty brutal for those of us prone to headaches this time of year. Ol' Fisk would know."

Hali nodded. "I will. Thank you, Fisk." Hali walked until making it to the trees. Once hidden in their cover, she ran back to Marilla's.

Hali jumped in the shower. Scraping away at stubborn sand that would have come off easier if she was dry. But she didn't care. The shower was one of the only places she could hide. Seeing her parents made her heart split into wooded splinters, poking at the rest of her chest in painful stabs. If that wasn't enough, Cas had to be there to witness her humiliating encounter with a sea creature, adding embarrassment to her already terrible day.

How did Cas even know where she was?

Hali hadn't been close at all to where the afternoon group fished, and she hadn't asked for his help. It didn't matter either way—she hadn't deserved his misplaced ire that had managed to rub off on her.

After Hali's tears had finished draining from her eyes, she got out of the shower to find Marilla waiting right next to the door. Hali jumped back a little.

"Are you okay, Hali?" Marilla's eyes crinkled with worry.

"Yeah, why do you ask?" Hali questioned, but didn't really want Marilla to answer.

Marilla cocked her head. "My dad said you ran back here. Said it seemed like something was eating you."

Darn Fisk.

"I'm fine Marilla, really." Hali knew she wasn't selling her answers, and Marilla certainly wasn't buying them, but Hali was too emotionally depleted to put forth the effort of a believable performance.

Marilla nodded suspiciously. Hali walked past her to the bedroom, wrapped in a towel, moving closer to her escape with every step. Just a couple more steps and she could close the door on Marilla, and on her day, that had gone from bad to worse. But as her right leg crossed into the bedroom, she was stopped in her tracks when Marilla asked, "I thought you were fishing leprechaun style, what made you go out into the water today?"

Hali whipped around, confused of how Marilla knew.

Hali dropped her head down, resting her back on the doorframe as she sighed heavily. She knew then she wasn't getting out of the conversation. "I saw my parent's boat out in the water. They had crossed the barrier. I yelled but they never saw me. And then they were gone." Hali avoided telling Marilla about the sea creature and Cas, saying only what needed to be said. It took every last bit of her energy to even do that much.

As Hali spoke, Marilla's shoulders relaxed, and her suspicious expression wilted into remorse. "I'm so sorry, Hali. I thought ... never mind, it doesn't matter."

Hali lifted her head up, curiously. "What is it, Marilla? What did you think?"

Marilla's eyes met Hali's. "I talked with Cas."

Hali's stomach lurched at the impending embarrassment she was sure to come.

Had Cas told Marilla about the incident with the sea creature?

"He told me that this wasn't the first time you've approached the barrier." Marilla paused, giving Hali room to tell her side of the story.

Gnawing guilt took the space Hali had reserved for her embarrassment. She opened her mouth several times to speak, but the words were caught in a net of lies of her own creation. Hali hadn't intended to lie, but in the end, intention didn't matter when the result turned out to be the same.

Why would Cas sell her out?

"Marilla, I'm sorry I didn't tell you when it first happened. The truth is, I didn't want to worry you or disappoint you. I had already messed up by going out in the water in the first place." Unruly tears sprang from Hali's eyes. As mad as she was at Cas and although she wanted nothing more than to confess everything to Marilla in that moment, she didn't. She had made a promise that proved to be more inconvenient than she could have imagined. But it was a promise all the same. She cried even harder because she knew that in order to protect Marilla, Ronan, and all the other Anchors, she needed to continue to lie, even if the guilt ate a hole through her.

Marilla spoke softly. "Hali, we all make mistakes. I understand why you didn't tell me. But I also want you to be comfortable talking with me about anything. We've all at one time or another tried to break through the barrier, but none of us have tried alone or have been shocked by it. I understand the desire to go home better than you think, but we do things in groups for a reason. Being unconscious in the water alone is a recipe for disaster."

Hali nodded frantically, her face flushed and puffy, the trials of the day catching up to her. "I'm sorry, Marilla."

"You have nothing to be sorry for. I'm just glad it all worked out okay today, and last year. If I'm being honest, I would have probably done the same thing if it was my parents. It makes sense why you were hanging out at the barrier now. Cas had thought you had a death wish. Guess he's come a long way in a year. I've never seen him that upset, but I know it comes from a good place. Now go get dressed and ready. We can talk some more if you want when you're done."

Death wish?

Before Hali could ask what Marilla had meant, she walked out of the hall, leaving Hali to dress and ponder.

Moments later, she stepped out of the room and walked the short distance to the living area where only Marilla waited. Once Ronan stopped being part of their fishing group he was rarely ever at home, opting to spend time outside with friends instead. He still helped Hali bake something at least once a week, but his appetite had grown so much over the past year that they had to increase the amounts of everything they baked just to ensure they would have enough to share at camp. Usually she missed Ronan's presence, but today she was relieved of his absence. Hali didn't need anyone else witnessing the mess she had become.

Marilla stood in the kitchen, holding a newly brewed cup of coffee as she looked up to see Hali approach.

"Feeling better?" Marilla asked.

"I am, thank you."

"Did you want to talk about it?"

The question alone left Hali's eyes stinging with fresh tears. She did want to talk, but not about seeing her parents. Steeling herself, she asked, "Marilla, how did you know I was at the barrier today? I wasn't near where you fish."

"I didn't. Cas did."

Hali's eyebrows rose.

"While we were fishing, he said he needed to check something out and handed me his three full skewers," Marilla continued. "I didn't even get a chance to ask him what before he swam off. A little later when we brought the fish in, I found him sitting on the shore brooding. When I asked him where he swam off to, he said he saw you swimming to the barrier. He mumbled something about you preferring death over life on the Eyes' Land. I don't think he meant for me to hear him, because when I asked what he meant he looked a little guilty, but then he told me about your incident a year ago with the barrier. To be fair, I don't think he wanted to tell me, but I was pretty persistent, and he knew I wasn't going to let it go. I still don't know how he spotted you from that far away; like you said, we weren't even close, and we were divided by an area thick with kelp. Guess he just has better eyes than the rest of us."

Hali grimaced, unsure of what to make of what Marilla was telling her, but not really in the mindset to continue talking about it. Changing the subject, she glanced at the clock and said, "Lunch should be ready soon."

"I can bring a plate back for you if you're not up to being around everyone right now," Marilla offered.

Hali was relieved that Marilla wasn't pushing the conversation any further. "No, I'll be all right," she lied. The last thing Hali wanted to do was eat lunch with all the Anchors, but she knew if she wasn't at lunch, there would be questions later. Anchors took roll in their heads at each meal, and any missing Anchor was fair game for gossip. Hali knew better than to put herself in a position to be a topic of conversation, and not showing up for a meal was practically a guaranteed slot on their list of discussion topics. For Hali, it was easier just to suck it up and go.

Hali walked into camp apprehensive of what she would say to Cas. She had to keep telling herself that she did nothing wrong—that Cas should be the one nervous, not her—but the reminders did little in easing her anxiousness.

"Is your head feelin' better, Hali?" Fisk asked, as she approached the table with dinnerware.

"Yes, thank you," Hali answered.

Fisk continued, without any prompting, "Cas was here just a few minutes ago. I think he had a *stubborn* headache himself. Never knew that boy to be one to get many headaches though. Must be the changin' weather and such. He was in a big ol' hurry to get his lunch and go. But I'm glad to see that you're recovered, Hali, maybe there's some hope for Cas yet."

Marilla glared at Fisk.

Hali nodded, smiling faintly, and said, "Maybe there is," before walking off to find a table. Cas's absence settled her nerves slightly until she thought about it and became annoyed. As irritated as she was that he had lashed out at her in the water, she was willing to put her feelings aside so they didn't become gossip for the Anchors looking for a source of entertainment. Hali looked at her plate, suddenly not hungry. But she knew better than to not eat—Anchors needed every calorie they were offered.

She maneuvered through the tables as her day replayed in her head. Her mind was like a tangled ball of yarn— knotted in sadness, anger, and disappointment. Not only was Hali battling her own emotions, she had the added bonus of having those same emotions mirrored back at her by each person she had encountered that day. Sadness etched her parents' faces with wrinkles that hadn't been there a year before; anger strained every muscle and tendon from Cas's stomach to his face; and disappointment— stemmed from not disclosing what she had experienced at the barrier a year ago—pulled Marilla's usually pleasant appearance into a slight frown. Of all the unnerving events that had taken place that day, what Hali couldn't understand was why Cas—someone she had spent the past year getting to know—thought she had a death wish? Sure, she had been near the barrier when she wasn't supposed to be, but why had his mind gone there? For the life of her she couldn't comprehend why he chose to get mad at her instead of talking to her first and why he refused to talk with her now? The entire day had been nothing but missed connections, miscommunication, and mistakes and on top of everything else, she learned firsthand how terrifying it actually was to be sought out by a sea creature.

24

THE IMPOSTER

As Hali searched for a table, she found Delphia sitting alone, looking glum. It was such a rare sighting to see Delphia without Carmya, that Hali had almost walked past her table without recognizing her.

Stopping in her tracks, she asked, "Hey Delph, where's Carmya?"

Delphia looked up at Hali. "On a walk ... with Kai," she answered, scooting fish around her plate with a fork, aimlessly.

Hali sat down at the table, forgetting her own problems for the moment, as she took in Delphia's pitiful state. She struggled with how to respond to Delphia's plight, feeling both concerned and entertained, now that she knew Delphia's issue wasn't anything too serious.

"Oh," was all Hali could come up with to say.

"I'm not upset. Really. I'm happy for the two of them."

Hali smiled slightly, tilting her head towards Delphia. "I can tell, you are just radiating with happiness."

Delphia huffed out a lazy laugh, rolling her eyes and

shaking her head. "No, really I am. I'm happy that Kai is finally coming around and maturing," she said through gritted teeth.

"But?"

Reluctantly, Delphia continued, "I just didn't think when he did, I would lose my best friend in the process. I've never seen Carmya so happy, but I just don't see why everyone is in a rush to grow up in the first place. I think I liked Kai better when he was unaware." Delphia abandoned her lunch and began playing with the ends of her hair in deep thought. "Am I being selfish?"

Hali's mouth drew up in an understanding smile, realizing how similar she was to Delphia. Though she had a nagging suspicion that Delphia's concerns weren't just about Carmya's and Kai's budding relationship, but of something deeper.

"No, you're not selfish. You just miss Carmya. But you and Carmya will always be friends," Hali reassured.

"But it won't be the same again. Everyone will pair up and become their own family with responsibilities. Sure, Carmya and I will remain friends, but it will never be like it was."

Hali wasn't sure what to say to that. No words of comfort came to mind, and she felt out of her realm discussing a topic to which she had little experience on either Emerald Cove or the Eyes' Land. Her own encounter with the sea creature had been a mortifying lesson on the outcome of signals she wished to never experience again. With her own mind still jolted, she said little, hoping Delphia only needed her ears, not her words. Luckily for Hali, that seemed to be the case.

"And Kai and Carmya have already sealed their link, so

it's a done deal now. Their connection is solid and unbreakable."

Hali scowled, confused by the latest development. "Sealed? How does the link get sealed?"

Delphia's eyebrows furrowed. "A kiss," she rushed out, as if saying the words gave weight to a truth she didn't want to believe. "What I don't understand, is the two already knew they were linked, so what was the rush? Why couldn't they have waited? If two people decide to not seal the link immediately, the pull to the other person doesn't go away. It's not like any of us can go anywhere."

Hali hadn't wanted to interrupt Delphia's stewing, or speak at all on the subject, but the new information sparked a question of her own. "Delphia, I know Carmya had said that she knew she was linked to Kai because she didn't mind him anymore, like green beans, but do guys emit signals the same way as girls?"

That afternoon, Hali had been so preoccupied by seeing her parents' boat, she hadn't considered she might truly be in her fertile time. Though even if she had been aware, it wouldn't have changed her reaction. Her attempt to speak to them had not gone well but seeing them made it all worth it. Even if that meant she had nightmares of the sea creature's slimy arms wrapped around her waist for the rest of her life.

The memory made Hali shudder. During their interaction, Hali wanted to get away desperately, but her skin had buzzed with a sensation unrelated to her lawpnies. Despite the feeling being subtle, it terrified Hali to think that she might actually be linked to the sea creature. She hadn't felt specifically drawn to him as he held her, but the tingle confounded her, nonetheless.

Marilla had told Hali that sea creatures cared little about

compatibility when they sensed a fertile signal. Hali only hoped it was true in her case.

The incident had her rubbing away at the invisible impressions his fingertips left on her wrists a majority of the afternoon. For some reason, her repulsion towards him comforted her. Green beans still held no appeal in Hali's eyes and that had to be a good sign.

Delphia absentmindedly braided her hair, glancing from her brunette braid to Hali as she spoke. "I've never experienced any of it so I can't tell you firsthand, but I hear for guys it's like a current running through their bodies. At least that's what Kai says." Delphia stopped braiding her hair briefly and pretended to gag. Hali laughed and shook her head at Delphia's dramatics. Delphia smirked in response, carrying on with her braid and explanation. "But for women the pull is different. I heard my mom talk about it once, but I was too young to really remember most of it. I do remember her saying that she was drawn to my dad's right ear."

"His right ear? As opposed to his left one?" Hali joked.

Delphia giggled, her mood lightening up from when Hali first sat down at the table. "I know it sounds crazy. My dad had a little notch at the top of his right ear. He snagged it against a rock in the water when he was a kid, well before the Eyes' Land was here. He had it stitched up, but there was always a little slice taken out of the top where it healed. My mom, for whatever reason, was drawn to that."

Hali laughed. "Good thing for you then."

"I guess so," Delphia smiled, but her eyes held a hint of sadness. "Thanks, Hali."

"For what?" Hali asked. "I didn't do anything."

"You did, though. You listened. It helped me put things

into perspective. I saw how happy my parents were before the Eye attack and I, of all people, should know that life is too short. If Kai has finally figured out how amazing Carmya is, I'm not going to stand in their way. I want them to be happy."

"I know I'm not Carmya, but you can always hang out with me, too. I'm around."

Delphia smiled coyly. "Not for long."

Now it was Hali's turn to furrow her brows. "Even if we escape the Eyes' Land, I'd still want to hang out with you, Delphia."

"That's not what I meant, Hali."

"Then what did you mean?"

"I just mean ... I'd like to enjoy one friend for a little while longer before she is too *in love* to hang out with me anymore."

"Ugh," Hali groaned, cringing with embarrassment. Besides Cas, Hali thought she had escaped her encounter with the sea creature without any other witnesses, but apparently, she had been wrong. "You saw? I'm not sure if I'll ever get back in the water again after today. I guess it could have been worse; at least the sea creature didn't follow me out to land." Then Hali muttered, almost to herself, "He'd have to be conscious to do that."

Delphia examined Hali thoughtfully, ruminating inwardly, with a puzzled expression gracing her face. Several seconds passed between the two, before Delphia said, "That explains why Cas was so mad."

Hali blew out a breath. "That makes two of us."

Delphia smirked, mischievously.

"What is that look, Delphia?"

"I don't have a look," she lied.

"Oh, but you do. I'm scarred for life after what happened today and you are just sitting over there, judging and laughing at me in your head."

"I promise I'm not judging you at all, laughing, yes, but not judging."

As Delphia finished braiding her hair, a spark of energy lit her eyes, restoring her to her usual happy state. "Do you want to pick apples for a pie? We could also make some apple muffins for breakfast, too."

Hali raised her eyebrows at the idea, which required walking near the shore, where she feared the sea creature she had escaped, still waited for her. Sensing Hali's apprehension, Delphia clarified, "The sea creatures will leave you alone. They can't pick up your signal unless you're in the water."

Hali hesitated before nodding in agreement.

Thirty minutes later, they had a sack of apples draped around their shoulders, walking a safe distance away from the shore.

"Have you ever had a sea creature find you in the water?" Hali asked, adjusting the sack of apples on her shoulder.

"Twice," Delphia's face soured, while her shoulders shook with the heebie-jeebies. "Once when I was only fourteen, which was alarming, and once when I was seventeen, which was also alarming but I was better prepared to handle it then. But don't tell Carmya, she'd never let me live it down, especially since I've given her such a hard time about her encounter."

"I won't," Hali promised. "How did you get away each time?"

"By a stroke of luck the first time. The sea creature wrapped his arms around my waist, and as I brought my arms up to push him away, I sneezed instead, elbowing him right in his eye. He released me immediately, and I took the opportunity to swim away as fast as I could. The second time I knew what worked, and just poked him in the eyes, no sneeze needed."

"Seriously?" Hali laughed.

"Seriously," Delphia nodded proudly. "Thank goodness, too, because there was no one around to come to my rescue." Delphia nudged Hali's arm with her elbow in jest.

"Hey, I would have saved myself."

"Really?" Delphia crossed her arms. "How?"

"I have some tricks, too. Maybe I would have yawned and bit his ear. My yawns can be pretty aggressive."

Delphia shook her head. "Well, I'm glad you didn't have to resort to that ... for your sake more than the sea creature's."

The two girls, not quite ready to be considered women, walked back to camp, laughing and kicking up sand as they did. Hali had forgotten all about her troubles, until she glanced in Mr. Gruff's direction and almost stopped dead in her tracks. Hali couldn't believe what she was witnessing. Water rushed across his bare feet as he sat working on his stump—his feet remained, unchanged.

Why doesn't he have fins?

She watched on, her eyes straining, squinting, then widening to get a better look. He continued shaving as water moved over his feet, over and over again as if it was normal.

Maybe it was.

The entire year that Hali had been on the Eyes' Land, she had never seen him change into a merman.

How had no one ever questioned it?

Hali's eyes had seen clearly and Delphia was none the wiser of Hali's covert inspection as they walked side by side.

Urgency to get Delphia back to camp swept over her.

She needed to investigate how this was possible and Delphia couldn't be with her when she did.

"You all right?" Delphia asked warily. "What are you staring at?" she followed Hali's gaze, looking back and forth between Hali and Mr. Gruff.

"I'm fine," Hali said quickly, bringing Delphia's attention back to her. "I just feel bad for him, he's always shaving branches."

Delphia shrugged, obliviously. "I do, too. Even though no one asked him to. It's just something he's always done. Either way, it's very helpful that he does otherwise we would all have to chip in and make our own skewers before we fished."

Changing the subject, Hali raised her bag of reddish-yellow apples, that resembled the color of the sky when the sun made its descent on the western hemisphere, and asked, "Ready to get some baking done?"

"I sure am!" Delphia exclaimed, already forgetting about Mr. Gruff.

"I'll race you," Hali challenged.

After hours of baking in Delphia's kitchen, Delphia's mood improved significantly from when Hali first found her that afternoon. The two shared companionable silence most of the time they baked, but both for different reasons. Delphia remained focused on the baking tasks at hand, while Hali contemplated the various possibilities Mr. Gruff's feet didn't turn to fins—growing antsier every second she was stuck in the kitchen.

They had to bake pies of all things, Hali thought.

The pie dough on its own typically required four hours to chill in the refrigerator. But using Delphia's impatience in her favor, Hali easily convinced her that the dough was ready at the two-hour mark. Despite desperately working to get back down to the shore before dinner, the pie baking took until it was time to go, leaving Hali no time to visit Mr. Gruff.

Walking into camp, arms full of pies, stacked carefully one on top of the other, Mamie strolled up beside them.

"What did you girls bake today?"

"Apple pies," Delphia announced proudly.

"Mmm mmm, I just love when you all make apple pies. I think I like those just a little better than the cookies." Mamie's smile twisted into a cringe as she watched them carefully balance their stacks. "I'd offer to help carry some, but I'm not sure I can grab a few without knocking them all down."

"Hali and I got a handle on it, we only have a little ways to walk anyway," Delphia assured with a smile. "We have apple muffins ready for breakfast tomorrow morning, too."

"Oooooh, you girls were busy. Just think Hali, if you hadn't come along, we would have all stayed skinny."

Hali and Delphia laughed cautiously while they steadied their stacks.

"We've graduated from skinny to lean," Delphia added.

"Maybe this time next year we will be up to rotund," Mamie patted her stomach.

"We can dream."

Hali shook her head, smiling at their banter, while doing her best not to drop all the pies she was carrying to the ground.

When they finally reached the tables, Hali was relieved

to set her stack of pies down. Scanning camp, she spotted Cas sitting at a table with Fisk, Marilla, and Ronan talking and laughing as they ate. A flash of annoyance snaked through her skin as she watched him carry on a conversation with the others, completely unaffected by his earlier behavior.

"Hali, did you hear me?" Delphia asked.

Distracted, Hali uttered, "Hmm?"

"I guess not," Delphia grinned, her brown eyes illuminated with the descending sun. "I said, are you ready to get some dinner, so we can finally dig into our pies?"

"Of course," Hali answered, nodding her head a little too emphatically for the question. But Mamie saw right through her, smiling at her suspiciously, then glancing back and forth between Cas's table and Hali. Hali missed a lot of things about her old life. But one thing she missed the most was not having her every move scrutinized. As someone who relished autonomy, it was a very frustrating facet of life on the Eyes' Land.

Thankfully, Mamie kept her thoughts to herself as they plated their dinners.

"There is some room at Marilla's table," Delphia announced.

Fantastic.

Delphia walked to the table, waiting for no answer, with Hali and Mamie obediently following. Mamie smirked at Hali, but Hali quickly looked away, like she hadn't noticed. Mamie was enjoying Hali's discomfort all too much. Hali wanted to run, breathe, and escape curious eyes. Sitting felt like a surrender—a silent apology she didn't think she owed to Cas. But running would be cowardly, like she had been in the wrong. The blade sliced just as sharp on both sides.

Before her mind could make a decision, she found that

her legs already had. She sat on the opposite side and end of the table as Cas, being as far from him as she could. Ronan sat on her right with Marilla and Fisk next to him. Directly opposite of her was Mamie, then Delphia in the center, then Cas.

"What's for dessert?" Ronan blurted out.

"Hali and I made apple pies and there are some apple muffins to add to breakfast," Delphia answered. Turning her attention to Cas, she asked, "When are you going to cave and try a dessert? You have no idea what you are missing out on."

Acid rolled in Hali's stomach at the mention of dessert, as if she had consumed too many. No one on the Eyes' Land, besides Hali, knew the sacrifices Cas made monthly to satisfy their culinary desires. But ever since the vote on increasing the use of baking supplies had gone through, Cas hadn't complained once about their overuse, despite never eating any of it. His self-discipline only added to Hali's guilt. More than once she had wished he'd eat a baked good, if for no other reason than to assuage her own conscience. But he never did.

"Can't miss what you've never had," Cas said, taking a bite of fish. The muscle in his jaw twitched as he chewed, his eyes landing on no one as he looked past Fisk sitting directly across from him. Hali's mood turned somber, placating any appetite she had brought to dinner. The acid that rolled in her stomach moments before left a hollow space. Cas resumed eating like his words didn't have a hidden meaning. But after spending time with him for the past year, Hali could tell he was upset.

She didn't care if he was mad, she lied to herself.

Delphia shrugged at his answer, before asking, "Why would you assume you'd ever have to give up desserts in the first place? I sure don't plan on it." Cas drew another bite of fish to his mouth, appearing indifferent to Delphia's question, except for the twitch in his jaw that projected out, unrelated to chewing. Hali tried hard to remember that Delphia couldn't be held accountable for information she didn't know. Cas and Delphia were having two completely different conversations.

When Cas finished his bite, he huffed out a humorless laugh. "The enchanters haven't agreed to continue supplying us forever. I don't want to get attached to anything that can be ripped away, without any warning."

Fisk shook his head. "So serious boy. There's no joy to be had in a life lived that way. Eat the dang pie. You're just as likely to regret never havin' any as you're to miss it if it goes away.

"Before the Eyes' Land, when I was just a boy not much younger than Ronan, I'd ride my bike in the summers from sunup to sundown. And you know what? I'm not sittin' my days away thinkin', I wish I'd never road that darn bike, since now I'll never git to ride it again. Nope. I remember the sun in my face, frecklin' me all to heck on those hot, humid summers and not havin' myself a care in the world. Now that's really livin'. I wouldn't take those days back for nothin'. I'm not sayin' there ain't some pain that goes with the memories, but there was some happiness first. Not havin' any pain means you probably have never had any true happiness and that would be the real tragedy."

The table went quiet for several moments after Fisk's speech.

"If I could do life over, I'd probably skip learning to ride a bike," Mamie added, the eyes at the table shifted from Fisk to Mamie as the conversation took another turn. "Who would have thought sitting between two wheels could break so many bones."

Everyone besides Cas chuckled. He rose from the table, empty plate in hand, nodding a wordless farewell to everyone.

When he was out of earshot Marilla turned to Hali, whispering, "You need to talk to him."

"What? Why?" anger flared in Hali's chest at the demand.

"Because you know why. Now I'm not saying Cas is right. He's stubborn and pig headed at times, but also loyal and protective of those he cares about. If he feels betrayed in any way, he shuts down and is hard to reason with." Marilla paused, allowing Hali time to think on what she said. Hali pushed her food around her plate in contemplation, offering Marilla no assurances she would heed her order. Marilla changed her approach, deferring to blunt tactics. "One of you needs to be the bigger person and it looks like the bigger person needs to be you this time."

This time? Hali thought. *When would it ever be Cas's time?*

The rest of the table eyed her, awaiting a response. Hali wasn't even sure why Marilla had bothered whispering.

"Okay," was the only answer Hali offered, still looking down at her plate to avoid their invasive stares.

"Do you want me to go with you?" Ronan offered, sweetly. He was a boy destined to be as kind and pragmatic as his mother, surpassing the maturity of boy-men more than a decade older than him.

The grip of anger on Hali's heart loosened the slightest bit at Ronan's genuineness. "Thank you, Ronan, but I will go. Cas doesn't scare me." Ronan acquiesced with a nod. Hali stood up, tired of the expectant stares and exited the party.

Weaving through the tables, Hali never saw Cas. So, she decided to put her peace-making mission on hold. Instead, she used the opportunity to sneak off to the shore to find Mr. Gruff. Nerves plagued her as she moved swiftly into the woods. Her heart galloped in her chest at her sneakiness. She glanced backwards as she moved forward, making sure she wasn't being followed. Branches and leaves scratched at her skin like uninvited fingernails as she passed. The small invasions made her jump at every touch. Emerging from the woods, a figure sat in her peripheral, on her left, in the space where the sand began, and the woods ended.

Cas.

They both stared at each other for a moment before Hali spoke.

"Hey."

Cas lifted his head, giving the smallest of greetings, obviously not ready to give up his grudge.

Mr. Gruff would have to wait.

Hali sat down beside him, staring at his scar. She blushed when she realized what she was doing. Hoping that Cas didn't notice, she quickly turned, peering out at the ocean. She organized her thoughts, afraid that even the truth wouldn't do any good in assuaging his anger. She inhaled, letting out a slow exhale. Her attempt at being the bigger person, had her feeling small.

For the sake of harmony and unity, she told herself.

It was the mantra the Anchors lived and breathed. She would have never bothered explaining her actions to a stubborn recipient in her old life, there wouldn't have been a need. Her parents and Camille hardly ever challenged her motives and they were the only few people she cared about enough to worry what opinion they had of her. But as she was learning, that was no longer true. Cas had weaseled his way into the small, exclusive club.

Hali sighed. "I had no intention of going out in the water today."

Cas stayed quiet, unmoving, but his eyes moved from the ocean the slightest bit, so Hali knew she had his attention. Hali continued, "After I skewered my last fish, I saw a boat out in the water. Not just any boat—my parents' boat."

Cas turned to her, surprise etched into his features, but he still didn't speak. Hali stared out into the ocean as she recounted the details, attempting to keep her composure as she tore at the fresh scab of the memory.

"They crossed over the barrier and I yelled for them. But they couldn't hear me. They were gone not long after they came and then the sea creature showed up." Hali trailed off; the embarrassment still fresh. "You know the rest." A painful knot welled in Hali's throat, leaving her unable to swallow. They both sat there for several moments, not speaking, the approaching and retreating of the waves the only sound.

Hali pinched grains of sand between her fingers, distracting herself from her bobbing throat. Suddenly, Cas took her left hand in his right, intertwining their fingers and resting them in the sand. The act was so innocent, yet Hali flushed at the newness of it. She hadn't held hands with anyone since playing "Ring Around the Rosie" in elementary school, but this was different. Hali was sure Cas only held her hand out of compassion, but his intent to comfort her produced the opposite effect.

They sat long enough to see the sky transformed into darkening swatches of oranges and pinks. Cas's thumb moved gently along Hali's thumb, back and forth, and Hali struggled to keep the lawpnies at bay while she basked in Cas's affection.

Cas finally spoke after what felt like an hour of sitting hand in hand. "I'm sorry, Hali. When I saw you out there, I just assumed the worst. And then when I got to you ... it doesn't matter, I was wrong."

Hali smiled faintly. "You are forgiven." Cas gave Hali's hand a quick squeeze, then turned his attention back to the ocean. Turmoil brewed in his eyes.

"Cas, what's wrong?" Hali asked.

He swallowed, then asked, "What happens if you break the barrier, Hali? What happens to the Eyes' Land and everyone here?"

Cas's question surprised Hali and his vulnerability gutted her, as she realized that leaving the Eyes' Land to Cas, was similar to Hali's arrival: foreign and terrifying. Hali had known all along where she would go once the barrier was broken, but she hadn't considered where the rest of the Anchors would end up. But Cas had.

Life anywhere was unpredictable at best. The Eyes' Land was no different. Hali couldn't provide any assurances of their well-being on the Eyes' Land, so how could she make any promises outside of it?

"I don't know," she uttered.

Cas glared at Hali in disbelief, irritation returning to his features. "Well, don't you think you should, before you go and rip the homes away from all of the Anchors?" Cas ripped his hand away from Hali's and came to a standing position.

Hali mirrored Cas's movements, just as annoyed. "Where is this coming from, Cas? I thought we were on the same page with this. You know as well as I do that as long as the Eyes' Land exists, the Eyes will have control. It's called the Eyes' Land for a reason," Hali repeated the words Cas had said to her just a year before.

Cas shook his head. "We've fought them once, we can do it again."

Hali's mouth fell as she stared at Cas in disbelief. "Cas, you can't really want to be trapped here forever. Think about what you're saying."

Cas wouldn't look at Hali, instead, he stared out at the wide ocean, his expression hard as his lips pressed into a line of stubbornness. He shrugged, detached and apathetic to the validity of her questions.

Hali sighed. "Cas, I can understand that it's scary to change everything you know. I know all about that. But change isn't a bad thing."

She couldn't believe her own words.

"It's easy for you to say. You have a whole other life to go back to. A home."

"It's not easy for me to say, Cas. And if and when we break the barrier, you won't be alone afterwards. We will all be in this together. We can all help each other."

Cas scoffed. "You mean the rest of us will all help each other while you run back home to your parents, so you can forget all about the Eyes' Land and the past year."

Anger festered under her skin. Hali struggled to keep her lawpnies contained. She moved herself into the path of Cas's stare, glaring back into his eyes. "Forget! Are you kidding me right now?"

"Don't pretend that's not what would happen," he challenged. "You have a home to go back to, the rest of us don't. Are we supposed to stay in the water and become sea creatures? How do you plan on explaining to mortals the sudden arrival of hundreds of Anchors showing up to Emerald Cove? How am I supposed to create housing on land that is owned by someone else? Have you thought of any of these details, Hali?"

Despite Cas's many valid points, Hali couldn't understand why he was only bringing them up now and why he was so furious with her. It's not like she had created the barrier.

And what was wrong with her wanting to go home? Where did Cas expect her to go?

"So, you'd rather stay here forever, trapped, at the mercy of the Eyes whenever they should decide they want to pay a visit?"

Cas said nothing to Hali's question.

"What happens when they start flaying babies and children?"

Cas looked away from her again, grimacing. His arms crossed against his chest, tense and activated at Hali's suggestion.

Letting the idea sink into Cas's hard head, Hali turned towards the water. Mr. Gruff's hunched silhouette sat against the background of the changing sky.

"You know it's only a matter of time until they come back," she said softly. "The longer they are away, the more prepared they will be."

Cas ran his hands through his hair, turning further away from Hali, but he didn't leave.

"There is something else I need to tell you."

Cas turned back around to face Hali, his face filled with trepidation.

"I don't think Mr. Gruff is a merman at all," she stated. Cas's eyes widened, urging Hali on. "When I was walking back from picking apples with Delphia earlier today, I noticed the water rolling over his feet, but they didn't change into fins."

Without a word, Cas stalked off in Mr. Gruff's direction. Hali chased after him. "What are you going to do?"

"I'm going to see what he is for myself."

As they approached, Mr. Gruff shaved branches, aloof to their presence. A pile of skewers, most likely intended for tomorrow's breakfast, sat next to him, but to the side of that were flatter pieces, shaved smoothly. The flatter pieces were not fit to be used as skewers or weapons—just like the two-by-fours she noticed beside him a year ago hadn't been. Cas and Hali looked at each other, both appearing to share the same thought. The tide was low and Mr. Gruff's feet sat in dry sand with no threat of water lapping over them. He was positioned closer to the shore-side of the trunk than he had been when Hali saw him earlier. Impatient, Cas scooped up water with his hands and threw it onto Mr. Gruff's feet and legs.

Nothing.

Cas did it several more times. His pace grew more frantic at each attempt, his aim less accurate.

Finally, Hali wrapped her arms around one of Cas's to pull him away.

Mr. Gruff had stopped working during Cas's experiment, his shoulder length hair hung in wet tendrils. Mr. Gruff's eyes were a golden brown that Hali imagined were once alive and vibrant, but now appeared bloodshot, murky, and weathered in a way that only a difficult life could produce.

"What are you?" Cas demanded.

Mr. Gruff stared Cas down as Hali tried adding the information up in her head. Unlike Cas she had had the entire afternoon of baking to mull over the possibilities. Ones she hadn't had a chance to share with Cas, but she had her suspicions.

"I am nothing anymore," Mr. Gruff muttered. His voice

cracked, sounding dry and harsh from years of not speaking. He coughed immediately after.

Once his coughing fit ceased, Hali passed a furtive glance Cas's way, then brought her attention back to Mr. Gruff.

"Rowina?"

25

A PROMISE

CAS STEPPED BACK, releasing himself from Hali's hold, disbelief striking his features like a lightning bolt. He looked back and forth between Hali and Mr. Gruff, unsure of what to make of either of them.

"Who sent you?" Cas demanded, his tone deep and controlled. Changing into the leader he was expected to be on the Eyes' Land whenever a threat arose. It was the same role he took on the day Hali had arrived. His purpose was the same then as it was now, to protect the Anchors at all costs from outsiders. It had been over a year since Hali had seen that side of Cas, she almost forgot it existed.

Mr. Gruff glared at Cas apathetically picking up a shell and branch to resume his work. Cas's fists clenched and his forearms bulged at Mr. Gruff's indifference, revealing a tangle of muscles and tendons. Tension buzzed in the air that Hali could physically feel. Reacting on instinct alone, she jumped in front of Cas, breaking his death stare and inevitable slew of rage. Her palm landed on his chest. Cas peered down at the hand splayed across his heart, his head tilted, and his expression widened with the slightest hint of shock, before looking at Hali. Suddenly aware, Hali pulled her eyes and hand away, rubbing her palm against the cloth of her dress nervously.

Summoning her courage, she glanced back up at Cas, who now peered at her with curiosity. "You won't get anything useful from him that way," she whispered. "He's had nineteen years' experience of not answering to anyone. Let me try to talk to him and see what I can find out."

Cas sighed before reluctantly nodding his head in agreement.

Hali walked towards Mr. Gruff, who had retreated back to his log when she had convened with Cas. She took a seat on the dry sand near him, while he continued working like no altercation had taken place.

"I'm Hali. My birth mother was Arcelia and my birth father was Murchadh. Did you know who they were?"

Coils of wet hair hung in Mr. Gruff's eyes as he shaved the branch in the methodical pace he shaved all the branches.

Swish Swish.

"Yes," he uttered without stopping.

A wave of nervous excitement swept through Hali as she hovered on the brink of an answer to her hunch. Though Mr. Gruff hadn't officially admitted to being Rowina, Hali had a strong inkling her guess was right. With Rowina, it became possible to break the spell.

"Are you Rowina?"

Irritated, Mr. Gruff stopped working, peering down at Hali as he blew out a breath. "You know the answer already. There is no apology I can offer you that will undo any of *this* —" he waved the branch he was shaving through the air. "It won't bring your parents back and it won't undo your being captured and brought here."

"I'm not looking for an apology. I think you can help break the spell that holds the barrier in place."

Mr. Gruff let out a calloused laugh that went from dry to gurgly to full blown hacking, sounding like a car engine about to explode. Hali stood up from the sand, because it felt a lot less heartless than sitting down and watching him struggle to breath, despite her ability to help him being just as ineffective either way. She didn't even have water to offer him. Suddenly, Cas was by her side, watching Mr. Gruff like his coughing fit had happened out of some ulterior motive, and not the nineteen years his voice hadn't been used. Mr. Gruff rolled his eyes at Cas's presence, exasperated, as he regained control of his coughing. He cleared his throat once more for good measure, before responding to Hali.

"I don't know if you've noticed, but I don't have any powers left. Haven't had any for a long time. The only helpful contribution I've made in my life since coming here is sharpening branches into little points. Any attempts I've made to be useful have always resulted in failure. So, you see, I am of no use to anyone."

"Are we supposed to feel sorry for you?" Cas chimed in. Hali wished he hadn't. They needed Mr. Guff ... or Rowina.

"But you can be useful," Hali interrupted, her words hurried like a car salesman about to lose a potential customer. "You don't need to have powers to help break the spell. You just need to be at the wall with me, since I carry the blood of Arcelia, and I technically have Cillian's blood running through me since Murchadh was Cillian's brother. Together, you and I have the power to break the spell." Hali hoped, more than knew for certain, that was all that was needed to break the barrier.

"I may not have powers anymore, but I know how spells work, child. What you are not understanding is that when the spell unravels it will draw from the sources of the original spell, but it will also need to pull power from the sources to make it work."

"What does that mean?" Cas crossed his arms, suspiciously.

Mr. Gruff didn't even glance at Cas but kept talking to Hali like he wasn't there. "It means that Hali's magic will be sucked out of her, weakening her—just like Arcelia's had by Cillian. And we all know how that turned out."

The lawpnies bubbled on the surface of Hali's skin before she could control them. Sadness briefly flitted across Mr. Gruff's eyes at the sight of the little lights. If Hali hadn't been looking at Mr. Gruff at that exact moment, she would have missed the brief flash of sorrow that filled his eyes. Whether the grief stemmed from losing his own magic all those years ago or Hali's predicament, she really wasn't sure.

He cleared his throat again. "So, you see, it can't be done. I already have your mother's and father's deaths on my hands. I will not add yours to my list of repentance."

Hali stared at him dumbstruck as her lawpnies proceeded to swim around her. Anxiousness hadn't allowed her the control to reign the lawpnies back into herself that she normally possessed. Her thoughts flittered and her concentration was shot. The answer she had been waiting for for over a year sat right in front of her and she couldn't do anything with it.

Or maybe she could.

"Hali, no," Cas interrupted, as if reading her mind.

Hali turned her gaze at him, guiltily, as he scrutinized her. "What?" she asked, even though she knew what Cas was thinking. His awareness caused her lawpnies to surge. She closed her eyes, willing the lawpnies to retreat, needing to feel some sense of control over the situation.

"You're still thinking about doing it, even after everything you've been told," Cas accused.

Ignoring Cas's accurate judgement, she turned her attention back to Mr. Gruff. "Are you sure it would kill me?"

Cas scoffed beside her, but she chose to ignore him. She had waited too long for this opportunity to walk away with stones unturned.

Mr. Gruff nodded. "Like I said, I already have two deaths on my hands, I will not be responsible for another. Life on the Eyes' Land hasn't been easy, but it is more than I deserve. If there is nothing left to discuss, I need to get back to my work."

And just like that, the flicker of hope Hali had nursed all afternoon was out before it could even become a flame. Mr. Gruff resumed his tireless work, shut off from any further conversation. He was an impenetrable wall once again. Unless Hali could figure out a way to break the spell without dying in the process, arguing the matter further would be useless.

With nothing left to say, Hali walked away, defeated. Cas followed, stealing glances at her as they walked side by side. Luckily, he didn't lecture her, but Hali could sense he was mulling over something and was either too afraid to vocalize it or afraid of her response. Probably both.

"Is it so bad here, Hali?" he finally asked.

She said nothing at first, opting to stare down the pine trees just in front of her, flustered. For the past year the third key to break the barrier had sat right in front of her, shaving branches. She had been clueless. But it didn't matter either way, since she couldn't do anything with the information. The day had been one disappointment after another.

"I know it's not what you are used to, and you miss your

parents, but is it so bad that you would sacrifice your own life for it?" Cas tried to reason.

She considered his point, and she considered hers. The information formed a twisted web in her brain, creating connections that led to dead ends and more uncertainty.

What did she want? If she died in the process, would it have even mattered that she tried to escape the Eyes' Land? Would her parents want her to if they knew the risks?

She wasn't ready to give up, but she didn't have a death wish either. Hali allowed her head to turn away from the trees and her eyes to float up to Cas's. He looked sad, which made Hali feel even worse. He was a person that had known loss from a young age. A loss that no child should ever have to experience. It's not that she had forgotten about his trials as a young boy with the Eyes, but it was the first time she had noticed how much it impacted him.

Cas hadn't become a leader out of a desire to be important. He was a leader out of some inherent responsibility he had put on himself to protect those he cared about. The full moon ritual was a prime example of this fact. Marilla had spoken of his loyalty just at dinner—but Hali had been too mad at him to hear it then. But now she could *see* what Marilla had been talking about. Cas was worried about Hali sacrificing her life to the barrier, just as he would be for any Anchor who thought about attempting the same stunt.

Hali grabbed his hand, feeling responsible for the agony she saw on his face. Thinking of sacrificing herself wasn't a thought Hali took lightly, but seeing Cas hurt from the idea bothered her just as much. If she stayed, her parents would never know what happened to her. If she broke the barrier, but died in the process, she would have to hope that someone would relay her story to her parents. She assumed it would provide better closure than a memorial by sea had.

But even still, Hali wasn't sure her parents would believe a random messenger, and Neilan had already skirted the topic when she had brought it up to him in the woods a year ago.

Hali squeezed Cas's hand as tears threatened to escape her eyes. Cas remained intent on her, waiting for her to speak.

"I'm not trying to break the barrier because I'm unhappy here. I want to break the barrier because I want my guilt to stop reminding me when I'm content. Every time I experience any happiness here, I know that my parents are just across the water, worried about me. And after seeing them ..." Hali exhaled, desperate to gain some semblance of composure. They had made it to the trees. "What would that make me, Cas?" Hali wiped her tears with the back of her free hand. "I'll tell you. It would make me the most selfish daughter there ever was."

Cas removed his hand from hers, turned her to him and grabbed both of her shoulders, his arms outstretched as he leveled his eyes to hers. "Hali, you are a lot of things, but selfish isn't one of them."

Hali scoffed, shaking her head as more tears fell.

"Hali, look at me."

Watery and bloodshot, her eyes struggled to peer back at him.

"I'm serious," he persisted. "Promise me you won't try to break the spell."

"It's not like I can without Mr. Gruff's help," she reasoned.

He tilted his head and gave her a quizzical look, saying, "Promise me anyway."

With his blue eyes staring into her hazel ones, Hali conceded with a nod.

"I want to hear you say, you promise."

Hali rolled her eyes. "Really?" Cas's glare never wavered. Hali sighed. "Okay. I promise."

His face softened and he let go of her shoulders. "Good."

"You need to make a promise to me now."

Curious, Cas's eyebrows rose. "What's that?"

"You need to promise to not get mad at me anymore before you hear my side of things. You owe me that."

"And why do I owe you that?" he grinned, impishly.

"Because I'm your friend and I would extend you the same courtesy. You have a knack at jumping to conclusions and shutting me out."

Cas appeared perplexed. "When have I shut you out?"

Hali chuckled at what she thought was Cas's attempt at sarcasm, her cheeks still tear-stained. When his expression didn't change, Hali's laughter faded. Befuddled, she asked, "You're not joking? Do you not remember my first day on the Eyes' Land or less than two hours ago?"

"I don't know what you are talking about, Hali." Cas paused, frozen with the same confused expression before a smile crossed over his face: victorious, mischievous, and handsome.

Hali grumbled. "Cas, what the heck?" giving him a gentle shove. He held up his hands in surrender.

"I had you going there for a second."

"You're infuriating sometimes. You know that?"

"You wouldn't have it any other way."

Hali smiled but said nothing. She wasn't going to let Cas know he was right.

26

UNRAVELING

Night descended on the Eyes' Land as crickets chirped, frogs croaked, and Anchors retreated back to their dwellings.

"Did you and Cas patch things up?" Marilla greeted as Hali stepped through the front door, making her way to the kitchen. Marilla's hand was already clad with a cup of coffee. Hali couldn't remember a time over the past year she hadn't seen Marilla with a cup of joe in hand while in the cabin. She wondered if Cas had ever tried to limit the amount of coffee Marilla consumed, and if he had, how quickly he must have lost that battle. Hali smiled to herself, imagining Marilla tackling Cas for her precious beans. Not much rattled Marilla, but the rationing of her coffee might be her undoing.

Shaking the image from her mind, she replied, "We did."

Marilla grinned. "Good."

Moments later, they turned as Ronan stepped through the front door—slamming it a little harder than necessary.

Marilla raised her eyebrows to Hali with a smile, not seeming at all surprised by Ronan's foul mood.

"You all right, Ronan?" Marilla asked, her tone hiding the smallest amount of exaggerated sweetness.

"No," he fumed. "Petra keeps following me around. Toru and Jett keep calling her my 'little girlfriend' and making it worse."

"Oh, that's not so bad," Marilla said. "There are worse things," her nose wrinkled at Hali, a playful grin on her lips.

"Not for me," Ronan replied. "Everywhere I go she is there. Anytime I talk to Delmar she is spying on us, listening. I hate her."

Marilla frowned. "Now, now, Ronan, I don't want to hear you using those words ever again. There is no place for it in the world, especially on the Eyes' Land. You may not like the unwanted attention now, but one day you might not mind it so much."

Ronan sighed out a "Yes, ma'am," as his head hung down in defeat. "I'm going to go shower."

As Ronan trudged off, Hali was fraught with guilt that the only place in the house he could brood in peace was the bathroom, since she had taken over his room. Ronan was growing up and he needed his own space. Hali's stay on the Eyes' Land was no longer as temporary as she had first thought. It was time for her to begin looking at a more permanent living situation. Hope still existed within her that one day she'd find a solution that would enable her to break the spell without dying in the process, but today wasn't that day. After speaking to Mr. Gruff, she felt broken down and helpless. She needed a break from wishful thinking.

Hali showered when Ronan finished and headed to bed early. Not to sleep so much as to give Ronan and Marilla some mother-son time. They had never complained, but

Hali presumed that it wasn't easy always having a permanent guest in their space all of the time.

While she lay in bed with her arms folded under her pillow where her head rested, she waited for Cas's portal to appear, staring at the ceiling as she did. As usual, she pondered the various ways to break the barrier, despite resolving that very day to live in the present. She mused out of habit more than desire. Stuck between hope and guilt, hope was the easier of the two. Hali couldn't function with the kind of guilt a lack of effort would have on her conscience, no matter how tiring it was.

Once the portal appeared, Hali hid Cas's red blanket—that smelled more like her and less like him now—under her pillow.

As she left Marilla's cabin and entered Cas's, he met her with a smile.

"What's up, Cas-a-fras?" Hali said her typical greeting, that she wouldn't dare utter outside of his cabin. Cas, as usual, shook his head and rolled his eyes. But Hali knew that it didn't annoy him as much as he pretended it did. Either way, his reaction never prevented Hali from using the redundant greeting. On the contrary, it just gave her all the more reason. Though tonight Cas appeared distracted.

"What's going on?" Hali asked, earnestly. She took a seat on the couch, opening the spell book that sat on the coffee table to the *Unraveling of Spells* section. It was a section she had become well versed in but not well practiced. In fact, she hadn't been able to attempt most spells due to the sacrifices they required and the lack of space in Cas's cabin. On top of that, the power needed for most spells put them at risk of being sniffed out by Eyes. This limited Hali to work with what was readily available in Cas's cabin—which wasn't much. To Cas's chagrin, one of Hali's favorite spells was body swapping. Every time Hali switched bodies with Cas, he would get very uptight and demand that Hali change them back immediately. After a little taunting, she eventually would. But other than body swapping and other smaller spells, Hali still didn't know how far her magic muscle could stretch.

"Kai and Carmya are getting married."

Hali's mouth fell open as easily as the spell book had to the *Unraveling of Spells* section. "Wow, really?" she asked. Hali wasn't surprised that Carmya was ready to get married, but Kai?

"Yep," Cas answered as his eyebrows came together.

"Are you upset?" Hali found herself asking, as she took in Cas's distracted state.

Did he wish it was him marrying Carmya and not Kai?

Hali remembered that not too long ago, before Kai matured, that Carmya had her sights set on Cas.

Maybe the feelings had been mutual after all.

A sinking feeling sprung into Hali's belly out of nowhere. Unaware of Hali's inner battle, Cas contemplated her question, while she tried to figure out the new unwelcome feeling that was wreaking havoc within her.

"No, just surprised is all. Kai hasn't always been the most mature of our group, but I'm happy for him. Honestly, I'm a little envious."

The words burned Hali like a seer.

What right did she have to be ... jealous?

Hali and Cas were only friends. She had no business being territorial, especially since she had spent the last year waiting for her chance to leave the Eyes' Land with or without any of them. Her rationalization did nothing in easing the ball of copper that coiled in her stomach: tight, strong, and metallic to the taste.

"Oh," was the only response Hali could think to utter, as she stared down at the spell book, pretending to be completely engrossed in what she was reading, but not comprehending anything at all.

"Hali?"

"Uh-huh," she answered, afraid to look up and give herself away.

"Can you look at me?"

Hali exhaled, doing her best to compose herself as she slowly raised her eyes to Cas's, fighting to control her lawpnies. She cursed herself under her breath, battling an emotion she had no business having. Hali wished she had never stepped through the portal in the first place.

Cas's gaze never faltered, taking her in in a way that made Hali more self-conscious than she would have liked. She considered using a masking spell but thought hiding would only make her jealousy more obvious.

Cas tilted his head, leaning his back on the kitchen island with one leg crossed over the other, studying her. "I'm not envious because he *has* Carmya, I'm envious because he doesn't have to hide the way he feels about her anymore."

The coil that had gripped at Hali's stomach released. She was swaddled in a new sensation that bathed her skin in warmth. Hali immediately looked down, unsure of Cas's meaning, and unsure where her own head was at.

"Why would he feel the need to hide what he felt for Carmya in the first place?" Hali spoke into the spell book, attempting indifference, but her hands trembled in her lap.

Cas didn't say anything for several long seconds that felt like minutes. The air felt heavy with anticipation. So much was being said in the silence ... *but what?* In her head it didn't seem as intimate of a question as it did out loud.

Cas shifted, moving his crossed leg to be parallel with

his supporting leg, as if what he was about to say required balance. "Anchors take commitment seriously. Even though Kai picked up Carmya's signal a while ago, he wasn't ready to seal the relationship quite yet. If he went ahead and sealed their bond before he was ready for everything else that goes along with it then it wouldn't have been fair to Carmya or himself." Cas finished, appearing torn, as if he had either divulged too much to her or not enough.

Hali breathed slowly, doing her best not to squirm on the couch, exposing her awkwardness. The conversation had her feeling like she was back in middle school listening to the birds and bees talk given by Mrs. Garcia, her seventh grade P.E. teacher, who was just as uncomfortable giving the talk as the students were hearing it. But despite how uncomfortable Hali was, the questions just kept falling out of her mouth.

"Seal the bond?" she asked, before remembering her conversation with Delphia. Her ears grew hot and she slid her shaky pointer finger across words in the spell book to keep her hands busy, even though she didn't absorb any of it. If Cas asked her, she probably couldn't even tell him what section of the spell book she was studying.

"A kiss, Hali," Cas stated matter-of-factly, not sounding the least bit uncomfortable with the turn the conversation had taken.

Over the past year, Hali had enjoyed learning magic from the spell book, but enjoyed Cas's companionship more. She would never admit it to him, but their nights of training and talking were always the highlight of her day. But the situation would have never been possible had she not been desperate to learn what her magic could do. But somehow, over time, Hali relaxed, and a friendship bloomed between her and Cas. The time they had spent together had purpose that trumped possible awkwardness—at least before she stupidly decided to step through the portal that night. Now, her brain raced and sputtered like the engine of an old car, searching for something to say to fill the awkward silence she had created, but only creating more. And she couldn't make it stop.

"So, I g-guess Kai and Carmya have sealed their bond then," Hali stuttered out. She wanted to smack herself.

Why was she still talking? And why was she being weird about this conversation?

Despite being attracted to Cas, their interactions had been strictly platonic. In the last year Hali could barely think past trying to find a way home, Eyes coming after her, and harnessing her abilities to conquer the former two points. Cas hadn't shown any interest in her beyond training. Until recently, it could even be said that he still held reservations about her, since she was part leprechaun. Hali at times wondered what Cas got out of meeting with her. But then she realized he got what she got from it: someone to share his ability with, whether that someone was leprechaun or not. Their common ground gave them a reason to meet but over time they found that they actually got along and shared more similarities than just magic.

Cas let out a low chuckle. "Guess so," was his response. But Hali didn't stop there. Nope. The word vomit just kept spewing from her mouth. She blamed her lawpnies.

"What would happen if two people kiss that aren't linked by the signal thing?"

Cas laughed at that. "'The signal thing?' Jeez Hali, I thought your parents were both veterinarians and the best term you can come up with is 'signal thing?'"

"Hey, it's not like I'm a veterinarian, and you still haven't answered my question."

"Nothing happens. The kiss is just a kiss. It's like trying to cook fish over a nonexistent flame. You'll get what you need from it, but it won't taste nearly as good and it could make you sick in the end."

A chuckle burst out of Hali. "Wow, did you just come up with that?"

"I sure did." Cas beamed while he laughed, proud and a little surprised by his own explanation.

"That's good, I think I'm going to write that down. That sounds like something Fisk would come up with."

Cas shook his head and huffed out a laugh, followed by Hali's rolling giggles. Their combined laughter helped Hali forget why she felt awkward moments before.

Once their chuckles subsided, Hali peered up from the spell book, asking, "So, where will Kai and Carmya live?"

"They will move into Jett's family's cabin that has been vacant since the Eye attack. Why do you ask?" his head angled, curiously.

"Does that mean that Delphia will have a free room, then?"

"Yeah, I guess so ..." Cas waited for Hali to number the rest of the dots for him.

"Sooo, I was thinking that I could move in with Delphia after Kai and Carmya are married, so poor Ronan can get his room back. He's never complained about me taking over his room, but he's getting older now and would probably like to stop sleeping on the couch."

Looking a little disappointed, Cas said, "That makes sense," but his expression shifted back so fast that Hali questioned whether she had imagined it.

"I'll let you know if and when it happens, so you aren't sending your portal to the wrong place."

Cas nodded, his forehead pinched together, revealing a

line in between his eyebrows while his lips pursed together in concentration. "Okay," he said evenly, not giving away his thoughts.

Hali regarded his subtle change in mood, discreetly. Keeping her next question light, she asked, "When are they going to get married?"

"Tomorrow evening, after dinner," he answered, shifting one leg over the other, resuming the position he had started in.

"Wow, that was fast."

"It usually is."

"So how do weddings usually work on the Eyes' Land?"

Wind rattled at the windows, as soon as she asked. Hali jumped up from the couch ready to pounce. Summer storms weren't unusual, but when the Eyes weren't too far off, one couldn't be too careful. Her heart pounded and her eyes dilated, despite knowing it was only the wind. Getting her bearings, she slowly straightened from her crouching position.

"It's only the wind, Hali." Cas assured tenderly. Hali exhaled deeply, but her heart didn't slow. "Are you okay?"

Hali inhaled and exhaled once more, alleviating her lungs. She nodded her confirmation, her back to Cas as her eyes remained fixed on the windows.

Suddenly, a hand landed on her shoulder and Hali turned quickly, meeting Cas's gaze. His hand dropped from her shoulder as she twisted and he brought it to the back of his head, scrubbing the nape of his neck with his palm. Hali's breathing hitched at the contact, while Cas grimaced, embarrassed.

"Sorry," he uttered. "I wasn't trying to scare you even more ... bad timing."

"It's okay," Hali said, shaking it off with a grin. "I'm just jumpy."

Cas nodded, dejectedly, despite doing his best to smile back at her. He had tried to comfort her, and she had spurned him unintentionally in return. And now he thought she was disgusted by him. Needing to mitigate the awkwardness—or if nothing else, level the playing field— she put herself out there, spreading her arms wide for a hug, tilting her head down and raising her eyes up to Cas in an apology. He sighed, shaking his head with a grin, pausing only briefly before stepping into the embrace. Hali tentatively wrapped her arms around Cas's waist, but he confidently pulled her into his chest, wrapping one arm across her upper back and holding her head to his chest with the other. He was warm and his heart beat steady and fast. He gently massaged her scalp as Hali breathed in his scent that always comforted her, easing her into a fog.

She grinned lazily, as his hands worked through different sections of her head. Cas usually had a wall up, but in the moments they were alone, Hali got to see a light-hearted side to Cas that he never revealed in front of the other Anchors. The glimpses Hali got from Cas's more relaxed side always made her feel privileged—like they were hers and hers alone to enjoy.

"Your scent relaxes me," Hali said nonchalantly as she slipped further into a sea of tranquility. But his closeness kept something awake inside of her and she struggled to step away from their embrace that had carried on for longer than a typical hug should.

Cas froze at Hali's honest statement, his ministrations halting. The moment gave Hali just enough time to come to her senses, but before she could peel away from him, he pulled away from her.

He left the hug, leaving Hali cold and embarrassed.

Had her honesty freaked him out?

The playing field had not only been leveled; Hali was now on the losing side of it. But the feeling didn't last long as Cas sat on the couch and put a pillow on his lap.

"Lay your head down and I'll massage your head," he said easily, like he was offering her a glass of water.

Hali hesitantly walked to the couch with uncertain steps, with legs that must have belonged to someone else. She could almost hear her lawpnies' faint giggles. Whether she surrendered or was possessed, Hali rested her head back on the pillow all the same. It wasn't until she looked up into Cas's eyes, that she knew her mischievous lawpnies' must have played a role in having her go through with the idea. At least that's what she told herself.

Cas reached his arm across the back of the couch, picking up a familiar red blanket, the only one he had left in his cabin, since Hali had the other. Fanning the blanket across her, he brought the top corners down, meeting Hali's hands to takeover. Her skin tingled at his touch, producing a wave of goosebumps across her skin that she was grateful remained hidden by the blanket she kicked around until it fully covered her feet. She curled her hands at the top edge of the blanket, holding it to her chin to be sure. Hali was covered in his fresh scent that had dissipated long ago from his blanket that was back at Marilla's.

"I still need to return your other blanket," Hali said, barely able to hold eye contact at so close a distance.

"It's okay," Cas said. He gently pulled the hair tie off the ends of Hali's hair and began untwisting the auburn tendrils of her braid. "I still have this one." With every scratch, tug, and movement of her scalp and hair, Hali's eyes fluttered closed and her body relaxed, forgetting any reservations she might have had.

"Tell me how weddings work here," Hali said sluggishly, as Cas continued sedating her with his hands.

"Well, it depends on the couple," he said. "Kai and Carmya have chosen to have their wedding tomorrow evening after dinner. To be honest that's when most couples choose to have their weddings. Makes things a little easier."

"Makes what easier?" Hali dumbly asked.

Cas hesitated, an awkward silence fell between the two, his fingers stopped massaging briefly before continuing.

"To go home," was all he said and all he needed to say.

"Gotcha," Hali replied. It wasn't lost on her that every time she attempted to fill the awkward silence, she made it worse. But she was no quitter, so she kept going. "I guess what I'm curious about is if there are any traditions here that are the same as back home or if it's different. Are special outfits worn? Is there a wedding cake? Are vows exchanged?"

"Mortals find any excuse for dessert, don't they?" Cas stated more than asked. "To answer your questions, weddings here have always been simple. Fisk or Troy usually officiates. I think Fisk is officiating Carmya's and Kai's. A couple can either have their wedding underwater or on land—depends on the couple. Brides usually wear white if they're doing a land ceremony and grooms wear khaki shorts and a white button-down short-sleeve shirt. As far as vows go, the couple can either come up with their own or they can have the officiant say the standard vows."

"Sounds similar to back home." Hali felt heavier, her hair wilder and undone, as each wave stretched and released from its hold. Even with the knowledge that her hair probably resembled a lion's mane, Hali couldn't bring herself to care. The massage soothed her to the brink of slumber, and she wasn't sure how she would be alert enough to train with Cas when he finished. Hali knew she should get up. But she felt a good kind of heavy—her body fixed but her mind afloat. As she felt her breathing become deeper, she thought talking would help her stay awake. So, she asked more questions while enjoying not only the massage but the scent of the red blanket and Cas's voice that lulled her to sleep as much as it kept her awake.

"How do weddings in the water go?" Hali yawned.

Cas yawned in response, but his hands never ceased. "Well, the ceremony is the same underwater as it is on land, other than everyone being in either mermaid or merman form and marine life popping in when they are nearby."

"Is that a bad thing ... the marine life popping in, I mean?"

"No, it's not a bad thing but it could be distracting. I wouldn't want to be married underwater. There was one underwater ceremony where a school of fish nearly took out the bride."

Hali laughed, which prompted Cas to tell her about other undersea wedding disasters. He recounted one incident where dolphins shrieked in the water, barely making the vows audible, and another time a sea creature charged into the middle of the ceremony because one of the guests was going through her fertile time but didn't want to miss the wedding. After everything Cas had told her she couldn't imagine why any of the Anchors would want to get married underwater, but Cas had said the sea was such a big part of who they were that for some Anchors it didn't seem right to leave it out of their big day. They talked for a while, but at some point, Hali completely drifted off.

It wasn't until she had rolled, almost dropping to the

floor, that she realized she had made the mistake of falling asleep. Sitting up quickly her head got woozy. She placed her palms on the couch, closing her eyes to steady the whirling in her head. Once she opened her eyes again, she noticed Cas to her right, upright, but his head hung down, breathing slow steady breaths. He had fallen asleep, too. Sudden panic flared within her, making her movements careless. She propped up on the couch, twisting to peak behind one of the window curtains to gauge the time. She was thankful to find that it was still dark outside. Relief flooded her and the breath she exhaled released a flock of pent up nerves that sent her heartbeat fluttering. Cas startled awake from Hali's movements. His body straightened as soon as he saw her, appearing taken aback.

Cas's confusion quickly jolted into awareness before he was jumping up off the couch rubbing his eyes and running a hand through his hair. "How long have I been sleeping?" he asked.

"I have no idea, I just woke up, too. Are you awake enough to make a portal back to Marilla's?" Hali turned her head to the wall clock that read 2:23 a.m.

Cas nodded and stepped around the coffee table. Hali followed. Her legs wobbled beneath her like a newborn fawn as blood found its way to her longest limbs, stabilizing her movements.

Cas rubbed his eyes, then looked at Hali. A low chuckle sounded in his throat. "Wow, I did a number to your hair."

With no mirror nearby, Hali grabbed her hair, pulling it to the front of her face to assess the damage. Her normally loose dark auburn waves looked like they had been struck by a bolt of lightning.

"Looks good," Cas said, sleepily.

Hali glared at him, dropping her shoulders, not

believing a word out of his mouth. It only made him laugh more.

Moments later, Cas produced a portal. It was a spell that Hali had yet to master. Not because she hadn't wanted to, but because if she wasn't precise, she would risk giving up the fact that Cas was an enchanter. Portal spells left a trail of where they came from and where they ended up, like breadcrumbs. Meaning that if Hali ended up in the forest when an Eye was watching, that Eye would be able to trace where she had come from, leaving Cas compromised.

Cas bid her "Good night," and not long after Hali was back in her room at Marilla's. She lay in bed wide awake: twisting, turning, thinking. She thought about her parents, thought about her day and the sea creature, thought about Kai and Carmya getting married, thought about moving in with Delphia, thought about the spell on the barrier, but mostly, she thought about Cas. Their friendship meant a whole lot more to Hali than she would have liked to admit. She wondered what Cas had meant when he said that he envied Kai for finally getting to admit that he had feelings for Carmya and if that meant that he was holding back his own feelings for someone. That thought scared her more than the others. Mostly, as she had come to realize, that she wanted to be that someone to Cas. But the Eyes' Land operated differently than what she was used to, and Cas might already be linked with someone else. She was stuck in a limbo that made moving forward and holding back feel like a betrayal to her parents.

Would her parents want her to stop living? she wondered.

After more than two hours of restless contemplation, Hali didn't fall asleep until after 5:00 in the morning, managing to sleep for about two hours. Surprisingly, she didn't wake up too tired.

When Hali entered the living area, Marilla's eyes lit up from the kitchen, causing her to take pause.

"Oh, good, I'm so glad that you're up. I just got word from Ronan that Carmya and Kai are getting married tonight after dinner. Do you think you and Delphia could whip up a dessert?"

"I think we can come up with something," Hali agreed, mustering as much enthusiasm as she could for the subject, despite it being morning.

"Great! I'm going to head out for breakfast and see if there is anything I can do to help with the ceremony, but I wanted to talk to you before I left. Ronan and Delmar already agreed to take your places fishing this afternoon, so you have more time to get dessert together."

"Thank you," Hali said, doing her best not to yawn. "I appreciate you making the arrangements."

"No, thank you, for agreeing to make the dessert. Well, if you need anything let me know. I'm going to head out now, so take your time. Remember, there are muffins if you want something to hold you over before breakfast."

Marilla flitted out of the cabin like a bumblebee leaving a flower, taking her excitement with her like a bumblebee takes pollen. The sun filtered through the windows leaving streaks of warmth on the wooden floors. Hali moved to a slice of sunshine on the wooden planks and let it warm her feet. She stood in the quiet cabin, enjoying the silence for a few moments, before launching herself into all the chaos a wedding usually brought.

After eating an apple muffin that she had made with Delphia the day before, Hali got ready and headed out thirty minutes after Marilla. Once arriving later for the camp breakfast, she said her congratulations to Carmya and Kai, ate some fish, and found a blubbering Delphia.

"Oh, Delphia," Hali said while pulling her into a hug. "What's the matter?" she asked, more out of rule than need.

"Other than losing my best friend?"

"You're not losing her," Hali tried to console.

"You don't understand, Hali. I've never lived by myself before. When my family died after ... the Eyes ... Carmya and I moved in together because there just weren't enough adults to look after all the little ones, because most of them were killed in the attack. The adults that were left decided that they would put the older kids together and check in on them from time to time. Kai, Toru, and Jett were grouped together too. But at least Jett and Toru will still have each other when Kai gets married. So, you see, we are more than just roommates, we are practically sisters."

Hali couldn't imagine living with only Camille at only twelve-years-old, especially after such a tragedy. She wondered if Cas had always lived alone or if that was a more recent development. Hali thought it was interesting that Kai, Toru, and Jett shared one cabin and Cas had one all to himself.

"I'm afraid to live alone but I'm not sure how I could live with anyone else, either. You know what I mean?"

So much for asking to live with Delphia, Hali thought.

"I think so. It will be a big adjustment for both of you I'm sure, but you have to think of the positives. What's one thing you have always wanted to do but couldn't because you shared the space?"

"Play my fiddle through the night," Delphia answered immediately. Her tears were the only hint of sadness left on her face.

"Wow, that literally took you no time at all to answer. Are you sure you're sad that Carmya's moving out?" Hali joked.

Delphia snorted with equal parts laughter and sadness.

"No, I really will," she sniffled, wiping puddles from her eyes. After a few breaths, Delphia said, "I'll be fine, once I get over the shock of all of it. Everything is just happening so fast. I knew they were going to get married, but I thought I would have a little more time to live with Carmya." Delphia wiped the back of her hand to her nose.

"I think I have something to help get your mind off being sad for a little while."

"What's that?" Delphia sniffed, an expectant gleam lit her eyes as she waited for Hali's idea.

"Marilla asked if we both could make dessert."

Straightening, Delphia's frown morphed into a smile. "What are we going to make?"

Hali couldn't believe she was talking to the same girl who was crestfallen only seconds before. But she wasn't complaining. Being an emotional support was not in Hali's wheelhouse. She could barely understand her own emotions half the time, even though her empathy for others had grown in the past year. Being captured, hunted, and surprised with magical abilities had a way of making a person more in tune to the woes of others. But she still lacked the openness to show compassion as easily as many did.

"I was going to ask you just that. What do you think Kai and Carmya would like?"

Delphia contemplated for only a second before she answered. "Do we have time to make a multi-layered cake?"

"If we get started now, then maybe."

Delphia grabbed Hali's hand, pulling Hali along urgently to her cabin. She stopped suddenly and Hali had to hop off to the side to keep herself from slamming into Delphia's back. Oblivious to the almost collision, Delphia scowled. "Shoot, we need to fish in the afternoon."

Hali shook her head while waving her free hand in a similar motion. "Marilla already took care of it. Ronan and Delmar will be taking our place."

Delphia's scowl transformed into a huge grin, but it did nothing to loosen the death grip she had on Hali's hand as she resumed running.

"Where are you both off to in a hurry?" Jett yelled as Delphia maneuvered through tables, dragging Hali not too far behind.

"Gotta make cake Jett, no time for small talk," Delphia yelled back, annoyed.

"Hali!" a male voice called out, reluctantly slowing Delphia's pace down.

"Cas, we have to make cake," Delphia asserted.

"I need to talk to Hali for just a minute."

"Fine, but just for a minute," Delphia heaved out a sigh, not disguising her frustration.

The lawpnies tingled under Hali's skin as soon as Cas's eyes met with her own. They flooded her like the blush appearing on her cheeks. Cas had a way of balancing her and putting her off balance at the same time.

Hali walked to Cas, with her back to Delphia, just outside the tables of camp. Delphia crossed her arms and stared at Cas, her foot serving as a timer as it tapped the passing seconds. As Hali stood in front of him, a million thoughts running through her head of why he was singling her out, she couldn't help noticing the blush of his own cheeks.

"Hali, did you already ask Delphia if you could move in with her?" he rushed out.

Hali tilted her head, the lawpnies danced under her skin. "No, I didn't ask," Hali answered, leaving out the detail about Delphia not being ready for a roommate quite so soon.

Cas sighed in relief, releasing his shoulders as the tension he carried flew out like birds from a cage.

"Good, I have another idea."

"This cake isn't going to bake itself, unless you've learned how to cast a spell, Hali," Delphia hollered from behind. Hali and Cas looked at each other on the verge of laughing.

If only Delphia knew.

Everyone on the Eyes' Land was aware that Hali was part enchanter, but no one besides Cas knew that she was actually able to use her abilities. Marilla knew about the lawpnies, but after Hali wasn't able to secure a spell book, Marilla hadn't pried any further into the matter.

"What idea?" Hali asked.

"We can talk about it tonight, after the wedding."

Hali squinted at Cas for his vague answer. He smirked. If Hali didn't have Delphia breathing down her neck she would have probed further, but as Delphia's toe tapped the dirt in the not so far distance, so did time. Hali almost wished to do as Delphia suggested and conjure a cake with magic, but that would have raised too many questions and would take all the fun out of the process for both Delphia and Hali.

"Go on before Delphia murders me," Cas pointed his head in Delphia's direction.

Hali chuckled, nodding in agreement. She smiled up at Cas once more, his scar once again luring her. Moments passed as they both looked at each other, unmoving.

"Hey, I'm still back here," Delphia called, breaking Hali and Cas from their trance. Hali quickly waved to Cas and turned around feeling bashful.

Delphia just shook her head when Hali returned, but didn't say anything about the weird interaction between her and Cas. "I hope you're ready to run."

Hali huffed, surging with pride. "I'm always ready to run."

"Good. But I'm still going to beat you." Without warning, Delphia sprinted—like a cheater. Hali followed, milliseconds behind. Delphia was fast, but Hali was faster. The girls zigged and zagged through the trees. Both too concerned with winning, they didn't notice that the trees rattled above: looming, waiting, watching.

27

A WEDDING

MANY HOURS and baking supplies later, the "wedding cake" was finished. The cake had three round tiers which included a top layer of strawberry with chocolate frosting; a middle layer with chocolate and vanilla frosting; and a bottom layer with vanilla and chocolate frosting. Knowing that the one cake wasn't going to feed all of the Anchors, Hali and Delphia decided that it would be faster to make sheet cakes for everyone else and use the layered cake as the centerpiece. Thus, they didn't just make one wedding cake they made several.

Thankfully, Marilla brought them lunch and dinner so they didn't have to stop working. She also delivered more baking supplies—since Hali and Delphia had underestimated the task they had taken on. Marilla even moved the completed cakes to the lodge so Hali and Delphia had more room to work in the small kitchen. But the end result would hopefully be worth the two scales Cas would undoubtedly need to remove from himself to replenish the baking supplies at the next full moon.

Once Marilla took the last completed cake to the lodge,

Hali looked down to see she was covered in flour. She only had an hour and a half to run back to Marilla's, shower, do her hair, and get dressed before it was time for the wedding.

When Hali stepped out of Delphia's cabin it was bright and humid, causing her to take a step back and raise an arm to shade her eyes. It was at least a twenty-degree difference from the crisp and cool morning it had been when she entered. Despite the heat and the brightness, big puffy rain-clouds blotted the sky, threatening to pour. Hali just hoped that the storm would stay away until at least after the wedding. The indoor lodge would house the wedding cakes regardless, since the humidity was enough to melt them into puddles if kept outside too long.

As Hali walked to the shore, she came across Mamie step-ping out of her cabin.

"Hali girl, you look beautiful," Mamie exclaimed with a gleam in her eyes.

Marilla and Ronan had left early for the wedding to help with setup, while Hali fussed with her hair up until the last minute, trying to tame her waves that she normally braided. Hali wore a simple, pale violet dress with a boat neckline that cinched at her waist and flowed to her knees.

"Thank you, Mamie. So, do you." Mamie smiled a toothy grin, holding her arm out for Hali to take. Hali wrapped an arm around Mamie's, escorting her down the path.

"Your hair looks nice too. Can't say I've ever seen it down before," Mamie complimented, eyeing Hali suspiciously.

"Thanks." Hali looked ahead to avoid Mamie's scrutiny, but her gaze could still be felt in Hali's peripheral. "If there was any occasion to wear it down, this would be it." Hali laughed nervously, hating that she felt the need to explain putting an effort into her appearance. She raised her arm displaying a new hair tie—since she left her other one at Cas's—wrapped around her wrist. "I came prepared in case I change my mind, though."

Mamie's eyebrows rose as she nodded slightly and said, "I see that." Hali could feel her dark auburn waves hitting the middle of her back as she walked, tormenting her. If Mamie thought she was trying to impress at this wedding, then others might too. She didn't want to care, but she did.

Thunder rumbled in the distance, breaking Hali from her own frets. She jumped at the sound and looked at Mamie who appeared unconcerned.

"That's not good," Hali voiced.

"Eh, a little rain never hurt anyone," Mamie shrugged.

"A little lightning will, though."

Mamie cackled with the vigor that would give a Halloween witch a run for her money.

Another rumble of thunder rolled through the air. The lawpnies quaked beneath her skin. Hali pushed back, reasoning that her lawpnies were only reacting to her body's jolted response. A line of Anchors walked the path to the beach, where the ceremony was going to take place. Mamie's arm remained wrapped around Hali's as they walked and made it to the clearing out of the woods and onto the sand. Hali spotted Ronan, Marilla, Fisk, and Cas talking. She continued rationalizing the uneasiness that had crept under her skin as they approached the group—insisting the thunder was the reason. But she still couldn't shake the feeling no matter how much she tried.

"My Hali, you clean up real nice," Fisk declared, unbothered by the changing weather.

"Thank you," Hali said, dropping her head down to

inspect her hands that didn't need inspecting. All while avoiding the temptation to look at Cas for approval.

Fisk cleared his throat. "Well, if you don't mind, Hali, I'd like to escort Ms. Mamie down to the shore, if it's okay with Ms. Mamie, of course. My daughter and grandson have partnered up and I reckon you will look better on Cas's arm than I will." Fisk lifted his elbow for Mamie to take. "May I have the honors, Ms. Mamie?"

"You may." Mamie unwrapped her arm from Hali's, letting Fisk's arm take its place. Mamie winked at Hali before the two walked off and Marilla and Ronan lined up behind them. Marilla looked at Hali pleased before turning around to face the beach, arm and arm with Ronan.

Ronan looked back at Hali. "What's for dessert?" he whispered.

Hali shook her head and laughed. "Lots of cake."

Ronan, "Mm mm mmm'd" his approval as Marilla glared at him in disapproval.

"For Pete's sake boy, will you think of nothing but your stomach these days?"

"It's a wedding, mom. I need something to look forward to."

Marilla rolled her eyes, exhaling a heavy breath as she did. Hali bit the side of her cheek to prevent herself from laughing, not wanting to undermine Marilla's attempt at discipline.

"One day, Ronan, you may feel differently," Marilla chided.

"That's what you keep telling me," Ronan countered before walking off, Marilla's lecturing words trailed off with them.

Hali was still smiling at their banter when she looked up to see Cas gazing at her, holding up his elbow for her to take. He was wearing khaki pants with a pale-green button-down shirt. The green complemented his blue eyes and Hali became aware that she was staring.

"You look beautiful, Hali," Cas smiled. "But you always do."

Her stomach flipped. Cas had never paid her such a compliment before or looked at her with such adoration. The lawpnies tingled warm beneath her skin, as her fear from the thunder disappeared.

"Thank you, so do you."

Hali smiled, took his arm and they began walking to the shore. Goosebumps erupted on her skin, as their arms intertwined. She felt short of breath as her heartbeat quickened and pounded against her chest. They didn't speak, opting to take in the wedding scene, as they started down the shell-lined path. At the end of the path were chairs where most of the Anchors were already seated. The dark gray clouds that hung over the horizon were outlined in an explosion of pinks and oranges with wisps of blues and white. An energy buzzed between them that was similar to the feeling Hali had the day in the water with the sea creature, but stronger.

It was only nerves, Hali reasoned.

They found seats in the last row. Cas stepped out of her grasp and let Hali take the inside seat before sitting next to her. Their shoulders touched as the wedding guests chatted and laughed around them. Cas and Hali were in their own bubble, still not saying a word to each other. Her cheeks flushed at their closeness.

Thunder rumbled in the distance as the sky darkened, followed by the nervous murmurs of wedding guests. Fisk stood up from the front row, peering up at the clouds with a grimace.

"Well, I suppose we should get this shindig started

before we need to postpone it. I'm not sure how much our bride and groom would appreciate that." The crowd laughed in agreement.

Delphia stepped up from the front row and began playing Canon in D with her violin. She appeared nervous initially but after the first few measures, she became completely immersed in the music as if no one was around. Hali had never heard Delphia play and now understood why she would want the cabin to herself. She was mesmerizing to watch and hear.

Kai stood up from the front row at the same time as Delphia and took his place on the right side of Fisk, staring down the aisle with excited anticipation in his eyes. He had come a long way since Hali first met him, from arrogant and immature to confident and less immature.

Baby steps.

The crowd turned and waited with him, watching for the first glimpse of Carmya.

Stepping out from the trees, Carmya was a vision in cream. The little bit of sunshine that hadn't been bleated out by clouds or squashed by the incoming darkness of night, cast a warm pleasant glow on her advancing figure.

She walked down the seashell-lined aisle towards Kai on her own. Her parents, like most parents on the Eyes' Land, hadn't survived the Eye raid more than a decade before. There were no groomsmen, bridesmaids, best man, or maid of honor. In fact, no one was given an honor higher than anyone else. Anchors viewed each connection a person made, good or bad, as equally important. The living existed in the foreground, while the deceased fell into the background. A person was equally shaped by both parts.

Instead of Carmya filling the unoccupied space on her arm by another important person in her life, she intentionally left her arm empty, as a remembrance to her father and mother. Bringing her background to the present, like stars in a darkening sky.

Collective "oohs and ahhhs" sounded in the crowd as Carmya drew closer to the guests. Fittingly, her satin gown was mermaid style, hugging her figure and belled out at her feet; the short train dragged through the sand as she walked. Carmya looked happy. Kai beamed, like he had won the lottery. Despite not always having the best interactions with Kai, Hali smiled for the both of them.

As Carmya made it to the end of the aisle, Delphia's violin gently came to a stop as she played her final note. She smiled at Carmya, tears brimming in her eyes, and gave her a quick hug, which Hali knew from experience, probably squeezed all the air from Carmya's lungs. Delphia wasn't known for doing anything halfway, which is why Hali shouldn't have been surprised that she had played the violin so well.

Fisk began speaking after Delphia took her seat and Kai grabbed Carmya's hands to hold. But Hali didn't hear a word, because at that moment, Cas decided to take her hand in his own, intertwining their fingers. When he did, Hali noticed the hair tie she left at his place the night before, wrapped around his wrist.

What did this mean?

Before she knew it, the ceremony was over and Carmya and Kai were running down the aisle. Everyone stood from their seats clapping, chatting, and slowly making their way back to camp to take part in the reception. Before they stood up, Cas unclasped his fingers from Hali's. Delphia approached with red-rimmed eyes moments later.

"You played so well, Delphia!" Hali complimented.

Delphia flicked her hand in an "oh please," gesture in return.

"You did, Delphia, and you know it," Cas added evenly. The three walked, with Hali in the middle, while Delphia talked about how beautiful Carmya looked, how nervous she was to play in front of everyone, and how weird it was going be to go back to an empty cabin. She said the latter with a mixture of sadness and excitement.

"I'm going to run my violin back to my place. Wow, it is so bizarre to say that. I'll catch up with you guys later." Delphia skipped off like a fairy, not giving Hali and Cas a chance to ask her if she wanted company.

The party had already started once Hali and Cas strolled into camp. But they stood on the perimeter of it all, still not speaking. The longer they went, the harder it became, and small talk would have cheapened the significance of the silence. Something needed to be said, but Hali decided she would let Cas speak first. Mainly because she didn't know what to say, but also because after the previous night, she didn't trust that she wouldn't embarrass herself.

So instead, she peered around like she was taking in the scene. The happy crowd bleated out their silence and provided a much-needed distraction. She spotted Ronan and Delmar walking around the perimeter too. Delmar whispered something to Ronan and immediately started laughing when he did, but Ronan was left with a smile that didn't reach his eyes. Surprisingly, Petra sat at a table with her parents, not following Ronan around like she usually did. Mr. Gruff, stood near a barbecue grill, awaiting his dinner, just so he could exit. After learning Mr. Gruff's true identity, she resolved to continue thinking of him only as Mr. Gruff and not Rowina, to ensure she didn't reveal his true identity to the others. Scanning the mostly joyful scene,

Hali found Mamie, Marilla, and Fisk shooting the breeze at
one of the tables as Kai and Carmya made eyes at each other
at their own table, ignoring all of their surroundings.

Music erupted over all the chatter when three older men
began playing a lively Celtic song. One man played a violin,
another man began hitting a drum with his hand that Hali
had learned was called a bodhrán, and the last musician
played an Irish flute. Hali half expected fairies to appear
from above. The music was earthy and majestic, and the
Anchors wasted no time jumping from their seats and grabbing a partner. The night pushed towards the cloud-ridden
horizon only leaving a little natural light left. Thankfully,
the lanterns that hung from the trees as well as centered in
the middle of each table had been lit prior to the ceremony
in anticipation for the night festivities, casting a warm hue
that highlighted the darkness that surrounded them. Hali
smiled at the wild display she had never witnessed from the
Anchors. There wasn't even any alcohol involved.

Delphia's tranquil piece of music had almost been a
warmup of what was to come. The last time Hali had heard
music from instruments, or a radio had been over a year
ago, so the music overwhelmed her physically and emotionally. The sound invaded her veins, and the bodhrán's beat
made it difficult for Hali to decipher the sound of the drum
to her own heartbeat. She felt dizzy as the dancers began
circling like a tornado in the space that was cleared of tables
—grabbing new victims with every rotation.

"Hali," Cas began to say before she was swept up in the
circling wave. Annoyance lined his face as Hali was pulled
away from him. Jett and Toru bordered her on each side,
laughing and hooting at their conquest.

"Cas is going to murder you," Toru yelled over the music
to Jett.

"He's gotta catch me first," Jett yelled back. The fact that they were both having a conversation with Hali sandwiched between their elbows—like she didn't exist—wasn't lost on her. She had no idea what game the two meddling idiots were playing, or why they were involving her, but Hali wanted no part of it.

Hali only hoped that Delphia wouldn't eventually be linked to either one of them. Considering Delphia was in her early twenties and hadn't already, seemed like a pretty safe bet—but one couldn't be too careful. All Hali knew was that if she linked to anyone like Toru or Jett, she would become a sea creature just to avoid them.

Thinking of Delphia, Hali realized she hadn't come back from returning her violin. A sinking feeling, unrelated to her dance partners, filled her chest.

The song ended and Hali had the early beginnings of a headache from all the stimulation. Unwrapping herself from Toru's and Jett's arms she didn't even waste time to give them a dirty look before running off and scanning the crowd for Delphia. Jett and Toru snickered under their breaths when she left, but Hali had been too preoccupied to call them out on it. She only cared about making sure Delphia was safe.

The lawpnies mirrored her anxiousness as they hummed under her skin. After scanning the reception crowd and not finding Delphia, Hali made her way through the trees in the direction of Delphia's cabin. Dread crept into her bones with each step. Suddenly, a hand gripped her right shoulder. Instinctively, Hali whipped around as her hand connected to warm flesh with a loud thwack.

"Damn!" the flesh grumbled, as the silhouette stumbled backwards into the trees, grabbing its face. Gaining composure, the figure quickly moved out of the trees, showing his face to avoid another hit.

"Neilan! What are you doing here?!" Hali whispered through clenched teeth.

"Hello to you, too." Neilan rubbed his cheek some more and looked down at his palm as if the pain Hali just inflicted was removable. "I came to warn you."

Panic ignited within Hali. "Where's Delphia?!"

Out of nowhere, Neilan was being tackled to the ground by none other than Cas.

"Why are you here?" Cas spit out, his legs straddled on top of Neilan, pinning his arms to his sides with his legs. Neilan bucked his hips and before Hali knew it the two were wrestling, kicking up the sandy dirt as thunder rumbled low in the distance. The open spaces of the trees with views of the horizon displayed the sky darkening from navy to black.

"Cas, stop! He came to warn us."

Surprisingly, Cas did. When he stepped away from Neilan, his face was lined with rage. Neilan's chest heaved at the tussle, as he spit into the trees and wiped dirt from his face with the back of his hand. Neilan was as equally enraged as Cas. "Do you know this *Eye*?" Cas accused, unquestionably livid.

Cas said *Eye* like it was equal to a serial killer.

"Yes," Hali answered quietly. "I've known Neilan my whole life, but I didn't know he was a leprechaun until I got here." Hali didn't plan on discriminating against all leprechauns like Cas had, just the ones who planned on hurting Anchors or any other innocent. It saddened Hali to have to explain that she didn't know Neilan was a leprechaun, like being a leprechaun was enough cause for her to resent him. How could she resent someone for a bloodline she shared herself? But Cas's anger wasn't without cause, so she made no argument with him about his feelings towards leprechauns.

"What do you mean, since you got *here*?"

Oops.

"I've known for about a year, but I didn't say anything," Hali answered, chancing a look at Cas to see rage shift to betrayal. A look she never wanted to be responsible for placing on someone's face, especially Cas's. His expression left her feeling like a hypocrite, remembering how she had chastised Neilan for withholding information from her just over a year ago.

"Cas it wasn't my secret to tell." Hali countered, using the same words that Neilan had used on her. They didn't work for Hali then and they certainly weren't working for Cas now.

"*Anchors* don't keep Eyes' secrets, Hali. We aren't trying to make it easier for *them* to come after us." Cas spoke through gritted teeth, emphasizing that Hali was either with the Anchors or against them.

"Enough," Neilan interrupted. "We don't have time." Cas and Hali turned towards Neilan, who carried himself with the same authority as his tone. "The Eyes are coming for you Hali and there is nothing I can do to stop them. This time they are coming prepared."

"Where's Delphia?" Hali asked again, but this time there was no fear in her tone, just anger for having to repeat herself.

"She's safe," Neilan answered, his tone clipped.

"And we are supposed to trust that you are telling us the truth." Cas stated more than asked, glaring at Neilan.

"Would I bother warning you, risking my own safety in the process, if I was lying? I'm not exactly getting anything out of helping Anchors."

"So why are you helping us, then?" Cas didn't falter, as his eyes bore through Neilan's like an Eye lie detector, ready to pounce at the first sign of dishonesty.

Neilan exhaled a defeated breath as his head, shoulders, and eyes dropped. "Because it's the right thing to do. Hali is my sister's best friend and like a sister to me too. But even if Hali wasn't the reason the Eyes were coming, I'd still help."

Cas exhaled, but his body remained tense, his scowl unyielding. "When do the Eyes plan on attacking?"

Without missing a beat, Neilan answered, "Within the next twenty-four hours."

28

RECEPTION

Laughter and music drifted through the air as Hali, Cas, and Neilan gathered in their impending huddle of doom that only emphasized what they were trying to protect. Hali almost wished she could be oblivious like the other Anchors. Less than an hour before, her biggest annoyance was being pulled into the dancing circle by Jett and Toru.

"We need to warn the others," Cas ordered.

"I need to remain unseen," Neilan countered. "I am no help to any of you if the other Eyes realize I'm helping you out."

"So where will you go?" Hali asked. "Won't the Eyes know something is up if you aren't part of their attack?"

Neilan just shook his head. "O ye of little faith. The other Eyes know I'm here. They sent me to scout out the situation and report back."

Cas moved forward ready to pounce on Neilan, but Neilan just held up his hands. "Calm down there, Hulk. I'm not going to tell them anything that puts the Anchors in jeopardy. Plus, I have my own interest to protect."

"Hulk?" Cas stumbled on the foreign name. "What *interests* do you have to protect?"

Hali wondered the same thing.

"Oh yeah, I forgot, you've probably never read a comic book. And it's more like *interest*, and no worries Cas, my *interest* will not impact yours in the slightest."

"A what book?" Cas asked, truly confused, completely ignoring the latter part of Neilan's statement. Despite the Eyes' Land having books, the books kept in the school room at the lodge were either educational or classics. Sometimes Hali forgot how little the Anchors knew about the happenings of the outside world, until she made a reference to something common from her previous life, only to be met with confusion. Honestly, Neilan's mention of comic books was the only part of what he said that made any sense to Hali. She had no clue what Neilan's *interest* on the Eyes' Land could be, but her twinge of curiosity hadn't let her forget there were more pressing concerns ... like a missing friend and a slew of Eyes about to invade.

"Jeez, Hali, how have you been here a year and not imparted any pop-culture knowledge to these poor souls?"

"I don't know, Neilan, I guess it slipped my mind when I was busy trying to survive the Eyes and find a way home."

"Touché," Neilan acquiesced.

Cas rolled his eyes impatiently, "We don't have time for this," he said, quoting the same words Neilan had said moments before. "Is there anything we need to know, other than they are going to attack? Are the Eyes watching us now? How exactly do they plan on using Hali? It's not like they can take her off the Eyes' Land." Cas paced as he spoke.

"I've disabled the trees for the moment, so that the other Eyes can't see, but I don't have long before they start getting suspicious. When an Eye travels through the trees the viewer automatically gets cut off because all the energy goes to getting the Eye to where he needs to go. I haven't closed off the tree I traveled through yet." Neilan sighed, running his hand over his light brown hair that was no longer shaved as it had been a year ago, but cropped short.

"As far as the Eyes' plans, I'm not privy to all the details, but they don't need to take Hali off the Eyes' Land to get what they want from her," Neilan replied. "Once they get all the Anchors out of their way, Hali will be an easy target."

Cas's fists and jaw clenched, and the lawpnies throbbed under Hali's skin demanding to be set free. But she resisted the temptation, knowing that even with Neilan's assurance that he had blocked the Eyes' ability to see them, they weren't far away.

"So, the Eyes plan on killing all of us, is that it? I thought you weren't privy to all the details. Could have fooled me. Sounds like you know exactly what they plan on doing," Cas challenged, not hiding his fury.

He really was like the Hulk.

"I don't know what spells or other plans they have for Hali once they clear the Eyes' Land. But all I know is we are running out of time. Every minute you waste second guessing my motives the Eyes are that much closer to closing in on this place and ripping the scales from every Anchor they see."

Neilan was right. He wasn't the enemy. But if the Anchors couldn't leave, how could they protect themselves from an influx of Eyes out to kill them? The Eyes had the advantage of knowing how many they were up against, along with knives meant for fighting. They wouldn't be slinging kitchen utensils around or pointed pieces of wood, but crafted metal designed for killing. But of all the advantages the Eyes had, the biggest was their ability to come and go, on and off the Eyes' Land as they pleased.

Lightning rippled through the sky, in a formation that looked like the talons of a hawk. Thunder cracked, not long after, shaking the Eyes' Land. The time had come. Hali could no longer hide. Terrified shivers took over her body.

"I need to go," Neilan said, "and you both need to prepare the others. The Eyes can do a lot of damage with the energy the sky is supplying."

This time Neilan didn't leave through a tree, but ran off, disappearing as stealthily as he had appeared. Only Cas and Hali were left. The music in the distance had ceased after lightning crashed into the ocean. Cas walked back the way he had come, without saying a word.

"Cas, where are you going?" Hali asked desperately.

He looked over his shoulder but didn't stop moving. "To warn the others."

Hali had to practically run to catch up to him. "Cas, wait!"

Cas turned around, facing Hali with so many emotions crossing his face. Anger, frustration, betrayal, and a hint of fear boiled in his blue eyes that mirrored the color of the night in the dark shadows of the trees.

"What is it, Hali?" Cas's voice was irritable and hurried.

"Why are you running from me? I'm coming with you."

"Suit yourself."

"Why are you treating me like I'm the enemy here? I have just as much at stake in this as anybody else, if not more."

"Well, aren't you, Hali?"

"Aren't I what?"

"The enemy? It's not *you* who the Eyes plan on getting out of their way."

Hali's mouth dropped open in disgust of what she was hearing. "You're right, because being tortured is so much better."

"Well, maybe if you had given me a heads up a year ago, that Nielson had paid you a visit we could have prepared ourselves a little better."

"It's Neilan! Not Nielson. And what do you call what we've been doing this past year? It's not like we didn't know that this has been a possibility since the day the Eyes arrived looking for me. The only advice Neilan gave me was to get a spell book if I could, and that is the last I saw of him. You act as if I'm harboring some big secret from you that would have saved us all from this fate. Because you and I both know that as long as we remain trapped here, we are nothing but sitting ducks at the Eyes' disposal whenever they want to pay the Anchors a visit. If you had just let me try to break the spell, then maybe we would all be free from this place."

"Oh, I know you just can't wait to leave and go back to your mom and dad, right Hali? It's so terrible here you'd risk dying to get away. Sorry, I was trying to save you from sacrificing yourself to a lost cause. I've watched enough people die in my life. I'm not going to watch another person die at the hands of the Eyes if I can prevent it."

"What if I can do it? I can't just sit by and watch the Eyes kill everyone, just like you can't."

Cas's eyes softened as rain began falling from the sky in pellets. Drenching them both instantly, Cas's shirt darkened, and clung to every line in his upper body, while Hali's dress grabbed at every curve she tried to hide. Vanity took a back seat to their own immediate concerns.

"Hali, we can fight the Eyes off. We have before and this time we are older and know what to expect," Cas pleaded.

"What if we can't fight them off?"

"We will, because we have to. The only power they have on us, is the ability to use the elements collectively. Otherwise we are equally strong, if not stronger than they are. Think about it, they want you because you are powerful. If neither of us holds back and we use all the power between us, we can protect all of the Anchors.

"How is that possible, Cas?" Hali asked, as she pushed her messy wet hair—that she had spent so much time perfecting that night—out of her eyes.

"Because we don't need to be careful with how much power we use, like we have been during training."

"But Cas, then the Eyes will know that you are an enchanter and you'll put yourself at risk."

Cas huffed out a humorless laugh. "At risk for what, Hali? I'll take my chances of the Eyes discovering me and torturing me for life. If that turns out to be the case, at least you'll have company."

Cas began walking again, but this time his hurried pace was not as aggressive as it was before. The slower pace allowed Hali to follow along beside him without having to run.

"What are we going to tell the others?"

"I don't know yet," Cas said, uncertainty coating his tone. "I'm still trying to figure out what spells would be best to use."

"What if we use a masking spell to hide everyone?"

Cas contemplated the idea. "That could work, but masking comes at the cost of one scale for non-enchanters and it wears off after a time. Plus, being invisible takes away physical power, so you're like air. We won't be able to inflict any real damage on the Eyes when we're in an invisible state. Enchanter law."

Hali cringed thinking of everyone needing to remove a scale from themselves.

"But ... it could help us buy some time; and one scale is better than being flayed of all of them by the Eyes," Cas added.

"Enchanters are a lot more noble than I ever imagined them to be. You know ... before I believed they existed and that I was one."

Cas shrugged. "Well, with power, comes responsibility."

Hali's lips curled up and her nose crinkled.

"What?" Cas asked, noticing her amused expression.

"Are you sure you've never read a comic book?"

Cas looked puzzled by Hali's question.

"Never mind," Hali finished, shaking her head.

Once they reached camp the merriment had dwindled, and the Anchors were nowhere in sight. The lanterns flickered, swaying back and forth in windless air as if possessed. Hali's lawpnies tingled in alarm. Before she could take in the whole scene Cas was grasping her wrist and pulling her to him, ready to make a run for it. But he was too late.

"I don't think we've met." A gravelly voice spoke as the silhouette it belonged to stepped out from the trees, standing in front of Hali and Cas. "Hali, I presume?" It was the same older Eye with shoulder-length, salt and paprika-colored hair that had faced-off with Mamie over a year ago, looking for Hali. A year had transformed more red strands to gray and up close she could see the man's skin was leathered and freckled. She imagined in his younger days his skin used to be a healthy rose color.

"Who are you? Where are the others?" Cas growled. The Eye took a step back, raising his hands, a gesture that showed he was there to speak peacefully, but Hali and her lawpnies knew that it was only because he was alone. People were always more cooperative when they didn't have backup.

"The name is Jimmy and the others are fine ... for now."

"What do you mean *for now*?" Hali questioned, while struggling to contain her lawpnies. The effort to keep them at bay was usually uncomfortable, but now it felt impossible, like holding a waterfall back with the palms of her hands. Hali just hoped her internal struggle wasn't apparent to Jimmy.

"It means, if you come with me willingly, then maybe the others don't need to get hurt."

Jimmy didn't finish his sentence before Cas was stepping in front of Hali, like a pawn protecting his queen.

"That's not going to happen." Each tendon in Cas's forearm flexed against his skin in anger as he pointed a finger in Jimmy's face. Hali's cheek found the recess of Cas's back, pressing between his flared shoulder blades that threatened to rip the drenched shirt on his back to pieces with each muscle puffed in frustration.

Jimmy stepped back again, holding his hands up as if to say, *don't shoot the messenger,* but Cas didn't let up on his pursuit.

"Listen, I'm trying to help," Jimmy said, his tone and expression too agreeable to trust anything coming out of his mouth.

"Really, how is giving you what you want going to help us at all?" Cas interjected.

"Because, Exalted only wants Hali."

"Exalted?" Cas and Hali said in unison.

"Yes, Exalted is the superior of the Eyes, very few know his true identity and he has been waiting a long time for Hali to come of age. The rest of you are just obstacles. If you can prove to not be obstacles, you can spare many lives from fighting a war you can't win."

Cas moved forward like a lion about to strike his prey. Hali moved with Cas—her head never leaving the cocoon of his shoulder blades—hugging him from behind, until her hands were grabbing his shoulders from the front.

"Cas, stop!" Hali pleaded. Cas froze in place at the contact. "Think about what you are doing," she whispered, as her hands rose up and down with every breath Cas took. He inhaled and exhaled deep heavy breaths, like he had already been fighting.

"Hali, you need to let go," Cas enunciated each word slowly, his tone low and controlled.

Hali bit the side of her mouth, struggling to move, gripped by fear, burdened with responsibility. She had no desire to die or be used by Eyes, like Arcelia had been. But she couldn't risk the others, especially Cas. He had made an unbearable year bearable. She cared about him. A lot. She knew he cared about her too. She wouldn't let the others take on her burden.

Her insides quaked as she whispered into Cas's back, "So do you." She clung to him as the words reverberated in her chest. Their heartbeats connected them—Cas's in Hali's ear and hers into his back. Hali always thought that getting older meant not being afraid, but she learned she had been wrong. Fear still existed within her, maybe even more than when she was little. "I need to do this, Cas."

Cas's shoulders tightened, and he brought his hands up to grab Hali's, tightly. He never took his eyes off of Jimmy.

The rain picked up again, and thunder rumbled in the background of the dark blue night. "Hali, no."

"Cas, I have to."

"You don't," he gritted out.

Jimmy cleared his throat. "Well, how about this. I'll give you two a moment to sort out whatever this is while I go back and sort things out with the others. Hali, if you agree to my terms, you need to come down to the shore that follows the path from camp at midnight. If you are not there, or if you try to pull any funny business, we will murder all Anchors, no questions asked. I'm a fair man, but I won't be crossed. Is that understood?"

Hali peered from behind Cas's back and replied, "Yes," straining to speak over the knot that had built up in her throat.

"Good," Jimmy answered, as he retreated into the dark abyss of night, becoming just another shadow.

Hali's heart pounded at the ultimatum, pushing blood and logic out of her head. She couldn't think or stand straight. The weight of her body collapsed against Cas's back, afraid to meet his glower face-to-face. He must have felt the same, because he made no immediate move to look her in the eyes.

"You can't surrender yourself Hali, it's only a trap. They will kill us all anyway, with or without your help."

"I can't take that chance, Cas. You heard what Jimmy said."

"I don't care what Jimmy said," Cas's voice elevated, while his hands tightened around Hali's. "Why are you being so stubborn?"

"I don't want to argue with you, Cas," Hali stated, strained from the argument.

"Then stop talking crazy. We'll be fine. The Eyes are just

using intimidation to scare you into making it easier for them. You can't give in. They won't be able to kill all the Anchors without a fight."

"Are you trying to convince me or yourself?"

Cas pulled Hali around him, until they were face-to-face. He let go of her hands, exchanging them for her shoulders. "You are the most exhausting person I've ever met. What was the point of training if you were just going to give up as soon as the Eyes asked you to? Can you answer that question?"

Hali's lower lip trembled. "Because," she said, "I love you and I can't watch you and the others die if I could have prevented it." The words spilled out of her mouth effortlessly, escaping from the confines of her ribs. The proclamation wasn't planned. How could it have been with such awful timing? But she doubted she could have said it at all under perfect circumstances. Death hung over all of the Eyes' Land, urging the truth out of hiding. A truth she had ignored until it grew too powerful to cage any longer. Her lawpnies couldn't even be blamed. It was all Hali.

Cas didn't move and it felt like time had stopped. His long, dark eyelashes had droplets of rain hanging from them, but he never wavered from holding Hali's shoulders to wipe them away. The rain fell in sheets. Cas squinted, and Hali wasn't sure if his grimace was the result of the assaulting rain or her declaration. Either way, Hali couldn't handle him looking at her anymore. She lowered her eyes from his, vulnerable and exposed by her honesty. Her shoulders got lighter as Cas removed his hands. Hali stubbornly avoided his gaze, expecting when she allowed her eyes to meet his again, she would be met with pity. His silence was answer enough.

"Hali, I—" Hali was snatched from the ground so quickly, she blurred on her assent.

"Toodle-oo," two Eyes said in unison from the top of a tree. Their fingers waved at Cas, while they sandwiched Hali between them, each holding one of her arms hostage. Cas shot his lawpnies at them with both hands, being careful to avoid Hali. But by the time the white flames reached the two Eyes, they had disappeared. Hali was gone.

29

THE HONEY MOON

ALL BETS WERE OFF as Cas transported himself to the shore, without a care of who saw him. Hali wasn't there and neither was Mr. Gruff. He brought his hands up to his head, slicking his wet hair back, as he scanned the area, looking up to the almost full moon that had a small sliver missing from the outside. It floated just above the horizon, golden honey in color, highlighting the waves and the rain that fell from the sky. The moon loomed over the Eyes' Land, taunting it with its borrowed light from the sun which wasn't sufficient enough to expose the evils that were occurring below. Cas felt sickened and helpless by it all. What good was he if he couldn't help those that he cared about? He couldn't help his parents and he couldn't help Hali.

He trudged rapidly up the shore, looking for some kind of clue. Footprints, signs of a struggle, anything that could lead him to Hali and the others—but saw nothing. Knowing that they couldn't leave the Eyes' Land gave him a little hope, but he knew better than to underestimate the Eyes. His lawpnies pulled at his skin, breaking free to draw an arrow circling itself a foot in front of his face.

"What are you trying to tell me?" Cas asked the lawpnies. The circling lights straightened out, pointing their arrow at Cas's hands, before circling once more and pointing at his hands again. In times like these he wished his lawpnies could speak. He watched in frustration as the lawpnies continued their repetitious cycles, until he finally understood what they were trying to communicate.

A tracking spell.

He had spent his whole life only using measured amounts of his abilities, that not holding back was a foreign concept.

"Ahh, lawpnies, you're geniuses." The little orbs flashed like fireflies in approval before retreating back into Cas's skin. Cas turned away from the moon and the ocean, ready to return to his cabin for his spell book, when a figure approached out of nowhere.

Cas jumped back a few feet, squatting in a fighting position, ready to attack the intruder, when he saw that it was only Mr. Gruff. "Where the hell did you come from? Where are the others?"

Mr. Gruff wore the same indifferent expression he had worn since he had become Mr. Gruff almost two decades before, not at all fazed by Cas.

"The Eyes took everyone," Mr. Gruff answered, as if commenting on the weather.

"Why didn't you stop them?" Cas gritted out, his body straightening.

Mr. Gruff watched Cas curse to himself while kicking sand at the ocean, resulting in a sprinkle of moonlit grains of sand and rain plummeting towards the earth in a clouded haze.

Mr. Gruff held his spot in the sand, remaining unperturbed. "Cas, I could have acted brave and demanded that the Eyes—which were many by the way—release all of the Anchors and been killed heroically in an instant. But I decided to hide instead."

"Well, isn't that convenient," Cas huffed, shaking his head in disbelief at Mr. Gruff's unabashed honesty.

"I have no fear in dying. In fact, I welcome death most days, when it will finally decide to give me mercy. But I thought that maybe I could be of some use before that happens."

Cas's eyes never shifted from Mr. Gruff's and his expression never swayed from irritation. "Well, if you have some other use, besides wooden spears, you need to speak up now, because if you haven't noticed I'm a bit preoccupied."

Cas granted Mr. Gruff all of three seconds to speak, before walking away.

He had trudged six steps when Mr. Gruff finally spoke. "I'm assuming you need help with a tracking spell?"

Cas turned back around, his interest peaked, waiting for Mr. Gruff to continue.

"It's funny what you can observe when you don't speak. It's almost like becoming invisible. People assume if one doesn't speak that they can't see, when it's quite the opposite. The past nineteen years have become an education on the magic of silence." Cas began to open his mouth, but Mr. Gruff cut him off before he could talk. "Don't worry, I've done enough malice for one lifetime. Your monthly humanitarian efforts are safe with me. I'm only here to help. That is, if you want my help. Obviously, I cannot produce any of my own magic, but I'm a living, breathing spell book. The enchanters didn't take my knowledge away, only my powers."

It took Cas no time to decide. "What do I need to do?"

After only a few moments, Cas had clipped five scales

from himself in quick succession, teetering on excruciating. "What now?" he asked through clenched teeth. If Mr. Gruff was only goading him, he'd have no issue pulling him out into the ocean and leaving him there to find his own way back to shore.

"The moon is strong tonight, so we'll use its power. Offer the scales up with both of your hands and repeat after me." Cas did as he was instructed, listening for the words he had to repeat:

"*Whether hither or yon, you're here, not gone.*
Disappearing midair, lead us to where."

After Cas repeated the incantation, his hands tingled in the air. When he brought his hands down to his face, he found he no longer had his five scales, but he also didn't have the information he needed.

"Did it work?" he asked Mr. Gruff.

Mr. Gruff nodded his head to Cas's hands. "Look."

Cas peered down at the lawpnies that had gathered in his palms in an orb of concentrated light that lit his face. An image appeared that at first he couldn't make out. His eyes worked hard, shifting between widening and squinting to adjust to the constant change in lighting and rainfall. Finally, he was able to make out the image of a cabin that belonged to Toru's family. The small cabin hadn't been occupied since Toru's parents and sister passed away in the Eye attack eleven years before, leaving Toru to move in with Kai and Jett. Despite not being used, it still had running water from the well, and electricity from the windmill Cas's parents had installed near the orchards when the cabins were created.

The dwelling was one that he had planned on making Hali's, only if his original idea took longer than he wanted it to ... but Cas really hoped it wouldn't. The idea had come to him after Hali had mentioned a desire to return Ronan's room back to him, believing herself to be a burden. Cas knew that wasn't true and that both Marilla and Ronan enjoyed having her live with them, but he could understand Hali's reasoning for wanting a place to call her own. But when Hali brought up living with Delphia, Cas couldn't say he was thrilled with that option, for a couple of reasons—all selfish. But the least of his selfish reasons were to maintain the anonymity of his enchanter side. He didn't want Delphia to barge into Hali's room one night and discover she wasn't there. Once that happened it would only be a matter of time before Delphia figured out that Hali was training with Cas and his secret would be exposed.

Preserving his secret was also the prime reason Cas insisted not to live with anyone after the Eye attack, despite encouragement from the elders to do so. They would say things like, *it's not good for a young man to live alone* or *your parents would want you to have company.* Cas's reply would always be the same. *I'll manage.* There were simply too many orphaned children for the elders to fuss too long over him, that they finally gave up. But living arrangements mattered little now, if he couldn't figure out how to fight off the Eyes.

Focusing in on the image, he saw Hali sitting in the middle of the floor, her hands bound behind her back and her legs wrapped from her ankles up in what appeared to be duct tape. Her dress laid over her wrapped legs and Cas's blood pressure rose the more he took in the flickering image. Modest Hali, who had been so uncomfortable about undressing to fish, was being manhandled by Eyes with duct tape. At that moment, the lawpnies disintegrated in his palms, like the sand had after he kicked it in the air. With the intel he needed, Cas began to run to the cabin, even though he knew a portal would get him there faster. He couldn't risk appearing from thin air in a forest that likely had Eyes stationed in the shadows. Besides the Eyes that had taken Hali, the other Eyes didn't know he possessed magic—at least, not yet—and he needed every advantage he could get, if the Anchors had a chance against them.

Cas had become so engrossed in his next steps that he had forgotten Mr. Gruff was following behind. "Where is she, Cas?" Mr. Gruff hobbled briskly behind but not fast enough to match Cas's pace. Cas didn't answer. His brain was too busy formulating a plan to form the words necessary for an answer.

"You know boy, it might be helpful if you have a plan in place before you go and get yourself killed. You won't be any help to anyone then."

"What do you think I'm trying to do?" Cas whipped around fuming at Mr. Gruff.

Mr. Gruff studied him for a moment longer than Cas had the time for. Cas shrugged, turned away and resumed running, while Mr. Gruff stayed put.

"You know, if only there was a spell you could use for a situation like this?"

Cas's shoulders fell with his head, before turning back around to find Mr. Gruff planted where he left him. "If you have something to say, I suggest you say it now. I don't have time for these games."

"Very well then," Mr. Gruff said, unmoving. Irritated, Cas jogged back to him. Once Cas stood in front of him, Mr. Gruff asked, "What do Eyes covet?"

"I thought I said no games," Cas protested.

"Do you want my help or not?"

Cas shrugged, answering anyway, "Power."

"Right, they want power. And where do they get their power from?"

"The elements. Is there a point to this?" Cas would have bolted if he had any other ideas, but his thoughts were irrational, desperate even. He wasn't himself. Mr. Gruff's indifference to the situation made him the only logical one of the two.

"Yes, and we're getting to it. Other than the elements, how do Eyes gain power? Think about what the Eyes want from Anchors, so much so, they are blinded by their greed for it."

"Scales," Cas said without hesitation.

"Exactly," Mr. Gruff ended.

Cas threw his arms up. "But I already knew all of this. How is this new information?"

"Because, you're as blinded by anger and fear as the Eyes are by power and greed. They're using your weakness against you. You have enchanter powers Cas, the Eyes don't. And what you're forgetting is that Hali has enchanter powers, too. Both of you need to use them. If you go in like an enraged mortal, you will lose, not only for yourself but for Hali and all of the Anchors. The Eyes didn't come without a plan, so don't be foolish or it will all be for nothing."

Cas looked down at the sand, letting Mr. Gruff's words seep into his stubborn skull. In the past year Cas and Hali had studied the spell book and worked on their fighting skills nightly. The spell book alone could take a century to go through and an enchanter would still not learn everything in it, which is why most enchanters read it like a recipe book, knowing that memorizing the entire book in a year's time wasn't practical or possible. Their plan of attack hadn't gotten much further than learning how to strike the Eyes down with their lawpnies. Practicing or using any other magic would have come at a cost that Hali and Cas couldn't risk without being caught. All of these reasons they hadn't been more proactive in using their magic seemed ridiculous now, since the Eyes were prepared, and the Anchors weren't.

As Cas mulled over everything Mr. Gruff said, an idea occurred to him like a lightbulb flashing over his head. "I have an idea!" Cas announced.

"I was hoping you would," Mr. Gruff said sarcastically.

"I think I liked you more before you talked. Come on, I'll tell you on the way." Without waiting to see if Mr. Gruff followed, Cas began jogging to the cabin that held Hali.

Moving his legs faster than he had in close to two decades, without an utter from Cas about his plan, Mr. Gruff wheezed out, "Is part of your idea ... to kill me ... or are you trying ... to keep me in suspense ... on whatever you've come up with?"

Cas rolled his eyes to himself. "I'm going to do what you said and lure the Eyes with their own greed," he called over his shoulder.

"Okay. After you *lure* them ... then what?" Mr. Gruff coughed on the oxygen entering his lungs at a much faster rate than he had been accustomed to.

"I'm thinking about it. That's as far as I've gotten on the plan," Cas stated, almost embarrassed. Usually his mind was sharp when it came to strategy, but with Hali thrown into the mix his mind couldn't follow a line of thinking without going off track to think of her in danger. His fear overwhelmed him.

"Well then ... you're in luck."

Cas twisted his head over his shoulder to look at Mr. Gruff, yet again. His neck was beginning to ache with the amount of times he needed to turn around for the laggard.

"I happen to know … what we can use … to trap some …
Eyes," Mr. Gruff rushed out between gasps.

"What?"

"I'm glad you asked … I've been working on something
… for a while… that could use … a little more help."

They didn't speak anymore until reaching the woods.
Cas stopped once they entered. Mr. Gruff finally caught up
and walked alongside Cas showing the tiniest hint of enthusiasm across his face.

Switching roles, Mr. Gruff said, "Follow me," before
walking into the part of the forest that was dense with trees,
leaving Cas behind without waiting. With no other means to
trap Eyes by and with time ticking on, Cas followed. After
what felt like five minutes of getting lost, they came to a stop
in front of a large pile that Cas struggled to make out, since
the trees concealed a fair amount of light from the moon.

Cas looked down, his eyes adjusting to see massive piles
of moss-covered wood, dank and muddy, in various sizes.
"What is it?"

Holding out his arms like a game show host showing off
a new car, Mr. Gruff answered, "It's a boat."

Cas cut his eyes towards Mr. Gruff, leaving no confusion
of what he thought of his idea. "The hell it is," he argued,
grabbing the top of his head in frustration at the time they
had wasted.

Ignoring Cas, Mr. Gruff continued, "With the proper
spell it will be the perfect boat to capture Eyes with. Repeat
after me:

"*Bow to the sun and sea, pointed and free.*
Stern to the trees and sand, back to the land.
Starboard hugging the right, holding on tight.
Port supporting the left, nothing bereft."

Cas obeyed, on the off chance the sad, rotten planks could

be transformed by the spell and not all was lost from their journey into the woods. The lawpnies danced to the incantation, creating a cloud of light around the stacked planks. After the last word of the spell was spoken the lawpnies cleared, finding their way back to Cas. A massive boat was left in the place where the wood stacks sat seconds before. There was no time to be in awe of his work, but the boat was the most complex creation he had ever assembled with his magic. What made the boat even more impressive was that Cas didn't even need to use any scales to make it happen. Since all the pieces were already available, it was just a matter of assembly.

"What made you shave pieces for a boat?" Cas asked.

Mr. Gruff shrugged. "I'm not the greatest swimmer. Thought it might be a good idea to have a place to wait it out when the Eyes came back. My project has just taken a little longer than I would have liked. Guess now I don't need to work on creating pegs for assembly."

Cas nodded in understanding. "Now what?"

"Now you need to move it out into the open so we can trap the Eyes, but we need to mask it so they can't see it."

"How am I supposed to do both spells at once?" Cas asked. It was the mortal equivalent of doing two math problems at once, except if you made a mistake on one problem you took a gamble of having a boat drop on your head.

But before Cas could work out the new obstacle, a new voice said, "I think I can help with that." Neilan appeared in the small clearing, looking amazed as he examined the impressive creation that took over the entire space. Cas wasn't sure what he thought of Neilan, but he wasn't in a position to turn down help. "Where do you want it?"

With his contribution completed, Mr. Gruff passed the responsibility over to Cas with a glance. Cas accepted with a nod before turning to Neilan. "The Eyes have Hali in an empty cabin that sits just a little off from the occupied ones. Will you be able to move the boat if you can't see it?"

Neilan scoffed. "I can move anything."

Annoyed by his unearned bravado, Cas challenged, "Okay, then—*move* your ass." Cas crossed his arms, staring Neilan down.

Neilan's eyebrows quirked up, as he turned to an apathetic Mr. Gruff and asked, "Is he always this hostile?" Mr. Gruff only shrugged in response.

"What are you waiting for?" Cas pushed.

"I'm waiting to *not* see a boat," Neilan gestured to the out-of-place vessel.

"Why can't you start moving it while I'm producing the spell?"

Neilan sighed. "I could, but then that would defeat the point of making it invisible, now wouldn't it?"

"I doubt you can move it faster than I can make it disappear."

"Want to try me?" Neilan challenged.

Cas snapped his fingers and the boat vanished; smug confidence oozed from him before nodding his head to Neilan. "Well, come on then."

Slightly defeated, Neilan mumbled, "And Eyes are supposed to be the cheaters."

Rain had drenched their bodies to a point that clothing stopped being effective at providing any shelter. Luckily the night and rain were warm, otherwise hypothermia would have become a problem. Which in Cas's opinion, would have still been a more preferable death than death at the hands of the Eyes.

The lightning and thunder rumbled on consistently in the background, hardly noticeable when compared to the storm of havoc the Eyes were wreaking.

Neilan sucked in a breath of storm that puffed his chest full, reddening his cheeks from exertion. The trees rattled, as the invisible boat levitated.

"Lead the way," Neilan choked out through restricted breaths.

The journey to the cabin felt nothing short of a Herculean effort, but Neilan didn't complain once and Cas said nothing snarky about the task appearing harder for Neilan than he had boasted.

With the boat placed where it needed to be, Cas ran up to the cabin windows that held Hali hostage to get a peek inside. Neilan and Mr. Gruff sat below Cas's feet listening and acting as backup.

The Eyes who'd taken Hali were inside, their heads hung low, like two children being scolded for misbehaving. Cas peered in from one of the windows behind the couch, but he couldn't see Hali or who was doing the scolding. Cas went to the other window a few feet away, parallel to the one he had been looking through to get a better angle. He saw Jimmy—the Eye who had attempted to coerce Hali to come on her own to the shore at midnight—chiding the two Eyes.

"I thought I told you two nitwits to let me handle it, but instead you had to go and take her, making a liar out of me. All I asked you to do was to keep an eye on her and listen and you couldn't even do that. We could have had all the Anchors in the same place at the same time, and now we have no idea where Cas is." Jimmy was so furious that Cas almost felt sorry for the two nitwitted Eyes. Almost.

"We're sorry Jimmy, we thought we were helping. Honest," one of the naive Eyes pleaded.

"Well, you didn't. Now we have Eyes dousing the girl in ocean water in a bathtub. Why do we have Eyes dousing her with ocean water in a bathtub when we are near a perfectly good ocean for crying out loud? Don't you know an Anchor can't transform in any place besides the ocean? Why is she even being transformed right now? Exalted wants her for her magic, not her scales! We have an entire island of Anchors we can pluck scales from, you idiots!"

The other Eye spoke up this time. "At first, we wrapped her up, well, not us, but the others did. But then she shot fire from her hands, like the fella she was with, so we had to knock her out so she wouldn't kill us. That's when we got the idea to put her in the bathtub. We thought plucking some of her scales might teach her a lesson."

Jimmy's eyes went from annoyed to murderous. He paused, clearing his throat, with a measured voice that held an eerie calmness and asked, "What do you mean, like the fella she was with?"

Both the nitwits looked to one another, not sure if answering was only going to get them both into more trouble.

"I th-think he had magic too. He b-burnt my arm," nitwit number one, with orange-red hair stuttered, holding up his arm to show Jimmy the scorched band of skin across his forearm.

Cas moved away from the window, stepping in a hole that once held a tree. His arms instinctively slammed into the cabin walls to regain his footing. The crash echoed through the cabin, but luckily thunder rattled the sky at the same time. The Eyes remained unaware.

"Shit, that was close," Cas whispered. Neilan grimaced at

Cas's flub and Mr. Gruff closed his eyes, knowing how close Cas was to making a mistake that could have cost them all. "We need to move on this now! Move to the front door," he demanded.

Cas had kept the masking spell in place so long that it had made him clumsier than his usual sure-footed self. And now he needed to create another. For the confetti spell he didn't need Mr. Gruff's help. He had worked on it with Hali many times. It was one of the few spells that he could do in the confines of a cabin that didn't require scales.

He remembered the first time he had taught Hali the spell. It was a few months after she had settled on the Eyes' Land. The weather had cooled, the days had become shorter, the nights longer and Hali sat on his couch quietly thumbing through the spell book, not asking half the questions she usually did during their nightly trainings. After some badgering, he learned that the day would have been the start of college for Hali and her friend Camille. Life had kept moving forward and Hali felt left behind, though she never said it. Cas knew all too well what it was like to have your life rearranged unexpectedly. But as he watched a disheartened Hali, he thought of a way to cheer her up.

His idea stemmed from one of their previous trainings months before. It was during the thick of summer, when they were both worn down by their daily dose of sunshine and humidity. Hali's cheeks were flushed even though they had been sitting in Cas's air-conditioned cabin for a while. Reluctant to exert themselves any more than they already had during the day, they talked instead, neither one moving to do anything training related. Hali mentioned that the brutal heat reminded her of how much she missed and loved to visit the snow. Adding that it rarely ever snowed in

Emerald Cove so her family would go to the mountains every so often but hadn't been for some time.

Months later, Cas remembered this conversation as he watched Hali resting her chin on the palm of her hand, apathetically flipping through pages of the spell book with the other. Cas laughed to himself as he watched Hali's eyes cross when the first snowflake fell on her nose, catching her attention. Peering up from the spell book, she found snow falling from everywhere. A confused smile cracked through her melancholy as Hali's eyes met with his. As she stood up from the couch to take in the scene, Cas placed a hot cocoa in her hands. She tilted her head towards him, her smile making his own breath hitch in his chest.

"You didn't make any cocoa for yourself?" Hali asked.

Cas shook his head, and Hali's eyes responded with a flicker of disappointment.

Changing subjects, she returned her gaze back to the snowfall as she wiped snowflakes from her lashes with her free hand and asked, "What is all this?"

"It's a confetti spell," Cas answered, remaining focused on the spell, so he didn't smile back at her like an idiot. "Ready to learn how to do it yourself?"

Hali's eyes lit up and her head nodded in quick agreement. Cas taught her the spell and she learned it easily. He remembered how happy and in awe she looked as the snowflakes landed on her hair, melting into her braid that fell over her shoulder.

The memory choked him up, as he was brought back to reality with Neilan's voice.

"You all right?" Neilan asked, genuinely concerned.

Cas shook away his memories, and the worry that they would be the only memories he'd ever have of watching

Hali enjoy the snow. "Yep, let's do this," he responded with more calmness than he felt.

They had discussed their strategy briefly, Cas just hoped that it would all go smoothly even without practice.

Lightning streaked the lavender background of the sky once again. The bold-illuminated cracks like scratch marks from a cat's outstretched paws on a wooden floor.

Neilan hid behind a nearby tree, nodding to Cas that he was ready. Cas closed his eyes as wind whipped at his back. Mr. Gruff stood beside Neilan, as cool and calm as usual, ready to call out incantations if needed.

The rain ceased as the wind grew stronger in intensity. The front door of the cabin was the first to come off, flying off the hinges effortlessly, and disappearing into the night as fast as it appeared. Seconds later, the turbulent winds slowed to a gentle breeze, indicating it was time for Cas to work his magic.

With glowing palms, he chanted:

"*Let Anchors' scales scatter like autumn leaves, on the ground, through air, and the rooftops' eaves.*"

Scales swirled down from the sky mixed with the light drizzle that had resumed after Neilan stopped pulling from the elements. Neilan's eyes rounded at the sight of the colorful glimmers that held the promise of power.

"Hold your pants on boy, it's only an illusion. Not the real thing," Mr. Gruff whispered, harshly.

"But it looks so real," Neilan said, watching the scales above him in a daze.

Mr. Gruff whacked Neilan across the back of his head. "That's the point, now get it together or you'll end up with the others and leave something important behind."

Neilan rubbed the back of his head and looked at Mr. Gruff with surprise. "What do you—"

"Know?" Mr. Gruff finished. "Everything. What? You think Eyes are the only ones who pay attention?"

Neilan began to open his mouth, looking like a fish out of water, but Mr. Gruff cut him off again.

"Don't worry, I care very little of the secrets that float around here. But you just make sure that you return things back the way you found them, or I'll be forced to speak."

Neilan nodded in silent agreement, sobered by Mr. Gruff's threat. Moments later, Eyes poured from the cabin, just as enthralled by the floating scales as Neilan had been.

Neilan sucked in the nearest rain cloud that was responsible for the drizzling conditions. Cas and Mr. Gruff watched on as Neilan blew out a soft breath that brought the colorful scattered scales together, creating a path. The Eyes followed the scales, tripping over themselves as they lost track of their feet. The vibrant scales twinkled under the moonlight and the Eyes grabbed greedily at the twirling illusions, unaware that they were being led. The next cloud Neilan sucked in inflated him like a balloon one pinprick away from popping. Neilan slowly released his breath with a number of small exhales, the strain on his face lessening with each puff.

Once the Eyes were safely in the invisible boat easing into the water, Neilan took in another storm cloud bigger than the last. This time, releasing the breath without holding back, like a five-year-old blowing out birthday candles. When Neilan was finished, he tipped his head to Cas, letting him know that the work was done.

Cas's shoulders lowered, as he released his grip on both spells. The scales that danced in the air vanished and the Eye-filled boat appeared against the backdrop of the moon, just before tipping over the horizon.

"Will they turn back around when they realize they've been tricked?" Cas asked.

"No. They will be on the other side of the world before they regain any control of the boat. I sent them on their way pretty fast."

"Thank you," Cas struggled to say.

Neilan just pointed his head towards the cabin and said, "Go get Hali."

"Hali," Cas called out as he charged into the cabin. A thud sounded from the bathroom in response. Reaching the bathroom within seconds, he found Hali's mouth taped, her eyes masked by a black bandana, and her arms tied behind her back with rope. The bottom half of her dress was soaked, appearing a darker purple. The Eyes' attempts to submerge her in their makeshift ocean in the bathtub, left the dress threadbare and her legs reddened from the duct tape that had been violently torn from her skin. Cas fumed.

Hali looked wild, ready to attack the next person who got in her space. The ropes tied behind her back were hanging on by a literal thread from her own efforts at burning them with her lawpnies. Hali was within seconds of setting herself free before Cas arrived.

"Hali, it's Cas," he announced warily. Hali's head fell backwards with a sigh.

"Thank God," Hali cried. "I thought you were another Eye."

Cas uncovered Hali's eyes and used his lawpnies to sever the last bit of rope holding her hostage. Her eyes softened when she saw Cas, but then she looked down quickly, as if embarrassed. Hali's quick change in emotions confused Cas at first, until he remembered their last conversation. Hali rubbed at her rope-burned wrists, all while avoiding eye contact with him.

There was too much going on to say all he needed to say to Hali, so instead he settled for a hug, relieved she was alive. Wrapping his arms around Hali's back, he savored the feel and smell of her. But the connection was over much sooner than he would have liked as Hali broke from their hug first, leaving her hands at Cas's elbows.

With seriousness and fear in her eyes, Hali asked, "Where are the other Anchors?"

Cas shook his head. "I don't know, but we need to move fast."

Cas grabbed for Hali's hand as they made their way outside. They didn't make it to the trees before Cas suddenly stopped.

"What's the matter?" Hali asked. Her lawpnies crawled up her spine to her neck like spiders escaping a demolished web.

He held his pointer finger up to his mouth, silently shushing her. She heeded his order, following Cas's gaze. The rain and wind had stopped. Crickets, frogs, and cicadas didn't cry their mating calls. The only sound to be heard was the pipping and popping of rain droplets, diving to freedom from their leaf cocoons into the newly formed puddles that rested beneath the trees. It was dark and quiet. Eerily so. Cas glanced around aware of Hali watching his every move, sensing his unease.

Cas turned his head to Hali and said, "Neilan and Mr. Gruff are gone."

30

CROSSING THE THRESHOLD

CAS WHISPERED into Hali's ear, "We need to mask ourselves, or we're going to give ourselves away to the Eyes. Do you remember how?"

Hali nodded as she muttered the incantation to disappear:

"Protect my body with a mask, if it's not too much to ask."

After the last word had been spoken, Hali held up her arm, examining to see if it was still visible. It wasn't. One thing Hali had learned about enchanter magic, was that it wasn't to be used haphazardly. Many of the basic incantations sounded more like a request rather than a demand that would be met with certainty. Cas had said it was because enchanter law didn't want magic to be taken for granted. By asking permission, it humbled enchanters into accepting that the power they were bestowed was not their own but borrowed, and could be taken away if misused.

"Hali, you there?"

"Yes," she said softly.

"Good, grab my hand, so we stay together. This will help

buy us some time to find the others, but we'll need to unmask if we need to use our lawpnies."

"Okay," Hali agreed, as she waved her arm around to find Cas's hand. Once their hands clasped, they made their way down to the shore without speaking. They weaved around the trees like two ghosts in the night, the wind whistling through them. Hali's body had become a mist in the sticky air, but her thoughts were still intact as if she were whole. Like ashes, she felt like she was a breeze away from dissolving into the air and sea forever. But despite their vaporized state, Cas's hand felt solid in hers.

"How's it possible that we're part of the air, but I can hold your hand like we're whole?" Hali instantly regretted the innocent question that sounded more meaningful aloud than it did in her head.

Cas's mist buoyed like a warm, ocean spray beside her own. After admitting her love for him earlier that night without him saying anything in return, she was glad to be invisible. Her timing for her unfiltered honesty hadn't been the best, considering she was snatched from the ground almost immediately after. If there hadn't been more important matters to worry over, *seeing* him and holding his hand might have been unbearably uncomfortable. She could barely look him in the eyes after he had pulled the cloth covering her eyes free. But the words were out nonetheless and that knowledge both contented her and riddled her with anxiousness.

As Hali cringed at her question, Cas surprised her with his answer. "That's because we're connected by something more powerful than our physical beings."

"Like what?" Hali asked quickly as she scanned the Eyes' Land from above. For the life of her she couldn't understand why she seemed to have no filter with Cas. They hovered just above the ground like helium balloons the day after a party. Deflated, but still holding on.

Before he could answer, lights flickered in the distance where the orchards stood, catching both of their attention. Cas quietly asked, "Do you see that?" Hali squeezed his hand in response. Without a word, they both glided in the direction of the orchards.

Once they made it to the trees, they found the Anchors held up in nets, hanging from a few matured oak trees that had sturdy, thick branches. Standing silent and still, the Eyes surrounded below each oak tree with knives sheathed to their hips, keeping watch over the Anchors. Hali estimated the Eyes outnumbered the two-hundred and four Anchors by one hundred. A sense of foreboding buzzed around her mist.

"Where are the others? They should be here by now with Hali," a deep familiar voice asked. Hali knew that voice. It was a voice that she had heard all of her life. Shivers went down her misty spine as she squeezed Cas's hand harder. Hali's heartbeat drummed faster. The increased pace pulsed around her like millions of small hearts beating in unison. The warm breeze blew through her ghostlike body as if she was a strainer full of holes. She searched the crowd of Eyes frantically for the face she knew matched the voice, but found nothing.

Could it be a coincidence?

Deep down, Hali knew it wasn't, but she still didn't have proof. Suddenly a man stepped out of the shadows of a tree set off from the other Eyes and Anchors.

Hidden.

If Hali wasn't afforded the advantage of floating above the trees, she would have never caught a glimpse of the man and confirmed her fear.

A girl Eye, who looked younger than Hali by a couple of years, with shoulder-length, blonde hair and big, brown, doe eyes stood next to him. "Exalted, we lost track of the others ... and Hali."

"What do you mean, you lost track? We're on an island. Find her. And while you're at it, find Neilan. But not before you find Hali."

"Yes, Exalted." The girl skittered off into the trees with one of her ears pointing out from her blonde bob, appearing even more doe-like than before.

As Hali remained hidden with Cas in their masked states, Hali straddled between wanting to gather intel and wanting to act. Cas must have sensed her dilemma, because he gave her hand a little squeeze.

"Hey, we need to have a plan before we do anything. We need to distract the Eyes hovering around the trees so we can cut the others loose."

"How are we going to do that?" Hali questioned. Just as she asked, leaves rattled from a nearby fig tree. Turning, she scanned the active tree and noticed a figure bunched at the top. At the base of the tree, Hali saw a less agile figure, using the trunk as a hiding spot.

Mr. Gruff.

So, if Mr. Gruff was hiding at the base of the tree then that only meant that Neilan was hiding up in the tall branches. Hali watched as Mr. Gruff shook his head in annoyance at Neilan's clumsiness. Hali grinned an invisible grin to herself.

"We look like ghosts—" Cas started.

"So, let's act like ghosts," she finished.

"Exactly, but I'll need to turn back to my solid form to cut the others from the trees."

"Actually, you don't."

"How's that?" Cas asked, oblivious to the happenings in the fig tree behind them that Hali had borne witness to.

Hali got close to where she thought Cas's ear would be and whispered, "We have backup in the fig tree, behind us."

His hand twisted in hers as he moved to see what backup Hali was talking about. Cas chuckled quietly, "All right then, are you ready to stir up some trouble like a proper enchanter?"

Hali exhaled. "As ready as I'm going to be."

"Don't come out of your masked state no matter what happens, Hali."

"But—"

"No buts, you can't protect everyone. You're who the Eyes want. They may try to use the Anchors against you as collateral. Don't let them. Hold strong."

Hali became nervous at Cas's warnings. She wanted to be oblivious to all the possibilities, but now it was all she thought about.

How could he expect her to promise something like that during battle? If only she could break the barrier.

Her mind always circled back to that one factor in this entire mess. How could it not? The Anchors could have the entire ocean and world at their disposal rather than live as prey for the Eyes to access in the fishbowl that was the Eyes' Land. As scared as she was, she didn't feel right protecting herself, when certain death was on the line for the others.

"Hali, do you hear me?" Cas asked, breaking into her thoughts.

"I do ... but I can't make any promises."

"Hali—"

"No. I won't protect myself at the expense of the others here if there's a way I can help. Please don't ask me to make a promise I won't be able to keep."

There was a long breath of silence after Hali spoke. Cas's hand remained in hers, so she knew he hadn't left, but he said nothing. As a mist there was no way to gauge what he was thinking, since she couldn't see him. It was the most annoying side effect of masking. The enchanters made sure to balance some powers with a weakness. Hali understood why, but invisibility was turning out to be more inconvenient than helpful. Especially now, when Hali desperately needed to see Cas's face.

Suddenly, without a word spoken, Cas began flying through the air over the Eyes, clutching Hali's hand. She wanted to ask him what he was doing, but she couldn't without being heard by Eyes below. When Hali did have a chance to ask, Cas soared too fast for her to breathe, let alone speak. They glided faster in the air as mists than they did swimming as mermaid and merman. Cas flew for miles, deep into the uncleared section of forest without cabins, that was densely packed with trees. Hali had never been that far into the forest before. Her walks from the shore to the cabins, where the trees were sparser, was the most experience she had with the forest. That's why for the life of her, she couldn't imagine why Cas was taking her there now and how it helped their plan of attack.

"Cas, why are we here?" Hali finally asked, when he slowed down.

He remained silent, despite no one being around.

"Cas!" Hali's voice grew louder.

"Just trust me," Cas said as they stopped at a pine tree with an unusually large trunk. Floating in the middle of the air, Cas brought Hali's hand that he was holding up to the tree and placed her palm against the trunk, while his hand splayed firmly over hers.

"What are you doing?" Hali asked. But Cas ignored her,

muttering something so low that she couldn't understand what he was saying.

Before Hali could make sense of what Cas was doing, her viewpoint changed. No longer was she outside surrounded by trees, the night sky with the almost full moon, and Cas all around her, but inside a small, dark space, illuminated by artificial light.

"What the hell?" Hali said.

"Hali? Is that you? I hear you, but I don't see you."

"Delphia?" Hali questioned with a mixture of relief and confusion. "Where are we? Where's Cas?" And then it dawned on her what Cas had done. "Cas! Why am I inside of a tree!" Hali dropped the masking spell, not wasting her energy on being invisible when she needed it to murder Cas.

"Hali, I'm sorry, but I won't let you sacrifice yourself. You made your choice and I've made mine. I need to go."

"Cas!" Hali yelled at his departure, not even attempting to whisper. "Cas!"

After the hundredth time of Hali's pleas going unanswered, she stopped. It was no use. Cas was gone and Hali was trapped inside of a tree. Hali turned to see Delphia, lit by the yellow glow of the solitary lamp that sat on the floor, shaking her head.

"Am I to assume you were dispensed here because the fighting has officially begun?"

"Just about," Hali answered, leaning her head against the inside of the trunk. "So, how did you end up in the tree? I went to look for you during the reception when you hadn't come back from putting your violin away, but that's when everything had gone crazy."

"That's a whole other story," Delphia huffed, rolling her eyes.

Hali squinted at her for a moment, curiously. But Delphia gave nothing away. Hali dropped the topic. But she couldn't help but wonder, if all the wedding guests were at the reception, including Cas, then who put Delphia inside of the tree?

Cas flew back to the fruit trees so quickly he worried that part of his mist would be left behind, and he wouldn't be whole when it was time to turn back to a solid. Trapping Hali in the enchanted tree wasn't Cas's first choice to protect her. Originally, he planned on fighting against the Eyes alongside her and the other Anchors. But when she basically declared to sacrifice herself to protect the other Anchors, Cas knew what he needed to do.

Had she learned nothing from Arcelia's story?

Even if she didn't speak to him for months or years after it was over. At least she would be alive. Now all Cas needed to worry about was making sure the Anchors won, and hope Hali didn't find a way out of the tree before the coast was clear.

Literally.

The Eyes huddled around the trees as they had before Cas left. The Eye referred to as Exalted stood apart from the other Eyes. His ears were so pointy they almost looked like knives glued to the sides of his head. Exalted was middle-aged with gray hair cropped short that belied his still youthful face. He was lean while still being muscular. Based off appearance alone, Cas could see why he would be a leader.

Examining what was before him, Cas swooped in, pushing Exalted in the back, lurching him forward. Cas saw the moment Exalted's intimidating glare slipped and was replaced with bewilderment. Exalted circled himself in search of the trespasser, frantically, like a dog chasing his tail. But Cas had no time to bask in his triumph. He needed to move fast before the other Eyes figured out enchanter magic was being used against them.

Cas swam in the air, too high for the Eyes to catch him, especially when they couldn't see him. The Eyes huddled beneath the Anchor-filled trees were still unaware of the attack on Exalted. Good. Cas needed them clueless. Outstretching his hand and with all the strength he had in his invisible state, he looped around the Eyes, knocking each one down with whacks to their heads as he went. The Eyes fell one by one like dominoes pushed down by a strong wind. Cas flew to the next tree and the next until all the Eyes were on the ground grabbing their heads. Some of the stronger ones shot up from the ground searching the night sky for a predator but found none. Soon they would.

Needing to get the Eyes away from the trees, Cas released the masking spell, while ensuring that he stayed above ground when he did—appearing from thin air. Cas saw the moment the Eyes noticed him. Their expressions went from dumbstruck to deadly. An opponent you could see was far less intimidating than one you couldn't. The Eyes' grins proved that they didn't think he was much of a challenge, but Cas would prove them wrong. He wasn't the biggest, but he was smart, strong, and had abilities that the Eyes could only dream of.

The Eyes began running for him like he was a bubble to catch before it made its final assent towards the sky. They jumped for him, but Cas was too far off the ground. He began moving away from the trees, allowing himself to be bait. Cas moved quickly enough to appear to be trying to get away, but slowly enough that the Eyes didn't give up on their pursuit.

As soon as the Eyes were far enough away, Neilan jumped out of the fig tree that he and Mr. Gruff had run to while Cas was getting Hali from the cabin. They hadn't meant to leave them behind, but Mr. Gruff had heard screams in the distance—Anchors' screams—that they couldn't ignore. Neilan ran to the first oak tree that held Anchors. His heart pounded in his chest, knowing that time was of the essence. Especially since he was going against his own kind. Mr. Gruff hobbled along, holding the thick rope while Neilan cut at it with his knife in one hand and the rope with the other. The Anchors dropped to the ground like a blanket full of apples. Luckily, the drop wasn't too high, since neither Mr. Gruff nor Neilan had the strength to help the Anchors come down gently from the net. Neilan and Mr. Gruff released every Anchor. The younger Anchors, like Kai and Carmya, appeared unaffected from the treatment, but the older Anchors, like Mamie and Fisk, looked the worse for wear.

"Go down to the shore," Neilan instructed. "Cas is leading the Eyes there."

"Why should we listen to you?! You're one of them," Kai challenged angrily.

Neilan stepped forward, pointing a finger in Kai's face. "Because I just saved your ass. Now go!"

Kai darted a death glare at Neilan, but Carmya grabbed his arm and whispered into his ear until his demeanor relaxed as much as circumstance would allow. The Anchors were anxious and on edge. Neilan could understand why they didn't trust him. But when they began moving towards the shore, relief washed over him. The fight wasn't over, but Neilan had just won the most important battle if the Anchors stood a chance against the Eyes—a fair fight ... or at least as fair as it could get.

"You know, I don't have enchanter blood or anything, but I've been in here for several hours and I don't think there's a way out from the inside." Delphia watched as Hali pressed and zapped—what she called lawpnies—at every square inch of the inside of the tree.

"There has to be," Hali said. "And I thought you were supposed to be the positive one. How can you be okay with being trapped in here? And are you going to tell me how you ended up here in the first place?" Hali sat down next to Delphia, dizzy from making circles for over an hour. Pulling her knees to her chest, she rested her head on her kneecaps.

"Are you okay, Hali?" Delphia asked.

"Yep, just a little dizzy."

"Do you need some water?"

"Nope, and don't change the subject," Hali demanded, her words muffled with her head down.

Delphia sighed. "I don't want to talk about me right now. I'm as mad as you are and I'm trying to stay optimistic. If I talk about my situation I'm only going to rant and that's not going to help anything. Maybe another night when I don't feel like I've fallen into another dimension."

Hali's head shot up from between her kneecaps. "What did you say?"

Delphia's eyebrows came together. "Which part?"

"The last part," Hali rushed out as an idea bubbled in her head.

"I feel like I've fallen into another dimension?" Delphia repeated with her eyebrows raised.

Hali nodded emphatically. "Yes! Thank you, Delphia!" Hali rose to her feet, no longer dizzy, her energy renewed.

"Am I missing something?"

"I think you just figured out how to get us out of here."

Delphia twisted her head, waiting for Hali to explain.

"Grab my hand," Hali instructed, then she closed her eyes and began chanting while the lawpnies glowed in her free hand. Delphia's eyes widened at the new sight.

"In a secret dimension, inside out, please release us back where we know the route."

Hali shot her lawpnies to the ground, squeezing Delphia's hand to make sure she wasn't left behind. The lawpnies blinded them both until the lit cloud cleared and Delphia and Hali realized they were no longer inside of the tree. Delphia gasped as she looked herself up and down, amazed that she was still in one piece.

"Come on, let's go," Hali said.

"Where?" Delphia choked out.

"The shore."

31

FIRST FIGHT

WHEN HALI and Delphia arrived at the shore, the Eyes and Anchors were already fighting. Cas flew above it all, shooting lawpnies like lightning bolts from his hands. Spears flew from both directions. The Eyes still outnumbered the Anchors, but with Cas at work in the air, the playing field was a bit more leveled.

Immediately, Hali regretted bringing Delphia to the battle as she watched on in horror. Eyes used their powers to push Anchors into piles. But before their knives could plunge into the Anchors, a second force blew the Anchors out of harm's way. *Neilan*. The Anchors looked like feathers in the wind, trying to stay afloat while swaying back and forth.

While Neilan and Cas were at work, the Anchors fought with spears, their eyes crazed with despair. Hali and Delphia hid behind a tree, waiting for the right moment to enter the battle.

Hali looked over to Delphia. The panic she wore on her face mirrored the dread that Hali felt inside. "Delphia, you don't need to be here."

Delphia turned to face Hali, hiding her reservations with bravado, as if accepting a dare, but Hali knew the truth. "You are the one the Eyes want. I *should* be here ... you shouldn't."

Hali closed her eyes a moment longer than a blink. Delphia wasn't wrong, but she wasn't right either. Delphia had every reason to be there, but so did Hali. Hali conceded to Delphia's point with a nod. Coincidentally, it was the same argument that Hali had with Cas only a couple hours before. Delphia nodded back, forging a silent truce on the matter.

"I guess that means we're both stubborn," Hali said.

Delphia's lips turned up in a fleeting grin that didn't hide the fear that quaked within her. "I guess so," she replied. Hali didn't miss Delphia's neck muscles tense as she struggled to swallow, her throat most likely dry from terror. But it didn't stop Delphia from asking, "So what's our plan?"

Cas didn't know how long he had flown around shooting his lawpnies, but it was long enough for his forearms to tremble. In all his time as an enchanter he had never exerted his powers so much in such a short time span. Cas was mentally, physically, and emotionally strong. But magically he wasn't as strong as he needed to be. The battle with the Eyes made it glaringly apparent that he had spent a lifetime concealing his magic, because he was exhausted in a way he had never experienced. He promised himself that if he survived this trial that he would keep his powers strong and practice every day. But that was a big if. Either way, Hali would be released from the tree. He had made sure to add a loophole to ensure at least that much when he had muttered the incantation.

The Anchors fought tirelessly, spearing Eyes like they were fish. The Eyes had underestimated the Anchors savage fighting and hunting capabilities, since those skills were hidden by the ocean. The Eyes had also never fought the Anchors when they were prepared for a fight or awake for that matter.

When the Eyes gained footing on the Anchors, Neilan helped counter their pull. As great of hunters as the Anchors were, Cas honestly didn't know what they would have done without Neilan's help. The Eyes' had the advantage of utilizing the elements to bunch the Anchors together, and more than once Cas thought he was going to have to witness a mass slaying of his own kind before he could intervene. But then Neilan would push back, freeing the Anchors over and over from their clusters.

Cas looked over to Neilan in the midst of shooting his lawpnies and having knives thrown at him, noting that Neilan's movements were becoming more and more labored the longer the battle lasted. With no end in sight, Cas felt just as tired and helpless as Neilan looked. But he wouldn't quit. He couldn't.

Just when despair started to seep in, he caught sight of a large bird flying in his peripheral, but he kept his attention focused on the dark battlefield below, which presented a challenge all on its own. For starters, distinguishing between Anchor and Eye silhouettes in the overcast night sky wasn't an easy task. He thought about doing an oil and water spell to separate the Anchors from the Eyes, but not only was the spell temporary, his lawpnies would be suspended while the spell was in effect. Leaving the Anchors with the same advantage as the Eyes. It was a pointless diversion at best. But with no side leading, Cas was running out of ideas on how to gain an edge on the Eyes.

As Cas contemplated his dilemma, lightning flashed in the corner of his vision, too close for him not to look. But as his eyes jumped to the bolt, he realized the source didn't come from the sky.

Hali flew around, shooting her lawpnies that immediately dropped five Eyes. The problem with lawpnies as their main weapon, was it only shocked its recipients, so the stricken Eyes would eventually get back up ready to battle unless an Anchor ended them with their spears. But fighting in the night also made it difficult for Anchors to recognize a downed Eye from a dead one. Especially since the Anchors reused spears after each kill. Thus, not every dead Eye had the marking of a spear to make it easier to distinguish the difference.

It didn't take long for the Eyes to realize that their prize dangled in the air before them. Cas's heart sputtered with a new kind of fear, as his adrenaline gave him a second wind. The Eyes licked their chops, as their stares hungrily followed Hali like she was the first meal they had seen in weeks. Despite Cas being part enchanter and Anchor, the Eyes weren't as enticed at what he had to offer as they were Hali and that worried him even more. When she arrived, their focus turned singular.

Hali's presence renewed energy on both sides as she fiercely zapped and zinged the Eyes. They fell into piles and the Anchors wasted no time spearing the zapped Eyes before their bodies could hit the sand.

Hali shot her lawpnies like silly string, and she feared that like a can of silly string, she would eventually run out. The fact that Cas had been fighting much longer than she had, gave her hope that her lawpnies could withstand the battle until the end. At least that's what she hoped.

Hali squashed any thoughts of how Mamie, Marilla, Ronan, and the others were fairing down below, concentrating only on the task at hand. She just hoped that Mamie and the other elders followed protocol of what to do when the fighting began.

Hali's concentration suffered a setback when a woman's scream broke through and pierced the night. The pitch rose and fell, curdling and rasping, into desperate depths. Hali halted mid-flight, scanning the ground to find the source. Her gaze happened on an Eye holding Marilla from behind with a knife grazing her throat. A trickle of blood dripped down to her collarbone and Hali lost her breath as her heart took pause. Hali flew closer and saw that Marilla wasn't crying out for her own life, but Ronan's. He too was held by an Eye in the same compromising position. Hali's body froze as blood flooded her brain like lava. She could feel her heartbeat throbbing in her temples. There was too much to process and her brain moved liked sludge to find a solution, panic fogging her thinking. It was as Cas said it would be.

The Eyes were using the Anchors against her.

The battle forged on around them because the Eyes knew that they had Hali trapped in fear, life's most effective cage. The fighting kept the Anchors adequately distracted, so the Eyes could pursue why they had really come.

The Eye holding Marilla hostage, a taller man with red skin that looked sunburnt, looked up at Hali and Cas. "If any of you zap me, they will both die."

Hali nodded, her tongue pushing against the roof of her

mouth, unable to form words. She floated, frozen in space like a spider in an invisible web. Her heart beat impossibly fast and she looked over to Cas for answers she hoped he had. When their eyes met, there was a flicker of uncertainty in his eyes, unnoticed by the Eyes, in which he gave nothing away.

"Now listen here"—the Eye holding Marilla called up —"this can all be over if you just come down and stop this nonsense."

Without question Hali began to descend from the sky, the Eye's lips curled up in victory. Hali kept her distance, mostly because Cas moved to her side, holding her arm.

"Set them free and then I will surrender," Hali announced. The word "surrender" echoed in her head like an old church bell.

"Come closer and lose the boy toy," the Eye holding Marilla shot back.

"Not happening," Cas growled. "You get us both or not at all."

"Exalted doesn't want you," a weaselly Eye, short and thin, with pale skin and black hair bit out. It was the same Eye that held Ronan. As soon as he spoke, he slumped back in on himself; his bout of confidence extinguished with his last word, like flour on a fire, leaving only a puff of smoke.

"I don't give a damn if he wants me. He's going to get me whether he likes it or not. That's the deal!" Cas's voice boomed.

The Eye holding Marilla began caressing her neck with the blade, testing Cas's resolve. "Are you sure about thaaaa ..." he suddenly face-planted into the sand, a wooden spear poking out from his back. The weaselly Eye's mouth hung agape before he was down just like his friend, a matching wooden spear in his back. Seconds later, a set of blue fins dipped into the ocean.

Hali stood still, "What did I just see?" she whispered to Cas. Whatever she saw wasn't an Eye, but it also wasn't an Anchor ... *or was it?*

"It was a sea creature," Cas confirmed.

W*hy would a sea creature come out of the ocean to help?*

There was no place for her confusion as the fighting carried on around them. The Eyes hardly noticed two of their own were taken out by a sly assailant, who killed swiftly, and slithered off without anyone the wiser.

Cas grabbed Hali's arm and pulled her up in the air again, no captives left to ground them. They shot their lawpnies at every being with pointy ears for what seemed like hours, while the Anchors on the ground finished them off.

Zap and kill, zap and kill.

It continued on that way until three Eyes turned on Neilan. Two of the Eyes held Neilan's arms behind his back while another held a knife to his heart.

"Any last words, traitor?" the Eye holding the knife questioned. Neilan opened his mouth to speak but was interrupted.

"Hey, over here," Delphia called out, laying on her side at the edge of the shore in mermaid form. Waves lapped over her shimmering orange tail and top as she rested her head in the palm of her supporting arm, looking completely at ease. Delphia smiled coyly at the Eyes, contradicting the fear-ridden girl Hali had witnessed before they entered the battle. The stoic face Neilan wore moments before crumbled, turning to anger. His nostrils flared as the Eyes turned their attention to Delphia. If looks could kill, Neilan could level out all the Eyes and Anchors with one glance.

"A few of my scales would be worth a lot," Delphia

giggled flirtatiously while flapping her fins for effect. The Eyes' grips loosened on Neilan, along with their willpower. Entranced, the Eyes forgot about Neilan and stalked towards their siren. Neilan's jaw and forearms tightened. If Delphia was nervous, she didn't let it show as they began charging for her.

One Eye down—speared.

Two Eyes down—speared.

Three Eyes down—knifed.

The preying Eyes dropped to their knees before collapsing on their faces in the sand with Neilan, Jett, and Toru standing behind them. Jett and Toru moved on to their next kills immediately, but Neilan stared at Delphia with fury in his eyes. Delphia's eyes mirrored Neilan's, but she smiled at him briefly without humor before slipping quietly back into the ocean.

Another hour of fighting went on, before it fizzled and died. The few Eyes left could barely hold their arms up in surrender they were so fatigued. Cas and Neilan escorted the remaining sullen Eyes off the Eyes' Land, watching as they vanished into the trees. Their stamina had worn out and the fighting was finally over.

When they Eyes' Land was cleared, the Anchors collapsed on the sand like seals, exhausted, but also not ready to leave the comfort of unity. The horrors of the night still loomed over them, and no one, even Kai and Carmya, who had the biggest excuse for alone time, was ready to separate from each other.

Some of the older Anchors and children that weren't fit for battle, including Mamie and Fisk, emerged from hiding in the ocean, settling on the shore with the others after the fighting had been over for some time.

"Ooooh weee, I thought I'd be a sea creature 'fore I ever

saw the light of day again," Fisk exclaimed, as he sat on the shore with the others. "After they trapped us up in nets, I thought that was the end of ol' Fisk. But then by the grace of God I got my chance to slip off into the water 'fore the battle began. I'll tell you what, I haven't been on that long of a swim for some time. I can't imagine how you youngins' are feelin' after battlin' from night 'til dawn. It was hard to watch. The Eyes are pretty scrappy. Even after bein' zapped, they were jumpin' up like cockroaches that had been stepped on time after time. I didn't know if it would ever end. And as for you Mr. Cas, you certainly surprised me with all your floatin' 'round like a ghost and shootin' fire out of your darn fingertips. You've got some secrets to tell, that's for sure. I'm a little tired to truly appreciate a good story at the moment, especially sittin' amongst the dead. Don't need the Eyes comin' back to life to haunt me. You think you could do somethin' about that, Hali? Not straight away," Fisk amended. "We need to make sure we pay our respects to our own, but after that, when the sun's up, we should clear everythin' up."

Hali nodded at the request, too tired for anything else. The shore was peppered in corpses. As far as Hali could tell, none of the Anchors seemed to be missing and no one appeared visibly upset from losing a loved one.

Could all of the Anchors have survived or was everyone just too afraid to look?

As Hali took inventory of the living Anchors her eyes ran across Marilla sitting closer to the shore than everyone else. Hali ventured over to her, partly to see how she was doing, but also to have some quiet from Fisk's constant yammering. Normally it didn't bother her, but her brain needed some time to reflect on everything that had happened and what came next.

"Is it okay if I sit with you?" Hali asked hesitantly, not wanting to encroach on Marilla's privacy.

"Of course," Marilla said, patting the sand next to her.

"How are you holding up, Marilla?" Hali asked as she sat down.

Marilla wiped tears from her eyes with the side of her pointer finger. "I'm doing all right, you?"

"I'm okay."

Hali had a question she wanted to ask Marilla, though she wasn't sure if it was the right time to ask. After sitting in silent contemplation beside Marilla for a beat, Hali resolved that there probably would never be an appropriate time.

"Hey, Marilla," Hali started, uncertain.

Marilla looked at Hali, patiently.

"Who saved you and Ronan from the Eyes?"

Marilla smiled a sad smile and looked away, looking out at the horizon coming into view as the sun lit the sky into a new day. "My husband," Marilla shared. "Ronan's father, but I don't think Ronan recognized him, since he camouflaged himself and it has been years. Ronan was just a baby the last time he saw him."

Hali did her best to not let her mouth hang open. "But I thought your husband died?"

Marilla shook her head. "No, he didn't, which is almost worse. After the Eyes attacked us all those years ago, he didn't like the idea of being left vulnerable for future invasions. As a sea creature, you lose your humanity, but your other senses and abilities are heightened. He thought the only way to protect us was to sacrifice his humanity. I disagreed. But it turns out he was right, because here he is saving us from Eyes all these years later."

Hali sat in shock at the revelation. "Do you ever see him when you go out in the water?"

"Sometimes I think I do, but I don't know if it's just because I *want* to see him or because I *am* seeing him. I've been spending more than a decade trying to forget about him after he left. But I still love him, sea creature or not. We are bound together for life whether we spend that time in each other's presence or not. Before he left, he told me that love requires sacrifices otherwise it's not love, it's convenience. When he said he would spend his life in the ocean protecting us because that's the sacrifice he needed to make, I almost didn't believe him."

"I mean no disrespect when I ask this, but why didn't you go with him?" Hali asked, truly baffled.

"None taken. I would have loved to go with him, but I thought Ronan deserved a chance at humanity—to learn, grow, and experience all the things life could offer even if trapped on an island."

Hali's eyes grew hot from tears threatening to spill out, and she wanted nothing more than to fix Marilla's situation for her. "Is there not a way that you both can be together even if he's a sea creature and you're an Anchor?"

Marilla tilted her head in concern for Hali. "Sad to say, it doesn't work like that Hali. The sea creatures stay in the water full time and we're in the water a brief amount of time in comparison. It's the price we pay for our humanity and the price they pay for their abilities."

"But you *are* in the water some of the time. Can you two not meet up?" Hali desperately sought a solution, to make her feel better about a problem that wasn't even her own. But maybe in a way she felt somewhat responsible. She didn't create the Eyes' Land, but the fact that she knew a possible way to dissolve it nagged at her. Every story of sacrifice she encountered always led back to the same solution—breaking the spell on the barrier. Being part of the key to the solution only made her feel selfish. But she had promised Cas she wouldn't try. Keeping her promise to Cas was feeling impossible, considering how things could be easier for the Anchors as a whole if she succeeded in breaking the spell. Mr. Gruff and Cas believed it wasn't possible to break it down, but Hali wasn't so sure.

"Sometimes I wish we could, but he keeps his distance. There are more barriers within the Eyes' Land than the ones that keep us apart from the rest of the world, Hali. This is just one of those barriers that shouldn't be crossed ... at least for now. I need to be here for Ronan and my husband believes he needs to be out there for us." Marilla's words were measured as she spoke. As if she was attempting to convince herself it was the way it needed to be. "Please don't tell Ronan, he believes his father is dead. It was just easier than the truth. I know it's wrong, but I needed to protect him."

"Does anyone else know?" Hali asked, wondering why Marilla trusted her with such a secret.

"No, not even my dad," Marilla paused, a small smile graced her lips but not her eyes. "Ol' Fisk can be quite the talker when he wants to be. If he knew Lyle didn't actually die and chose to be a sea creature, I'd never hear the end of it. My dad is a skilled ranter if you hadn't noticed." Marilla huffed out a sad laugh. Hali responded with a weak smile.

"My lips are sealed," Hali assured. As they sat in silence for a few moments longer, Delphia walked up.

"Carmya and I were talking about making pancakes for breakfast. Maybe some bacon and sausage if we have any. We thought a good breakfast might help lift everyone's spirits, especially the kids, since no one seems to be going to sleep anytime soon. Well, except for Cas, that is. He's zonked. Would either of you want to help?"

"Sure, that sounds nice," Marilla agreed as she stood up.

"Is Cas okay?" Hali asked, standing with Marilla. After the fighting was over, she had lost track of him after he had gone with Neilan to make sure the remaining Eyes left.

"Yeah, he's breathing. We checked, but he doesn't look like he's going to be waking up anytime soon. So, are you in?" Delphia asked.

Hali's brows furrowed with worry, that didn't escape Delphia's notice. "Yes, but I need to check on something first and then I'll head over to camp."

Delphia smirked knowingly. Hali crinkled her nose back at her in return, relieved Delphia didn't pry any further.

"Be careful walking to camp, Hali. Ask someone to walk with you just to be safe," Marilla cautioned.

"I will," Hali complied.

After parting ways with Delphia and Marilla, Hali headed over to Cas. He lay on his side and Hali carefully knelt down on her knees, bringing an ear down to his ribs that faced up, confirming with her own ears that he was in fact breathing. She exhaled a breath, long and slow, as relief washed through her.

"Are you checking every sleeping person this way?" Cas mumbled.

Hali bolted her head off Cas's ribs, but before she could sit upright, Cas wrapped both arms around her, hugging her close.

"So, are you?" Cas repeated as Hali relaxed against him, both comforted and surprised by Cas's playfulness.

"I am, actually," Hali teased.

Cas squeezed her a little tighter. "Oh, you are? Guess, I'm not very special then."

"Guess not," Hali continued, "but lucky for you, you were the only one asleep."

"Ahh, so I'm special by default," Cas quirked a mischievous smile at Hali.

Hali looked up to Cas's face and smiled back, peering down just as quickly after remembering all that she had shared with him and he'd yet to respond to any of it. Hali couldn't think of any of it now. Her mind needed a break and she wasn't ready to have a conversation of why he was snuggling her, when he knew she loved him. Hali never thought she'd be the kind of girl that would announce her feelings, not have them returned, and still talk to the guy. She thought she'd have a little more respect for herself than that. But apparently, she was wrong, because instead of getting up and walking away like she would have expected of herself, she lay her head back down on Cas's chest, savoring the first moments of peace after hours of battle. He may have not loved her, but he sure held her like someone who did.

As Cas massaged Hali's scalp with his fingers, she moved her head to provide better access for his hands. When she did, she noticed bloody sand stemming from Cas's leg.

"You're hurt," Hali stated more than asked.

Cas looked down at his pants, grimacing at being discovered. Hali waited for his response, her eyes widening with worry.

"I cut my leg on a tree."

Hali wasn't convinced. "If that's true then why aren't your pants cut, too?"

"I cut my leg while I was masked?" Cas tried out another excuse, but Hali was sitting up now with her arms crossed across her chest.

"Cas, tell me what really happened."

Cas just stared at Hali. "Do you know you have very beautiful eyes?"

"Cas!" Hali warned, but his compliment broke her resolve a little as a small smile peaked through her scowling lips. "Don't change the subject, I will not be charmed."

"Are you sure? I think I can do better. I never got to tell you where I thought you could live instead of Delphia's."

Hali was intrigued and frustrated that Cas's charms were working on her, but she wasn't going to let him know that.

And was he being flirty with her?

Maybe he was loopy from the blood loss. That had to be it, because Hali had never seen this side of Cas before. She couldn't take anything he was saying too seriously, or he might crush her heart for a second time in one day.

"You can tell me that after you tell me why your leg is bleeding. I think you owe me some information after leaving me to rot in a tree. Lucky for you, I'm giving you a pass on that blunder under the premise that you were scared and not in your right mind. But I'll have you know that I've held a grudge on lesser infractions for much longer." Hali stared Cas down, narrowing her eyes with as serious of an expression as she could muster, with arms crossed and no smile. But deep down she had no desire or energy to be mad at anyone after the night she had, especially Cas. Though she would keep that card close to her chest, for the sake of their current argument.

Cas sighed. "Fine. I did a protection spell over all the Anchors that required some scales."

"When did you do this?" Hali questioned.

"After I left you in the tree, before the battle began. It's not a full proof spell and will not stop an Anchor from getting hurt but will speed up healing and recovery exponentially. A gash from a knife will feel like a scratch," Cas explained.

"How many scales did you need?"

Cas looked down to the sand, circling his fingertip around into a figure eight.

"Cas?" Hali prodded.

Cas huffed. "One ... per Anchor."

"Oh, Cas," Hali's face fell. "How are you even awake right now?"

"I wasn't, somebody laid on my ribs and woke me up," Cas joked, but Hali didn't laugh. Cas pulled Hali's shoulders down with him, bringing her head to his chest while still holding her gaze. Giving her a reassuring look, he said, "I'm only teasing, Hali. Plus, I protected myself too, so I'd heal faster and be able to fight, but I used a lot of scales so it's going to take a little longer."

Hali couldn't imagine all the pain Cas had to be in.

How had he battled in his condition?

Her own skin ached thinking of clipping one scale, let alone two-hundred and four.

"Is there anything I can do to help?" Hali asked, looking up towards Cas.

Cas's eyes were closed, and his chest rose and fell with each breath. He was asleep before he ever told Hali where he thought she could live. As she listened to him snore softly, she decided it could wait.

Ronan hesitantly walked up to Hali as she sat up to greet him. "Sorry to interrupt, but Delphia was asking if you could remember the recipe for pancakes off hand, she is a little nervous to go back to her cabin and grab the recipe card right now."

"That's right, shoot!" Hali exclaimed. "I'd forgotten about breakfast. I'll come and help."

Ronan's expression relaxed. She came to a standing position not wanting to leave Cas sleeping out in the open even with all the Anchors around. Fisk must have noticed Hali's conundrum.

"Go on, Hali," Fisk waved Hali off as he approached. "I'll keep an eye on Cas, so you can go make a tasty breakfast. I may not be much of a fighter these days, but I've been told my big mouth still works. If there's any trouble, you'll hear about it."

"Thank you, Fisk," Hali chuckled, comforted that someone she trusted would be looking out for Cas.

"My mom told me to walk back with you," Ronan said as he walked alongside Hali.

"That works for me. How are you holding up, baby Ron Ron?"

"Ugh, please, not you too. I get it enough from Mamie," Ronan shook his head in mock annoyance. Hali knew that he secretly loved the pet names, but she wouldn't call him out on it today.

"Sorry, just trying to lighten the mood. But really, how are you doing?"

Ronan contemplated Hali's question. "I'm okay. Still trying to figure out who saved me and my mom. It just seems weird that a sea creature would go through the trouble. I've only seen a sea creature come to the shore when he was chasing a ... signal," Ronan spit out. "I just don't understand why a sea creature saved us without anything in return."

Hali knew what Ronan meant. *Anything in return* was another way of saying an Anchor to take back to the ocean with him. Ronan was smart, so Hali wasn't surprised that he questioned the turn of events, but she wished that she could truly play innocent to knowing anything. Lucky for her, Neilan walked up before she had to feign ignorance.

"Where are you guys headed?" Neilan asked as he

plodded along the sand with less grace than an Anchor, kicking up heaps of sand as he walked.

"To breakfast, want to come?" Hali asked.

"Sure, I could eat."

As they walked, Hali asked, "Where will you go after this?" Neilan had burned more than a few bridges when he decided to help the Anchors.

Neilan chuckled. "We'll see."

Hali had so many questions for Neilan, but she wasn't sure how open he would be to answer most of them in front of Ronan, so she made a mental note to save them for later.

Suddenly, water splashed on Hali's cheek as the three walked to camp. As Hali wiped it away, she looked up to where the rogue droplet had fallen from, only to find herself staring into big, brown doe-eyes. The very same eyes that belonged to the female Eye with short blonde hair that Exalted had sent to find Hali. As soon as their eyes met, Hali was pulled up, as if being sucked up by a powerful vacuum. After a night of fighting, Hali was exhausted, but not exhausted enough to give up. With one zap, Hali broke the young Eye's pull.

The effects of the zap didn't last long, as the girl shot up from the ground, pushing Hali against the nearest tree with her powers. Powers that hadn't been tested and worn thin throughout the night from battle.

The impact hurt Hali more than she would have liked and definitely more than she expected. Adrenaline fought against her body's need for rest and nourishment.

Hali zapped the girl twice more, lawpnies bolting out of each of her hands. When the girl fell to the ground, Neilan and Ronan stepped in to help. Neilan held the girl down with his powers while Ronan attempted to tie her arms behind her back with his own belt. But the girl was strong, and knocked Ronan down with one swift kick to his head. He fell on his side grabbing at his ear—stunned by the strength of her kick. Before the blonde Eye could stand up, Hali helped secure her legs with her own elemental powers, breathing in a wisp of a nearby cloud. Neilan held strong, not neglecting his hold on the girl for even a split second.

The girl had a classic angelic face but wore a devilish glare pointed at Neilan.

"You don't have to do this, Mac," Neilan reasoned. They all just stared at each other for a moment as Mac's teeth clenched and her stomach rose and fell with each breath. Stubbornness ingrained in each cell of her makeup.

"Not all of us are traitors," a deep voice said, revving Hali's lawpnies.

Exalted came into view, stepping out from behind a tree, not far from their tussle with a malicious look on his face. Neilan's eyes grew as big as saucers, his nostrils flaring at the new force that stood before them, his confidence noticeably crumbling. Mac must have noticed because the death glare she wore transformed into a smug smirk, watching Neilan's Achilles' heel exposed. A moment later Mac was pulled from the ground by Exalted and placed next to him—a short inhale from Exalted was all it took. Neilan, Hali, and Ronan stood helpless.

"Dad?" Neilan growled out the question, betrayal tracing lines in his forehead as his eyebrows rose. Neilan's world disintegrated before their eyes, much like Hali's had a year before.

Not another word was uttered before Hali was pulled by the force of Exalted and abducted for the second time in one day.

32

COMPROMISE

Cas woke up to a frantic Marilla. Marilla didn't get frantic without reason or even with reason most the time. That's how Cas knew that whatever was going on couldn't be good and probably involved Ronan.

"What's going on, Marilla?" Cas asked, shooting up to his feet. Despite feeling better, he struggled to stand upright.

Marilla's red-rimmed eyes were panicked as she spoke. "Ronan and Hali are missing. They were last seen walking with that Eye fellow, Neilan."

"I just knew lettin' an Eye help us was a bad idea," Fisk gritted out.

"We don't know that yet," Cas said, wanting to believe his own words. "Why would he have helped us this long only to turn on us?"

"Well, aren't you a changed man," Fisk noted. "My talk a year ago helped, didn't it?"

Cas shook his head. "It's not that Fisk. I just don't want to waste our time seeking out the wrong enemy. I fought along Neilan all night. The Eyes could have easily taken us out if it hadn't been for his help. If he was going to turn on us, he would've already."

"Well, who is it then?" Marilla asked urgently.

Cas thought for a moment before speaking, recalling everything he could remember from the night before. And then a flash of memory ignited in his brain.

"There was a girl Eye with short blonde hair that was ordered to look for Hali before the fighting began. I'd forgotten about her once the fighting started but I don't remember seeing her during the battle, so that probably means she's still somewhere on the Eyes' Land. And if she's here, that means the Eyes' leader, Exalted, is still here, too."

"Did they mention where they would take her when they found her?" Marilla asked.

"No. How long have they been missing?" Cas questioned.

"Delphia and I waited for Ronan and Hali to come back to camp. We had sent Ronan to get a pancake recipe from her, but they never came back. I'd say they've been missing close to a half an hour at this point."

"I'll survey the Eyes' Land. You all wait here in case they come back," Cas said hurriedly. Masking, he disappeared from sight, not waiting for a response from Marilla or Fisk.

Hali had wondered the night before if Neilan had known all along who Exalted was. But after seeing Neilan's eyes widen at Exalted's—or Bram O'Riley's—presence, and Exalted's eyes flash in revulsion towards Neilan, Hali had her answer. The small glimpse that Hali had caught of Exalted hours before was by chance. Floating in the air like an apparition granted her a much different vantage point than Neilan and Mr. Gruff had in their positions at the fig tree that Hali hadn't considered until now. Neilan and Mr. Gruff hadn't been able to see Exalted or his scheming from where they were hidden.

Exalted had stayed in the shadows, letting Mac and the others do his bidding. Fighting, seeking, and tiring themselves while he remained fresh and ready to deliver the final blow when the time was right. The Eyes were nothing more than Exalted's minions, doing his dirty work so he could reap the reward. He sent Mac around the Eyes' Land as his spy. But he had made one mistake that would cost him dearly.

He had underestimated Hali.

Exalted was strong and so was Mac, but Hali was stronger. Stronger than even she had anticipated. At times during the fighting she felt that maybe she could have used even more power than she was outputting. But she held back, afraid the blast of her lawpnies would hurt more than her intended targets; unaware and preoccupied was what she had been. Exalted had planned it that way all along. The Anchors won the battle, but Exalted planned on winning the war.

And for the second time within a day, Hali was abducted. But this time she allowed herself to be taken, so that Neilan and Ronan would be left behind, unharmed. While the two evil Eyes led her away to work their plan, she created hers. It had become apparent that as long as she was alive, that the Anchors—while on the Eyes' Land—would never be safe or free. They would constantly have to battle the Eyes.

"Here we are," Exalted said. He towed her to a deep part of the woods, traveling swiftly by way of the elements. They had moved as if they were standing on a moving sidewalk at the airport.

Hali looked between Mac and Exalted, observing their relief and victorious expressions. She said nothing. Gave away nothing—watching and waiting for her moment.

They tied both Hali's legs and arms to a tree. She let them—biting the sides of her mouth to stop herself from laughing at their fruitless attempt.

Yesterday, the Eyes had been successful in strapping her down, using her fear against her. But today was a new day and Hali's skills were no longer untested or reserved.

When Hali was sufficiently tied, Mac brought a knife to Hali's throat. "If you try anything, we will kill every last Anchor on the Eyes' Land. Do you understand?" Mac warned.

"Yes," Hali answered, not risking being impaled from Mac's blade.

Mac removed her knife, glaring into Hali's hazel eyes with her brown ones. Hali smiled a toothy grin in return, before letting it fall back into a scowl. Mac scoffed at Hali's show before turning to Exalted for her next orders.

Exalted approached Hali, embracing her cheeks gently with both of his oddly smooth calloused hands. "You've made me a happy man today, Hali. You have no idea all that you possess within you." Mac's eyes rolled, jealousy over-taking her features. Hali felt sorry for her ... a little. Mac was probably just as used by him as he planned on using Hali.

Exalted stepped away from Hali, examining her like a painter would his work. "I'm going to be the first of my brothers to harness Arcelia's unyielding power and live to tell about it."

Hali's uncaring facade faded as she attempted to under-stand what Exalted meant when he said, *first of his brothers.*

In all her life, Bram O'Riley had been a figure in the background, her best friend's dad who was always gone fishing. He wasn't around often, but that was the typical life of a commercial fisherman and it was the reality accepted by Camille's family and Hali.

Whenever Mr. O'Riley was home, the family resumed being a family like he had never left. Never in Hali's craziest thoughts could she imagine Mr. O'Riley capable of hurting her. But as she stood roped to a tree, observing him mentally plot out the spells he planned on forcing her to perform, his expression morphing into something of the demon variety —red-faced and ears like horns—she couldn't see how she ever missed it. This side of him had been there all along, but she had been too inside of her own head to notice.

"Your biological mother received a powerful gift from her mother that has been passed down to you. All enchanters have powers but not all enchanters have unlimited abilities to cast multiple spells without resistance. Cillian got careless when he used Arcelia. If he'd given her a moment to breathe between spells, he could've kept her around a lot longer. My idiot brother didn't know how to pace himself and he weakened her magic when he bound her from using it directly. Had he not been a coward, he could've made her cast the spells directly, instead of extracting her magic and trying to use it himself, suffocating her as a result. But even after she collapsed from being out of air, it took the sun to kill her. That's how powerful she was."

Exalted's words began adding up. Hali had wondered the whole time why the Eyes had sought her over any other enchanter. At first, she had told herself it was because she possessed a trifecta of genetics: enchanter, mermaid, and leprechaun. But then Hali began figuring what the Eyes wanted from each part of her. The Eyes didn't need her leprechaun abilities for obvious reasons, and there were plenty of Anchors on the Eyes' Land with scales, which only left the enchanter part of herself they would be after. But even then, Hali wasn't the only enchanter around, or on the Eyes' Land for that matter. So, why the pursuit for only her unless some part of her magic was unique? And now she knew. Exalted wanted limitless power and Hali had to find out from him of all people, the depths of what she possessed. She had only wished she knew the night before, so she could have used it to her advantage.

"My brothers were idiots. Murchadh fell in love with Arcelia and Cillian wasn't careful. I will make no such mistake," Exalted paced.

Hali's mind swirled as the ropes rubbed at her wrists. If Murchadh and Cillian were his brothers, then that meant that Exalted was her ...

"It worked out perfectly really. It just took a little more patience. Arcelia made sure of that. Casting a binding spell over you until you were an adult ... very clever of her if I do say so myself. But in the end the result will be the same."

Hali struggled to keep her expression neutral. Her skin itched as her lawpnies clawed underneath, idling and purring like an engine to a sports car.

"The funny part of the story is that when Arcelia ran off with Murchadh, I was the one that clued Murchadh in that Cillian was after them. He was so trusting. He just assumed that since I had gotten married and had two children that I must also be on the straight and narrow. Arcelia decided then that the only way to protect you was to hide you amongst a mortal family. What she didn't realize was the mortal family she chose just happened to be good friends with my wife." Exalted laughed at the serendipity of the events.

"One of the perks of being the black sheep of my family is that I flew under the radar for so many years undetected. You were practically handed to me on a silver platter. I just had to wait for the spell your mother had put on you to wear off. When that happened, I knew exactly where to find you. Had you moved or gone away, the lighthouse wouldn't have pulled you here, but you hadn't—so now, here you are. As clever as Arcelia was, she hadn't planned for that." Exalted's gray eyes were devoid of compassion. His intent for her was clear, but the outcome he planned for her wasn't.

"So, as you can see *niece*, it's destiny after all."

Hali's stomach roiled at the word "niece" and she was sure her face was just as sour. Exalted laughed maniacally, turning his face and his ears a deep red that Hali thought might ignite into flames. He needed to be stopped. Hali glanced at Mac who looked almost disgusted by Exalted. Hali felt the same way, but probably not for the same reason.

As Exalted laughed, Hali muttered an incantation quietly to herself, unheard over Exalted's booming hysteria. It was apparent that he either felt safe from being heard by the Anchors or that he felt confident that the others were not a threat. Either way, Hali took advantage of his distracted state to mask herself. She just hoped it gave her enough time and distance to get done what she needed to.

Hali made it through the trees without incident. If Exalted and Mac were after her, she didn't know. She never looked back on her flight. Suddenly, she heard her name being called from somewhere below which made her do a double take of herself to ensure she was still masked.

Looking down she found Mr. Gruff. Hali floated down to him as he followed her wisp with his eyes.

"How did you know it was me?" Hali asked without unmasking.

Mr. Gruff sighed. "I may not have my powers anymore, but I still have my sight."

"Was I that obvious?"

"Not to the average eye, but my eyes are a little more attuned to magic."

A pregnant pause sat between them.

"Are you ready for our fallback plan?" Hali reluctantly asked, expecting her question to be immediately rejected. After Hali had promised Cas that she wouldn't attempt to break the spell on the barrier, she had gone back to the shore later that night and had a private conversation with Mr. Gruff. Mainly, because she thought she would get more intel from him without Cas making him defensive. She had been wrong, but she was able to get him to agree on one thing.

Mr. Gruff huffed. "I suppose the fallback plan has been the only option from the beginning."

A branch snapped under the foot of a trespasser. Hali's heart peddled faintly. The usually strong beat interspersed throughout her mist. Ronan peaked out from behind a tree. Hali's floating figure dropped a foot from the air in relief.

"It's me Ronan, you can come out," Hali reassured. Ronan tentatively stepped out from behind his tree and then Neilan stepped out behind another.

"Whatever you're planning on doing, I'm going to help," Neilan stated. The shock he had worn earlier was now gone, leaving only a troubled look in his eyes.

"Me too," Ronan chimed in, searching the air for Hali as he did.

Hali broke her spell, reappearing. She placed her hand on Ronan's shoulder and looked him in the eyes. "Ronan, your mother would kill me if anything was to happen to you."

"I'm going to help," Ronan said indignantly, bucking Hali's hand from his shoulder with a shrug. "It's not your choice."

Hali sighed at his testiness but didn't argue, turning her attention to Neilan. "Where did you guys go after I was taken?"

"We've been tree hopping, trying to find you. Some of us are better at tree hopping than others," Neilan poked at Ronan.

Ronan glared at Neilan. "Hey, let's go for a swim and see who's talking."

Neilan scoffed. "No problem. I'll just rearrange the ocean a bit."

Ronan rolled his eyes. "That's cheating."

"Yes, it is," Neilan mocked, "and we never agreed that cheating was against the rules, now did we?"

"We don't have time for this nonsense!" Mr. Gruff raised his voice louder than Hali had ever heard him. It wasn't quite at the level of a yell or a scream, but it was definitely the most emotion she had ever seen come out of him.

Even Neilan's and Ronan's mouths fell open slightly by Mr. Gruff's little outburst, prompting them to voice hasty apologies in unison.

After a brief, uncomfortable amount of silence had passed, Mr. Gruff bent his head in Hali's direction, indicating for her to speak.

She cleared her throat, filling the awkward silence, as a

bright green lizard crawled up the side of the tree nearest Neilan. The agile reptile did a poor job hiding against the deep brown trunk. "Well, if everyone plans on helping, let's get started."

Cas had circled the Eyes' Land and flown over the densely packed trees but saw no signs of Hali, Ronan, or Neilan. He suspected that they must have been hidden within the cover of the trees, a tracking spell being his only hope in finding them.

As the idea occurred to him, he heard a loud rustle from down below—louder than any squirrel or other rodent could make. Lowering himself to the ground, he scanned the area and found nothing out of the ordinary. He remained still and listened. But the birds chirping to each other from tree to tree was the only sound. Cas waited, tuning out the birds and listening to the space in between their conversations. Nothing. But Cas knew he had heard something. Then he realized that the birds had, too. Their calls were not in conversation, but in warning to each other of danger. The shrill shrieks he mistook as simple chirping filled the air. He no longer tuned out the sounds but tried to decipher their meaning. Still invisible, he remained rooted in place, waiting out the unknown predator that lurked nearby.

Suddenly, a tree only a few trees away from where he hid, separated from itself as if molting a layer of skin. The molting layer that removed itself from the tree turned out to not be a layer of tree bark at all. A sea creature emerged, sleeking off like a snake, camouflaging itself with its surroundings. Cas remained motionless, never seeing the sea creature's face as it slithered off. He followed after it, not really sure what he expected to find. He couldn't understand why a sea creature would come out of the ocean in the first place if not following a signal and even that was rare.

It was an anomaly that a sea creature had helped Marilla and Ronan during the battle. Cas couldn't figure out the strange occurrence, but he had a suspicion the sea creature would lead him to where he needed to go. So, he followed.

Exalted and Mac didn't have to go far to find Hali alone in the woods. She had gotten herself tangled up in a net much like the Anchors had the night before. Her hands caught within the rope openings like handcuffs, the net encasing the rest of her body like a pearl in a shell.

"Well, well, well, I guess destiny has spoken." Hali glared at Exalted and his sidekick over her shoulder with vehemence, attempting to wiggle free from the net. "Cut her down, but don't free her," Exalted instructed Mac.

The net lowered to the ground but wasn't opened. Hali was balled up in the shape of a raindrop, crouching with her head collapsed over her knees. Mac and Exalted pushed her along with energy from the clouds, and the raindrops collected by the leaves from the previous night's storm.

When they reached their destination, the same one from earlier, Exalted wasted no time, demanding Hali cast a spell.

"Make me fly, Hali," he demanded, readying himself for takeoff. His request was met with derision. Exalted moved closer to Hali, coming as face-to-face as the net allowed. "I said—Make. Me. Fly." His voice was low, measured, and angry. Hali didn't budge. Exalted shifted his weight from one foot to another, agitated. He growled at Hali's obstinance, but was not deterred from his goal. Mac's eyes flitted between Hali and Exalted, unsure how the scene was going to play out. Hali's head tilted and her eyes blinked. Her tongue darted swiftly from her mouth and back in. Exalted took a step back, his neck reining in his head as he took in Hali's peculiar behavior. Her tongue dashed out of her mouth once more, pulling back just as rapidly.

Exalted's head tilted. "Stop screwing around and make me fly!" His voice rose but his confidence wavered. Feeling deprived, Exalted turned to violence to get what he wanted. Unsheathing his knife, he approached the net and held the sharp blade under Hali's chin. His eyes were crazed as he spoke. "Don't make me ask you again." Hali blinked and her tongue shot out and back into her mouth, unfazed by Exalted's order. Her antics only made him angrier as he pressed the knife deeper into her skin. Before the knife broke through flesh, Hali vanished into thin air. Exalted lurched forward, falling into the net, cutting his cheek with his own knife as he did. Both Mac and Exalted got into a fighting stance, their heads whipping around them in search of her. They made circles trying to find the girl who had fooled them into believing she was a victim of circumstance. As they twirled around frantically, a nearby lizard transformed from bright green to the same deep brown as the tree it plastered itself on. The lizard had finally learned the importance of camouflage. Gripping the tree, the reptile's tongue jetted from its mouth back and forth, tasting the air, before crawling down from the tree to safety.

On another part of the Eyes' Land a lizard transformed back into its human form. Hali hopped from Ronan's hands abruptly, her feet finding the sand awkwardly when she did.

"Thanks for carrying me, Ronan," Hali said as she rolled her neck and shoulders around. Ronan gave her an affable smile and nodded in return.

They had made it to the shore, away from the other Anchors. The other Anchors were small in the distance but not invisible, which meant their group of four wasn't either. Hali just hoped no one noticed them.

Hali hadn't expected to make it that far before her body returned to her, but she gladly welcomed the head start she was afforded by the unassuming lizard. She knew the body swapping spell she used would leave the lizard she borrowed unharmed. And if—or when—the lizard encountered any danger, the spell would break with both resuming their usual forms. But she still felt a pang of guilt for putting the little critter through any anguish.

"Are you ready?" Hali asked Mr. Gruff. He grumbled a reluctant affirmation. Hali drew the elements into her nostrils, feeling the cool ocean breeze tickle her nose and burn a little from the salt. She exhaled out slowly. The energy from the air and the power within her mixed as she pushed it out of her mouth. The waters parted, creating a sliver of a pathway. Neilan mimicked her previous motions, pushing his breath out to create a bigger divide. A pathway now connected the shore to the barrier.

She had made an impossible promise to Cas that she had to break. There was too much at stake not to. After spending a night being hunted down by Eyes; discovering Anchors coiled up in nets with Eyes down below with knives; watching Ronan, Marilla, and even Neilan held at knife point; and finding Cas lain out on the beach, unaware that he was bleeding out all over the sand, she knew something needed to be done. That's why she had secretly gone to Mr. Gruff and made him promise her that if there came a point where the Anchors were out of options, that he would help her break the spell on the barrier. After many refusals, Mr. Gruff finally conceded.

That didn't stop the smallest hint of guilt from nestling its way within Hali's gut as the group of four walked the path of the unknown. She didn't feel guilty of what she was about to do—because like Marilla's husband had said long ago, love required sacrifices. She loved Cas, but she had also come to love the other Anchors like family. Nevertheless, she didn't take promises lightly, and Cas was the last person she wanted to betray. It pained her to do so. Still, it was what needed to be done, and she regretted making the promise to Cas in the first place. It would be the first promise in her life that she had to break.

Hali trembled with each step closer to the barrier. With each footstep she reminded herself that no matter what happened, it was the right thing to do. As she talked herself out of her panic, she heard Ronan yelp. The remaining three turned around to find his neck gripped by Exalted's hand. Mac stood by his side, but she didn't look as devoted to Exalted's cause. Instead she cringed, shifting her glance to Exalted then Ronan—uncertain, but too vested to leave. Exalted lifted his blade and as it made its journey to Ronan's heart, it was blocked by an arm—a sea creature's arm. Ronan's father, Lyle.

The blade sliced Lyle's arm. A crimson slash appeared against the surrounding blue skin. But the wound didn't stop Ronan's father as he took hold of the blade and stabbed it through Exalted's chest.

"Noooooooo!" Neilan yelled as Bram O'Riley fell to his

knees and onto his side. Neilan went to his father, dropping to his knees while placing a hand on his heart to test for a beat. But the drum of life ceased. Mr. O'Riley's hands covered the blade that impaled him, as if he had attempted to pull it from himself before it took his life. His eyes were open, but gray and vacant. The angry rouge that had colored his face and ears prior to being stabbed were gone, and his face was left a chalky white with a glean of sweat still covering it.

Mac shook violently, as Lyle moved towards her, grabbing her neck with one hand.

"Stop," Ronan demanded. "It's done. You don't need to kill her. She isn't a threat to us anymore."

Lyle turned his head towards Ronan, but his body remained towards Mac, his grip firmly on her neck. He stared at Ronan for a few seconds. His nostrils flared and he puffed a breath out in exasperation, before releasing Mac's neck. The blonde Eye cried in relief, sitting on the newly created path, hugging her knees to her chest—from menacing Eye to frightened little girl in a span of minutes.

Lyle slithered back into the water without anyone noticing, as Neilan cried silent tears over the father he never really knew—fresh blood coated his hands. Hali, Ronan, and Mr. Gruff stood behind him, unsure of what to say or do to console him.

Suddenly, Delphia popped up out of the water and onto the path. Neilan looked at her with swollen, bleary eyes and she looked at him with sympathy that Hali didn't think any Anchors were capable of having for an Eye, especially one whose father was a tyrant.

Delphia grabbed Neilan's hand and placed something inside his bloody palm that Hali couldn't see, before closing his fingers back around it. Delphia quickly dipped back into the ocean, while Neilan gripped his fingers tightly around the object, possessively. He stood up and slid the object covertly into his shirt pocket closest to his heart and buttoned it closed. Still turned away, he wiped his tears away with the back of his hands and turned around to face Hali, Ronan, and Mr. Gruff.

"Let's do what we came to do," Neilan said, his voice hoarse.

"Neilan—" Hali started.

"No Hali, this needs to be done, so no one ever has to go through this again."

Hali nodded. Her heart broke for her cousin.

"Ronan, your job is to keep an eye on Mac," Neilan ordered.

"Okay," Ronan agreed.

Mac continued sobbing quietly, unfazed at the idea of Ronan watching her like a guard watches a prisoner.

Mr. Gruff remained reticent as the group began walking to the barrier. Hali wondered if he was apprehensive about what life held for him once the barrier was gone or if he was concerned that they would be unsuccessful in their attempt.

The barrier bubbled and buzzed like an electric fence. Hali's pulse quickened at the sight of the water jetting along the barrier in figure eights. Her lawpnies ignited under her skin and shot out in front of her eyes, making a figure eight like the water. Hali watched as her lawpnies conjured an image within the figure eight. She squinted her eyes in an attempt to make out the new image that swirled along. Once Hali's eyes adjusted, she realized that the new image had fins. Following the fins with her eyes for several seconds she had an epiphany.

Her music box came to mind with the elegant mermaid swimming back and forth against the waves in figure eights.

The nightmare that had slipped from her memory once Cas pulled her to shore—after her first attempt at the barrier a year before—came to the forefront of her brain. She remembered the Eyes looking down at her with their blades ready to spear her scales while at the same time her lawpnies delivered an unfinished message. Hali squeezed her eyelids tightly closed, searching her mind to remember what the message had said.

"Why is your magic making the infinity sign?" Neilan asked, pulling Hali from her contemplation.

"The infinity sign?" she questioned, forcing herself to look at the message differently.

"Yeah, the sideways eight is the math symbol for infinity."

"It's also the sign enchanters use to indicate unlimited power," Mr. Gruff said with a grunt.

The music box came back to Hali's mind again. This time she remembered the poem scrolled across the top. While unconscious after being blasted by the barrier, her lawpnies wrote one word, *boundless*, but she awoke before they could finish. Now she knew what they were trying to communicate:

"Boundless as the sky at night.
Kindred as the stars.
Cherished as the sun is bright.
Burdened as the moon."
That was it!

The little, pale box that sat on her desk all those years contained a message of who she was all along, including the music that Mamie hummed. She was an enchanter with unlimited power, just as Exalted had said. The answer had been right under her nose her entire life. But who had gifted her parents with the music box? Could it have been from Arcelia and Murchadh, her biological parents, all along?

"Why do my lawpnies feel the need to tell me this now?"

Mr. Gruff sighed. "Because they want you to know that you have nothing to worry about."

Cas surprised everyone when he ran up from behind on the pathway in the ocean. "Don't do it, Hali! Please!" he begged. "The threat is gone. We can just live here in peace now. No one will come after you or us again."

"Yes, they will," Mac spoke up, shifting everyone's attention. "As long as there are Eyes, there will always be a threat to Anchors, especially ones with unlimited enchanter power."

"Then we'll kill you," Cas threatened, glowering at Mac.

Hali grabbed Cas's shoulders. "Cas, I can't let everyone go on living like this, always worried that an Eye is going to sneak up on them and destroy their life. That's no way to live."

"We've been living that way for years, Hali, and it's worked."

Mr. Gruff grunted. "For pity's sake, you young ones are dense sometimes. She's not going to die, Cas." Silence swept over them.

"What do you mean?" Cas asked, while a deep groove formed between his eyes.

Hali was just as confused by Mr. Gruff's announcement, since he stated the information like it was common knowledge.

"The barrier won't kill, Hali," he clarified.

"But this whole time you've led me to believe that it would," Hali said, removing her hands from Cas's shoulders.

"I lied," Mr. Gruff stated unapologetically. "I wasn't ready to leave the Eyes' Land. But I guess now I have no choice, so if you both are done with your love quarrel, I'd like to get on with it now."

Hali looked back at Cas, relieved, while his face remained coiled with apprehension. Hali reached out and squeezed Cas's hand one last time, before approaching the barrier with Mr. Gruff. Neilan attempted to walk with them, but Hali held her hand up for him to stop.

"What are you doing?" she asked.

"I'm going to help," he said.

"Why? I can cover most the links to break the barrier. There is no need for you to get hurt in the process, when we already know I won't die from the magic holding it in place."

"Hali, we may only get one shot to get this right. Each link needs to be as strong as possible and it will be strongest if there's only one being for each link. I'll be fine. I'm doing this."

"You're not thinking straight, you just lost your father."

"My thinking is as clear as ever, Hali. Stop stalling."

"He's right, Hali," Mr. Gruff inserted. "It will be stronger if he helps, even with your unlimited power."

Hali lifted her head to the sky, silently acquiescing, before exhaling a breath and moving on.

The three walked to the barrier. Standing before it, Hali felt a tremor of nerves run through her. She prayed that Neilan would be okay, because she had witnessed enough grief for one day.

"On three," Mr. Gruff instructed.

"One, two, three," Mr. Gruff, Hali, and Neilan said as they placed their hands on the barrier. Hali's body felt electric as the barrier lit up like the sun. The light so bright she was blinded from seeing anything else.

33

MAKING UP

HALI AWOKE from the blast in an unfamiliar setting with people she hadn't seen for over a year. She looked up into the tear-filled eyes of her mom and dad, Abigail and Theo. As soon as her eyes had flickered open, she was embraced by her mother as her father hugged around both of them.

Abigail released from the hug a little just so she could look into Hali's eyes. "You have no idea how good it is to see you," she said.

"Yes, I do," Hali countered. Abigail beamed as she embraced Hali once again for a squeeze.

Abigail quickly released Hali as something occurred to her. "I'm not hurting you, am I?"

"Not at all," Hali reassured.

"How are you feeling?" Theo asked, finally getting a word in.

"I'm feeling, all right. A little out of it," Hali admitted as she pushed up to a sitting position.

Her parents stared at her as she took in the sterile room. It had one large window covered by closed horizontal blinds that barely contained the brightness of the sun. It also had walls that could be considered gray or blue depending on the lighting—at that moment they were blue. The sound of Hali's heartbeat filled the room, beeping in the silence. The sunlight lit Hali's memory down a dazed path, highlighting fragments of vivid memories that had her wondering if it had been only a dream after all. She must have stared at the window for a while because her dad moved towards it.

"Would you like me to open the blinds, Hali?" he asked.

"Sure, thank you," she replied as she worked through her confusion.

When Theo was finished, he walked back over to the hospital bed where Hali rested and sat in a chair next to Abigail.

"Is there anything we can get for you?" she asked, "water, food ...?"

Hali couldn't remember the last time she had eaten, but her stomach wasn't complaining. Plus, she had too many questions surfacing to the forefront of her mind to even consider it.

Hali shook her head. "How long have I been here?"

"Just a day, you were found on the shore," Theo answered.

"Hali ..." Abigail started.

Hali looked at her mother's beautiful face that held so much love. A face that struggled to hold back happy tears because the tears would get in the way of seeing her daughter for the first time in over a year.

Tormented, Abigail hesitantly asked, "Where did you go? There's a young man named Cas who's been trying to see you." Abigail paused, worry glazing her eyes. "Did he take you and hurt you in any way?"

Hali laughed abruptly at the ridiculousness of the question. Abigail's insinuation couldn't be further from the truth.

If her mother only knew Cas, she'd know that he was just as much a victim of circumstance as Hali, taking on so many burdens to protect the Anchors, including Hali. But as Hali took in her mother's expression, riddled with uncertainty, Hali realized that her mom and dad didn't know Cas, and their question was a fair one, despite what Hali knew to be true.

Hali steadied her breaths, willing her laughter away. "No, I wasn't taken by Cas and he has never hurt me," she managed to say evenly. Theo and Abigail twisted their heads at her, unsure if Hali was telling the truth. "I promise I'll tell you everything, but can we go home first?"

Theo grimaced.

"What is it?" Hali asked.

"There have been detectives waiting for you to wake up. They need to talk to you before you leave."

After hours of answering question after question at the hospital then again at the police station after leaving the hospital, Hali finally got to go home. In the end, she only had to leave out a little, but she kept her story as close to the truth as she could, so she wouldn't have to remember so many lies. She left the hospital and the police station without ever seeing Cas or any other Anchors. Her mother had told her that once the police came around he disappeared. Hali smiled a little at the thought of him evading police but was also worried where he and everyone else had gone.

Up close, Hali was able to really see her parents. When she saw them at the barrier, she had noticed their heads were full of gray hairs and their eyes carried sorrow lines where laugh lines should have been, but now she could almost feel the grief they had been carrying in the air around them. It was this fact that made giving her parents the full version of the truth, not the abridged version she had given the skeptical detectives, a no-brainer.

A girl leaving home at eighteen years old to live on a remote island for a year by choice and returning unharmed was not the typical story the Emerald Cove detectives were used to hearing. When asked why she left without telling anyone or calling, Hali was quick to answer that she was in search to find her birth parents and didn't tell her adoptive parents because she didn't want to be stopped. Hali felt a little bad for throwing her parents under the bus, but she didn't think her story would be very believable without that piece. She needed a motive for leaving and that was the best she could come up with on a whim. When asked if she had found her birth parents, she quickly added that they were both deceased, but she had found her great-grandmother, which is why she stayed on the island. Hali also made sure to add that Mamie had no idea that Hali had left home without telling her parents, so that the detectives would hopefully leave her out of it.

Though with Mamie's sharpness, Hali doubted she would have any trouble navigating the detectives' questions. Because Hali was eighteen when she left and her answers were consistent, the detectives had no other choice but to drop the case. However, they didn't fail to lecture her on the consequences of her choices, how much anguish her parents had been through, and how many resources were pulled together in an effort to bring her home when a simple note or phone call could have prevented it all. It was hard for Hali to argue with their points, even if she didn't deserve the lecture. But she knew it was either that or to explain the unbelievable truth and have them think she was crazy. She chose the former instead.

After the detectives were done asking questions, she went home with her parents where she knew the real grilling would begin. With a box of Otis's doughnuts in the center of the kitchen table they had picked up on their way back from the police station, Theo, Abigail, and Hali sat down. Hali's parents hadn't been able to go into the interrogation room with her, so they were still in the dark of even the basic version of Hali's story.

On the car ride back to the house, Theo and Abigail had tried to get the truth from Hali, but she told them that it would be best if she explained at home, where they were not in danger of swerving off the road and into a tree. She had had enough of being in the hospital ... and of trees.

Also, during their car ride home, Theo and Abigail reluctantly divulged that Mr. O'Riley had passed away, and that Neilan was in a coma at the same hospital Hali had left that morning. The story being told was that Neilan and Mr. O'Riley were out fishing not too far off the coast of Emerald Cove when their boat caught fire, according to their "shipmates" who had survived the incident. The investigation was ongoing since neither Bram nor the burned ship had been found.

As they sat at the kitchen table, Hali inhaled and exhaled a deep breath. Theo's and Abigail's eyes burned with anticipation, as worry lined their faces, waiting for Hali to speak.

"Okay. What I'm about to tell you is going to sound crazy. But I promise, I'm telling you the truth and I can prove it."

Over the next several hours and doughnuts later, Hali's parents learned just about everything they needed to know of Hali's whereabouts over the past year. Starting with the

Emerald Cove Lighthouse and how it drew her in, only to capture her; ending with her final moments on the Eyes' Land where she broke the barrier with Neilan and Mr. Gruff. Hali explained to her parents how Mr. Gruff was really an Enchanter in his past life named Rowina and how he shaved branches daily as punishment for unknowingly aiding in the deaths of her birth parents, Arcelia and Murchadh, along with the creation of the Eyes' Land. It was at this point in Hali's story she saw remorse cross their faces. Her parents apologized profusely to her for not telling Hali they had adopted her, to which Hali accepted immediately. After having a year to process the information, Hali had come to terms with the fact that she was adopted, as much as a person could for her situation—which she doubted there were many cases like her own.

Theo and Abigail listened to Hali's retelling intently, but they still seemed a little unsure if Hali's story was authentic, or if she was suffering a mental break from reality. That's when Hali showed them her lawpnies, and then demonstrated her masking skills. As it turned out, disappearing without warning was not an impressive magic trick to show parents whose child had vanished for over a year. But Hali's magic had achieved the desired effect of making her parents believers in her unbelievable story. All was good in the end when Hali reappeared, but Theo and Abigail made her promise to never mask without telling them again.

The Shawn family stayed up late that night, with a visit from Camille and her mother at one point. The reunion was bittersweet. The families cried over Hali's homecoming, and of the loss of Bram O'Riley, and for Neilan, whose fate was still unknown. Camille and Mrs. O'Riley didn't stay too long, but long enough considering their own circumstances.

Before they left Camille pulled Hali to the side and

handed her a gift bag, while Theo and Abigail chatted in the kitchen with Mrs. O'Riley.

"I got this the day after you had gone missing and have been holding onto it since. It's not much, but I figured if there was a present waiting for you, then you'd eventually have to come back."

Hali looked at the bag, curiously. "Thank you, Camille."

"Well, don't thank me yet until after you open it," Camille gestured to the bag. "For all you know it could be nothing but dead cockroaches."

Hali smiled, then opened the bag, pulling out a vibrant, bright-green sweatshirt, identical to the one she had lost the day she was captured by the lighthouse in the largest size it came in. Hali set the bag on the floor and held the sweatshirt up to her body. "Thank you so much, Camille." Hali embraced her friend, with the sweatshirt in between them.

"You're welcome. Now don't think this means that I've completely forgiven you for taking off the way you did. I know you better than to buy the story that's going around," Camille lectured, pulling away from their hug.

Hali nodded in understanding, knowing that eventually, when Camille's grief of losing her dad wasn't the only thing preoccupying her mind, she would want to have a conversation with Hali. And that conversation would turn things upside down for Camille all over again.

After Camille and Mrs. O'Riley left, Theo turned up the television volume, which had been playing the local news in the background on mute. Hali was the Emerald Cove headliner for the evening with a developing story about the O'Riley men's ship fire also cycling on the screen right after her story. It was evident to Hali that the information on the ship fire was weak at best, relying heavily on eyewitness accounts from people on the shore, who would have been miles away from knowing what truly happened if there was such an incident. Unsurprisingly, the Eyes or "crewmates" that had concocted the fictional ship to hide the truth provided the local news only the basics: there was a fire, they escaped, Bram didn't, Neilan did ... eventually.

Also tied into Hali's story was the Emerald Cove Lighthouse. According to some nearby locals the lighthouse briefly lit the Emerald Cove sky on the morning of Hali's return, shining a light so bright one man thought it was a meteor. Some nearby locals swore by it, while others believed it was just lightning. Those who believed the former, also believed the lighthouse to be haunted, since the beam had also gone off the same night Hali had disappeared. That addition to her story made her laugh—not because it was ridiculous, but because it was so close to the truth.

It took Hali a while to convince her mom and dad that she could be left alone in her room. Her mother would have slept on Hali's bedroom floor had Hali not explained to her several times that the spell that had pulled her the first time had been extinguished, and the Eyes' Land was no longer a threat—or at least she hoped.

While Hali was relieved to be home, worry twisted in her gut about the well-being of Cas and the other Anchors as soon as she closed the door to her bedroom. The spell blasted the barrier to bits, but what did that mean for the Anchors? What would Neilan's outcome be? She tried not to think about Neilan's situation, because she really didn't know what she would do if he didn't come out of the coma. His family was already dealing with so much grief with the loss of Mr. O'Riley, that the guilt was too much for Hali to comprehend. She knew the Anchors were resourceful, but it didn't sit well with her that she sat in her cozy, messy room of abundance, while the others were out there somewhere. As the thought of the other Anchors took hold in her head, she turned for her door to let her parents know that she needed to go look for the others, when her window rattled.

She whipped around as a breeze lifted her white transparent curtains up like the arms of a ghost.

"Where are you going?" Cas asked as he unmasked, standing near her window as he did.

Hali ran to him, her arms outstretched for a hug. Cas pulled her in, breathing in her hair.

"I was just going to go find you and the others. Did everyone make it out okay? I can ask my parents if they can open up the aquarium for the Anchors to sleep in until we can figure out a more permanent solution." Hali spoke with her ear still pressed to Cas's chest, listening to his heartbeat thrum.

"Everyone is fine … mostly," Cas answered, his head still resting on top of Hali's head as he combed his fingers through her scalp.

"Mostly?" Hali looked up into Cas's eyes, with concern in her own. "I know about Neilan, but who else?"

Hali listened to Cas's lungs release a sigh. She stepped away from him to get a better read on his face. His scar looked redder than usual, which made Hali wonder how his scales were healing after he intentionally cut them to help protect the others.

Without thinking she reached up and ran her thumb across his scar. "Cas?"

Before she could pull away Cas placed his hand on top of hers, a look of sadness crossed the pools of his blue eyes.

"Mr. Gruff is gone. After the blast, all that was left of him were his clothes."

Hali's knees weakened on the news, as she sat at her

window seat. Cas followed, sitting next to her. "I thought he said nothing would happen to him because he didn't possess magic anymore."

Cas shrugged. "I don't know. In all my time reading my spell book, I've never found a case quite like this. Honestly, I'm not sure in the history of magic there's been such a complicated circumstance with so many types of magical powers mixed in. But under the *Consequences* section of the spell book it mentions that Enchanters who escape one punishment will be assigned another."

Tears began rolling down Hali's cheeks. In the year she spent on the Eyes' Land, she had thought about her home-coming and how wonderful it would be. She hadn't thought of the ramifications it would have on anyone else; believing that any issues could be resolved easily because they would be free.

"What's wrong, Hali?" Cas asked.

Hali grabbed a tissue from her tissue box, then had to grab another because the first tissue had been covered in a year's worth of dust. "You were right."

Cas's eyebrows raised. "About what?"

"I didn't think of any of the consequences of breaking the barrier. When we were being hunted by the Eyes it seemed like the only solution, but maybe I was wrong. Mr. Gruff is gone, Neilan is in a coma, and there are hundreds of homeless Anchors who can't just decide to setup camp on a public beach. Has anyone even eaten? What about Mamie and Fisk? I feel terrible that I'm in a house right now, like I'm deserting everyone."

"Hali," Cas interrupted. "Everyone's fine, including Mamie and Fisk. As far as eating goes, the Anchors will just eat in their mermaid or merman form until they get settled. It's not ideal, but no one is starving. And something you're forgetting is that some of the Anchors have existed outside the Eyes' Land before and still have assets. Also, I'm still part Enchanter with a few tricks up my fins."

Hali laughed at his last point. "How was it to eat raw fish?"

"Eh, not my favorite. Had to stay in the ocean a little longer to digest it, but not too bad overall. We found a section of beach that wasn't populated and took turns going out into the water to eat, while the others stood watch. I would have zap cooked the food, but we would have still had to bring all the fish up onto the beach. Mamie and Fisk said it might bring too much unwanted attention if we brought that many fish out of the water, especially if I cooked them with my lawpnies."

"That makes sense," Hali nodded. Relief and remorse see-sawed in her mind. But in the end, she came to the conclusion there really was no other way it could have all played out, without some adjustments and changes to everyone's lives. Living a free life was always worth the risk of upending an imprisoned life that was comfortable.

As they passed moments in silent reflection, Hali noticed that Cas seemed to be mulling over something else, almost appearing nervous. For a moment she worried there was some other bad news he had to brace himself to tell her, but she didn't think so. Cas's expression didn't hold the same stress as a person who had foreboding news to share. As if listening to her thoughts, he grabbed her hand, holding it between the two of them in the middle of the bench seat, igniting the feelings Hali had suppressed ever since they made their way out of her mouth. Hali looked down at their hands intertwined, her heart full even without the confirmation that Cas shared the same feelings towards her as she did for him.

"Did you mean what you said?" Cas asked with doubt in his eyes, breaking the silence. "Now that the fighting is over and you're back home, do you still feel the same way about me?"

Hali peered up from their clasped hands with watery eyes, tilting her head with a smile. She didn't even need to ask what he meant. She already knew. "Of course, I do."

He exhaled, relieved, but he didn't smile. "Hali ... I never told you why I was so angry that day you went out into the water. The day the sea creature found you while you were looking for your parents." Cas released Hali's hand, standing up from the bench seat. Hali remained seated, leaving her hand on the seat where Cas left it. She watched Cas pace in front of her, collecting his thoughts. A nervous excitement bloomed in Hali's chest.

"The day that you had gone to the barrier, I had been fishing like usual. When all of a sudden it felt like my body had grabbed onto the end of a live wire that I couldn't shake off. I thought I would go into cardiac arrest; the buzzing was so powerful. But as soon as I felt it, I knew exactly what it was.

"So many thoughts entered my head all at once, but the one thought that kept coming around, was that it wasn't your signal. It couldn't be, because you were on the shore, far away from me and I was in the ocean. I was crushed, knowing I was being led to someone who wasn't you, because you're the only one I've ever wanted. Little did I know at the time that you had gone out into the water.

"Initially I ignored the signal and fought the urge to follow it. But the more I fought, the more powerful the signal got. My ears wrung louder, my body tensed, my head pounded harder, but I wouldn't go. After a while, the signal rang like a warning and I couldn't ignore it anymore. It was like the person on the other end of the signal was in trouble. I finally gave in and followed it. But when I got to the other end of the signal and found you were next to the barrier with a sea creature wrapped around you ..."

Hali stood up, grabbing both his hands in hers. When their eyes met, she raised her eyebrows, nudging Cas to continue.

"I saw red, Hali. Not only was there a sea creature all over you, but you had gone out to the barrier in the first place. At the time, I believed you would never feel for me what I felt for you, because I wanted you and you wanted nothing more than to go home, back to your old life without me. The worst part was, I couldn't kiss you without sealing our bond, which was why I never tried. Over the last year I'd been tempted many times, but I wasn't sure if you would even want me to. I told myself I'd leave it in your hands, but I already knew that you would never initiate anything past a friendship. That's why when you told me you loved me, I was speechless. I more than love you, Hali. I'm bounded to you."

Hali clutched Cas's hands tighter. "How long have you known?"

Cas chuckled. "That I've loved you?"

"Uh-huh."

"Longer than I'd like to admit."

They both smiled at each other. Their eyes shining.

"Cas?" Hali said, her eyes meeting his. "You never did tell me where you thought I could live on the Eyes' Land, when I was thinking about living with Delphia."

Cas's gaze left hers, appearing shy. He groaned, smiling but looking conflicted. "Hali, you just got home, the idea I had then may not sound too good to you now." He let go of her hands, turning away from her slightly. Hali watched him, then grabbed his arm gently, forcing him to meet her eyes.

Hali smirked, raising her eyebrows. "It must be some idea if it's getting you this worked up. Are you afraid I won't like the idea, or have you decided that you no longer like it?"

Cas glared at her, like she had just insulted him. "Of course I still like the idea."

"Then I would like to hear it," Hali smiled.

Cas's eyes crinkled suspiciously. "Why are you goading me? Do you already know what my idea is?"

Hali smiled coyly. "I have my guesses, but I don't know for sure."

Cas's expression turned to relief as he fell to his knees, grabbing both of her hands. "Hali, will you marry me? I know that you just got back home, and you'll want to spend time here, but will you eventually marry me? I don't care if I have to wait years. I don't want to, but I will."

Without saying a word, Hali bent down to his eyes and gently placed a kiss on his scar. They both stared at each other for a moment when she pulled away, still only inches from his face. Cas's chest rose and fell with each breath he took. Hali's heart kicked up, as did her lawpnies, before she answered his question by pressing her lips to his. A kiss that made her forget where she was. Once she did, Cas took no time to pull Hali to him to reciprocate the gesture, cupping her face with his strong, but gentle hands. They carried on until their lips were swollen and chapped. Their kisses performed a push-pull dance like the waves did with the shore. At some point during the kiss she did answer "yes" in words, but the action was much stronger than any words could ever be. Their lawpnies swirled around them, sealing them forever and always, whether together or apart. Their love was young, but not untested; their stubbornness strong, but their hearts still loyal. They were anchored to the land and sea—and most of all ... each other.

"You were wrong about one thing," Hali said between breaths.

Cas looked at her through hooded eyes, willing to be wrong about anything if it meant they didn't need to stop kissing.

"What's that?"

"You had thought I wouldn't want anything to do with you once I got home."

He smiled. "I've never been so happy to be wrong in all my life."

EPILOGUE

AFTER CAS LEFT, Hali's heart felt fuller and heavier than it had ever been. She had already told her parents about Cas, but she knew that getting married would deliver one more shock to them. But she wouldn't worry about that quite yet. Now, she would bask in the happiness she was feeling, while she could.

As she sat at the window seat, her eyes happened on the little, wooden box that sat in the corner of her desk. She walked over to it, hesitant but determined. Hali slowly sat down at her desk chair. Reaching her hands out she clutched the box and brought it to her, opening it with the emerald-cut, violet gem that marked the center. The mermaid swam in its figure eights as the tune Mamie hummed filled the air. For a moment Hali worried that the music would wake her parents, so she snapped the box closed. But as she did, something shiny shimmered at the back of the trinket.

Hali slowly reopened the box ajar to try and see what she saw without activating the music. The glimmer of silver she spotted was actually a chain that was hiding in the underside of the lid. Hali pulled on the chain that had loosened from its hiding place gingerly, which popped the top layer of the lid out, exposing a good section of the chain. The silver link extended past the cover of the music box all the way to the base. Unable to keep the lid only ajar, Hali opened it fully, filling her room with its music as she followed the path of the chain under the base of the music box where the mermaid swam. Tugging on the chain popped the water structure right out, but the mermaid stayed fixed. The chain led to the gem in the front, which unhooked from the slot it was in when it had served as a knob, becoming the beautiful, violet stone of a necklace.

Hali brought the necklace up to her chest, looking at it glimmer on her neck in the mirror that hung on the wall above her desk. As she looked down at the box, she found a folded piece of paper. Setting the necklace down she picked up the paper, unfolding it to find a letter addressed to her.

Our little Hali,

We hope when you find this letter you are more ready to receive it than we were to write it. We'll start by introducing ourselves. I am your mother, Arcelia O'Riley, and your father's name is Murchadh O'Riley. I am an Anchor and an enchanter, and your father is a leprechaun. This means that you are an Anchor, enchanter, and leprechaun. As lucky as the combination may seem, it makes you very desirable for greedy leprechauns. There is good and bad of every type of being, Hali, but some leprechauns, like Cillian, who is currently hunting me for my powers, are bad seeds. Your father is not like his brother, he is one of the good ones. I tell you this for two reasons. The first is I want you to be aware and protect yourself from those who look to harm you. The second reason is I don't want your awareness to cause you to judge others before you know their character. If I had judged Murchadh based solely on his being a leprechaun, you wouldn't be here. I am very glad that I didn't. I haven't held you for more than a few hours and I can already tell you are one of the good ones. I hope that being comprised of so many unique qualities will help you and not hinder you in your life. But just in case, I've cut off your abilities until you turn eighteen, so that Cillian can't find you and so that you have an opportunity to grow up as a normal human being without powers to complicate your life.

One day I hope we can meet you under better circumstances and we can introduce you to family members without putting you at risk. But until then, just know that we love you more than we can express in a letter. You are the best gift your father and I have ever received. We want no harm ever done to you. It is because of this reason we realized that you are a gift we can't keep, no matter how badly we want to.

We've placed you in the care of Abigail and Theo Shawn. They are good people with good hearts. I've watched them care for marine life on my swims around Emerald Cove, so I know that they will both be good to you. When I found out they struggled to have a child and desperately wanted one, it seemed like fate had spoken.

I have so much to share with you and so little time to do it. Even though you will be with a family other than me and Murchadh I wanted to leave a piece of us behind. The music box plays a tune, sung to me when I was a little girl by my father and my grandmother, Mamie. It was a tune I wanted to pass on to my children, since it was a song I remembered singing so much when I was growing up.

The mermaid in the music box is no ordinary mermaid. She symbolizes you and all the power you will have when you reach *your eighteenth birthday. We come from a line of enchanters that have no caps placed on their power. It is a huge burden and responsibility to carry, and the reason I'm being hunted and have to give you away. What we possess is rare and not to be taken lightly, so keep that in mind when you come of age. Whenever you need reminding just read the inscription on your music box— I wrote it just for you. Please be careful who you share this information with, since greed is the demise of many.*

The chain of the necklace is white gold and from Murchadh. The beautiful gem has been passed down from my mother and her mother before her. It is an amethyst, the same color of our scales and of the few Anchors who have unlimited power. The stone holds no special powers or magic of any kind. It is simply to serve as a reminder. You see, the amethyst stone represents a purity of spirit and a withdrawal from negative influences. I hope when you look at this stone in the future you remember that the true magic you possess does not come from magic at all, but in being authentic in spite of your power. The weak-minded lose themselves when given any amount of power; it corrupts them rather than strengthens. I hope that never happens to you, Hali. Always own your power, don't let your power own you. I hope that makes sense.

These gifts will hopefully bring you comfort when and if you think of us. We are leaving it up to Theo and Abigail to decide when they tell you you're adopted. So hopefully you don't find this letter until after that has happened. This box is spelled to not reveal its secrets until your powers are active, but we needed you to know that we love you, now, forever, and always!

∞

Arcelia & Murchadh

· · ·

P.S. Look inside the music box again. It's a limited edition—the only of one of its kind—just like you. I am passing it on to you now. Protect and use well!

Looking inside the music box, Hali found an iridescent string, that wasn't there when she first peered inside. Instinctively, she tugged at it, watching as a small tornado twirled in front of her eyes. Moments later it settled, and on the desk in front of her sat a book. She recognized it immediately, despite never seeing it before. It was her family's spell book. Picking it up, she hugged it to her chest. Hali instantly felt the spell book embrace her back with warmth. She closed her eyes, overjoyed.

Over a year ago, she had learned she was adopted on the same day she learned she would never know her birth parents. But today, she was left with more than she could have ever imagined and more than she deserved. As her eyes shed in appreciation, she heard the faint beginnings of a song. The spell book glowed in her arms, as the sound grew in volume. A woman's voice struck Hali's core like a déjà vu, singing the song of the music box. The voice sounded a little like her own, but richer. The sound was woven into the fabric of her own being though she had never heard it before. It was the voice of her biological mother, Arcelia. Hali had no idea what the future held for her or the Anchors, but in that moment, she had never felt more loved and complete.

ACKNOWLEDGMENTS

Like many strange ideas, the concept for *Limited Edition* came to me in the middle of the night. After a cycle of writing and trashing my earlier drafts—with many pauses in the beginning stages, and plenty of revisions later—I finally finished. But not without some help.

First, I'd like to thank my family for their love, support, encouragement, and patience. More specifically, I'd like to thank my husband for being the first reader, and the second, as well my sounding board and live-in grammar checker. Without you, *Limited Edition* would have far more commas than necessary—none of which would be the Oxford variety.

A huge thanks to my younger brother, Hugo, for volunteering to read *Limited Edition* and giving his youthful perspective, honest opinion, and fresh eyes on the story. Your contribution was extremely helpful ... and humbling.

I'd also like to thank David Drummond from Salamander Hill Design for taking the time to create and design the awesome cover.

Last but not least, I want to thank you, the readers. I realize that reading is an investment of your time and there are plenty of other options available to choose from—so thank you! If you have taken the time to read this far, please consider leaving an honest review.

ABOUT THE AUTHOR

S.C. Wiles has always had an interest in understanding what makes people tick, which led her to earn a BA in Psychology and then an MS in Counselor Education. After taking a long pause from work to stay at home with her children, she channeled her love of good stories, and curiosity of the human condition into writing.

S.C. grew up in California and now lives on the East Coast with her husband and three children. When she is not writing, S.C. enjoys reading, taking walks with her family, traveling, and baking. *Limited Edition* is S.C.'s first novel.

For more information and updates:
www.authorscwiles.com